KT-475-064

"I am a great admirer of Kunal Mukherjee ... He's a very poetic writer with a lovely literary style, has wonderful characters, a beautiful setting, an exotic (to American readers) culture, all brought to life in an interesting way ..."

– Alan Rinzler, Executive Editor, Jossey-Bass/
John Wiley & Sons, Founding Editor, *Rolling Stone*

"The book evolved ... from a story of loss to a complex and multi-layered themes of love, loss, forbidden love ... breaking the rules to follow your heart."

–*Times of India*

"A sensitive read that gathers steam as you turn the pages, this book goes beyond being 'gay' literature--rather it's a study of eternal dilemmas that defy boundaries."

– *HarmonyIndia.org*

"Replete with Indian cliches like 70's mentality, hairdos, parental pressure ... placing religion ... family honour above all ... hard to put down, once you start"

– *Indian Express*

"My Magical Palace may be Kunal Mukherjee's maiden venture, but his foray into .... writing has made veterans sit up and take notice."

– *Millennium Post*

"Not very often does one come across a book which highlights sensitive issues in a stark yet subtle manner ... "

– *Bengal Post*

"It is ... a sensitive tale of a boy coming of age, and the many hurdles he must cross to find and heal himself ... the chronicler of loss from San Francisco ..."

– Mail Today UK

"A simple story written with an endearing simplicity, this one is undoubtedly one of the best debuts of the year.. Kunal is a stupendous storyteller."

– The Tales Pensieve

"It is about ... a constant sense of being an outsider; of being different and being punished for it."

– The Tribune

"If the moral ... "to follow one's heart, one has to break the rules sometimes" -- sounds a little sentimental, well, it is; but then, sentimentality -- even innocence -- runs through Mukherjee's first novel ,.. remember The God of Small Things?

– Hindustan Times

"Set in the 1970s in Hyderabad and San Francisco, the book takes a route less travelled and narrates a sweet love story..."

– Deccan Chronicle

My Magical Palace

KUNAL MUKHERJEE

First published in India in 2012
by HarperCollins *Publishers* India
a joint venture with
The India Today Group

Copyright © Kunal Mukherjee

ISBN: 978-0-9911847-0-5
Library of Congress 2012339503

Kunal Mukherjee asserts the moral right to be identified as the author of this work. This is a work of fiction and all characters and incidents described in this book are the product of the author's imagination. Any resemblance to actual persons, living or dead, is entirely coincidental. All rights reserved. No part of this publication may be reproduced, stored in a retrieval system, or transmitted, in any form or by any means, electronic, mechanical, photocopying, recording or otherwise, without the prior permission of the publisher.

Kunal Mukherjee Inc.
373 Moultrie Street
San Francisco, CA 94110
USA

Dedicated to people everywhere who
break the rules to follow their heart,
Linda Watanabe McFerrin
and my parents Durga and Parijat

'Don't forget love;
it will give you all the madness you need
to unfurl yourself across
the universe.'

– Mirabai (1498–1550)

(From *Love Poems from God* by Daniel Ladinsky)

I dreamt of my magical palace again last night. I glided over the marble floors and through locked rooms, my body light and ethereal. I heard the shrill cries of lapwings and koels as they rose in black clouds from the canopy of gulmohar trees, warning me that I must leave. I felt a deep sigh from the very heart of the palace walls, and in one last shudder, the stately pillars and rooms, the exquisite trees and flowers all vanished. I cried out, my arms reaching out to the receding walls. The darkness of despair engulfed me. Hot tears burst through a clenched fist in my chest. I felt a wrenching sense of loss as Andrew shook me awake.

1

Saturday morning. San Francisco.

'Rahul,' Andrew murmured, 'are you having nightmares again?' His arm draped protectively around me as he squeezed hard. He kissed the back of my neck, holding me tight. I felt the warmth of his body as he snuggled closer.

I sat up, my head in my hands.

'What is it?' he asked, shaking his head. 'You were so distant at dinner. I wanted to ask you if you'd had a bad day at work, but figured I'd give you some space.'

I looked at the digital face of the alarm clock. It was 6 a.m. The foghorn sounded forlorn, booming across North Beach and wafting up Russian Hill. The rumble of an early cable car, soon to be filled with tourists on their summer vacation, shook the apartment building on its way from the wharf on its first run of the day.

Andrew put his hand on my knee as my feet hit the hardwood floors with a thump. His fingers caressed my skin. Would he understand? I felt myself start to numb. I thought about the email from my mother in Bombay that I'd received just before leaving work the day before. It had weighed on my mind all evening and stirred old memories.

'Dear beta,' it said. 'We are getting old. It is time we saw the face of our grandchild before we die. Your father and I are healthy by the grace of God. But before we close our eyes, we would like to see you settle down. How I wish you would come back here, but you have decided to settle in America. Here is a picture of a lovely girl we met—Anu. She reminded me of Mallika. She was visiting her relatives in Bombay recently. Remember how Mallika wore her hair down to her waist, and that beautiful smile of hers? I thought of her when I met Anu. And we ran into Dr Bose at the supermarket. She said that Shubho's wife has divorced him. Such a lovely boy—so unfortunate that his marriage has ended this way. Anu lives in San Jose with her uncle, Dr Ganguly. They want to visit you on Sunday. I hope you will be able to meet her. I am sure you will like her a lot …' I turned on the lamp. Colonel Uncle and Claudio smiled at me from the photograph framed on my dresser. I reached out and touched their faces, then turned to look at Andrew. He looked very boyish, squinting in the sudden brightness. The tips of his early morning beard glinted blond in the light. He looked so beautiful that I had a sudden desire to put my head in his lap and cry.

'My parents want me to get married,' I said abruptly.

'What?' Andrew sat up. 'What do you mean? I thought…

Don't they know you're gay?'

'Well … no,' I said. 'Not exactly. They used to ask me to meet girls they had picked before I met you. You know, for an arranged marriage. They would be happy if I found someone myself, but since I wasn't making any effort to get married on my own, they consider it their duty as parents. I always met the girls they picked and then told them I didn't think we'd be compatible. It seemed to work. But then this email arrived yesterday … The girl they've picked, Anu, and her uncle would like to visit on Sunday evening.' I paused, assessing the rising panic in Andrew's eyes, then breathed deep and took the plunge. 'I'm very sorry, Andrew, but can you please leave for the evening? I promise I'll get them off my back quickly, and then you can come back …'

Andrew jumped off the bed, his eyes shining with unshed tears. He was struggling for words. 'I … Do you know how much it hurts to hear you say that? You're my lover, for God's sake, my partner for life!' He kicked the nightstand and the force sent a little statue of Ganesh crashing to the floor. 'Well, screw you,' he said after a while. 'How can you ask me to make myself invisible, even for an evening? You are not out to your parents! I don't believe this. You know what I've been through. If I had known this, I would never have moved in with you last month. Are you so ashamed of me that you can't tell your family that you have someone who loves you and adores you? Or are you ashamed of yourself? Are you going to hide all these pictures of us too?' Flying in an angry arc across the top of the credenza, his hand swept all the carefully arranged pictures of us, and they crashed to the floor.

'No, it's not like that …' I tried to explain, but then stopped. He would never get it, I thought bitterly. It was easy for him to live his life openly. His parents were divorced. They had broken his heart as a child and there was very little he could do to earn their disapproval. No matter how I explained this, it wouldn't be good enough for him.

Choosing my words carefully, I said, 'I love you, Andrew. Of course I do. But you don't understand—my parents are not American. They would never understand if I told them I was gay …' My breath caught in my throat as a familiar fear rose at the ominous words. I reached out to Andrew, but he moved away, nostrils flaring and lips set in a tight line above his stubborn chin.

'Look, Rahul,' he said softly, 'I understand that we all have issues, but we need to deal with them. I had mine and dealt with them. Why can't you?'

I shook my head. How could I make him understand the shame and humiliation of being an outsider and outcaste in the society I'd grown up in, a society where the individual comes last?

Annoyed by my reluctance, he said, 'I need some space to think.' He walked out of the room, slamming the door shut.

I sat on the bed wishing I had not asked him to leave this way. I'd had no idea that he would be so upset and hurt. We had been living together for barely a month, although we had been together for six months before that—and I had managed to avoid such a situation so far. I knew that there was no point in trying to talk to him right then. Andrew needed his space when he was upset.

After what seemed like aeons, Andrew came back.

'Wow, Rahul. I never saw this coming. It just doesn't feel right. I know something is up … You're always hiding what is going on,' he said, his voice shaking. 'You cry in your sleep and are in a foul mood all morning afterwards. What is bothering you? Am I a dirty secret that you have hidden from your world?'

'Andrew, please stop,' I begged. My carefully constructed life was falling apart. I felt thirteen again, powerless against the tide of life. I was back in my seventh-grade classroom.

'Well, you know what? I don't need to take this crap from anyone, least of all from you—the man I love and want to spend the rest of my life with.' Andrew turned away, his blue eyes filled with pain. 'I'll leave. But I'm not coming back. Either you're in this relationship with me, fully and openly, or we are finished.'

'Where are you going? Please, Andrew, don't leave!' My voice broke as he grabbed a bag and started pulling out clothes from the closet. Andrew didn't answer. He shoved the clothes into the bag as he ran out, tripping at the door.

I stood there, paralysed. The door shut with a bang and I heard his footsteps receding down the hallway. The hum of the lift started and ceased and the accordion doors shut with a clang. I heard it start its descent to the lobby.

I lay back on the bed and stared at the ceiling, not able to believe that he had actually left like this. I had not meant to hurt him. I felt the old ache rise within me—the pain of losing Shubho. Once again, I was an adolescent in love, and I could do nothing to stop the love of my life from leaving me.

Saturday afternoon. San Francisco.

I had called Andrew several times, but he hadn't answered the phone. The last time I tried calling, it was switched off. 'Andrew Borgese. Leave a message and I will call you back.' His clipped accent offered little comfort.

The day crawled by. I dozed on and off, unable to move. In my dream, I saw the Nizam's grandmother screaming as she saw a dead bat lying on the floor of the palace. Then the air was thick with flying bats and shreds of their blood-stained skin.

I saw Mallika, her face bruised and bleeding, her arms stretched out to me, begging for help as I stood frozen. I woke up heaving dry sobs, missing Andrew's comforting embrace. Desolate, I dialled his number again, hoping that he would pick up.

'Hello?' Andrew's voice was subdued.

'Baby, it's me.'

'Yes?'

'Baby, come home please.' My voice cracked with emotion. 'Please come home. I'll tell you about the nightmares, about the things that happened many years ago, the things that make me. I'll tell you how I learnt to hide myself from the world so I wouldn't get into trouble.'

'Rahul,' Andrew said, his voice wary, 'on one condition—that you'll tell me everything. There can be no more secrets between us. Otherwise, we cannot be together. I love you, but I've been through too much hell coming out of the closet. I can't be with you if your life is a lie.'

'Where are you?'

'At the Travelodge Motel, on Lombard Street.'

'Come home? Please?'

'Tell me your story first.'

'All right.' I sighed, trying to compose myself. He wasn't going to come home until I'd told him everything, I realized. 'But I wish you could hear it from me in person ...' I took a deep breath as I readied myself to tell him what I hadn't ever told a soul.

'I need to tell you first about the amazing place where I grew up. It's where I learnt to live and love,' I said.

'Okay.'

'You know that I grew up in Hyderabad. What I've never told you is that I grew up in a palace called Mint House. It was a grand old house ... Every time I came up the driveway and saw the imposing facade, the Corinthian pillars rising to the sky, the royal gardens, the elegantly laid out flowerbeds and orchards, I felt like a prince ... A real prince, not the prince of my father's mockery. "Prince of Kuchh Bhi Nahi State, the Prince of the Kingdom of Nothing," he'd say, and it would annoy the hell out of me. But I was so happy, enjoying the wonders of that palace and its grounds ...'

'Hold on, Rahul. Why are you telling me about this place? I want to know what happened to *you*.'

'I have to tell you about Mint House before anything else—it sort of ties everything together.'

'Oh, okay,' Andrew said. 'Was it a real palace? How big was it? How many acres, how many rooms?' My dear Andrew could be such an American—obsessed with statistics and numbers. 'I had no idea you came from such a privileged background.'

'Wait, there's a lot to this story, and I haven't got to it yet. And no, we weren't royalty, but I did have the privilege of living there because my dad was a government servant,' I said. 'The palace had two storeys and forty rooms ...' It was going to be hard for Andrew to understand how different my childhood had been from his; he had grown up in a tree-lined suburb in the Midwest.

I put on a kettle of water on the stove and then curled up in my favourite armchair, just like I used to in Hyderabad, except that this one was bigger. Leaning back, I closed my eyes and, like the vision in my dreams, my magical palace appeared before me, so clear that I could reach out and touch the wrought-iron gates, see the sunlight glinting off the bayonets of the sentries who always stood at attention, warning the world to stay out.

'It was like a jewel in the midst of the thirty-acre grounds,' I continued. 'Tall pillars lined the facade and there was a large portico tiled with marble. The palace was surrounded by orchards, woods, a wading pool, a lake, ancient trees and all kinds of birds and animals. I had lived in the palace since I was born. It was the only home I knew. I wish you could have seen it ...' I swallowed the lump in my throat because Andrew would never see my magical palace. 'So much happened that year, but the palace never lost its magic.'

'How did your family end up living in a king's palace?'

'Because of my father's job. Even though there were several myths surrounding the palace, I know for sure that it was built for the fabled Nizams of Hyderabad in 1880. It lay unused for several decades until the Indian Government decided to use it as officers' quarters.'

'The Nizams?'

'The Nizams were one of the fabled dynasties of India, known for their incredible wealth. Here's something that might interest you: in the 1940s, the Nizam was featured on *Time* magazine as the world's richest man.'

'Wow. That's incredible. So you got to stay in this guy's palace?'

'No, probably his great-great grandfather's palace. But they never lived in it. There's a fascinating legend about why it was abandoned before anyone moved in.'

'Lucky you,' Andrew said, and I breathed a sigh of relief that my story had caught his fancy and the tension between us had lessened palpably. 'Can't imagine what that would be like,' he continued. 'I grew up in a small house on the outskirts of Cleveland. Wasn't the palace falling apart after being abandoned?'

'Actually, most of it was in decent condition. But yes, part of it lay in ruins. Anyway, when the government took possession of all property owned by kings after Independence, it renamed the palace Mint House. They cleaned the place up and made it the official living quarters for the Mint Master—the person in charge of the India Government Mint. My father was the Mint Master, and so we lived in the Nizam's old palace. As far as I was concerned, it made me a prince.' I laughed, and Andrew chuckled. But the kettle started whistling, its strident sound harsh in the fog-muffled afternoon, breaking the mood.

'Tell me about your childhood,' Andrew said, his tone growing serious again. 'From what little you've told me, you were a happy kid. Then why are you so tormented? Sometimes, you know, I feel like a stranger is sleeping next to me. At least you're lucky you didn't have to deal with living in two homes and being used as a pawn by your parents! God, I hated how things changed after their divorce.'

I took the kettle off the stove and poured myself a cup of tea. 'When I was growing up, the only people who got divorces were film stars and models. We were middle-class folks and divorce was just another word for a loose woman. Growing up, we didn't know even one divorced couple. All our friends lived in families that remained intact despite the fact that not all the marriages were happy. Our parents had all had arranged marriages—no one questioned the system.' I paused, my mind running through my perfect childhood and family experience until I turned thirteen. 'My father was a patriarch, you know. Born and raised in West Bengal. Which means he was very traditional and very strict—not a fan of western influence. He was absolutely clear about what we were supposed to achieve in school and later in life, and negotiating with him about these things was not an option.

'My mother, on the other hand, was quite easy-going and very sophisticated. She was an independent and modern-thinking woman, but she kept her ideas to herself and avoided getting into arguments. On one thing, both of my parents agreed: they expected nothing less than top marks at school from my sister Rani and me.'

'Sounds rough,' Andrew said.

I laughed and continued. 'Rani was, even then, poised, clever and very quick-witted. We argued and fought endlessly, and she always won by some means or the other. She defended me fiercely from the outside world, but when the two of us spent time together, she completely dominated me. I guess the fact that she was two years older made her feel all confident and assured—she was, I'm afraid, a bit of a know-it-all.

'Mr Banerjee was my father's best friend. And his wife, Mrs Banerjee, was my mother's confidante. Their daughters Mallika and Shyamala were close friends of me and Rani.'

'Hmm.'

'Is this all too confusing?' I asked.

'A little—I don't know who these people are. But go on.'

'When I was growing up, there wasn't the kind of money in India that there is today.'

'It's kind of hard to think of India as anything other than a major world player,' Andrew said.

'Well, everything was quite different in those days. I mean *everything*. There wasn't much money and India was not engaged in world commerce in any way. No call centres or outsourcing operations! Society was segregated. People of different religions—or even different castes—were not supposed to marry each other. If they crossed those lines, there were severe consequences. And some things haven't changed—we still have honour killings.'

'What?'

'Yeah. But that's another story. Basically, the India of my childhood was a different world from the India of today. Anyway, let me tell you how it all began, the end of paradise in my magical palace …'

And so I began my tale of a time and place that exist no more.

2

April 1973. Hyderabad.

'Pay attention, Rahul!' A resounding slap on the side of my head accompanied that whip-like warning as Mr Swaminathan glared at me. My ear and head throbbed with pain.

I was in the seventh class, and it was my first year at my new school. And, as usual, I had been daydreaming about Rajesh Khanna, the famous matinee idol. In my mind, I was watching him in *Anand*, the film that started it all for me. Rajesh Khanna had never looked as fine as he did in *Anand*. He pouted and did this irresistible thing with his eyes, looking away and gently tilting his head towards his upraised hand in a move that kept his fans rapt with joy. I loved that moment—and in my private fantasy, it was just the two of us, in the gardens of my home, under the gulmohar tree. He moved closer and I leaned against the trunk, eyes closed, waiting to feel his warm breath against my cheek and the soft brush of his lips, before I pulled away in mock dismay, just like the heroine.

Mr Swaminathan's voice, however, snapped me out of my reverie. The close-clipped, military moustache that lined his upper lip shone from the thin layer of perspiration that covered his face. Though he was of medium height, his deep voice and terrible temper made him seem larger than life. On that day, his tie appeared to be too tight around his neck and his face seemed to swell with the heat and his rising irritation. Fearful, I shrank back in my chair as he stood in front of me, grimly smacking the ruler against his palm.

The classroom we were sitting in was a beautiful one, intricate Islamic designs painted in arches around the walls. Mahatma Gandhi smiled beatifically down at us from a gold-framed oil painting at one end of the room, as did Jawaharlal Nehru from a similar frame at the other end. The ceiling fans rotated lazily, almost as if in slow motion. The hot sun blazed outside on the baked earth. A sparrow flitted from branch to branch of a jamun tree, its mouth open, occasionally emitting a distressed chirp. A fly buzzed at the window, trapped in the hot room, and the low hum of its wings filled the room, tormenting us. The playground was deserted. The building that housed the senior students shimmered in the afternoon heat, its scalloped arches etched in light and shadow in the merciless sunshine. No students were visible anywhere, for we were all trapped in class. Only two weeks of the school year were left and I could not wait for them to be over. They would be followed by the exams. And then the summer vacations would begin—days of freedom and the time to watch lots of films. But Mr Swaminathan had slapped me into harsh reality. Shaking off my sense of disorientation, I tried to focus on what was happening in the classroom.

I took a quick look around. The boys in my highly competitive class, dressed in neat khaki pants and white shirts, with blue ties looked alert, delighted to have a diversion. I tensed with frustration. They were older, already adolescent, and picked on me endlessly. I was a year younger than my classmates since I had been given a double promotion when I was transferred to this historic school, built for the princes of the various principalities and members of the court of years gone by. I was the star student of my class and they were enjoying my punishment.

'Rahul? I will repeat the question one more time. How is the state government different from the central government? What in the name of God are you thinking about, boy?'

Confused and dazed by the stinging slap delivered by Mr Swaminathan's hand, I wanted to shrink from the view of my classmates. In horror I heard my voice say, 'Rajesh Khanna ...'

Ranjan Bose, the boy I thought was my best friend, could not repress a snicker.

'Did you just say Rajesh Khanna?' Mr Swaminathan's voice was icy. Apparently I had said the name loud enough for the entire class to hear. 'My, my,' his voice was scathing, 'so obviously film stars are more important than the civics class.'

My stomach knotted in confusion and humiliation. A few muted titters rose in small waves behind me.

'Silence!' Mr Swaminathan's voice thundered and the class fell quiet.

'Stand up and hold out your hands,' Mr Swaminathan barked at me.

I stood up slowly, fearing the punishment. Rajesh Khanna had deserted me. I held out my hands. Swish! The ruler came down, slicing the air in an angry arc, followed by another smack and yet one more. I swallowed my pain, trying to hold on to my pride and not cry out. My ears burnt with shame as the rest of the boys in the class laughed softly, unable to keep their pleasure at my humiliation to themselves. The ignominy of my punishment was worse than the burning brands of pain left on my hand. I fought to keep the hot tears that threatened to spill out from coursing down my cheeks.

Mr Swaminathan, fortunately, seemed satisfied with the punishment. Perhaps he was feeling somewhat compassionate because it was almost the end of the class. Or maybe he had to finish teaching the last chapter before the end of the session. He continued his lecture, his voice droning on: 'The Panchayat seestem is the seestem of village administra-yay-shun, by yelected villagers.' His strong South Indian accent drilled into the summer afternoon. The students soon forgot about me. Now that the entertainment was over, they all had a glazed look in their eyes.

I looked out of the window. In the distance, the football fields looked lush and green. The welts on my palm sent daggers of pain shooting up my arm, reminding me that I needed to pay attention. I reluctantly tried to focus on the lesson, hoping that the rest of the class would finish without any further incident. Without thinking, I looked over at Amit, who glanced back at me.

I felt another surge of embarrassment at having been humiliated in front of my hero. Amit was fifteen and the captain of the cricket team. He had won countless matches for the school and never made fun of me like the other boys did. I wanted him to pick me to be his friend, but naturally, I never dared to approach him. Instead, I watched him wherever I could—at cricket matches, at elocution competitions, at football games. I would hang around, hoping to be able to say, 'Hi, Amit!' and get his attention for a brief moment before he turned around to laugh at what his friends said.

Suddenly, there was a knock at the door. The headmistress, Mrs Joshi, swept into the room, looking grim.

The entire class went silent at once.

'Follow me to my office please, Amit.' Mrs Joshi's voice was deathly cold.

Taken aback and curious, we wondered what she could possibly want. Her calling the class hero out like this did not make any sense. Amit looked surprised for a moment, but then he shrugged. As he stood up, his chair scraped the stone slabs of the floor, sounding unnaturally loud in the silent classroom. His khaki pants were bunched up and wrinkled at his knees in the heat and his white shirt was crumpled, the tails escaping from the back. He placed his notebook and pen on the desk and followed Mrs Joshi out. So did Mr Swaminathan. As soon as the door closed behind them, all the boys started talking.

All around the room, everyone was speculating about why Amit, the class idol, had suddenly been called to the principal's office. Was he in trouble?

Suddenly, Suresh Khosla got up, looking very pleased with himself. I was not surprised; he always rejoiced in the misfortunes of others. He cleared his throat. 'Silence, boys,' he said grandly, clapping his hands to get our attention, 'I know what has happened.' With a sly grin on his face, he said, 'Amit wrote a love letter to Rohit. Rohit showed it to me after football practice. And I told Mrs Joshi.'

As soon as Suresh had said this, there was a huge commotion. 'Arre, yaar, Amit is a bloody homo!' several of the boys shouted indignantly. I did not understand what it meant or why everyone was getting so upset. The class got quiet again when our geography teacher walked in.

'What is a homo?' I whispered to Ranjan. He looked at me with scorn, delighted by my ignorance. Lips curling, he spoke in a patronizing voice: 'Amit wrote a love letter to another boy. Of course he is a homo. It's not normal.' Grimacing, he pretended to vomit.

'Oh ...' was all I could say, embarrassed by my ignorance, feeling the blood rush to my face. 'Oh, a homo.' I bit my lip.

Later, in the middle of civics class, looking harried, Mr Puri came into the room and collected Amit's bag and books. A professor in Osmania College, where Suresh Khosla's father also taught, he was tall and athletic like Amit. It was a shock to see his shoulders stooped in shame. He did not look at any of the boys who were his son's friends. As he left, I felt afraid for Amit.

Jolted out of my ruminations by the loud 'clang-clang-clang' of the fire alarm-like bell indicating the welcome end of the class, I streamed out of the room with my classmates.

That evening, when I went home, my mind was in turmoil. This was the first time that I had seen such disgust directed at anyone for doing what I had done—write a love letter. But in the films, the hero and heroine always wrote love letters to each other. No one ever said that was dirty. This must have something to do with a boy writing a love letter to another boy. It was obviously something disgusting enough to make Ranjan pretend to vomit. I thought of Mrs Joshi's chilling tone as she spoke to Amit. How could the hero of the class have fallen from grace so easily? I wanted to ask Rani, but dared not. I would have to find out on my own.

'Arre, why are you not paying attention? What is the matter?' my father asked me with irritation as I made careless mistakes doing my mathematics homework. He was an impatient man and always asked these questions. However, he never waited for an answer.

'I am tired,' I muttered as I stifled a fake yawn and shut my notebook.

'Oph ho! If you are that tired, then why are you not in bed? I am going to listen to the news. Don't slack off so close to the end of the first year at your new school,' he said, getting up from the table to go to listen to the news on All India Radio.

His words reminded me that my exams would start soon and my stomach tightened at the thought of what would happen if I did not come first. I went to bed with many unanswered questions.

The next day, Mrs Joshi announced at assembly time that Amit had left the school. Her prim mouth was pursed in a tight grimace.

'Amit Puri is not coming back to school. He … ah … he … ah,' Mrs Joshi stammered. Then she paused and spoke again, choosing her words carefully: 'He behaved in a manner not befitting the high standards of the school.' Her glittering eyes surveyed each of the boys, the horn-rimmed glasses perched menacingly at the end of her nose, looking for anyone unfortunate enough to be standing out of line or whose hair touched the edge of his collar. I shrank back as she gave me a cursory glance.

My fascination with Rajesh Khanna would most certainly be my downfall. I had written a love letter to him—if the school found out, I could be expelled. How foolish I had been! Mrs Joshi must never know about it, I decided. Like Amit, I too would be in trouble if anyone found out. The boys would call me a 'bloody homo'! It was hard enough being younger than the other boys—if I were a homo too, life would be unbearable at school and at home. 'Chhee … chhee …' my parents would say, shaking their heads sadly.

I was suddenly seized with fear. The letter I had written to Rajesh Khanna was at home. I might have left it on my desk. Or hidden it in my secret hiding place in the garden. As Mrs Joshi's gaze fixed on me, I knew I had to go home and destroy it before anyone discovered it.

I looked back once more at Amit's empty seat before I forced myself to turn away. The chair sat vacant for the rest of the week and felt to me like a gaping hole, a wound that had bled dry but never healed. The teacher skipped his name during roll call. It was as if he had never existed.

Saturday Night. San Francisco.

There was silence. Then a series of loud beeps started.

'Damn. My mobile is dying,' Andrew muttered. 'I have to charge it. Hold on.'

I heard him fumble with the charger. 'Come home, Andrew.

Please,' I begged.

'No, call me on the motel land line. The number is 922-3000. I am in Room 323.'

I called the Travelodge and was connected to the room.

'So, what happened after that?' Andrew asked.

I exhaled slowly, trying to sort the events of that year out in my head. 'I discovered over the next few months that I was not the only one in danger. But first, I need to tell you about more—the Banerjees, our family friends, and Colonel Uncle.'

'Okay. There is a lot here that is new to me, so please explain as you go along.'

I took a deep breath, trying to figure out how to explain the complicated relationships, and then continued my story.

'The Banerjee family was the closest to us among our friends. Mr and Mrs Banerjee had two daughters—Mallika and Shyamala. Mallika was the older of the two sisters, and I adored her. She loved me too and never made fun of me like her younger sister Shyamala or Rani. I called their father Binesh Kaku and their mother Anjali Mashi—kaku is what one calls one's father's younger brother in Bengali and one's maternal aunt is mashi. Anjali Mashi and my mother were very close, like sisters. There is a saying in Bengali that one's mashi is as good as one's mother—my mother used to called her Anjali Didi—older sister.

'Binesh Kaku was a very stern man. He rarely smiled and almost never laughed. He was tall, gangly and had grey-black blotches on his skin. A thin, close-clipped moustache lined his upper lip and tufts of hair sprouted from his ears. He wore square-framed spectacles, which made his eyes look distant, as if they were fish swimming in a big glass bowl. He was always dressed in white kurta-pajama, like most of my father's relatives in Calcutta.

'Anjali Mashi, on the other hand, was a very sweet person. Hailing from Calcutta, she ran her household in the traditional Bengali way, observing customs that my mother never did—my mother had grown up in Kanpur in Uttar Pradesh. Anjali Mashi had been trained at Santiniketan, the university established by Rabindranath Tagore, and so she preferred Bengali films and music to Hindi or English. But she tolerated our interest in popular Hindi and American films and stuff with good grace.

'Shyamala was Rani's age and they were classmates. She would turn out to be a late bloomer like her sister—at that time, she still had acne and wore glasses and braces. I used to hate the way she and Rani ganged up against me!

'That summer, we made a fateful visit to the Banerjee household, when I made a discovery that would change our lives forever ... And then, of course, there was Colonel Uncle.'

'Who was he?' Andrew asked.

I was silent for a moment and looked at the picture on my nightstand. 'Colonel Uncle was the most amazing person a boy could ever hope to know. I met him that summer and I don't know how I would have made it through that year without him. He used to live upstairs.

'Colonel Uncle was a rarely seen mystery to us, almost a phantom. An older gentleman, impeccably dressed, he walked with a military gait. Rani and I used to find him very intimidating. He had maintained his living quarters at the palace by special arrangement with the Indian government, but had only recently started living there. He used a different entrance, one to which we had no access. "The Ghost Who Walks", Rani and I had dubbed him, the name that the pygmies in Lee Walker's *Phantom* comics called the Phantom. Every time we called him that, we would giggle, delighted by our cleverness. But that was before I got to know him as a friend over the summer ...'

April 1973. Hyderabad.

Ahmed Uncle and Shabnam Aunty visited a few days after the incident in school. They had been friends of the family for as long as I could remember. Ahmed Uncle, tall and formally dressed in his Nehru jacket, and Shabnam Aunty, in her embroidered salwar kameez from Pakistan, were childless and always indulged me. Just before my summer vacation started, a few days before they moved to Pakistan to return to their estate, they came to the palace—it was to be the last time that I would meet them.

'Let me take the snacks in please? Please?' I begged my mother, anxious to show Ahmed Uncle and Shabnam Aunty that I was a grown-up boy.

Elegant and poised in her sea-green silk sari, my mother smiled as I looked adoringly at her. Her hair was swept up in a bun, in the style of Sharmila Tagore, with carefully arranged curls framing her face on each side. Her sleeveless blouse, made flawlessly by our family tailor, showed off her smooth arms adorned with matching glass bangles. Mother always carried the tray. She created and enforced the house rules, but relaxed them if I begged hard enough. Moved by my pleas, she said indulgently, 'All right, just this once, beta. But be careful—this is my favourite tea set.'

I ran to the mirror to make sure my hair was neatly arranged, tucked my shirt into my shorts, and brushed the twigs and dried leaves I had acquired while wriggling around in the grass as I tried to catch a ladybird. I sighed, wishing that I was wearing neatly pressed trousers like the older boys in school.

Then I picked up the tray and started walking. I stopped for a moment at the doorway to the sitting room to steady my aching arms.

My father and our guests sat in the centre of the sitting room, around the dark teak table polished to a shine. A copy of the *Deccan Chronicle* lay folded under the table surrounded by past issues of *Life* magazine. A rainbow of lights glittered from the crystal chandelier hanging above.

As I got closer, I heard my father talking. 'What is the world coming to these days? I tell you, it was the right thing they did, expelling that boy, Amit Puri. This sort of behaviour must never be tolerated. God knows what kind of blood runs in the family. I am glad that this bad influence has been removed from Rahul's class ... I just got a call from Mr Khosla from Osmania College. His son Suresh told him what had happened. Mr Khosla said that Amit's father was going to send him to a mental institution, where they will give Amit shock therapy to cure him of this revolting condition ...'

My heart stopped beating for a second and then started hammering in my chest. What would my father do if he knew that I had written a love letter, just as Amit Puri had? Oh no, I had forgotten about the letter! I had returned home from school and had not been able to find it. It had worried me for a bit, but as was often the case, I was soon distracted. Once I found it, I would destroy it, burn it to a crisp that very day. Then no one would know my secret.

Shabnam Aunty and Ahmed Uncle sat side by side on the sofa, their expressions concerned. I looked away from them at the dark-wood ball-and-claw feet of the sofa, which contrasted with the plush crimson carpet.

My father stopped talking abruptly when he saw me and changed the topic. 'So, Ahmed Bhai,' he said, 'you are now going to leave us all and return to Pakistan. We will miss you.'

'Arre, we are not going forever. We will visit you often, you will see,' Shabnam Aunty said soothingly. 'Rahul will be unrecognizable when we see him next. Look, he is already such a big boy—he is carrying the food in all by himself.'

I went forward with the tray laden with tea, tantalizingly crisp samosas accompanied by emerald-green mint chutney.

'Careful, Rahul,' my mother murmured.

My father chuckled as I set the tray down. 'So the Prince of Kuch Bhi Nahi State is now serving his own guests!' he said.

Ahmed Uncle and Shabnam Aunty chuckled in unison. I was annoyed. Again, he had called me the Prince of Nothing Kingdom. So what if there was no state to rule? I still lived in a magical palace built by kings, the fabled Nizams of Hyderabad.

'I am sure your father will find you a lovely princess to be your bride when you grow up to be a handsome prince and you will have lots of children to rule your kingdom.' Shabnam Aunty smiled lovingly as she held my face with one hand, her plump fingers digging into my cheeks as she moved my face from side to side. I squirmed and escaped.

A princess? No thanks! I thought to myself, my mind returning to the troublesome love letter. I would find the letter and burn it. I ran off to the kitchen to get a box of safety matches and slipped them into my pocket.

I could still hear their laughter as I approached my desk in the study room. I opened the drawers, looking for an envelope with the letters 'RK' written on it in an extravagant flourish. It was nowhere to be seen. I sifted through the drawers' contents: feathers from the birds that had visited the lake, multi-coloured stones I had collected from a visit to a riverside, glass marbles, stamp collections—they were all there, except for the letter. I tore open my school bag, searching the pockets. Still no luck. The feeling of dread spread. What if someone at school had found it? No, I reasoned, it had to be around somewhere.

I remembered a part of the letter: 'I imagine you close to me, singing to me just the way you sing to Sharmila Tagore.' I blushed with shame as I imagined the boys in my class reading it. Perhaps it was in the garden—I had many secret hiding places there. I ran out to the garden.

I had spent hours trying to write the perfect letter to Rajesh Khanna. Once he read it, he would surely understand my admiration and longing. This is what I had said in my letter: 'Dear Rajesh Khanna, I have watched all your films. I think you are the most handsome man I have ever seen. I think about you all the time … Will you come to see me in Hyderabad? Or will you send for me from Bombay?'

Saturday Night. San Francisco.

'God, I was so naive. Of course, we had no internet, no television and no pop culture-induced cynicism. So imagination ruled my reality.'

'Like it does still.' Andrew laughed. 'Is that why you are so dramatic when you dream and cry? Does your imagination run away with you still?' Surprised by his nasty tone, I fell silent. He got like this when he was upset, and I hated not being able to see him. Talking on the phone right now felt like eating with a fork and spoon instead of with my fingers.

Andrew was quiet too. I could hear the foghorn from the bay in the background. 'Sorry, Rahul,' he finally said. 'That came out wrong. It's not funny. Please go on.'

'Apology accepted,' I answered. 'I'm not a drama queen. And what happened was real ...' Feeling defensive, I stopped.

'Go on,' Andrew urged, his voice gentler.

'I first heard about the legend from my mother. She had heard it from a servant whose grandmother worked for the Nizam's family. Mother said that she was so disturbed by it that she had a Hindu priest come in and purify the house after they moved in. I thought about that story often, recreating it in my mind. Somehow, it made me feel as if I belonged to the royal family and that the palace was mine. I guess that is where I started identifying with being a prince.'

'I can imagine that,' Andrew said, and I could hear the smile in his voice.

'The palace, as I told you, had been mysteriously abandoned after it was built. It had taken many years to build the imposing two-storey structure and lay out the elegant gardens and orchards. So the palace was not ready for habitation for the Nizam until 1880, decades after work had begun. Begum Razia Banu, the Nizam's mother, a tough and tenacious old lady who ruled the household with an iron hand, insisted on making the rounds of the palace to make sure it was ready for the royal family.

'As a child, I could imagine the grand old dowager going from room to room, marvelling at the tall ceilings, the marble floors, the spacious portico and the delicate balustrade that ringed the open terraces upstairs. "Bahut khubsurat," she probably said as she gave her regal approval to the beautiful work done by her minions. In my vision, Razia Banu was dressed in a glorious sharara—the floor-length ensemble worn by Muslim women—loose and shimmering with silk thread and sequins. Her head was covered with a fine muslin veil made by legendary weavers from Dhaka. Her fingers were wrinkled, liver spots liberally sprinkled over the parchment-like skin. Rings encrusted with precious diamonds, rubies and sapphires from the Golconda mines weighed down the fingers that firmly clasped a walking stick with a jewel-studded head in the shape of a dragon's visage. She made her way through the royal palace that was to be her personal domain, planning every last detail of the big move. Then she came upon a bat on the floor of the upstairs bedroom. The bat lay sprawled, dead, in the centre of the mosaic pattern on the floor. She screamed dramatically, backing away. "Toba! Toba!" she said, over and over again, her hands touching each side of her face.

'Her superstition ruled the day. The palace was condemned as a place of ill omen. The family packed itself into the horse-drawn carriage and left, the dowager muttering to herself that she would not allow bad luck to touch anyone in her family. I saw the handsome prince sulking as he sat facing the rear window of the carriage, his eyes brimming with tears, feeling powerless and angry, knowing that he would never be able to play in the garden and make friends with the trees and birds. Because, of course, he wanted to, just like me.

'The dowager cursed the palace. "*Hum nahin rah sakte hain to yahan koi khushi se nahin rah sakta ... Khandaan ke chirag ki zindagi barbad ho jayegi.*' A short and powerful curse: "No one can be happy in this palace if I cannot live here. The life of the heir of the family which lives here will be hell."

'My mother was afraid that our family would face misfortune because of the curse.'

'What a horrible thing for her to say! Such a witch,' Andrew interjected.

'Yes. Who knows why she was so evil.' I shivered even though the fire was warm.

'So what happened to the palace after she left?'

'It was shuttered and left empty for many decades, and nature crept stealthily into the grounds. Wilderness and chaos continued unchecked until the Indian government took over and the palace became the Mint House.

'In front of the palace that I grew up in were immaculate lawns and a lake, fruit orchards, the driveway and thickets of trees that surrounded the endless carpet of green. Over the years, shrubs and bushes had turned into trees and trees had grown into towering giants that stretched and wove their branches into the ancient canopy above. Behind the palace were the tennis courts, the dhobi ghaats, the giant banyan tree and the guava orchard. And the palace walls were patrolled by sentries day and night.'

'You lucky bastard! That sounds like a fantasy palace, complete with guards and walls.'

'Yes, I was lucky—until it all fell apart. So back to my obsession with Rajesh Khanna and the letter …'

3

April 1973. Hyderabad.

I would come home from watching Rajesh Khanna films, consumed with thoughts of him—how he looked and how he smiled—his every gesture a source of endless stimulation. Then, at night, I would lie awake in bed, seized with a nameless longing. Sometimes, I dreamt of him and me together, at home in the palace, sleeping in my bed. I would relive my dream all day and remember with pleasure how his body had felt next to mine.

But after what had happened at school the week before, my love letter to him—once a beautiful missive—had become a curse. I had to destroy it. I would be a 'homo' as long as the letter existed.

As I continued on my quest for the letter in the garden, I went to one of my usual hiding places. Looking carefully over my shoulder, I picked up a large rock at the base of a tree and removed a little metal box. I scraped the soil off the box. It was decorated with a print of Rajesh Khanna and Sharmila Tagore, the name of the 1969 hit film *Aradhana* inscribed across the cover. I opened it and took out the letter still in its envelope. I read it once more. The familiar words said farewell to me, as did my dreams of meeting Rajesh Khanna.

I hid behind the bushes as I tore up the letter, starting at the centre and rending each square into smaller pieces. I struck a match and lit the pile. My writing came alive one last time as the flames curled around each square. Fragments of words—'want to see you and be with you ... dream about spending time with you'—glowed as they disappeared in smoke. After the pile was burnt, I took each little piece and ground it between my fingers. I rubbed the ashes into the ground with my feet. There was no one around. The gardeners and sweepers were on their afternoon siesta.

The deed done, I climbed up the gulmohar tree to my favourite spot, surrounded by a carpet of dry twigs and red-gold flowers. I climbed the precarious footholds with ease and, once high up, I snuggled against the trunk. A koel tried half-heartedly to start its sweet crescendo of calls, but faltered and stopped. A faint wind blew towards me from the mango orchard, carrying with it the tangy smell of its raw fruit. I had destroyed the evidence. For the moment, it felt safe.

Hearing my father call me, I climbed down with a guilty flush. I returned to the palace to see Ahmed Uncle and Shabnam Aunty standing in the portico, ready to leave. They gave me one last hug before they drove off in their Baby Ford.

The shadows of the trees in the garden were long, casting accusing fingers at me. I knew that no one had seen me burn the love letter, but I felt a shiver of apprehension. Birds chirped madly in their last chorus before settling in for the night in the giant banyan tree behind the palace. A large flock of European wood pigeons that lived on the grounds swooped and climbed the sky in a silent grey cloud as mosquitoes buzzed in a darker cloud close to my head. Thousands of black, flitting shadows darkened the evening sky as bats left on their nightly excursion. I looked up at the upper storey of the palace and my heart beat with excitement. The silhouette of jagged, urn-shaped structures that once supported the decaying frame of a balustrade looked like a broken crown. Behind them, I could see shells of rooms, some without a roof, sprawling until I could see no more. Clouds of bats came pouring out of the abandoned rooms. Some of the still-habitable rooms were used by Colonel Uncle. I was desperately curious to find out what was there, but my parents had made it strictly out of bounds.

'Rahul, you always find a way to do what you want. But I don't want you to go upstairs—there are bats there. It is dirty,' my mother warned me. However, I feared another, darker terror upstairs, something menacing that I would do well to avoid. But Rani and I would make occasional, half-hearted attempts to go upstairs, she egging me on. 'I challenge you to go upstairs,' she would say scornfully at the end of an argument. These challenges were always at night, of course. 'I knew it, I knew it!' she would then crow in victorious delight when she would find me, each time, huddled on the tenth step of the winding wrought-iron stairs, unable to go any farther, frozen in terror of God-knows-what.

'Are bats dangerous?' I'd once asked my mother. I was fascinated by them. Each bat had a fox-like, mammalian face, except that the nose was shaped like a leaf. Every sunset, I saw them flitting around like little black butterflies, wheeling and diving. 'Ignorant people think so because they look so different from anything else that flies. Contrary to urban myths, flying foxes or bats are completely harmless to humans and certainly do not get entangled in our hair,' Mother had said. 'I just think that places where bats live are filthy and dark. You never know what else might be there.'

Anyway, the urgent matter of the letter handled, I went to my room and curled up in my favourite chair with a mystery by Enid Blyton. Turning on the lamp, I was soon engrossed in my own world when Rani burst in.

'Rahul, Rahul! Where are you?' Rani sounded annoyed when she could not see me. The large armchair in which I comfortably snuggled easily swallowed my thin arms and torso.

'I'm here,' I answered, wary and not quite sure whether Rani had a devious trick planned.

'Aren't you supposed to be studying and preparing for the exams?'

'Yes, I am, but I don't feel like it.'

'You better do well at school or Baba will be very upset. And then we won't get to go watch any films this summer.'

'What about you? Are you preparing for the exams?' I countered.

Rani raised a hand patronizingly. 'Please. As if I would ever neglect my studies. You are the one who is always daydreaming and wandering about in the garden. I'm surprised you haven't been hauled up by your teachers at school.'

I wished she would go away, but Rani continued: 'Talking about school ... I heard from Suresh Khosla's sister that someone called Amit in your class was expelled. He told her that he had alerted the principal about a love letter that Amit had written. I am sure Suresh made it all up. Such troublemakers, Suresh and his sister! I hate people who tittle-tattle and get others in trouble. His sister is always bullying the new girls.'

I sat up, attentive. 'Suresh is the same way,' I told Rani, happy we were in agreement about something, thinking about his hatred when accusing Amit. Surprised at how amenable Rani was being, I decided to push my luck and ask her the question that had been preying on my mind all day.

'Do you know what shock therapy is?' I asked.

'It is given to someone who has a mental problem. You know, they put these metal plates on your temples and send some high-voltage electric current through it. It zaps the brain and gets people to stop behaving a certain way. Some people go mad after the therapy. Why?'

'Oh, nothing …' I said, sick to my stomach at the thought of Amit gone mad. A stab of fear went through me. What if I were made to go through shock therapy? Misery wound itself like a tight rope through my gut and I thought I was going to vomit. But I decided to push further. Perhaps Rani would know why the boys were so disgusted in class.

'Rani, what is a homo?' I asked daringly.

'What? Where did you hear that word?'

'At school.'

'Shhh …' my sister cautioned me, looking around to see if anyone could hear us. Hearing a car coming up the drive, we both jumped up.

Ashamed of my question and grateful for the reprieve, I blurted: 'Who could be visiting so late? Ma will want us to seat our guests. I will go and tell her.'

'Don't mention that word again,' Rani said sternly before I ran off, wishing I had not asked her anything.

My announcement of visitors sent my mother into a flurry of activity to become presentable. I ran to the window that overlooked the garden and the driveway, trying to see who had come. I was glad that Rani had not responded to my question—maybe she would forget it. The automobile lights swept the front of the palace, casting long shadows on the portico as the car came to rest.

An old, familiar Bentley sat there, shaking with the effort of coming up the long driveway. 'Firdausi Uncle and Aunty are visiting,' I informed my parents. Mr and Mrs Firdausi alighted from the Bentley, followed by their daughter Dilnaz. I was happy to see them. We loved to play board games and hide-and-seek with Dilnaz who was a year older than my sister. She was boisterous and tomboyish and ready for fun at any time. Grasping for a tiny bit of normality after such an anxiety-ridden day, I looked forward to a fun evening playing in the garden.

Rani and I turned on the lights in the sitting room and quickly straightened the sofa and the cushions. 'Namaste, Uncle and Aunty,' we chorused, opening the door when we heard our visitors knock.

'Namaste, beta,' they answered.

I was shocked to see a few inches in height and budding breasts had transformed Dilnaz into a young lady. 'Hi, Rahul. Hi, Rani,' she said in a put-on grown-up voice.

We led them to the sitting room and my parents joined them. As we went out into the garden with Dilnaz, I tried to tell her about the Enid Blyton books we were reading, but she had other interests.

'Have you started reading *Mills and Boons* novels?' Dilnaz asked.

'Yes, I have. But I have to hide them because they are meant for adults and our parents don't like us reading such books,' Rani replied, looking over her shoulder.

'I have to hide them too. But we are grown-up now, aren't we?' Dilnaz said to Rani with a wink and a nudge of her elbow.

I stared at Dilnaz. Her new hairstyle, like the actress Aruna Irani's, made her look very confident. She no longer wore a simple hair band over her frizzy hair. I tried to talk to her again, but she ignored me.

'So, have your menses started?' she asked Rani.

My sister and Dilnaz laughed at a shared joke I did not understand.

'Yes, a year ago,' Rani said.

'What are menses?' I asked.

'Nothing that you need to know about,' Rani said sternly, making a face at Dilnaz to shut up.

Dilnaz leaned back and looked at Rani critically. 'What is your bra size?'

Rani frowned at her and shook her head.

'You're lucky. I bet yours are round.' She looked down at her breasts with disgust. 'Mine are pointy. I bet all the boys want to talk to you.'

'I need to go help Ma,' Rani muttered and left in a hurry.

I felt uncomfortable around the new Dilnaz. As she moved close to me, I backed away into a tree trunk.

Standing in front of me, Dilnaz said softly, 'Rahul, you have seen a girl's breasts before, haven't you?'

I shook my head, both fascinated and repelled.

'You remind me of my cousin. He is shy just like you and had never touched a girl's breasts until I let him touch mine. Go ahead, you can touch them too.' She moved closer. The bark dug into my back.

Dilnaz lowered her voice conspiratorially. 'There is a boy in my neighbourhood, about your age, who leaves a love letter for me under the doormat every day. Isn't that sweet? What about you? Has anyone written you a love letter?'

I thought about the letter I had burnt and remained silent.

'You don't know what fun you're missing,' Dilnaz said archly, moving even closer, pressing her body against mine. 'Arre? What's the matter? You know the boys in your class would do anything for this.' Her voice was mocking.

Once again, I felt like an outsider in a familiar world. Dilnaz took my hand and placed it on her breast. It felt soft and warm. As I jerked my hand away, feeling dirty, she laughed derisively.

'What is the matter with you?' she asked again. She turned away and adjusted her breasts. 'You and Rani are not fun any more.'

'Rahul. Come in and help serve snacks to Uncle and Aunty,' my mother called from the portico.

'Are you scared, Rahul?' Dilnaz's jeering voice followed me as I ran to help Ma, shaking my hands and tossing my head from side to side as I tried to rid myself of the feelings of humiliation and discomfort that the incident had brought back.

When I reached the kitchen, Dilnaz walked in behind me, looking nonchalant and humming a tune. Rani and Ma got the snacks and drinks ready and served them. I felt the agitation building in my chest and tried to talk normally with Mr and Mrs Firdausi. As my father opened the windows to let some cool air in, a bat flitted into the room. It swooped in a graceful arc, the black, lace-like wings fluttering like wisps of evening light under the vaulted ceiling. We watched, transfixed. Suddenly, it swooped towards the window, preparing to fly out, when a breeze blew the gauze curtain around it. Mrs Firdausi jumped up in a flash, putting her dish down with a clatter. She rushed to the window where the bat was fluttering, caught in the curtains.

'Oh, I hate these disgusting creatures! They look like monsters with fur and wings. They are an abomination,' she cried as she shook the bat loose from the curtains. It tumbled to the floor, dazed.

'Mrs Firdausi, stop! Don't hurt it!' Ma jumped up, as did my father, but it was too late. Before our horrified eyes, Mrs Firdausi whipped her shoe off, battering the poor thing to death.

'You dirty, dirty creature,' she said with each blow, her voice shaking with revulsion. I thought of the soft, furry body with its incredible wings, each tip of it like an extended finger, connected by a fine skin-like web—and then it lay smashed on the floor, bloody and limp. I was overcome by anger and repulsion. My earlier terror and the stress of the past few days rose in my throat and my eyes darted around the room. Dilnaz and Rani were looking away from the scene while my parents appeared to be frozen with shock. Only Mr Firdausi seemed unmoved by what had happened.

At that moment, Firdausi Aunty changed before my eyes from a lovable aunt to a bloodthirsty hag. Her senseless disgust had destroyed a harmless bat—one that had probably lived upstairs. Maybe it had baby bats waiting to be fed. I wondered why people killed things that they found ugly. What were they afraid of? The bat had not been about to harm anyone.

As I ran screaming from the room, I resolved to never, ever speak to Firdausi Aunty again. I buried myself in the comfort of my bed, sobbing. I recalled again my vision of the dowager leaving the palace in terror. Her finely woven white sharara was covered with splashes of blood and shreds of delicate bat skin. Her harsh voice echoed through the empty palace: 'Toba, toba, toba ...'

The next morning, I sat at the breakfast table, worried. The exams were going to start in less than two weeks. It was the end of my first year at the new school and my parents had high expectations of me. I could not wait for the summer vacation, my favourite time of the year, to begin. Breakfast was a long, leisurely affair of parathas, fried eggs, leftover curry and tea that morning. And Ma was allowing us to loll around instead of cleaning the table and wiping it down after we had finished eating.

'Do you think you are taller than me now?' Rani asked. I immediately snapped out of my daydream. The magic words had made it competition time again.

Rani and I measured our heights often, sometimes daily. I was convinced that in the summer I would grow at a faster pace than during the rest of the year due to the amount of time I spent each day hanging from the pole set up by my father. The pole was suspended from the rafters of the veranda. Hanging from it, I was about six inches off the ground. Jumping up and grabbing it with both hands, I would let gravity pull me down, occasionally twisting and turning, willing my spine to elongate, vertebra by vertebra. I was sure that if I did it often enough my bones would grow longer and longer until I was as tall as Rani, who had measured a full five-feet-four the last time. I had been trying hard to catch up all through the school year, but I was still five-foot-three.

'Yes, I am,' I said in answer to Rani's question.

'What if you're wrong?' she said.

'I'm taller than you,' I said, now feeling less confident. But there was no turning back now.

'All right. But if you are still shorter than me, you will have to go upstairs. All the way this time. And if there are ghosts of dead members of the royal family, or even the Ghost Who Walks, you will have to face them. Otherwise, I will tell all your friends that you are a cowardy-custard.' Her face was menacing as she said this, her eyes thin slits. She was leaving me no room to negotiate. I swaggered over to the doorframe where we measured our heights, acting more confident than I felt.

'Ma,' I yelled. 'Please come and measure our heights.' I did not put it past Rani to doctor the results. I secretly hoped that my mother would skew the measurements in my favour, but she never did.

My mother appeared. 'Do you think I have no work to do?' she asked in mock annoyance. I knew that she secretly enjoyed this game of ours. 'All right,' she said. 'You first, Rahul, and then you, Rani. Hurry up, I don't have all day.'

I stood against a post in the veranda barefoot. Ma placed a ruler on my head, taking care that it was parallel to the floor and perpendicular to the post. She took a pencil, marked the column and wrote my name next to it. Rani hovered suspiciously, making sure that I was not getting an unfair advantage by error or intention. Then it was Rani's turn. To my mortification, I was still shorter by an inch.

'I knew it, I knew it!' Rani jumped up and down in victory as Ma went back to her work. 'Now you must go upstairs.'

'No, I won't.'

'Yes, you will. You will, or else I will tell Baba that you were asking about shock therapy and also about homos.' She whispered the last word.

'All right,' I conceded as fear descended on me again. 'Just don't tell anyone. Swear?'

'We'll see,' she said coyly and ran off.

I dreaded the coming of night that day, when I would have to go upstairs. I knew that Colonel Uncle lived up there. I wondered if he had a wife.

I went to the kitchen. 'Where is Colonel Uncle's wife?' I asked Ma.

'Colonel Uncle is a confirmed bachelor,' she answered.

'What is a confirmed bachelor?'

'Someone who never marries,' Ma said in a funny tone that made it clear that bachelors were a set of people quite different from regular people.

'Why do bachelors not marry?'

'Usually because of a broken heart. Or if they have waited too long and realized it is too late. But you don't have to worry about that.

Your father and I will find you a lovely bride. Your grandmother found brides for all your uncles and a groom for me. We don't have any bachelors in our family, so don't be concerned about becoming one.' Ma seemed determined to save me from a bachelor's fate.

'But what if I don't want to marry?' I thought about how I had felt no interest in Dilnaz, and her reaction to my disinterest. What if I did not want to marry when my parents thought it was time? I felt frustrated that I could not share my fears with my mother. I had always felt close to her, but for the first time, I was scared to tell her how different I felt from everyone at school.

'What is this madness? Everyone marries. You will too,' Baba said with a note of finality in his voice. He had just arrived home for lunch and I had not realized that he had been listening to our conversation.

'Why does Colonel Uncle live upstairs?' I asked my father.

'Colonel Uncle has lived here for many years. He was a colonel in the army in the days of the Second World War and was highly decorated. The government allocated the upstairs to him before we arrived here. He used to travel a lot earlier, but is here most of the time now.'

'Do you know who gave you your set of cooking utensils?' Baba asked Rani, who had just arrived as well.

'No,' she said.

'Colonel Uncle gave it to you when you were a little girl.'

I developed an immediate interest in Colonel Uncle when I heard that he had gifted Rani my favourite toy set—the shining stainless steel miniature cooking utensils including pots and pans, a stove, plates and cutlery.

'So how was your day at work?' I would ask Rani when I played with it, bustling around the make-believe kitchen as I ground spices, sautéed vegetables, boiled rice, rolled out perfectly shaped chapatis and created a culinary masterpiece out of thin air, accompanied by a lot of banging and clanging of the utensils.

'Fine. How was yours? What did you make me?' she would demand.

'Oh, I have made pulao, dal, chapatis, curry, sweets and so much more,' I would explain, ladling out large portions of air and heaping them on the toy plate.

Rani wielded this girlish interest of mine with great political skill whenever she wanted to get me to agree to something. She threatened me at the end of every fight, forcing me to concede defeat, saying, 'I will tell all your friends that you are a girl and play with my dolls and cooking utensils.'

That evening, after dinner, Rani and I went to the back of the house. I looked up at the iron stairs that spiralled around a metal pole, dark and beautifully wrought. I had never gone past the tenth step before.

'All right, then, here you go,' Rani said, handing me the old Eveready family torch and pushing me up the stairs. I clutched the thick, red plastic torch and pushed the button forward. As it slid on with a bump and a click, a watery beam of light shone ahead. The lights around the tennis court were on and might have illuminated my path, but their warm glow was devoured by the inky blackness of the summer night before it reached the stairs. The restless wind blew in the banyan tree, making whooshing sounds. The mango trees shivered in response as dry summer lightning forked through the sky, followed by deafening rolls of thunder. Back and forth, the trees swayed, as if speaking to each other. In my terror, I wondered if they were trying to warn me. I paused and then stopped altogether. Maybe I should just return and call the whole thing off? But I was too proud to back out.

I placed one foot in front of the other, forcing myself to go on. Soon, I had crossed the tenth step. By now, my eyes were used to the semi-darkness and I could make out each step before me. With the torch held in one hand and using my other hand as a guide, I moved up one foot at a time.

'Are you still climbing or just pretending?' Rani's jeering voice floated up from below. I was too busy climbing to answer. My hands were clammy and the torch felt slippery in them. Ahead of me was the first bend of the spiral staircase. Then I walked on to an open terrace covered with twigs, branches and leaves that looked as if they had collected over many years. The gusts of wind caught me off-guard and I staggered for a moment before steadying myself. Leaves churned in little vortexes at my feet and the wind felt cool on my sweat-drenched body. In the dim light of the night sky, I could see that there was a cunningly designed balustrade with urn-shaped railings all around the terrace. The terrace led to a number of darkened doorways. A glow of light came from a window at one end—it must be part of Colonel Uncle's living quarters, I thought. From where I stood, I could see the dark and cave-like empty rooms, and the smell of bat urine was faint but unmistakeable. I gingerly entered one of the abandoned rooms, my feet crunching years and years of accumulated debris, and was assailed by an unbearable stench. I shone the torch around and up at the ceiling. There were hundreds of fruit bats, or flying foxes as we called them, hanging upside down from the beams in the ceiling. Their black faces and snouts looked menacing and I retreated, frightened by the sheer number.

As I backed away, I tripped over some branches and fell. The torch rolled away, its beam illuminating damp walls with peeling plaster in a slow arc. I scrambled to my feet, picked up the torch and ran out to the terrace, my breath coming in short gasps.

I felt something soft and furry against my leg and then someone pulled my shirt. I yelled, trying to get away, and ran into a large urn, which fell over with a nasty crack.

'Kaun hai?' A voice cut through the air like a steel whip, asking the intruder to identify himself. A door opened and light streamed out. I was sitting on the ground, next to a furry jute bag and a broken urn. My shirt was torn and a piece was still hooked on a stray wire hanging from the doorframe of the room full of bats.

It was Colonel Uncle. His voice softened when he saw me. 'Rahul?' he asked. 'What is the matter? Come on in. Are you hurt?'

I was so surprised he knew who I was that I could not answer. I got up, feeling sheepish, and followed him.

'I was up here because I lost a bet with Rani ...' My voice trailed off. 'And then I saw the bats and thought there was a furry animal and ... I am sorry, Colonel Uncle. Please do not tell my father.'

Colonel Uncle was dressed in a gorgeous silk gown. The design was very intricate and reminded me of some tapestry I had once seen. He said kindly, 'No, I will not tell your father. Let me see if you have any cuts that need cleaning.'

I looked around. The room was beautiful, with the walls painted a warm beige colour. The ceiling was high and vaulted just like the rooms downstairs and an ornate chandelier hung in the middle. The door that opened to the terrace let in a gust of wind and the chandelier swayed gently in the breeze, the crystals making a soft, tinkling sound. The furniture in the room was very old and the dark wood and exquisite upholstery caught my eyes. Everything looked shiny and clean. A dark-blue Persian carpet covered the floor.

'I hope I have none, and if I do, please don't use tincture of iodine …' My voice became faint at the thought of the burning sensation that the tincture would cause. It was the school nurse's favourite first-aid medicine and I hated it, preferring the coolness of Mercurochrome when applied on cuts and wounds.

Colonel Uncle laughed. 'Looks like you only have some scratches on your palms and knees,' he said. 'When I was in the army, we did not even have tincture of iodine. The doctors had to amputate arms and legs without any anaesthesia.'

I shivered. 'My father told me you fought in the Second World War. Is that true? Is that when you did not have anaesthesia?'

Colonel Uncle's voice grew grave as he said, 'Yes.' He was quiet for a few moments, not volunteering any information about the war. But I persisted, thinking of the war in Italy, of villas and gardens and Venice.

'Oh, you are so lucky!' I exclaimed. 'Did you ever ride in a gondola in a Venetian canal? And what about the statue—Michelangelo's David? Did you see it? And the Sistine Chapel? I wish I could go to Italy. I learnt all about it in school.' Meeting someone who could tell me about the wonders of Italy I had only read about in books was too exciting for me and I ignored Colonel Uncle's serious expression.

'The Italy you study about in school did not really exist when I was there. I was only twenty-one years old and the British sent me from here to fight in the war as part of the British Army. It was a difficult time. Several of my friends died. I was very lucky. Nothing is ever fun in the time of war.'

I pointed to the marble bust of Apollo on his dressing table. 'Is that from Italy?' I asked.

'Yes, it is one of the two things I have left. I gave away most of the things I had to my friends many years ago. In those days, wealthy Italian families abandoned their possessions. One family in particular preferred to give me some of their family heirlooms. They did not want the Germans to get their hands on them.'

'What else do you still have?' I asked.

'This picture,' Colonel Uncle said. It was a sepia print, brown and discoloured, set in a leather frame. The leather was dark brown and covered with a fine web of cracks. Colonel Uncle picked it up from the marble-topped table and brushed the cuff of his sleeve across the front of the frame. I looked at the picture. I saw Colonel Uncle, barely recognizable. His arm was wrapped around the shoulders of another handsome young man and they were looking at each other and laughing. They were dressed in army uniforms, the British insignia clearly visible on Colonel Uncle's uniform. I stared with fascination at the young man in the picture. He had short, dark hair and his smile was radiant. He looked rebellious and wore a devil-may-care expression like James Dean. Like in the poster in Rani's room, a cigarette was hanging rakishly from his lips.

'Who is this?' I asked.

'That is Claudio. My friend.' Colonel Uncle saw me looking at Claudio's picture with interest and added with a hint of laughter: 'He looks like James Dean, doesn't he?'

'Yes,' I said, unable to hide my admiration. 'Where is he now? Did he die in the war?'

'No, he is alive,' Colonel Uncle said, laughing. 'He is a very good friend of mine and we write to each other a lot. He lives in Montepulciano with his wife and children.'

'Why did you not stay in Italy?' I asked.

'The war was over. I had to leave.' He was quiet for a second as he placed the picture back. 'So why did you run out of the room on the terrace in such a panic?' Colonel Uncle enquired.

'I am very scared of the dark. Rani made a bet with me. I lost. So I had to come upstairs. Wait till she finds out I saw your sitting room!

Anyway, I saw the bats hanging from the ceiling and suddenly got scared.'

'Rahul, there is no reason to be scared of bats, you know.'

'I know, I know! My mother told me the same thing, but then I thought there was a ghost who was pulling on my shirt.'

I felt guilty suddenly about the jokes we had made about uncle by calling him 'The Ghost Who Walks'. Just like Phantom in the comics, Colonel Uncle was proving to be very wise and capable.

'Mrs Firdausi killed a bat downstairs yesterday. It probably lived up here,' I said angrily. 'She said that bats are dirty and strange creatures that get caught in long hair and bite.'

'That is one of the oldest myths in the world.'

'I thought all myths were lovely,' I said, thinking of all the beautiful Greek myths I had read.

'Some myths are beautiful, like the myths about Goddess Durga and Goddess Kali. Others are not so inspiring and are created in ignorance.'

Colonel Uncle was not smiling any more. 'Fear and ignorance are our biggest enemies. They blind us to the truth, make us hate those who are different.' He looked at the photo again and carefully adjusted it in its place.

'Is it true that bats are blind?' I asked. 'Rani says so. Then how can they fly?'

'By using sonar. Inside their brain—that tiny little bat brain—is a sonar device that is constantly sensing the world of objects. That is why a bat would never get stuck in someone's hair, because it would avoid it easily, given its highly precise sonar system.'

I felt a surge of anger again at Mrs Firdausi.

'And bats eat many times their body weight in insects, like those annoying mosquitoes,' Colonel Uncle added. Then he looked at his watch and said, 'It is almost ten. Your parents are probably getting worried about you. I will walk you downstairs.'

'Please do not tell my father I was up here,' I begged him again.

'Don't worry. This will be our little secret. You can visit any time you want. I have been travelling to my family home in Rajasthan to take care of the estate for the past few years, but I will be here a lot more in the future. You will find me almost any time you visit.' Colonel Uncle smiled and I felt comforted. He walked me downstairs, using the other flight of stairs that led to a separate locked door, which was his private entrance.

Rani was beside herself with worry by the time I found her.

'Where were you and what were you doing up there?' she demanded. 'I almost told Ma and Baba. Of course, they would have been furious! So, what is it like upstairs?'

'Oh, wouldn't you love to know! If you never tell anyone that I play with your kitchen toy set, I will tell you.'

Rani hesitated. Her eyes glittered and she said, 'I am not interested.'

'Fine. Now you will never know what Colonel Uncle showed me,' I said airily as I walked away, feeling a rare sense of power in our never-ending struggle for the upper hand.

Saturday Evening. San Francisco.

'I already like Colonel Uncle. He seems to be the coolest of the gang.' Andrew's words broke into my memories. 'Everyone else seems to be really hard to deal with.'

'Yes, as I said, he was simply amazing.'

'So tell me, how did Colonel Uncle end up not marrying? From what you say, no one can escape the marriage trap.' He laughed ironically and said with some bitterness, 'And you don't seem to be winning this battle.'

'Hey, Andrew. Chill out. Give me a break, okay? You promised to hear me out …'

'Got it.' Andrew changed the subject swiftly, much to my relief. I really did not want to get into an argument again. 'I wonder what it is about bats that makes people so afraid. I mean, even here, bats are associated with so much scary stuff around Halloween, but it's in a "Haha, funny!" way. Although, that stupid superstition that they get caught in hair is quite common. But I love to watch them flying around at dusk around Stowe Lake in Golden Gate Park.'

'I think they get a raw deal because they are different. They fly and are nocturnal.'

Andrew was quiet for a few moments. 'But then, so do mosquitoes. They are not associated with darkness and evil.'

I made no answer. Andrew had a point. I looked at the clock and then out at the San Francisco Bay. The fog was rolling in across the bay now, shrouding it with translucent wisps of grey. It would be dark soon—and there was still so much to tell. A cable car rumbled by on its tracks and the apartment walls shook slightly. 'Let me get back to my story,' I said. 'Are you ready?'

'Hold on, let me get a beer.' I heard Andrew stomp to the fridge, take out a can and flip the lid with a pop-and-fizz. He took a swig. 'Shoot,' he said as he stifled an unexpected burp, 'Sorry …'

4

April 1973. Hyderabad.

I spent the next week with my nose buried in my school books as the teachers relentlessly ploughed through the last chapters of the syllabus, barely giving us time to revise and catch up on the new lessons. That Saturday, I had to study for my exams all day. I thought longingly about the garden and wished I could embark on the 'royal tour' I took of the grounds each year. But I would have to wait until the vacations started.

The palace was flanked by the state secretariat building on one side and the India Government Mint on the other. I heard the clock on the secretariat building chime the hour. It was already five o'clock.

'Rahul, we will be leaving at six o'clock for the Puja Committee meeting.' Ma's voice wafted in from her dressing room. She was already putting on her make-up—I could hear the drawers of the antique dressing table open and shut as she took out her cosmetics. There was a Bengali Association meeting at the Banerjee home. All the local Bengalis were meeting to discuss the upcoming Durga puja celebrations.

I did not really like going to these meetings. But I would get to see Mallika this time, so I was looking forward to an evening of fun, games and food.

I decided to go to the lakeside for a little while and lay down on a big rock. I wondered if Mallika had ever been tormented by her classmates. No, I reasoned, because Mallika was a good Bengali girl. I could not imagine her doing anything wrong like I had done, and drawing such contempt from her friends. I wanted to confide in her about what had happened in school, but I dared not. I shuddered to think what Binesh Kaku would do to me if he were my father—he was stricter than mine and meted out punishment mercilessly to his daughters.

Rani came running up to me, rudely interrupting my musings. A family of ducks rose up from the reeds, flapping their wings and quacking in alarm as they moved to the far side of the lake.

'Look what you did,' I said crossly. 'You scared them away.'

'Oh, please,' Rani said, sounding annoyed. 'What are you doing, Rahul? Don't you know we are going to see Mallika Didi and Shyamala? It's almost six o'clock. You better get dressed right away. Baba will be ready to drive soon—and you know how he hates to be kept waiting.'

'All right,' I mumbled. 'Stop pushing me.' We walked hurriedly back to the palace. 'Look,' I said, pointing to a cluster of snowy white egrets sitting on one of the branches of the giant banyan tree. As I gestured towards them, they rose like a flurry of snowflakes, a luminous white against the emerald green leaves of the banyan tree and glided effortlessly towards the lake, sparkling against the silhouette of the mosque that rose behind the palace walls. 'They are lovely, aren't they?' Rani murmured as caught up in the beauty of the moment as I was. 'Anyway, hurry up, you slowpoke,' she said, soon back to her usual form. I followed her to the palace—she easily outpaced me with her longer legs and brisk stride.

I washed up and searched the almirah for a stylish shirt to wear. I found one designed like the shirts Rajesh Khanna wore in *Anand*. It had a high collar and was made of cotton, light and cool. In that shirt, I felt as if I could be in a movie scene with him right there. For a moment I saw us together, lost to the world, yearning to be in each other's arms. Then I heard the impatient sound of a car horn coming from the portico.

'Rahul, Rani, are you ready?' My father sounded irritated. He had already got the Baby Ford out from the garage.

'Go join your father, Rani. Rahul, please come and help me with the sari.' My mother was running late as well.

I ran to her bedroom, where she stood in front of the mirror. I always thought that my mother was the most beautiful woman in the world. She had high cheekbones, almond-shaped eyes and long, lustrous hair down to her waist. For me, she held the secrets of the universe.

'Your great-grandmother was from the state of Assam, Rahul. That is why we both have such high cheekbones and you have that special hue to your skin,' she had told me many times.

'That makes me part Assamese too,' I always replied, feeling a great deal of affection for all things Assamese—Assam tea, rhinoceri and tea plantations.

At the moment, Ma was busy putting on her jewellery. 'Please pull the hem of my sari down and make sure all the pleats are even,' she said.

I got down on all fours at once, adjusting the length of the sari.

'It is even,' I said, dusting my knees and elbows and readjusting my collar.

'Thank you, Rahul. Am I looking pretty?' Ma preened in front of the full-length mirror of the almirah, knowing she looked smashing. 'Come here, stand next to me.'

I did. A boy of thirteen with fine features and the beginnings of a masculine chin and jawline and large eyes stared back at me. His hair was carefully arranged with a curl resting on his forehead. He wore a light-brown shirt with a high collar and dark drainpipe pants. He looked remarkably like Rajesh Khanna, I thought. I pouted my lips and tilted my head to one side, just like him. I was pleased with what I saw.

My mother smiled at me, and I said, 'Ma, you always look pretty. Just like Sharmila Tagore.'

She giggled self-consciously, patting the bun piled high on her head. 'When you grow up, all the girls will come after you, asking you to marry them. You are a lucky boy.'

'What if I don't want to get married?' I asked, feeling no excitement at the thought of being chased by girls.

'Oh, you silly boy!' My mother laughed. 'What an absurd question! Everyone has to get married. It is the normal thing to do. Come on now, your father will get upset if we delay any more.'

I wanted to tell her so badly that I was not like everyone else. That I was different from the boys in my class. That I might have been doing something really wrong. And that I did not want to get married. But I was sure she would not understand. This was not like the time when I had refused to play cricket with the other boys and she had argued with my father to let me stay at home and help her in the kitchen. This time, she was clear about what was normal and what was expected of me. I turned away from her, feeling very alone.

We quickly walked to the car and I tumbled into the back seat next to Rani. My father was at the wheel, looking annoyed. 'Oho, Mr Late Latif,' he snapped irritably. 'Always late. I don't understand why you can't be like your sister.' His jaw tightened and he started the engine.

As we drove out on the long driveway—always dark and covered by a canopy of trees—I sat at the edge of my seat my head close to the window, ready to watch the sentries enact their ritual as we left the palace. They looked like toys from the veranda. I loved the way they would spring to attention every time we passed, their rifles held upright, the bayonets gleaming, a warning to the world to stay out. No one was allowed to enter the Mint House unless they were visiting us because it was a secured area.

As we drove towards Mallika's house in Banjara Hills, we crossed the secretariat building, tall and imposing. The Khairatabad neighbourhood sundry store and café, named Café Irani, was filled to the brim with the Saturday late-afternoon crowd. The traffic was crazy and cars drove by ignoring lanes and traffic lights. Scooters and motorcycles only added to the confusion, and cycle rickshaws and bicycles continuously rang their bells. Stray dogs expertly waited for the right moment to cross the street and cows moved placidly in the traffic, their expressions inscrutable. As we approached the main road that led to Banjara Hills, the traffic thinned out and cars drove in a more disciplined fashion. The crowded neighbourhoods around Mint House had smaller houses and flats, crammed together. But as the roads widened, stately trees lined more elegant neighbourhood streets. Peepul, gulmohar and neem trees towered high above, blocking the light from the sun. Soon, we were climbing up the steep roads of Banjara Hills. As we got close to the house, we saw lots of cars in the driveway. The gates were open and the chowkidars, in their navy-blue uniforms, were on guard as always. My father parked a little distance from the house and we all had to walk a steep path to the house. Finally, I rang the doorbell.

Binesh Kaku came to the door and we saw a crowd in the background, their words tumbling towards us in the torrent of sweetness that is Bengali. Trying not to look at the woolly tufts sprouting from his ears, Rani and I chorused together: 'Nomoshkar, Binesh Kaku.'

'Rahul, Rani!' a glowing Mallika exclaimed as she came running into the foyer dressed in a light summer frock, followed by her sister Shyamala.

Mallika's hair was thick and lustrous and flowed down to her waist. She had a lovely smile, radiant and impish, that made her dimples show and her eyes sparkle. It was like the full moon peering from a break in the clouds, breathtaking every time. With her oval face, doe-like eyes—slanting slightly, like Goddess Durga's—and soft complexion, she was the most beautiful person I knew—next to my mother, of course. 'If I ever marry anyone, it will be Mallika Didi,' I had once told my parents, who laughed as if it were a good joke. She was eighteen now and had just started going to college.

We entered the foyer and scattered in different directions, on different missions. In the sitting room, I was surrounded by a sea of white dhotis and kurtas, heavy black-framed glasses, tussar silk saris with red borders, clinking bangles of gold and conch with dragon heads, and an unending stream of 'nomoshkars'. Conversation about politics, football and gossip swirled around me. The air was redolent with the smells of Priya perfume and mustard oil. I had to greet the Roy Choudhurys, the Banerjees, the Bhattacharjees, the Senguptas, the Mukherjees, the Chatterjees and the Gangulys as they entered the house for the Puja Committee meeting. Kitchen-calloused hands and well-meaning pats ruined the carefully arranged curl on the middle of my forehead as I bobbed and weaved through the crowd, trying to get to Mallika's room.

As I emerged from the crowded sitting room, I stopped. I had to straighten my rumpled clothes. Rani and Shyamala were chatting with some other girls at the bottom of the stairs and I could hear the excited buzz. As I approached, their voices dropped to whispers.

'Rahul, go and play with the boys, not the girls,' Rani said to me. 'The Sarkar boys are playing outside.'

I was fed up of being urged to play with boys and participate in their inane games of football and cricket. Being a Bengali male meant that I had to show my prowess at these games, kind of like how Indian males wear the moustache with pride. While I loved to play hide-and-seek, I hated the idea of running around on a field, getting my shoes dirty and being pushed around. The last time I played with the Sarkar boys, they let the bullies on the other team trip me several times. After that, I swore to myself that I would never play football again.

To hell with the Sarkar boys and the stupid girls, I thought as I climbed the stairs to Mallika's room. I had Mallika to myself and could not care less about their idiotic secrets.

I entered the room without knocking. She was lying on the bed with a dreamy smile, holding something to her chest. As I entered, she jumped and thrust what she was holding under her pillow. I heard the thin rice-paper crackling.

I loved Mallika's room. It was elegant and eclectic, just like her. I looked around, taking in the colourful posters of my favourite film stars, Rajesh Khanna and Sharmila Tagore. I lingered for a moment, savouring Paul Newman and Gregory Peck. Our ritual at each visit was to play one of the board games kept in a well-stocked old chest. At other times, a steady supply of books from the crammed bookshelves fed my voracious reading appetite.

We had a lot of fun when Mallika would shut the door and play albums of The Ventures from her collection of records stacked on top of the phonogram. We would dance to '*Walk, Don't Run*' or '*Tequila*' and sing along loudly. Soon Binesh Kaku would be at the door, asking us to turn the music down because it gave him a headache. Even though we were sent to school to be educated in English, our fathers did not like us listening to western music. But Mallika was in college and was a good student—also very stubborn—so she had her way.

After she had regained her composure, Mallika looked at me and smiled. 'Are the girls being mean to you again? Don't mind them. Let us play Snakes and Ladders.' She pulled out the game and rolled the die.

We enjoyed our game. Mallika chatted with me about school the whole time. She loved to read just like me, and asked, 'What book are you reading now?'

'Enid Blyton's *The Five on Kirrin Island Again*,' I replied.

'I love that book.' Mallika's eyes lit up. She reached over and put her hand on my cheek, gently patting it. 'Would you like some dal, rice and butter?' she asked.

I had an insatiable fondness for hot, steaming rice, heaped with fragrant, freshly made tuar dal—the flavour of the dal mingling with that of the Basmati rice—and the best part was a dollop of Amul butter melting on top.

'Why don't you wait here while I get you a plate of dal and rice?' Mallika said to me. I nodded, not really wanting to deal with the annoying girls as Mallika went downstairs.

I thought of the letter that Mallika had put away so hastily. I got up from the foot of the old, teak bed and went around to the headboard. One end of the pillow was folded under where Mallika had hastily hidden the letter. I pulled out the crumpled letter and saw the words, 'My dearest, darling Mallika', written on top, followed by pages of declarations of undying affection and devotion. I quickly scanned it. There were references to trysts at different places in Hyderabad and even on campus at Osmania College. On the last page, I saw the inscription, 'Your dearly beloved, Salim'. Then, as I heard footsteps, I stuffed the letter back under the pillow and ran back to the other side of the bed and picked up a mystery novel lying on the end table. I stared at the writing on the pages, but could not read a word. Mallika was seeing a boy. His name was Salim. And Salim was a Muslim name. Mallika was having an affair with a Muslim boy. It was frightening enough that she was breaking the rules that all good Bengali girls were supposed to follow by seeing a boy, but this was crossing the one line that no Hindu family would stand for. What would Binesh Kaku and Anjali Mashi say if they found out? I knew that if Rani had a boyfriend my father would never tolerate it. In my parents' and Mallika's parents' world, dating was considered to be sign of a 'loose character'. Only 'fast girls' dated and others gossiped about them.

With the exception of Ahmed Uncle and Shabnam Aunty, we had no Muslim family friends. Throughout the years, I had heard people say bad things about Muslims—that they were dirty and cruel, ate beef and didn't like Hindus.

'Here you are, Rahul.' Mallika was at the door, the plate of food in her hand. She sat with me while I ate with great relish.

As soon as I had finished eating, Anjali Mashi's voice floated up the stairs: 'Mallika, Shyamala, come help me take the food and tea out.' We heard the clinking of cutlery and crockery from the kitchen.

Anjali Mashi smiled at me with great affection when she saw me. 'Rahul, you grow taller each time I see you. Soon you will be taller than all of us, just like your father. May the Goddess bless you.' Her heavy, gold bangles chinked as she embraced me. I beamed. Dressed in the traditional Bengali style, Anjali Mashi wore a large, red bindi on her forehead and her sari was looped in from the front with the household keys tied to the end of the pallu. She never followed the hairstyles and fashions of actresses like my mother; instead, she wore her hair down, oiled and fragrant.

We helped bring the food out to the dining room. The boring meeting was over and the president, the secretary, the treasurer and other officers of the Durga Puja Committee had been elected.

The guests feasted on samosas, kachoris and all kinds of Bengali sweets. I was too full to eat and was preoccupied with my scandalous discovery. After the Bengali Association members left, we sat around the dining table, planning our summer vacation activities.

'Are you coming for pickle-making this year?' Rani asked Mallika and Shyamala as we rose to leave.

'When are you going to make pickles?' Shyamala enquired.

'In a couple of weeks, as soon as we start our vacation.'

'I will be there,' Mallika promised.

'I have to go for my Rabindra Sangeet practice every day for the next few weeks, so I can't join you,' Shyamala complained. 'Music practice is so boring!'

'You girls have no respect for your culture. Rabindranath Tagore is like a saint to us and you do not appreciate him. I don't know what kind of people you will be when you grow up,' Binesh Kaku snapped.

My father nodded his agreement and turned to us in warning. 'Why don't you children follow our traditions and make your parents proud instead of going to watch movies and listening to all that nonsense English music? Don't forget your culture and start imitating others. I don't want to hear anything about going to school dances and dating, do you hear? Or I will put an end to all of this nonsense. You will go to school and come home and study. That's it. Understand?' Binesh Kaku and he walked ahead, turning away from us.

Mallika looked nervously at my father and then quickly looked away.

Binesh Kaku saw us off, muttering about the unappreciative boys and girls of the new generation. We waved goodbye to Mallika and Shyamala and Anjali Mashi. Mallika could barely muster up a smile.

On the way back, I thought about Mallika's stricken face as we left. The rules that we had to follow were not just a matter of keeping a good reputation. They were about family honour and our parents' ability to walk in society 'with their head held high'. Having a love affair, and with a Muslim boy at that, was as big a transgression as Amit Puri's love letter and the consequences would probably be as humiliating as his expulsion. Fear for Mallika paralysed me in the way that was fast becoming familiar to me.

To relieve my anxiety, before going to bed, I looked for the dictionary in the bookshelf where my father's engineering books were kept. It was old and heavy, the clothbound covers frayed and dog-eared. I opened the dictionary to the letter 'h'. Running my finger down the page, I finally found it. It said:

'**Noun: homo** 'homo-, [N. Amer.] [Brit.], slang for **Noun: homosexual** 'homo'sekul [N. Amer.] [Brit.]: Someone who practices homosexuality; having an attraction to someone of the same gender.'

I stared at the page as my insides churned. So that is what a 'homo' was. Amit was a 'homo' because he had written a love letter to another boy. What Ranjan had said finally made sense. But I still did not understand why everyone was so upset about it. It must be considered to be really bad. Maybe I was one too. But I had not intended to do anything bad, only write a letter—I did not want to be different from others. Maybe I wasn't really a 'homo'.

As I lay in bed that night, staring at the shadows on the wall, my doubts returned. What if I was not normal? Was there something wrong with me? Something that could only be cured by shock therapy? At least Mallika was normal, even though she had broken the rules. She was in love and wrote love letters to a boy. But she too would get into a lot of trouble if anyone found out. Of all the things she could have done, having a love affair with a Muslim man was absolutely the worst. I slept fitfully that night, anxious for myself, worried about how I would be punished if I did not fare well in the examinations and anxious for Mallika who would surely be in trouble if her secret got out.

May 1973. Hyderabad.

On the day of the last exam, I hunched over my desk, holding a pen between my slippery fingers. The classroom was hot and airless. I looked up at the clock, feeling the tension in my gut as I calculated that I had only half an hour to answer the essay question. I looked around the classroom. It was empty except for a few students and Ranjan Bose, who was chewing on his pen. He wiped the sweat from his glasses with his shirt-tails and looked at me with a strange expression.

I turned to my paper, feeling uneasy. We all wrote as fast as we could. I finally finished and flexed my stiff and aching fingers. 'Time is up,' Mr Swaminathan snapped and snatched the paper from my hand. There had been no time to double-check my answers.

Outside, in the afternoon glare, I squinted in relief. The last two weeks had been hard and they were finally over.

'Rahul, how did you do?' Ranjan asked. 'Did you think the exam was easy?'

'No, not too easy. But I answered all the questions.'

'Did you know the answer to the question about how many seats there are in the State Legislature?'

'Yes, I answered that correctly.'

Ranjan's face went dark and his lips tightened. 'I hate this,' he muttered. 'Mum and Dad will be so upset if I don't get full marks.'

I reached out to him, to reassure him that, regardless of the score, I was still his friend and wanted to see him over the summer vacations. He roughly pushed my hand away. I felt a rush of guilt.

'You never know. Maybe you got it right,' I said. He scowled, turning away.

And that is when I saw the first man I fell madly in love with.

'Ranjan …' A handsome young man with a deep voice approached us, his strides long and graceful. His deep, tanned skin glowed from the heat of summer and drops of sweat clustered on his forehead and smooth upper lip. His lips were pursed, giving his jaw a determined look—I was keenly aware of their berry-redness. Then they curved in a friendly smile, showing white even teeth. The half-sleeved shirt he wore was open at the chest, displaying more smooth skin, and his forearms were finely muscled, the veins outlined in iridescent blue by the sheen of perspiration that covered them. His hair was dark and matted against his temples and neck.

I stared at him as the cacophony of voices receded and time slowed down.

'Rahul'—I heard Ranjan's voice, coming to me from far away—'this is Shubho dada, my brother. Do you remember him? He just came back from a student exchange programme in Spain.'

'Hello, Shubho dada ...' Shubho had been a shadowy figure for me. Three years older than us, he was always busy with his own friends and had been a stranger to Ranjan's friends. Now, his face had thinned out and he looked more like a man than a boy, he was much taller and athletic. Shubho had been the new star of the football team before he left for Spain, having scored more goals for our house team than any other player in the history of the school.

I liked the change in him in the months he was gone. He seemed so confident, strong and dashing. How I wished that I was grown up and manly too—not so skinny! And yet, unbelievably, right in front of me was Shubho, shaking my hand vigorously, patting me on my back and tousling my hair as he said, 'Rahul, you are growing up to be such a handsome boy! Watch out for those girls, they will get you!' He laughed.

I was speechless. My eyes were glued to the skin showing at his neck. I forced myself to look away. I hoped to God that Ranjan had not noticed my mortification. But he was chatting casually with his brother, slinging his satchel of books on his shoulder and preparing to leave.

They made a fine pair. Ranjan was tall just like his brother, but he wore glasses and was thin. Not particularly athletic like Shubho, he was generally easy-going and good-natured. Except when put off—

then he had his mother Dr Bose's peevish personality. But he had befriended me when I joined Hyderabad Royal Academy and felt completely out of place and had been my best friend for over a year. Lately, though, he seemed to be more irritable than usual, especially during the exams.

As they waved and left, my mouth tasted funny—metallic and salty. I slowly unclenched my jaws and picked up my school box and walked to the bus. My mind was a flurry of crazy thoughts, nothing made sense. But of one thing I was certain—I had never felt this way before, not for Amit Puri, not even for Rajesh Khanna. My scalp and skin still tingled where Shubho had touched me.

The bus wheezed and groaned all the way to my stop. I jumped out, barely waiting for it to stop moving.

'Happy hols!' my friends yelled at me.

'Happy hols!' I yelled back.

My father was home early that day. I walked in, an extra spring in my step, ready for the holidays.

'So how did you fare today? Will you come first this year?' my father asked.

'Very well,' I replied, feeling my euphoria drain.

'Come, eat. The food is getting cold. I have made your favourite tuar dal,' Mother said, and I realized I was very hungry.

'Maybe you will grow taller if you eat lots of dal,' Rani teased.

I smiled back at her. I had not felt so good in a while—I was thinking of Shubho, his warm smile.

'So when are we going to watch *Aradhana*?' I asked, my mind turning to Rajesh Khanna films as usual. I had watched it once already, but I wanted to watch that scene again, where he serenades Sharmila Tagore as the little mountain train winds its way up towards the top of the range. Rajesh Khanna hangs perilously from the side of the jeep, mouth organ in hand singing: '*Mere sapnon ki rani kab aayegi tu ...*' Queen of my dreams, when will you come to me?

'Why go for it again? We just watched it,' my father said.

'Well ... because ...' I was stumped. Here was that complication again. I did not want to tell him that I thought about Rajesh Khanna all the time. The memory of my punishment at the hands of Mr Swaminathan was still fresh in my mind and I would rather die than talk about my fantasies. It wasn't fair, I thought. I yearned to be older so that I would not need my father's permission to do anything! As soon as I could, I ran to the garden and to my special hiding place, wishing I could run away altogether and forget about school and rules.

I heard Rani calling me from the swings. 'Rahul, I have a surprise for you.'

I climbed down from the tree and crawled out from behind the thick underbrush, breathless and covered with twigs. But I knew that my secret hiding place was still safe.

'What is it, Rani?' I asked suspiciously.

'Go get me some nimbu pani from the fridge first,' Rani ordered. 'Then I will tell you. It is a surprise.' She sat down on the stone bench.

Carrying a glass carefully from the palace, I walked out to the lawn where Rani was waiting, tapping her foot impatiently.

'Good, I am glad you are back. The surprise is that Mallika Didi is coming here and we can all go watch a film together,' Rani finally said. 'Binesh Kaku has to go out for some business and he can drop us off at the theatre. He just called Baba to set it up.'

I set the tray down on the bench and said excitedly, 'When is Mallika Didi coming?'

'Right now. Now let me finish my drink in peace. You can go get dressed.'

I ran back to the palace, thrilled. I hoped it would be a film showing at the festival showcasing all of Rajesh Khanna's hits from the very beginning of his career, starting with the film *Aakhri Khat*. Each film was showing for a full week.

Binesh Kaku arrived shortly after. We all piled into the car, Shyamala, Rani and I sitting together in the back.

'Oh, I am so excited about going to see *Kati Patang* at Roxie!' Mallika exclaimed, turning around and leaning towards us through the gap between the front seats. Roxie was one of the new film theatres in Hyderabad and the location where the Rajesh Khanna

Film Festival was being held.

'Oh, that's the Rajesh Khanna and Asha Parekh film from 1970!' I beamed. 'I never got to watch it then because Baba said I was too young to go. But I love the songs so much!'

'Of course. The music is by R.D. Burman. It has to be good,' Rani said in a superior tone.

Binesh Kaku, as usual, did not speak much. The rest of us chattered about the film. As we drove past Tank Bund, the lake looked like blue ice in the golden afternoon sunshine, and I felt supremely happy.

The name Roxie Cinema was written across the front of the bright yellow theatre in English and Telugu and could be seen from far away. There were giant billboards showing Rajesh Khanna, perfectly groomed, his complexion too light and his lips too pink. Asha Parekh looked fair and pretty, her large, dark eyes dominating her face. Bindu was depicted with lots of make-up on her face and showing ample bosom. My heart quickened in excitement at the sight of the actors' paintings.

Binesh Kaku pulled the car up to the theatre and let us out. 'Be right here after the film ends. I will be here to pick you up.' The words barely out of his mouth, he pulled away, leaving us in a cloud of exhaust smoke. We turned and went into the theatre, Mallika's arm entwined with mine. Behind us, Rani and Shyamala whispered conspiratorially.

We quickly got some potato chips and Coca Cola and found our seats. Rani and I sat on each side of Mallika, wanting to be close to her. Shyamala sat next to Rani. We had barely started munching on the chips and sipping the Coca Cola when the scalloped curtains rose. A black-and-white screen appeared and the numbers flashing on it counted down, signalling the start of the newsreel.

'Oh God! Now we have to sit through the news documentary,' Rani groaned. After the news documentary, the trailers began. I wished they would hurry up and start the show. Mallika kept looking at her watch. I had never seen her so impatient.

The film started off on a romantic note. I watched in rapture as Rajesh Khanna, devastatingly handsome, sang a drunken love song to Asha Parekh in the rain. I could not understand why she turned away from him—I would have run straight into his arms! Soon after, Prem Chopra, the villain, made his appearance, showing off his hairy chest. He was accompanied by his moll Bindu.

A few minutes after the start of the movie, however, Mallika got up from her seat. 'I will be right back,' she whispered to me.

'Where are you going?' I asked in surprise, but she left without answering, pushing me firmly back into my seat.

I wondered where Mallika had gone, but the movie soon picked up pace and I was engrossed. I was completely caught up in the plot before I realized with a start that Mallika had been gone for a while.

I leaned across the empty seat and asked Rani in a low voice, 'Do you know where Mallika Didi went? Should I go look for her?'

'No, don't. Stay here. Be quiet,' Rani snapped.

'Shhh!' an annoyed patron admonished from behind us.

Rani grimaced and held her finger to her lips. Just then, Mallika returned. Was she crying? I wanted to ask her what had happened.

As the actress Bindu danced seductively on the screen, singing, 'Mera naam hai Shabnam, pyar se log mujhe Shabbo kehte hain ...' someone sitting in front made a catcall. More whistles of appreciation followed. I thought about the boys in my class. They would have whistled too. But the sight of Bindu stirred no such reaction in me.

'Such roadside Romeos!' Rani muttered. 'What can you expect from the peanut gallery?'

I felt vindicated. This kind of behaviour was just not acceptable in decent society—there was nothing wrong with me not finding Bindu attractive.

In contrast to Bindu, the heroine, Asha Parekh, was a demure and beautiful woman—a victim of circumstances and destiny. And I knew that Rajesh Khanna would surely save her. But when he sang to her and proclaimed his love for her, the catcalls started again. I realized then that I had no interest in Asha Parekh either and my heart sank. A wave of loneliness swept through me—I was incapable of feeling for the lovely heroine what Rajesh Khanna, my hero, felt for her.

When the intermission came, people reluctantly got up to restock their snacks and returned to the show after quickly stretching their legs. Rani chatted with Mallika while I waited to ask her where she had gone and tell her about the parts she had missed.

'Mallika Didi, where did you go?' I asked her at last.

'Oh, I had to meet a college friend. We are collaborating on a paper. She was supposed to meet me, but did not show up. The paper is due tomorrow and I need to finish it.' With that, she got up again. 'Maybe she is there now. Let me go and check. I will be right back.'

'Let me go with you, Mallika Didi.' I jumped up from my seat as the lights dimmed.

'No, stay here with Rani and Shyamala. I will be back soon, I promise.' She patted me on the cheek and left swiftly.

Mallika clearly did not want me to go with her and I wanted to know what she was hiding from me. Could she be meeting Salim?

I waited for a few minutes and then walked out into the foyer, blinking in the watery afternoon light. There was no sign of Mallika, so I went upstairs to the balcony to check. When I saw them, I ducked back behind the curve of the stairs. There they were, standing together. Even from where I stood, I could see that Salim was very handsome. Dark sideburns outlined his jaw and he was dressed in a T-shirt and jeans with canvas shoes. I admired the curve of his athletic legs and the way his jeans stretched around his thighs. He and Mallika were staring into each other's eyes and he was saying something to her in a low voice. I slowly went downstairs and returned to my seat.

'Where did you go?' Rani whispered to me furiously.

'Oh, just to the bathroom,' I lied. Rani grunted and turned her attention to the screen.

Mallika was gone for a long time. Meanwhile, the plot took many twists and turns. Just when we were sitting up in our seats for the final showdown, Mallika returned. She was beaming and held a large, white envelope in her hands. 'Sorry, I had to talk to my friend,' was all she said softly as she settled into her seat. She clutched the envelope and I heard paper crackling inside as the lovers united at the end of the film. I wanted to be like the sexy moll,

I thought, living a life of danger and sin with complete confidence.

'So, did you like the film?' Mallika's soft voice broke into my thoughts. We were walking back to the place where her father had dropped us off, her arm comfortably hooked in mine.

'I wish you hadn't missed the fun parts,' I said, feeling happy that Mallika was asking for my opinion. 'It was very good. I really like Rajesh Khanna and Bindu. Do you think, if I went to Bombay I could go meet them?' I asked, the words tumbling out.

Mallika looked at me, 'I am sure you could …'

Rani caught up with us. 'What are you two talking about?' she asked suspiciously.

Mallika laughed. 'Nothing,' she said. Proud of our special bond, I smiled.

Ahead of us was a family of four—parents with a son and daughter. I thought nothing of them at first, but there was something very familiar about the broad shoulders of the boy and the tilt of his head. I hurried closer to get a better look, leaving Mallika behind. Walking with his mother, father and sister was Amit Puri.

'Amit, Amit!' I shouted.

Mr and Mrs Puri stopped and said something to Amit.

'Hi, Amit, how are …' I could not complete my question.

Amit turned around to look at me. His eyes were vacant. A flicker of memory seemed to ignite for a moment, but then he looked confused and his mouth opened slightly.

'Beta, this is Rahul, from your class.'

Amit looked at me and uttered my name. It came out thick and slow. 'Raahuul,' he said, 'Raahuul.' He looked around helplessly, unable to say more.

'Remember Rahul from your class? Say something to him, beta,' Mr Puri said gently. His eyes were filled with so much sadness that I wanted to cry.

Amit looked at me with the same empty expression and clutched his father's hand like a lost child. I stared at him as the smile faded from my lips. What had happened to his smile and laughter, his exuberance and confidence? I could barely recognize the stranger in front of me.

'Amit is not feeling well,' Mr Puri said to me quietly. He was trying to lead Amit away, but he just stood there, staring at me. Mr Puri looked years older than the last time I had seen him. Mrs Puri was wiping her eyes with the end of her pallu and Amit's sister held her mother's hand in silence.

'Come, beta,' Mrs Puri said finally, her voice a whisper as she put her hand in Amit's and turned from me, leading him away. Amit walked off in a slow shuffle. He never looked back.

Mallika, who had been standing a little way off, came up to me and asked, 'Who is that boy? Does he go to school with you? He seemed so disoriented—is he all right?'

I kept quiet, sick at heart. Where was the Amit I used to know? Is this what had happened to him after shock therapy? Would he be like this for the rest of his life? I wanted to tell Mallika everything that had happened to Amit, but I did not know how. How could I ever explain my fear that I would end up like Amit?

'I don't know. I thought he was someone I knew from school, but I was mistaken.' I lied for the very first time to Mallika.

Rani and Shyamala had already reached Binesh Kaku, who was waiting for us to catch up. He looked hot and annoyed. 'Hurry up and get in,' he said. We tumbled into the car. The others talked endlessly about how much they had enjoyed the film while I sat quietly, in shock.

'How was the film?' my father asked me when we got home. It was twilight outside and the chirping of the birds in the banyan tree was deafening.

'It was so much fun!' Rani replied as I mumbled something and left the room. I could not pretend that my outing had been fun. I sat on the veranda steps, trying to rid myself of the haunting image of Amit, the terror that I too could suffer the same fate. I sat there until night covered the palace with her mantle of darkness.

After dinner, the phone rang. I was curled up in my favourite armchair, reading a book, when I heard my mother answer the phone.

'Four-six-five-three-zero,' she said. 'Oh, Anjali Didi. How are you?' She paused and listened for what seemed like a very long time. Then she said, 'Anjali Didi, you must not listen to gossip—especially from Professor Khosla's wife. Mallika is in college now and I am sure she has a lot of friends. Drinking coffee in the cafeteria does not give a girl a bad reputation. Our Mallika would never do anything to embarrass the family. I am sure these boys are just friends.'

I edged towards the dining room. I wondered if Mallika's secret had been discovered. Ma lowered her voice and I could not hear what she was saying next. As I walked towards the dining room, I saw her looking around to see if anyone was within earshot. She saw me approaching and spoke fast, her voice urgent and pleading: 'No, no. Please do not say anything to Mallika about this kind of gossip. And do not tell Binesh Dada anything. He will do something rash. Children these days have their own will. You need to handle this carefully if you suspect that she is mixing with a boy ...' As I entered the dining room, she swiftly changed the subject. 'Oh, Anjali Didi, I cannot wait to taste the patali-gur sandesh you make,' she said. 'Yes, I will ask Rahul's father to take us to your house on Saturday night.' The sandesh that Anjali Mashi made from milk and date-palm syrup was legendary in the Bengali community.

I wanted to warn Mallika about the conversation, but I did not know exactly what Anjali Mashi had discovered. I thought of Mallika and Salim in the theatre and felt very afraid for them. It was sickening to think that Mallika, like Amit, might be helpless to protect herself.

I dreamt about the film that night. Mallika was the heroine. She was in great danger and I was unable to help her. Even Rajesh Khanna could not do anything. In the end, I saw her lying in a pool of blood. Surrounding her were little shreds of bat skin, mixed with blood and pieces of ripped veil. I woke up in the middle of the night, screaming.

'May I invite Ranjan to spend the day tomorrow?' I asked my father as he sat at the dining table to enjoy a leisurely Saturday morning, which was never complete without tea and Britannia Marie biscuits.

'Only if you score higher marks than him in the exams this year.

Are you going to?' he asked. 'You were admitted to class IX instead of class VII at your new school because we all had high expectations of you. I don't want anyone to say my son did not come first. Understand?'

'Yes ... yes, of course I will ... I will come first in class, baba,' I replied, praying that I would come first again.

'Did I ever disappoint my parents? Never! You must not disappoint me. Achha, I will call Ranjan's parents and arrange it.'

A 'Day Spend' with Ranjan was a great way to start the summer vacation. It was the name we had given to the day my friends would visit and spend with me. It was a rare treat.

Ranjan's family was also Bengali, but very modern and lived in a large house in Banjara Hills, the enclave of the very wealthy. They travelled to Europe frequently and, like many Bengali Christians, they were very westernized. My family on the other hand, was more traditional and followed Bengali customs despite being so far from West Bengal. I was quite envious of Ranjan's family even though his parents—especially his mother, who was a psychiatrist—were very strict with their sons.

Later that morning, the phone rang. It was Ranjan with good news—he confirmed that he would be coming for a Day Spend the next day. I badly wanted to ask him about Shubho, but was scared he would think it odd. I could not think of asking anything that would sound casual—when the boys were making fun of Amit, I had seen a different side of Ranjan and I was wary.

'Ranjan is coming for Day Spend tomorrow. Will you make something special for lunch?' I asked my mother.

'Of course, I will,' she said. She was very fond of my best friend.

The rest of the Saturday dragged on. I woke up unusually early on Sunday because I was so excited that I could not stay in bed. Once I'd brushed my teeth, I went outside to the garden.

It was a cool morning and the air smelt of freshly moistened earth, typical of a Hyderabad summer in the palace. Dawn had just broken and the sky was still streaked with fingers of pink. The garden was blanketed in a heavy layer of dew. The lawn sparkled, moisture catching the early rays of light, and birds twittered in every tree. My mother would say that they tried to get their song out to the world before the heat of the day silenced them.

When I ventured back into the palace, my parents were sitting at the breakfast table, reading the paper in silent companionship. The teapot sat between them.

'Scoundrels! Bastards!' my father suddenly muttered angrily under his breath as he banged his fist on the table, sending a spoon clattering to the floor.

'What is it?' my mother asked, frowning at him to be quiet and watch his language around me.

'Why don't those bloody Muslims stop this? The mosque in Khairatabad, which is next to the old Vishnu temple, wants to expand on the empty plot of city-owned land and the Hindus claim that the land is the site of an ancient temple that was destroyed a few hundred years ago. Why do they have to stir up trouble? Why can't they build the mosque somewhere else? That whole area is sensitive enough as it is. Do we really need more strikes, processions and workers' unrest? This country is going to the dogs.' Flinging down the *Deccan Chronicle*, he walked away, swearing under his breath.

'Ma, why is Baba upset?' I asked. He was often irritable and impatient, but rarely used bad words in front of me.

'He is upset because he will have to deal with labour issues in the factory if there are fights between Hindus and Muslims,' She sounded tired.

'Why do they fight?'

'It has been going on for many years and has never stopped, Rahul. You are a teenager—almost a grown-up now. I will tell you about it someday,' Ma said. I caught a glimpse of anger and sorrow in her eyes before she veiled them and poured a cup of tea for me. This was typical of her—she never showed her distress in front of her children.

'Have some tea, Rahul. Don't worry yourself with any of this so early in the morning. Always think of harmonious things at the start of the day. Besides, you need to get ready for Ranjan,' Ma said after a while.

I sipped my ginger-and-cardamom tea and watched the garden wake up.

Seized with a desire to walk through the lawn in my bare feet, I took off my slippers. The sensation was heavenly as the icy drops of dew tickled my toes. At the far end of the lawn, I stopped at the lake and looked up at the walls of the mosque. Through the high slits in the wall, I could see the bluish-green colour of the fluorescent tube lights. The voice of the mullah wafted over my head through the loudspeaker: 'Allah ho Akbar ...' From another direction came the sound of bells ringing and early morning bhajans from the Hindu temple. Calls to the faithful mingled harmoniously in the quiet of the morning.

I wanted everything to be perfect for Ranjan's visit. I made my way over to the ruins to see if the anthill had grown. It was much larger than the first time I had noticed it years ago. Streams of ants poured out of it onto the rust-red cone made up of grainy beads of mud. I walked through the garden, checking to see if there were any mangoes lying on the ground from the last storm. Overhead, the sky had turned bluish gray, getting brighter by the minute. The early-morning sun peeped in from over the palace walls, over the secretariat building, its rays bathing the dewdrops on the leaves of the trees with reddish-gold light.

Breakfast was a hurried affair. Ranjan showed up at ten on the dot. His parents were very punctual. His father, Mr Bose, was at the wheel, dressed in white pants and a golfing shirt. His cap was perched jauntily on the side of his head. He looked like the men in American magazine advertisements—like a young Arnold Palmer. I found myself wishing that Shubho was there too. I flushed with excitement as I remembered his good-natured teasing and an almost physical need to touch him rose in me.

Rani and I ran up to the car. 'Nomoshkar, Uncle,' we said, greeting Mr Bose.

'Have a good time,' he said genially, dismissing the three of us as he continued making small talk with my parents. Rani, Ranjan and I ran into the palace.

'What would you like to do first—play Monopoly or go outside to the garden?'

Ranjan looked undecided, so I made up his mind for him—though I would regret my rashness later.

'Let us go outside now,' I said. 'It will be too hot later. We can play Monopoly in the afternoon.' I was anxious to show off my palace gardens and did not want to wait.

'Go ahead. I will join you boys later,' Rani said.

We proceeded to the neem tree that grew in the courtyard among the ruins. Ranjan had always liked climbing it. Neem trees grow really tall, with thick, green leaves with jagged edges and a dark-brown bark. The sweet and musky smell of the fruit that looks like lemon-yellow grapes wafted up from the earth. I looked at the makeshift seat I had made last summer. It looked barely large enough to allow Ranjan and me to sit on—a year ago, it had seemed so big and sturdy.

We climbed high up, swaying with the branches. I closed my eyes and luxuriated in the feeling of being in the arms of the tree. I knew that as soon as I looked over the wall the spell would break—I would no longer be living in an enchanted palace that needed guards and had no world outside it.

But break the spell we did. Parting the thick fronds of the neem, we peered at the giant iron beams and girders spanning the cavernous roof of the open factory shed outside the palace walls. We stood precariously on tiptoe to see the corrugated metal roofs, large metal pulleys, hooks and machinery that would slide back and forth, accompanied by the occasional mechanical clank. The factory had many buildings where thousands of workers were employed. That was the world of my father—of his grown-up life and activities broken into phases by the daily sirens. The days of my world here, in my magical palace, were also marked by these sirens, the bhajans from the temples and the mullah's call for prayer.

We turned around and looked towards the palace. Looking at the tall Corinthian pillars gracing the large portico and the flight of marble stairs leading to the front door, Ranjan said with the deep sigh and frown of envy that I had come to know so well in the past few months, 'Oh, Rahul. You are so lucky to live in a palace! I wish my father worked for the Mint too. Then we would also live in a place like this.'

'But I love your home,' I protested, feeling nervous like I always did when Ranjan was upset.

'Yes,' he grumbled, 'but not as fun as your palace.'

My palace, I thought proudly as I looked at the imposing facade. Feeling magnanimous, I said, 'Come, let's see if we can find any new humming bird nests.'

I took Ranjan to the thicket of tall trees and shrubs by the main gate. I looked around, hunting for some sign that the humming birds were nesting. The nests from the year before were gone, blown away by the late-summer storms and rains. Then I saw it at the same moment that Ranjan did—a new brown nest, perfectly woven by the baya, the weaver bird.

'Wow, it's perfect,' Ranjan whispered under his breath. The nest swayed gently in the warm breeze. A long tube led up to the nest, which looked like a human stomach. I knew that the tube was made in such a way that it fooled predators so that they were unable to get to the eggs or chicks. Had the bird laid any eggs, I wondered as we sat quietly in the bushes close to the nest. Ranjan stared at the nest for a while, mesmerized, then shifted impatiently. Without a word, he walked over and reached out to touch it.

'Don't do that,' I whispered urgently, running up to him.

'Why not? I just want to see if there is anything inside.'

'No, you will hurt the baby birds inside. Besides, if you touch it the parents will abandon the nest and the babies,' I exclaimed, remembering what Rani had told me.

'That is just a story made up by old ladies.' Ranjan was scornful. 'So what if the story is true? The parents can make another nest and lay more eggs. Most of the chicks die anyway—you know that, don't you? I see dead sparrow chicks every time there is a nest up in the rafters. I would love to have this nest on the wall in my room.'

Surprising me, he lunged towards the nest and tugged at it, standing on tiptoe. Luckily, it was too high for him to grasp firmly. The nest was securely anchored to a branch of the tree—it bent sharply under the pressure, but did not come loose.

'No!' I pulled Ranjan away with more force than I had intended to use and we both fell back. I hit my head on a tree stump and was momentarily stunned from the impact.

'Ow! That hurt!' I was angry now and tried to get up, but fell back, feeling dizzy. Without offering me a hand, Ranjan got up and towered over me.

'Relax. Don't be such a girl. You know what they say about girlie boys at school,' he taunted me, his face turning ugly with disgust. 'Anyway, since I have touched the nest, the parents will abandon it. We might as well take it.'

'No, I won't let you touch it again!'I leapt up unsteadily and stood between him and the nest. I had had no idea that he could be like this. I wished I had never invited him over.

He pushed me again and roughly shook the nest. Something fell out onto the carpet of dry leaves and I went cold. It was a little baby. The feathers were still not formed and little black spikes protruded from the skin. It cheeped in distress, trying to hide. I ran over to see the chick. Its eyes were open as it moved around in little circles.

'Look at what you have done!' I shouted in anger as I knelt down. 'Now the bird will die.'

'Put it back in the nest if you care.' Without another word, Ranjan stomped off in the direction of the palace.

I tore some leaves off the mulberry tree with shaking hands and tenderly cradled the bird, taking care not to touch it. I slid it back in the nest and shook it gently till I thought it was back in the hollow.

'Rahul, where are you? Ranjan and I are waiting for you. Lunch is ready. Let's go eat.' Rani called out from the veranda outside the dining room.

I stayed for a moment, looking at the nest to make sure that the baby was safe. I washed my hands and joined Ranjan and Rani at the table. Ranjan looked sulky. He behaved politely with Rani and Ma, but ignored me completely.

The kitchen smelt lovely. My mother had made special dishes for Day Spend. Instead of regular rice, we had biryani. Made in the Hyderabadi style, it was seasoned and flavoured with cumin and saffron. The daily curries too had been replaced by slightly more formal ones—the sauces richer and more aromatic. The dal had been seasoned with special spices and crisp fried onions, just the way I liked it. The fish kebabs had been smoked all morning in the traditional style and the saag curry was moss-green and blended with a special sauce. As Ma served the food, I looked at Ranjan being his charming self and hoped he would not bring up the matter of girlie boys in front of Rani. She would never let me hear the last of it.

'You are so lucky,' Ranjan said to me and Rani. 'Your mother is such a good cook! I wish my mother was a good cook. She is too busy all the time at the mental hospital.' He sounded envious and I wondered if Dr Bose, his mother, cooked for him at all. I knew that, unlike us, his family had a cook. When I had visited him a couple of times, Dr Bose had never gone into the kitchen and the servants had done all the serving and cleaning.

'I feel like I am going to burst,' Ranjan groaned at the end of the meal, holding his distended stomach with both hands.

'Shall we play some indoor games?' I asked, ready to move on to the next item on our agenda for the day.

'Rani, will you join us?' Ranjan asked my sister.

I glared at him. I did not want to risk him telling her about my punishment at school. But it was too late. She accepted his invitation.

'Let us play Snakes and Ladders. Or do you boys want to play Ludo or Monopoly?' she asked.

'Monopoly,' Ranjan and I both said. We were fascinated by all the stories we read in school—they were set in London and made the names like Charing Cross and Mayfair and Pall Mall that were written on the Monopoly board appear super-attractive.

I got the Monopoly set from my room and we sat down on the carpet. Ranjan rolled the dice and we began to play.

After playing for a while, I was on my way to winning the game when Ranjan said suddenly, 'You are cheating, Rahul.'

'Of course, I am not,' I retorted.

'You know you are cheating. I bet you cheated in class too,' he said, sounding resentful. 'Hey, did you tell Rani what happened in class the other day?' he asked, his eyes glinting with a strange hardness.

'What? Nothing happened …' My voice faltered. 'Ranjan,' I continued, filled with terror, 'don't you dare tittle-tattle!' The spectre of my humiliation in class rose in front of me again and my heart pounded. Rani must never find out.

'Rani, did Rahul tell you that he got into trouble in class? Rahul, you better be careful. Remember Amit and how he got into trouble …'

'What? What?' Rani was very interested. 'What happened in your class, Ranjan? Tell me.'

'That's not funny, Ranjan.' I glared at him. 'Nothing happened, Rani.' I turned to her. 'Really, nothing happened. He is just teasing. Aren't you, Ranjan?'

'Rahul!' my mother called from the dining room. 'Help me set the table.' She entered the sitting room and we fell silent. When she left, I stayed, reluctant to leave in case Ranjan told Rani anything about school. But I was again saved by Ma, who came back and said, 'Rani, I need your help too with the cake. Ranjan, please excuse them for a few minutes.'

'Sure, Aunty,' he said.

Upset and angry, as I left I squeezed his arm as hard as I could, whispering in his ear, 'If you tell Rani about Mr Swaminathan, I swear I will never ever talk to you again.'

Ma had made everything I loved for high tea. Sandwiches made with green chutney, mango chutney, tomato, cheese and eggs were placed on a platter. There were also freshly fried samosas and alu tikias. And Ma had baked a pound cake and frosted it that very day. The frosting was already melting in the afternoon humidity. We tucked in greedily and, for a long time, no one spoke.

'Who wants to play on the swings?' Rani asked after we had eaten our fill.

'Go ahead, I will clean up after you,' my mother generously offered.

So off we ran to the swings. There were only two of them.

'Who is going to get on first? 'I am taking my favourite side,' Rani announced. She smiled coyly at Ranjan. 'As our guest of honour, you can swing on this one. Will you race me? Let's see if you are stronger than Rahul. I always win. Rahul, you can get on the swing later, since you are the baby.' I stared at Rani—my tomboyish sister was acting coquettishly!

Ranjan swaggered to the swing and jumped on, his chest puffed out as he gave Rani a flirtatious smile. He turned to me with a victorious look. 'Hey, don't feel bad, Rahul. That's what happens when you cheat at Monopoly. I always find a way to even the score.' He hissed the last part at me.

Neither of them noticed as I left to go to the gulmohar tree. I could hear them egging each other on and arguing about who was stronger and faster.

The sun slipped over the palace walls and the shadows lengthened soon after. The chorus of birdsong increased in volume and frogs started croaking in the pool. The crickets joined the symphony and the melody of nature preparing for dusk enveloped us. Tiny flecks of black lace flitted across the sky—the bats had started their nightly explorations.

A car came up the driveway, its lights sweeping the tree trunks. It was Ranjan's father's car. Ranjan was leaving and I was ready to forget the unpleasantness, wanting his goodwill back. As we ran over to the car from different parts of the garden, my heart stopped. Ranjan's father was at the wheel with Shubho in the backseat. I was surprised to see a young girl sitting next to him.

'That is Shubho Dada's girlfriend,' Ranjan whispered.

'Isn't your father angry with him? Does her father know that her boyfriend is Shubho Dada? How does he allow this? Isn't he just fifteen years old?' I asked.

Ranjan looked surprised as he said, 'No, he is sixteen. And why should either my father or hers be angry? Our parents expect us to date. My father dated my mother when he was in higher secondary school too, just like Shubho Dada.'

My head was spinning. I could not reconcile the openness and casual attitude of his family to the values that prevailed in mine.

'You are so lucky,' I said, thinking of all the times I had been told that dating was not respectable and that my parents would find Rani and me our spouses when we grew up. It was my turn to envy

Ranjan and Shubho and the freedom they enjoyed.

'Hey, Rahul, I really like Rani. She is so much fun and really beautiful, you know,' Ranjan said as he poked me in the ribs with a wink.

I shifted uncomfortably.

'Bet she has a boyfriend and you don't even know about it,' he said with a nasty laugh, as if he knew something I did not.

'Of course not. My parents would never allow it.'

'Sure. Whatever you say.' He shrugged as we reached the car.

Mr Bose smiled at us and got out of the car. 'I have left the keys in the car. Don't take off and leave without me,' he joked. 'Call me when you are ready to leave. I am going to chat with Rahul's parents.'

Shubho looked at us, his genial smile welcoming. All of a sudden, I felt really shy.

His strong jaw and chin were speckled with a faint shadow of an early beard. He reminded me of the old Amit in some ways, but he was older and manlier. I pushed away the heaviness I felt when I thought about my close call in front of Rani that afternoon. It wasn't too difficult to do that in Shubho's presence. I noticed his sinewy arms again, the veins outlined clearly against his rich brown skin. His shirt was open at the neck and I felt an irresistible urge to reach out and touch him and breathe in his scent. I felt a movement in my groin and turned red with embarrassment. I'd never got hard down there in the presence of a man—only in my dreams and fantasies.

'Rahul, this is my girlfriend Anamika,' Shubho said.

Smiling, she said, 'Hello, Rahul.'

'Hello,' I mumbled.

'Rahul is Ranjan's best friend. He will be a handsome fellow, I tell you. All the girls will be after him,' Shubho told Anamika as he reached out of the car and patted my head with his right hand. 'Hey, Rahul, got a girlfriend yet?'

I just stood there, tongue-tied. My scalp tingled at his touch and I wanted him to touch me again.

'Oh, Mr Bose, you must stay for a few minutes,' I heard my father say hospitably as he took Mr Bose towards the palace.

'Rahul, what is the matter with you? Are you frozen or something? Let's go. I have to go inside and get my bag,' Ranjan said impatiently as I stared at Shubho. He ran off and I followed him inside. When I realized that I had left my slippers by the gulmohar tree, I turned around. It was almost dark and I walked swiftly towards the garden. As I neared the car, I saw Shubho and Anamika kissing. It was dark enough that I could not see too well, and they certainly could not see me. I hid behind a pillar of the portico and peeped cautiously around.

I could hear soft kissing sounds and light moans. Shubho was holding Anamika's face in his hands. Her eyes were shut, like his. It was getting darker and I stepped out from my hiding place. The windows of the Fiat were down, so I could see inside. Hot and flushed, I wanted to see Shubho better. I wondered if his mouth was open when he kissed, like when James Bond had kissed the Japanese girl in *You Only Live Twice*. I had heard the boys in class talk about kissing girls and none of it sounded very interesting. But this was more than interesting—it was exciting.

As I watched, one of Shubho's hands moved from Anamika's face down to her shoulder and lay on the hollow of her neck. She sighed and arched her back. Shubho's hands moved lower down her body, towards her breast. I was as excited as I was scared. I wanted to see Shubho more clearly and I stepped a little closer. Just then, to my horror, I saw him open his eyes and look directly at me. My excitement was replaced by instant dread as I steadied myself for being scolded for spying. But nothing happened. Shubho's eyes sparkled in the dim light from the dashboard and he continued to look at me as he kissed Anamika and touched her breasts. I watched for a few more seconds more and then turned and ran towards the garden.

My heart was beating hard as I ran to get my slippers. I could hear Rani's voice: 'Rahul, Rahul, where are you?'

'Rahul, I'm leaving. Thanks, and we'll chat soon,' Ranjan's voice called out and I heard Mr Bose say goodbye to my parents. I could not bear to see Ranjan and Shubho right then. A minute later, I heard the Fiat start up. It turned around in the driveway and made its way out towards the main gate. I watched the tail lights grow dim and finally disappear. A faint smell of the exhaust smoke wafted across the garden as I made my way back to the palace.

That night, as I lay in bed, I kept thinking of Shubho and the way he had looked at me. I wondered what it would feel like to kiss him. I ran my fingers over my lips and wondered if Shubho's lips would be soft and yielding like mine or firm and hard. I wondered if his face would gently scrape mine and felt my groin harden again. Then I thought about Ranjan. If he ever found out about my feelings for his brother, he would make my life miserable. This was dangerous territory and I would have to be very careful not to let anyone know how I felt. As I thought of how Suresh Khosla and his gang would mock me and make sure that Mrs Joshi humiliated me, I felt hopeless. I thought about Shubho again and felt an unbearable craving to touch his body, to be close to him. I had never felt such longing before.

5

Saturday Evening. San Francisco.

'I don't want to keep talking on the phone. Let me tell you the rest in person,' I said as I poured myself a glass of water. 'Want to meet for a drink?' I wanted to see Andrew with an urgency that was almost physical in its intensity.

'Okay,' Andrew said after a few moments of silence. 'But I just want to hear the rest of the story. I am not coming home with you. Not that easily.'

'Let us meet at the Tunnel Top on Bush Street,' I said, trying to contain my excitement. 'They make the best cocktails and it's not too noisy. I'll continue my story there.'

I got dressed in a hurry. Though Andrew had warned me, I was determined to bring him back. I reached the Tunnel Top in half an hour. I had walked, not wanting to lose my parking space in Russian Hill. I figured we could take a cab home if I could manage to pacify him somehow. And then I waited for the longest twenty minutes of my life.

'Expecting someone?' the bartender asked me with a knowing smile.

'Uhuh.'

I stood up when Andrew walked in. He looked as strained and miserable as I felt. He gave me a perfunctory kiss on the cheek, turning away from my mouth. I hugged him, but he stiffened and I stepped back, feeling rejected.

'What will you have?' I asked after a moment.

'A Manhattan.'

I ordered two Manhattans.

'You look like hell,' he said.

'So do you.'

We raised our glasses.

'To no more secrets,' Andrew said with a grim smile.

I nodded silently, feeling a deep anxiety at the thought of spending a night without him.

May 1973. Hyderabad.

I woke up with a start the day after Day Spend—Rani was shaking me hard.

'Wake up, sleepyhead,' she said rudely.

I groaned. I had been dreaming about Shubho in the garden. We were snuggling high up in the gulmohar tree, hiding from Ranjan and Rani in a game of hide and seek. It was the perfect revenge after Ranjan's behaviour and Rani's complicity in excluding me from the swings. I blinked as I adjusted to the harsh morning light.

'Today is mango-pickle-making day. Mallika Didi is coming. Don't you want to get up and get ready?'

I sat up, excited at the thought of seeing Mallika. I quickly brushed my teeth and started to get dressed. It was cool inside the palace, even though I could feel the heat building up when I went out to the veranda.

Mallika arrived just after lunch.

'Sorry I am late,' she said as she got out of the car, smoothing her clothes and shaking her hair out. She was wearing a flowered skirt and a blouse, her slim shoulders and arms glowing in the sun. Her beautiful fingernails were polished ice-blue and she looked elegant and cool even on such a hot day.

'Those hooligans are making trouble again,' Binesh Kaku said irritably to my father as he prepared to drive off. 'We were stuck at a blockade set up by the police in the market. A crowd of some twenty people was about to get into a fight, but the police managed to stop it. After almost half an hour, we were finally allowed to leave. We got here by making a detour around Khairatabad market. More

Hindu–Muslim tension. I saw the police throwing a couple of goons into the van. They had been threatening a Hindu flower-shop owner and then people took sides and it turned ugly. The Muslims want to build a mosque extension on the holy ground of an old Venkateswara temple. Just out to make trouble. Nothing has changed after all these years.'

I thought about Salim. He would never be part of such a mob, but our parents wouldn't believe that. Mallika looked devastated.

'Let us go to the mango grove and spot the best mangoes to pickle,' Rani said. She linked her arm with Mallika's and walked off with her. I followed them quietly. Binesh Kaku's outburst had cast a shadow on our day.

One of the most stunning features of the palace was the mango orchard. The orchard had various old mango trees. Some of them were almost eighty years old, with mighty, gnarled trunks and many, many branches. Each winter, the branches would be bare, but in spring, tiny, pale peppermint-green leaves would grow in great clusters. Soon, miniature white flowers would appear, blossoming and then turning into little green knobs that would grow into full-grown raw mangoes in the summer.

There were many varieties of mangoes in the garden because, after all, it was a garden fit for a king. 'Phalon ka Raja'—the King of the Fruit—my mother called the mango, using a description that had stood the test of time.

One variety was the sinduri mango, of a rich shade of green. The point where the fruit was attached to the branch, had a sprinkling of bright, vermilion red (sinduri), as if someone had taken a pinch of the powder and dusted the end with it. And then there was the Alfonso, considered by connoisseurs to be the best for sweetness and flavour and named after Alfonso de Albuquerque, who established the Portuguese colony in Goa. Perfectly shaped and bright gold in colour, it was like a topaz that stood apart from all other varieties of mango.

It was still too early to pick mangoes for ripening, but it was the perfect time to capture their tartness in pickles.

'Rahul, go call Ma and Shankar so that we can pluck the raw

mangoes,' Rani ordered.

I sped off obediently to find Shankar, our gardener.

'Ma, Rani wants you and Shankar to come to the mango grove,' I said, breathless. My mother was busy drying stainless steel pots and mixing oils and spices in preparation for the pickling.

'Go and stay with the girls. I will be there soon with Shankar,' Ma said.

I ran back to the mango grove. As I got close, I heard a loud squeal of joy.

'Really?' I heard Rani exclaim. 'How romantic! Have you told anyone yet?'

'Shhh … No. No one knows. If Baba and Ma find out, it will be terrible.'

I slowed down.

'So, is Salim handsome?' Rani asked excitedly.

'Mm … he is very handsome, just like Shashi Kapoor,' Mallika said.

'Where did you meet him?'

'At Osmania College, in a political science class.'

'How long have you known him?'

'About three months. He writes me love letters all the time. I have to hide them carefully from everyone. I am in love with him. I want to marry him,' Mallika said shyly and yet with defiance.

'Are you crazy? He is a Muslim. You know they will never agree to a love marriage, let alone marriage to a Muslim! You just heard Binesh Kaku talking about them. He will disown you. That is, if he does not kill you first.'

'I know, I know. I wish these fights over the temple had not broken out. It is going to make it even harder for Baba to accept us. I don't know what to do. I only know that I cannot live without Salim.'

'I can't even imagine what my father would do if I fell in love with a Muslim boy.' Rani shuddered. 'He would be so furious! And your father has a much worse temper than mine. What if he goes to Salim's house and tells his father and they have a fight? He will forbid you from seeing him. He would arrange a marriage for you with someone right away. And can you imagine what all your relatives in Calcutta would say about your family?'

'I know, I know. But I am in love with Salim, Rani.' Mallika sounded desperate. Looking around her, she said, 'We better stop talking about it in case someone overhears us. I will see him again tonight at the film theatre when I go with you and Rahul.'

I wished they would include me in their confidence. I thought about Amit again. It was useless to fight our parents who were so powerful and ruled our fates.

They fell silent when they noticed me and then started talking loudly about mangoes. Shankar and my mother arrived soon after.

Shankar had two vertical lines, joined together at the base, like the letter 'U' painted on his forehead to symbolize his devotion to Lord Vishnu. He untied a little bundle tied around his waist and offered us prasad. The laddoos were sweet and crumbly. I raised the prasad to my forehead in reverence before eating it. Rani, Mother and Mallika did the same.

'Did you go to the temple?' I asked him.

'Yes, baba. I went to the temple today. We took an oath to protect our temple and defend it against the Musalmans who want to take over the sacred ground. We have to fight for Lord Vishnu.' Shankar looked determined, his nostrils flaring with pride.

'You have a young wife and children, Shankar,' my mother said with concern. 'Don't get involved in Hindu–Muslim riots. If anything happens to you, what will happen to them?' She softened her voice and said, 'Let politicians and religious leaders fight their own wars. In the end, it is always the women and children who suffer.'

'Memsahib, I have taken an oath to fight if we have to. Please don't worry about me. Vishnu Bhagwan will protect me and all his devotees from those who wish to defile his holy temple.' Shankar bowed his head with due respect, but his chin was set. 'We will teach them a lesson if they do not stop trying to take over our holy land.'

Rani looked at Mallika and raised her eyebrows. I went and held her hand in silent support.

'Where should I start, memsahib?' Shankar dusted his hands and rubbed them in preparation.

The mangoes used for pickles would have to be raw—but not too raw, or the milk in the mango would make them too caustic. And they could not be too ripe, or the flesh would no longer be milky white but yellow. Shankar had put together a clever little contraption. He had a long pole—tall enough to reach most of the top branches of the tree. A scythe blade was attached to the top and he was able to operate it by tugging on a rope that was tied to it. When he found a mango to pluck, he used this device to cut the stalk so it would fall into the bag attached below the blade.

My mother directed the entire operation with a confidence formed from years of pickle-making. Mangoes with blemishes, those that had been partially eaten by birds or mangoes that had fallen to the ground were unsuitable for pickles. As the afternoon wore on, we went from tree to tree, picking a few specimens from each.

We got to the trees with the chusnis or suckable mangoes. These were long and thin and had large seeds. But they were incredibly sweet and full of fibres. They were no good served in slices—the best way to eat them was to roll them between your hands, making the flesh soft and pliable, then biting an end and sucking all the juices out. A little pulp came out as well, and at the end, the mango looked like a withered breast, drained of milk.

After the bag was full, we stopped. Ma took some mangoes from the bag and put them in Shankar's tunic, which he was holding out from the waist.

'Shukriya, memsahib.' Shankar left, holding the bundle of mangoes to his waist.

'Mallika Didi, will you promise to come to the ripe mango harvest?' I asked, prompted by a sudden premonition. I did not know why, but I needed an assurance from her.

'Of course, Rahul. I promise.' She put her arm around my shoulders and kissed me on my forehead.

We walked back to the kitchen where the annual event was about to begin. Bengalis have their own style of making pickles. The mark of a good cook is one whose pickles never go mouldy. 'Aachar bichar', goes an old Bengali saying—meaning that pickle-makers need to be careful and judicious.

The kitchen had high ceilings and the walls were dark with soot from years of cooking. Large windows let in air and light and opened onto the veranda and one could see the servants' quarters beyond. But these were empty now, since we did not have any live-in help.

There were a number of rooms next to the kitchen: storerooms, pantry rooms, box rooms and laundry rooms. The kitchen itself was large and could hold many stoves. Counters lined each side and there was a large table in the centre. The bag of mangoes lay on the table.

My mother prided herself on her pickling success. 'I have never made a pickle that went bad or grew fungus,' she boasted. 'All right, children. First of all, I want you to wash your hands well and dry them carefully. Water is anathema to pickles, to be avoided at all costs. Mallika Beti, come and help me with the mangoes. Wipe them carefully—there is no need to wash them.'

Mallika reached for the bag that had been carefully placed on the table. She took the mangoes out and wiped them. 'Mashi, how do you want them cut?'

'Well, let's see. For the two savoury pickles, slice them like this, along the seed. Cut the two sides into cubes and don't peel the skin. Be careful not to eat the raw mango, or you will get boils. For the sweet pickle, slice the mango like this, in long slices. I will make mango chutney with the seeds later. Rani, why don't you take these small mangoes and dry them carefully? I will pickle them whole. And Rahul, sit here and clean the chaff out of the cumin and sesame seeds.'

Cumin, coriander, fenugreek, bay leaves, cayenne pepper and other fragrant spices lay in small mounds on a dry, stainless steel thali. My mother poured some mustard oil, dark and pungent, into a kadhai and it soon exuded raw mustard fumes.

'Actually, Rahul, before you clean the spices, use this dry cloth to wipe out the inside of the pickle jars,' Ma instructed me.

I loved the pickle jars—some tall and cavernous, some transparent and others opaque—that would hold the mangoes and spices once they were mixed. We sat around the kitchen table on stools as we worked. The conversation that followed was a defining moment for me because I heard from my mother for the first time what she thought of 'love marriages'.

It started with Mallika saying, 'I cannot wait to watch the film tonight. Rishi Kapoor is supposed to be really good in it.'

'I know. He is so cute,' Rani chimed in.

'What is the story about?' my mother asked.

'It is about this Hindu boy and Christian girl. They fall in love and run away, in the end jumping over a waterfall ...' Mallika said sadly.

'Oh, that is so sad. But those kinds of mixed marriages never work, you know.'

'Don't be so old-fashioned, Ma.' Rani sounded exasperated. 'Things are not like they used to be when you were young. If I had a Muslim or Christian boyfriend, would you not let me marry him?'

'I might. But you know your father. He would never, ever permit it. His family suffered terribly in the Partition when they came over from East Pakistan. In this world, society is still not ready for Hindus to marry Christians or Muslims. The scars from the Partition are still fresh. It is going to take decades, maybe even hundreds of years, before Hindus and Muslims intermarry and before love marriages are accepted.'

The slicing knife slid off a mango seed and buried itself in Mallika's finger. She pulled it out and it fell to the kitchen floor with a clatter.

'Oh!' Mallika cried and grabbed a towel and wrapped her finger in it even as it turned red. 'Oh no, this is bad luck!' she said, her voice full of pain and fear as she looked at Rani.

I felt a shiver of apprehension as I stared at the blood dripping onto the floor. The hopelessness of Mallika's love was overwhelming because she was truly alone. Rani, Mallika, Shyamala and I were powerless and had to do whatever our parents told us to.

'Don't be superstitious, Mallika. It is just an accident.' Rani tried to soothe her as she and I jumped up and went to see how bad the cut was.

'Oh, Mallika!' My mother was at her side in a flash. 'Show it to me.' She examined the finger, holding it tightly on either side of the cut. 'It is not too deep. Thank God. Your mother would never forgive me if you were hurt in my kitchen.'

'Here is some ice from the fridge. I am going to apply a tourniquet. I learnt how to do first-aid in my Girl Scouts class.' Rani had been anxious to use the word tourniquet, I was sure.

The cut stopped bleeding after intense pressure was applied for a while.

'Okay, that is enough work for all of you. Wash your hands. Mallika, rinse out the cut and let Rani apply some Boroline ointment and then tie a bandage. I will finish the rest. I will make the lime pickles later. Mallika, tell your mother I will give her some of my pickles when they are done.'

Mallika and Rani went off to wash their hands. I stayed behind in the kitchen, going through the spices, looking for chaff. It was hot outside and the crows sounded tired and cranky. A fly buzzed annoyingly above us somewhere. '*Jis gali mein tera ghar na ho, balama ...*' The hit song from *Kati Patang* on the radio reminded me again of Rajesh Khanna rowing a boat in Nainital while Asha Parekh blushed. My mother mixed the mangoes in the oil and heated them with the spices in the kadhai. Then she carefully poured the mixture into the jars.

She took some time with the sweet pickle, which was one of my favourites. It was made with summer berries. She tied a cloth over the mouth of each jar. The jars were then placed out in the blazing summer sun. There they would sit for the rest of summer, to be brought in each night and put out each morning. After about three to four months of being infused in the hot sun, the pickles would be on their way to the pantry, where they would stay for a year or two before being eaten. When ready, these pickles were dark and sticky with berries and mangoes—the promise of summer distilled.

I wondered what would happen to all of us in a year, when the pickles would be ready. Would Mallika still be in love with Salim? Would Binesh Kaku and Anjali Mashi accept their relationship? Would I be normal like everyone else at school or would I have to hide my feelings from everyone so that I did not get punished and expelled, and bring shame to my family? Would I become like Amit, vacant and slow, if I were administered shock therapy?

'Go see how Mallika is doing, Rahul' Ma said to me. 'I don't know how I would have made all these pickles without your help.' She smiled and pushed me outside the kitchen as she prepared to clean up.

Mallika and Rani were sitting at the dining table and talking in low voices. Mallika looked pensive. They stopped talking when I entered.

'How is your finger, Mallika Didi?' I asked.

'Much better. Thank God it has stopped bleeding.'

'I am so excited about the film we are going to watch this evening.' I said. I could not wait to see Salim again. I hoped Mallika would introduce me to him.

'I am too,' said Mallika, suddenly looking radiant.

'I will be bringing out tea soon. Rani, set the table,' my mother announced from the kitchen.

We snacked on hot, spicy tea, with crisp, savoury nimkis and a plate of gajas filled with nuts and raisins and shaped like half-moons.

'It is almost five in the evening,' Mallika suddenly exclaimed.

'Let us go,' Rani said. 'I need to get ready.'

'Me too!' I scrambled for the bedroom. I put on my new Rajesh Khanna-style shirt and pants. My favourite shoes with the big buckles were next. I arranged my hair carefully with a curl on one side, just like my hero and then, humming '*Mere sapnon ki rani kab ayegi tu ...*' to myself, I ran to meet the others.

My father was waiting at the wheel, ready to drive us to the film theatre. 'Rahul, stay close to Mallika and Rani,' he ordered.

'We will make sure of that,' Mallika said, squeezing my hand conspiratorially.

I smiled to myself, thrilled to be going to Ramesh Talkies, my favourite theatre. Grand and imposing, it had gigantic, painted posters with larger-than-life pictures of actors and actresses. We loved the potato chips, the spicy masala peanuts and the popcorn sold there—the roasted and sweet aroma would be heavy in the foyer when we entered. But most of all, I was excited because I would see Salim.

'Let us get snacks.' Mallika said as we walked to the stand selling Coca Cola and snacks.

'Oh, yes, let's go,' Rani said with a meaningful look at Mallika.

Mallika was paying the vendor when a voice behind us said, 'Mallika?'

I recognized him right away.

Mallika turned around. Her face lit up and she squealed with joy: 'Salim!'

'Are you here to watch this film?' he asked.

'Yes!' Mallika giggled.

I had not realized how impressive Salim was up close. He was over six feet tall and had beautiful dark hair. His hair was done in the latest fashion, nicely combed back and with sideburns. He was dressed stylishly too. His eyes were dark and soulful and he had a sparkling smile. Walking over to me, he placed his hand on my shoulder and said, 'And who are you?' I found myself looking into his eyes and stared at him, enjoying our proximity.

'This is Rahul. Rahul, meet Salim. I know Salim from college,' Mallika said. Salim's eyes twinkled as he squeezed my shoulder and said, 'Hi, Rahul.'

I knew a lot more about Salim already, but I also knew that it was supposed to be a secret.

'Hi, Salim,' I said, suddenly feeling shy. With the exception of Shubho, he was the most handsome man I had ever seen off screen. He was older than Shubho and there was nothing boyish about him. I stared at his brown eyes and was conscious of a desire to look at all of him—the pants that hugged his hips tightly, the dark curly hair that showed at the opening of his shirt, the strong forearms and the large hand that still squeezed my shoulder. I held on to Mallika's hand, feeling both bashful and excited.

Rani came up to meet us. 'Hello ... I mean, hi,' she stammered. 'Nice to meet you. I am Rani.'

I was conscious of a sense of disappointment as Salim moved away from me to greet her. 'Hi, Rani,' he said.

'Would you like to join us? What a coincidence, running into you here.' Mallika sounded perfectly innocent. Salim looked at Mallika and gave her a quick wink. Mallika blushed as she looked down, trying to hide her pleasure.

I knew that this clandestine meeting was no coincidence. I felt especially thrilled to be in the presence of a real-life romantic couple, just like the heroes and heroines in films. I thought about Shubho and his girlfriend. They did not need to hide their feelings for each other and meet secretly. A sudden stab of jealousy shot through me as I thought about how they had kissed and touched each other.

We walked into the theatre, our feet sinking into the blood-red carpet. It was dark and cool, the air-conditioning a welcome respite from the heat outside. Scalloped velvet curtains covered the silver screen. The stale air smelt of sickly sweet Priya perfume, Jovan Musk cologne and sweat, mingling with the aroma of popcorn and potato chips. Bags rustled around us. Mallika took us high up onto the balcony where it was not very crowded. Salim sat next to me on one side. On the other side, Mallika sat, flanked by Rani. The curtains lifted and the conversations became whispers all around as people tried to finish their talking before the show.

After the obligatory newsreel and trailers, the film started. Whispers quieted down further. The rustling and crackling of plastic died away as the snacks were put aside for a bit.

I glanced at Mallika, happy to be with my real-life heroine. She and Salim were looking at each other, bright smiles on their faces. Her eyes sparkling, she patted my cheek. I was elated to be sitting in between these two beautiful people who had committed their love to each other against all odds. I knew then that, no matter what opposition they faced, I would support them any way I could. I thought about Shubho, my real-life hero, and wished that I was sitting in the darkened theatre with him, my head on his shoulder.

The film we were watching, *Bobby*, was probably the best-known teenage love story ever made in India. Rishi Kapoor, handsome and dashing, was a Hindu boy. But his rich father was a scheming villain and inflexible about his son's love for a Christian girl, a Goan fisherman's daughter, played by the beautiful Dimple Kapadia. Thus the hero and heroine were in constant danger from their controlling parents. In the end, after an escape and chase, the lovers jump off a cliff, over a waterfall and into a deep gorge, because no one would accept their love. But a last-minute reprieve was granted when the girl's father, the poor fisherman, had a change of heart and jumped in to save them.

Mallika and Rani cried from relief and joy at the end. I did too, discreetly, feeling too old to show my tears in public. I felt Salim put his arm over the back of my chair. I looked over and saw Salim's hand on Mallika's shoulder, gently rubbing it. She looked at him and smiled. She stopped crying. So did I.

6

June 1973. Hyderabad

The day had dawned still and hot. As I relived our meeting with Salim from the night before, I sat outside on the veranda, my legs dangling a few feet above the ground, listening to the gusts of wind that made the trees bow and sway in sudden snatches. The storm that had been threatening to break had not arrived, granting us a temporary reprieve. The monsoons would arrive soon.

I thought about Shubho as well. I wanted desperately to see him again and wondered if I could convince my parents to let me visit Ranjan soon for a Day Spend. They would undoubtedly say that it was too soon. I racked my brains, trying to think of an excuse to be around Ranjan, so that I could be around Shubho too. I thought of the way he had looked right at me as he kissed his girlfriend and a familiar, warm sensation flooded my body. I wished I could read the letter that Amit Puri had written. Had he felt the same rush of desire that I did when he expressed his love for the captain of the football team?

The phone rang, breaking into my thoughts.

'Four-six-five-three-zero,' I heard my mother answer. 'Oh, Anjali Didi. How are you?' There was a pause as Anjali Mashi said something. Then Ma continued: 'Yes, of course I remember. We will visit you this Saturday. Don't worry so much. We can talk more when we visit. Rahul and Rani are here and I have to cook lunch for them. But we will see you later tonight.'

She hung up and turned around. 'We are going to see Mallika this evening,' she said to Rani and me. We nodded enthusiastically at the news and walked to the steps that led down from the veranda.

'I think Mallika Didi likes Salim just like Dimple liked Rishi Kapoor. They are boyfriend–girlfriend, aren't they?' I asked Rani, using the scandalous words I had learnt at school. And I had seen what Shubho did with his girlfriend and felt privy to a secret world that Rani had probably never seen.

'Don't be stupid! And don't mention this to anyone or else we will not be allowed to go out with Mallika Didi. If Binesh Kaku and Anjali Mashi find out, they will be very angry. So never, never mention this to anyone. Understand? I hope I have a boyfriend too. I cannot imagine being married off to someone I do not know, like our parents were,' she said, her voice holding a surprising urgency. Her face tightened with dread and she grabbed my arm.

I felt Rani's fear palpably as never before and it made me feel unexpectedly sad for her. I was newly aware of the precariousness of her position. I looked at her and noticed again how her body had changed over the past year and how she held herself differently, with a new modesty. I had seen Ranjan responding to her. Rani's hair was pulled up and her big hooped earrings gave her a mature look. She would have to follow many rules like other girls and her freedom was much more tenuous than mine. I had always assumed that Rani's place in life was stronger since she had bullied and threatened me for as long as I could remember. Rani had secrets too, and would have more, like Mallika, I thought. Just like me.

We visited Mallika that night. I was worried that Binesh Kaku would never allow her to see Salim if he found out what was going on. If someone saw them together and told Binesh Kaku, they would not stand a chance.

'Mallika, Chatterjee Mesho has arrived,' Binesh Kaku announced imperiously as he opened the door without a smile. After waiting for just a few seconds, he said impatiently, 'Mallika, come here, right now!' He sounded so angry that both Rani and I looked at each other, wondering if he knew. If he did, we would get into trouble too.

Mallika and Shyamala came running downstairs, looking scared. Mallika was wearing a salwar kameez, her hair flowing down around her shoulders. She greeted my parents nervously and, as they walked into the sitting room, she said to Rani and me, 'Come upstairs.' Her voice was low and agitated. She turned around and ran up the stairs.

The moment we reached the bedroom, she closed the door behind her. Taking Rani aside, she said to her, 'They are upset because Mr Khosla mentioned to Baba that I was associating with young men.' She looked nervously at me.

'It's okay. Rahul knows about it all. How did Binesh Kaku and Anjali Mashi find out?' Rani said, including me in the conversation. I felt very privileged at having their confidence for the first time.

'It is that nosy parker, Professor Khosla, who saw Salim and me having tea at the cafeteria at Osmania. He made it a point to mention it to Baba at the Lions' Club meeting. Next thing I know, there is a Spanish Inquisition here at home. I have never seen Baba so angry. I thought he was going to slap me. Ma said that if I persist like this I will ruin the family name. They said that if I continued this behaviour they would marry me off to the first eligible boy they find. Can you imagine me in an arranged marriage?' She paused, then continued with fear in her voice: 'I don't think they know about Salim. Oh God, if they find out, it will be hell. In any case, I will not stop seeing him!' Mallika sounded defiant and angry, her normally cheerful face stubborn, her lower lip jutting out obstinately. But she also looked worried, the lines on her forehead made her look older, like her mother.

She went to the dressing table and opening the bottom drawer, stuck her hand all the way in and pulled out a bundle of handwritten rice paper. 'Look,' she said, showing us the bundle. 'Salim says he loves me. He drops off a letter for me almost every day at college.' She held the bundle to her chest, a dreamy look on her face.

We were rudely interrupted by Binesh Kaku. His voice was rough. 'Mallika, serve Chatterjee Mesho tea and snacks,' he ordered from downstairs. I was reminded of the way my father ordered my mother to bring him tea. It was as if the purpose of women in life was to serve men. 'I'm coming,' Mallika replied, and we trooped down obediently. We sat in the living room, drinking tea and eating kochuri and alur dom. I wondered if Binesh Kaku and Anjali Mashi had said anything to my parents. He looked serious as always, so it was hard to tell.

After dinner, my father leaned back in his chair with a contented sigh and said, 'Mallika, sing us a song.'

Always acquiescent, Mallika went to Anjali Mashi's bedroom and brought out the family harmonium. She sang a famous Rabindra Sangeet, '*Aami chini go chini tomare, o go bideshini ...*', a haunting, lilting melody that took her parents and mine back to a place I had never been—Calcutta.

'Binesh Kaku, please let Mallika Didi and Shyamala come and visit us tomorrow. We want to go to the market and buy bangles.' Rani and I begged before we were leaving.

'No!' Binesh Kaku's eyebrows were furrowed and his lips were tight. I felt like leaving the room as I did when my father was angry.

'She can go, it is summer vacation,' Anjali Mashi said.

'Yes, Binesh Dada, let them visit. It will be a nice change for them to be at our place,' my mother joined in.

'What change? Don't they have plenty of fun at school and college? There is no need for such frivolous activities. They can stay home and help their mother. It is high time they learned some housekeeping skills.'

I felt helpless and angry. Without our parents' permission, we could not do anything. It was just not fair!

'Binesh, I am like Mallika and Shyamala's father. It will be good for them to come over and visit.' My father came unexpectedly to the rescue.

Unable to refuse his gentle admonition, Binesh Kaku relented. Mallika started clearing the table, breathing a sigh of relief. Accompanied by Shyamala and Rani, she went to the kitchen. I followed them.

'I will call Salim and tell him to meet us at the South Indian restaurant when we go to buy bangles. You must convince your father to take us to the bangle shop,' Mallika whispered to Rani.

'Remember, Rahul, not a word to anyone—don't be a blabbermouth!' Rani said.

'Yes, Rahul, remember this is our secret. We will have fun tomorrow.' Mallika's eyes sparkled mischievously for a moment as she took my hand in hers and squeezed it. I had never felt so grown-up and special and I knew that I would keep this secret—just like my other secret, my fantasies about Rajesh Khanna and now about Shubho. Perhaps things would actually work out for both of us.

The next day I woke up and lay in bed, luxuriating in the joy of the day ahead, full of anticipation. Mallika arrived just before lunch, looking like my old Mallika—excited about doing things with me. She looked stunning in a sky-blue churidar–kurta embroidered with little red flowers and covered with glass-work, her hair shining in the sunlight. I was thrilled. We were going to meet Salim and no one else knew about it.

'Remember to ask if we can go to buy bangles,' Shyamala said to Rani. 'After buying bangles, we will go to meet Salim.'

Rani nodded conspiratorially.

After we had eaten, Rani addressed Baba: 'I want to buy some of the lovely satin-glass bangles that Mallika Didi has. They are available at the shop on Abid Road. And then we want to go eat some South Indian food at the Udipi Palace, next to John's Bakery. Can you take us there, please, please, please?' We knew that Rani was the only one who could get my father to agree.

Unable to resist her pleading, my father said, 'Achha, but all of you must stay together. Mallika, please make sure you keep an eye on Rahul.' I felt like I was being treated like a child and almost declared that Mallika had shared her secret with me and that I was a big boy, but remembered just in time that I had promised her not to tell anyone. I had many confidences to keep.

'Remember to be right here when I come back,' Baba said as he dropped us off on Abid Road. 'Here, Rani,' he said, holding out a ten-rupee note. 'This is for your South Indian treat.' He laughed at the look on her face. I loved it when he surprised us like that. I felt a pang of guilt for lying to him. But we had to do this so that Mallika could meet with Salim. She was counting on us.

We went to Mohini Bangle Store on Abid Road. It was a tiny store and sold thousands of bangles. There were bangles made of glass, brass, gold, silver, plastic, lac, bone and bronze. The walls were covered with hundreds of tiny wooden drawers with shiny brass handles. In the front of the store was a glass case that held the more expensive gold and silver bangles. They were studded with glass, semi-precious and precious stones. Some were also enamelled, painted and carved.

'Namaste, Baby and Baba,' the shop owner said, bowing to us with folded hands.

'Namaste, Uncleji,' we chorused in unison. He was a kindly old man, always dressed in khadi kurta–pajama and a Gandhi cap.

'Uncleji, please show us some of the satin-glass bangles you have, just like these.' Mallika thrust her wrist out for him to see.

'Achha, Baby,' he said. He turned around and looked at the identical drawers with the identical brass knobs. I have no idea how he knew where to look, but he went straight to a brass knob in the middle of the wall and pulled. A dark-brown, varnished drawer slid out smoothly. He pulled it out of the wall and brought it over to us. It was full of a few dozen bangles, all shiny and satiny, made of glass.

'Uncleji, I want these blue ones,' Rani said.

'I want some too, the red ones!' I said, unable to help myself.

The shop owner turned to me and looked me up and down in bemusement. His voice was surprisingly sharp. 'Baba, you are not a girl. Only girls wear bangles. Who will marry a boy who wears bangles? I had a nephew who insisted on wearing girls' clothes and bangles when he was your age.'

Rani sputtered in the background and then started humming under her breath: 'Rahul is a girlie boy. Rahul is a girlie boy!' Shyamala started giggling.

He turned to them, looking serious. 'No, Baby, it is not a laughing matter. He never married, not to this day and his mother, my poor sister, died without a grandchild. Everyone made fun of him. It was very sad.'

'But Uncleji, I don't want to get married,' I stated firmly.

'Not marry? But everyone marries!' Uncleji looked shocked. 'Ram, Ram,' he muttered under his breath as he turned away. 'Who will make them understand? Children these days! Why don't they listen to their elders?'

'Don't listen to anyone,' Mallika said. 'You wear whatever you want, Rahul.'

I beamed. I loved it when Mallika stood up for me.

'Not all of us do what is expected of us by this stupid conformist society with its hoity-toity British mentality. How I wish I could break the rules!' Mallika's voice shook as she shredded a corner of her lace handkerchief in her frustration.

'Calm down, Mallika Didi,' Rani said in a low, appeasing voice. 'We don't want Uncleji to say anything about you getting upset to Binesh Kaku, or he will never let us go out together again.'

Mallika took a deep breath. I took her hand in mine and squeezed it and she smiled at me wanly. 'We'll show them, won't we, Rahul?'

Uncleji carefully wrapped a dozen of the electric-blue bangles in newspaper and then put them in a bag for Rani. Triumphantly bearing her spoils aloft, she led the way out of the store. We walked out, blinking in the afternoon light, the heat from the paving stones rising in a wave, making us dizzy.

'Let us go to the Udipi Palace,' Shyamala suggested, looking at her watch. 'It is nice and air-conditioned inside—it is so hot right now!'

'Yes, let's go.' Mallika's steps lightened at the suggestion. She led the group forward and we quickened our steps, the unrelenting heat following us. The Udipi Palace was a large restaurant and immensely popular during summertime in Hyderabad. We opened the darkened doors covered with greasy fingerprints and walked into a cool oasis. The blast of cold freezing was very welcome.

'Ah, that feels so good, doesn't it, Mallika Didi?' I asked.

Mallika was not listening. She was already ahead of us, scanning the tables, looking for someone. Salim.

'Oh, what if someone sees us?' Mallika's voice was fearful as she clutched at my arm when she saw him. We stopped for a moment as Shyamala and Rani moved forward.

I looked up at her and smiled and then pulled her along gently. Salim waved to us. He was wearing white cotton pants and a maroon short-sleeved shirt. I noticed his lean arms as he stretched his hand out over the table to say hello to us. Rani and Shyamala looked self-conscious. They giggled and looked away from Salim, suddenly gawky.

'Salim.' Mallika's quiet voice filled with pleasure. We stood awkwardly around the table, trying to decide where to sit. Mallika looked around nervously at the room and then slipped into the chair that Salim held out for her, next to him.

Shyamala and Rani looked around too. 'The coast looks clear,' Rani murmured. 'I will sit here so that I can look at the door in case someone we know walks in.'

The waiter came over and poured us tall glasses of icy water.

'So, Rani and Shyamala, how are you?' Salim leaned over the table, looking at them with his beautiful brown eyes.

Rani giggled and leaned forward to get a glass of water and, in a clumsy move, knocked it over. The water spilt and flowed towards Mallika. Salim jumped up in a flash, went to Mallika's chair and pulled her away. She blushed furiously and brushed his hands away. Shyamala started laughing and then I joined in and soon the rest burst out laughing as well. The ice was broken.

'Rahul, Rahul! Hey!' a familiar, deep voice resounded over the clink of the stainless steel plates and bowls, the only way good South Indian food was ever served. It was a serendipitous moment, for when I turned around, there was Shubho, sitting a few tables away with his girlfriend Anamika. 'Come over and say hello,' he invited.

I felt a wave of excitement go through my body and then felt acutely embarrassed.

'Who is that?' Rani's voice cut through my embarrassment. 'My, he is so cute.'

'Yes, he is,' Shyamala agreed with a muffled giggle.

'That is Shubho Dada.' I mumbled.

'What? Ranjan Bose's brother? The last time I saw him he was all gangly and awkward. He looks so ... handsome!'

'Yes,' I said, not sure what exactly she thought I was agreeing to.

'And who is that girl with him?'

'That is Anamika, his girlfriend.'

'Hey, Rahul!' Shubho was relentless.

'I'll be right back,' I said and walked over to Shubho's table.

Anamika was dressed in a short white tennis outfit. Shubho was wearing shorts that said 'Slazenger' on the side. His tanned calves were taut and his expensive tennis shoes were neatly laced up. A white polo shirt was open at the neck. They must have arrived just before us. Even though the air-conditioning was on, they both looked sweaty and flushed from their game of tennis and the torpid heat.

'Hey, Rahul, have a seat.' Shubho patted an empty chair next to him. I sat down awkwardly, both elated and unsure of what to do next. I looked at the table in front of me and examined the food stains that the waiter had missed. I focused on one that looked just like the map of Africa.

'So, how is your summer vacation going? Are you having fun? Who are you here with?' Shubho shot off a series of questions.

'You boys catch up while I go to the bathroom.' Anamika pushed her chair back and left the dining room as scores of eyes followed her out, glued to her bare legs in the short tennis tunic. A sight like this had probably been seen only in films by most of the patrons of the restaurant. I wondered what the men in the room felt when they saw Anamika. This was not the way the women in their families dressed. I knew that the boys in my class would have responded the same way as the patrons. But why did I not feel that interest? No matter—Shubho's questions demanded my attention.

'Yes, Shubho. I am having a good time,' I said, finally raising my eyes and looking at him, my breath caught in my throat. He was smiling at me with that same look in his eyes again. This was the look he had given me when he caught me spying on him as he kissed Anamika. 'I am here with my sister and some of our friends,' I blurted out, then looked down at my hands again. They were fiddling with the cloth napkin, folding it into various origami shapes. I stole a look at Shubho's hands. They were strong like his forearms, the nails nice and broad and neatly trimmed. Searching for something to say, I asked abruptly, 'So, how was your stay in Spain? Are you coming back to our school again this year?'

'Definitely. Spain was great. They have a great football coach in the school I attended. I made some really good friends in class. I was ready to come back in six months, though.' He smiled at the memories I had stirred up, a faraway but happy look in his eyes. 'So, are you going to join the football team when you're back in school?'

he asked. Then he shifted in his seat and uncrossed his legs and I felt the warm pressure of his shins against my legs. A wave of excitement travelled up my leg to my groin. I was embarrassed and hoped no one could see. He moved his legs so that his knees were between mine, touching my inner thigh. I liked the way his bare knees and legs felt, both smooth and hard at the same time, so I did not move away. Neither did Shubho, as he gently rubbed his knee against me and leaned in a little closer, a mischievous look on his face.

'Yes, I will join the team,' I promised, scarcely aware of what I was saying. I felt the familiar, enjoyable sensation in my body and stomach again. Except that it was so much stronger this time than when I would dream of Rajesh Khanna. I could smell Shubho's cologne, mixed with the musky scent of his skin. I had a sudden urge to bury my nose in the side of his neck and breathe in deep. I wanted him to hold me ... I looked up at him in confusion. Shubho's lips were slightly parted and he licked them with the tip of his tongue and I could still feel the pressure of his legs against mine. I was not sure at all of what was going on. But I knew that I liked it, even though I was scared that someone would think it shameful.

'I'm back.' Anamika was taking her seat again and the sounds and movements of the restaurant flowed back into my silent reverie. Shubho sat up suddenly and I felt a cool brush of air as he moved his leg slowly away from mine.

'I have to go back to the table.' I simply wanted to leave. I could not bear to see Anamika fawning over Shubho.

'All right, Rahul. You are such a lucky bugger. You will break some hearts one day, I tell you.' Shubho's confident and hearty laugh echoed around the restaurant as he patted my cheek affectionately with his hand.

'Bye, Shubho Dada. Bye, Anamika,' I said, pushing my chair back and standing up quickly as I saw Rani making all kinds of gestures with her hands, asking me to return.

'Bye,' they replied.

I walked back, casually pulling my shirt down, my mind a confused jumble of emotions.

'Gosh, Rahul. We were getting ready to go and rescue you. You looked totally trapped at Shubho Dada's table. What were you talking about anyway? Girls?' Rani let out a big guffaw, echoed by Shyamala. 'Can you imagine Rahul with a girlfriend? Who on earth would go out on a date with someone who spends most of the day climbing trees or playing with earthworms?'

'Oh, leave him alone.' Mallika's voice was firm. 'Don't you two have anyone else to pick on?'

'Oh, sorry, Rahul. I forgot that you are no longer a little boy,' Rani said. 'When did you start growing this?' She stroked my upper lip gently, outlining the peach fuzz that had appeared under my nose and on my chin.

'Stop it,' I muttered, suddenly shy.

'You know, one day you'll be a man and I will no longer be able to tease you,' Rani said, her voice unusually pensive.

'I remember when I started growing the beginnings of a moustache,' Salim broke in mischievously. 'Nothing was the same after that.' He raised an eyebrow as if to mean something, and Mallika laughed.

'Rahul, we have already decided what we want to eat. Did you even get a chance to look at the menu?' Salim, gracious and charming, just like Mallika, changed the topic. 'Bearer,' Salim said, summoning a waiter.

The waiter arrived. He used a towel to wipe the tabletop and then used a second one to polish it.

'I will have a masala dosa and a Madras coffee,' Rani said.

'Same for me,' I said, putting down the menu after giving it a quick glance, and settling for my favourite item.

'Copycat,' said Rani.

'You are one too,' I retorted.

'Now, now, let us not squabble right now, all right?' said Mallika.

Mallika ordered idli and sambar and so did Salim. Shyamala ordered vada and a masala dosa. They all wanted Madras coffee as well.

The waiter brought us our food quickly and, in no time, we were tucking in greedily. The chutney made with fresh-ground coconut was the perfect accompaniment to the crisp dosas.

The waiter then brought out the coffee and then went through the ceremonial pantomime with which South Indian coffee was served. He poured the chicory-flavoured coffee from one stainless steel glass to the next, back and forth, the glasses held an impossible three feet apart, as he expertly transferred the liquid. The coffee grew frothy and, at the exact moment when we were certain he would spill it, the waiter stopped and served it to us. He left his cleaning towel on the table.

We were quiet, each of us enjoying the meal, except for Mallika and Salim, who kept looking at each other and smiling. I thought of Rajesh Khanna and the way he looked at Sharmila Tagore in *Aradhana*.

'Oh, no!' Mallika's panic-stricken voice broke into my food and film-filled ecstasy. 'Mrs Khosla is here! She will tell Ma and Baba that Salim was here. I knew it. We should have never come here. Baba will be so angry!' Her face grew pale and she put her head down, trying to hide. Rani and I looked at each other as we thought about how much trouble we would get into as well for providing a cover for Mallika. Mrs Khosla saw us and made a beeline for our table. Salim jumped up and put the towel that the waiter had left behind on his shoulder and started cleaning the table.

'Madam,' he said to Shyamala as Mrs Khosla walked over, 'would you like more kaapi?' Her expensive silk sari was wrapped around her formidable body and rolls of fat hung from her waist, unable to stay within the confines of her too-small choli blouse. Since her son Suresh went to school with me and her daughter with Rani, she knew us all. She knew Anjali Mashi too because her husband taught at Osmania College. And of course, she knew Mallika. After all, *her* husband had told Mallika's father that she was associating with boys. She looked at Salim for a second and then, ignoring him, said in her loud voice, 'So, how are you all?' Without waiting for an answer, she continued, 'I took Suresh and his friends out for a treat after a film. *Diamonds are for Ever*, with Roger Moore. I really like Roger Moore—he is so handsome. And then that Sean Connery? Ohh!' She squealed with enthusiasm and her jowls quivered lustfully for a second.

'Madam, phor you?' Salim continued, as he asked Rani the heavily accented question.

'Mm ... nothing,' she said, giggling. Salim left.

'Why was that waiter sitting at your table?'

'Yes, Aunty, we were chatting with him because ...' I began, not really knowing what I was going to say.

'He knows my ...' Shyamala started at the same time, and then we both stopped.

Mrs Khosla frowned and cut in, silencing us. 'So you children are here alone? That is very dangerous. Bad, bad things happen to children when they are alone, you know. Do your parents know you are associating with low-class people with no one to supervise you?'

'Oh, no, Khosla Aunty, I am taking care of them,' Mallika replied, sounding nervous.

'So who is actually sitting here?' Khosla Aunty asked, pointing to Salim's empty chair, plate of food and glass of water. 'A friend of mine from school,' Rani said, just as Shyamala said, 'Anuradha.' We looked at each other and shut up in confusion.

Khosla Aunty looked suspicious, unable to solve the puzzle, She turned on her heel, saying very righteously, 'I don't understand why your parents let you go out by yourselves and associate with strangers and expose yourselves to riffraff. At least *I* don't let my children go out alone without me. Anyway, I have to go see my darling sona Suresh and his friends, they are waiting outside.'

We stared at her, unable to say anything more than 'Namaste, Aunty' as we realized how narrow our escape had been. Another word from Mr Khosla would have made things very difficult for Mallika. Her father would probably lock her up in her room until he married her off.

As Mrs Khosla left, swaying slightly from side to side in an effort to balance her rolls of fat, her sari billowing behind her and leaving a trail of expensive French perfume, our barely contained mirth could be restrained no longer. We exploded in paroxysms of laughter. Salim came up to the table, grinning broadly as he took his place.

'Wah, wah, kya acting!' Mallika said with a small flourish of appreciation to Salim for defusing what could have been a disastrous situation. They sat close at the corner of the table, their hands barely touching but close enough that he could whisper something in her ear from time to time, making her giggle and blush. 'Meri jaan,' he said once, loud enough for all of us to hear, and Rani and Shyamala simpered coyly. I loved seeing them at a loss for words. The time-honoured way of addressing one's beloved was passionate, teasing and flirtatious all at once. Only Rajesh Khanna could say those words with that much emotion to Sharmila Tagore. I felt an ever-growing affection for Salim. I looked over at Shubho's table to see if he had noticed the small commotion at ours, but Shubho and Anamika were gone. I missed him already. I did not know when I would see him again.

Salim paid the bill. He left first, after handing Mallika a letter that crackled with the sound I knew so well. Mallika looked sad the moment he left, but then brightened up as she felt the letter in her hands. She straightened her shoulders and said, 'Come on, it is time to go. Remember, this is our secret.'

We walked out, and I was overjoyed to finally be treated like a grown-up, the keeper of Mallika's confidence.

My father was waiting for us at the wheel of the Baby Ford. We piled in.

'So, how was the food?'

'It was great.'

'The dosas were tasty. Thanks for the ten rupees.'

'I love my bangles.'

We all chimed in together and Baba laughed as well, unaware of our scandalous behaviour, as we drove to Mint House. It was a happy group that spilt out of the car and onto the portico of the palace.

Shortly afterwards, Mallika's parents drove up to pick her and Shyamala up and our apprehension returned as the euphoria of the afternoon faded.

'We have to go soon,' Binesh Kaku said as they walked up the portico steps and towards the sitting room.

'So soon?' Baba would not let them leave. 'Arre, Binesh, how can you leave without cha and snacks?'

Binesh Kaku and Anjali Mashi came reluctantly into the living room.

'Chatterjee Dada, please find us a match for Mallika,' Anjali Mashi said abruptly.

I was walking very slowly to the dining room, taking my time. I stopped to look under the table by the door, as if searching for something.

'What? She is too young. Shouldn't she be finishing her college first?' Baba said.

'Well … yes … but you know. A girl's place is in her husband's home. We are just raising her to be part of another household, just like you are raising Rani,' Binesh Kaku said.

'Actually, Chatterjee Dada, the truth is …' Anjali Mashi started saying when her husband cut her short.

'Go help Mrs Chatterjee in the kitchen,' he barked.

Jolted by the sharpness in his voice, I jumped up, knocking over a picture frame. Everyone looked at me.

'What are you doing, Rahul? Go inside and play with Rani,' my father snapped.

I slunk out of the sitting room as quickly as possible, reeling with the news. But before I could tell anyone about it, my mother asked me to set the table in the sitting room. This time, I did not want to serve tea or snacks. I just wanted to get away and warn Mallika, but I would have to do it later.

Anjali Mashi left to join my mother in the kitchen. Her eyes looked puffy and red when she returned and she was quiet the rest of the evening. But my mother acted normal—she was used to the role of peace-keeper.

All of us sat in the sitting room, drinking tea and eating snacks. I watched for any further signs or hints of what Anjali Mashi had been trying to tell Baba, but Binesh Kaku talked politics the entire evening. As always, he dominated the conversation, cutting in whenever Anjali Mashi or his daughters spoke. It was as if no woman's opinion could really count.

'Mallika, stay here. We are leaving soon.' Binesh Kaku

commanded Mallika and Shyamala to sit with the grown-ups as we got up to leave, anxious to regroup and discuss the afternoon's escapade. It irritated me that we could not go and sit outside on the veranda without his permission. We looked at each other and silently reaffirmed our secret. Little did we know that we would never ever be alone together like this again.

After our guests left, I was helping to clear the sitting room of plates and cups when I heard my mother talking to my father in a low tone. I strained to hear while making noise with the cups and dishes as if I were clearing the table.

'Mallika is mixing with a boy,' she said in Bengali.

'Oh. That is terrible.'

'He is not a Brahmin. He is not even a Hindu. He is Muslim.'

'How did they find out?' Baba asked, sounding incredulous. 'Are they absolutely sure? Our Mallika is such a good girl!'

'Well, first of all, Mrs Khosla, the wife of Professor Khosla, mentioned something to Anjali Didi about her husband seeing Mallika talking to boys. Then Mr Khosla himself made a pointed comment to Binesh Dada at the Lions' Club meeting. When they asked Mallika about the boy she was with in the cafeteria, she denied everything. Anjali Didi searched her bedroom and found a bundle of love letters, written by a boy called Salim. She has not told Binesh Dada that the boy is Muslim and that she has read the love letters. She is scared that he will do something rash.'

'Chhee chee!' my father responded. 'A Muslim! How could she? Binesh is from such a good Brahmin family. How could she do this? What will people say?'

'But she is a young girl. I remember what it was like to be young and passionate,' Ma said, looking coy for a second. Then she grew serious. 'The boy she is seeing must have brainwashed her. He is six years older than her. He must surely know that if people find out no one will marry Shyamala.'

'So what are they going to do now?'

'They want to end this affair. Anjali Didi does not know what to do.'

'Did they confront her?'

'Yes, she did. When Anjali Didi asked Mallika about the boy, she said he was just a good acquaintance and occasionally accompanied her group of friends when they went to the cafeteria. They also worked on a class presentation together this year.'

'Do you think she told the truth? Binesh will want to get her married off as quickly as possible,' my father said. 'That's what I would do.'

'I think it is a mistake to get her married without talking to the boy. It is better that they invite him and his parents to their home and have a frank conversation.'

'You know Binesh would never do that once he finds out the boy is Muslim. Because of Muslims, his family had to move from Chittagong in East Pakistan to India. Their family lost everything. His mother died on the way to Calcutta, when their train was attacked and set on fire. The train arrived at the station with everyone in it stabbed to death and burnt!' Baba said, his voice heavy. 'He saw such terrible things. He told me of one particular incident—he saw a Muslim man take a baby from its mother's arms and tear it into two before her eyes.'

'Oh ... stop, stop. I can't bear to think of such cruelty.' My mother shuddered. 'I remember stories I heard when I was young in Allahabad. Bai, our nanny, told us terrible accounts too. Our driver was a man called Adam, he was a Christian. He converted to Sikhism because that was the only way he was allowed to carry a dagger. He fought back and tried to save many Hindu families.'

I walked through the dining room, into the kitchen, the dishes balanced carefully on the tray while my heart raced with horror listening to all the terrible things that had happened during the partition of India. This was the first time I had heard of my parents' experience of such atrocities. But Salim—Salim, who was so cultured and gentle—how could he ever be involved in such cruelty? I thought about his handsome face and loving eyes, and I was certain that not all Muslims could be so bad. I wished my parents could see him and understand this.

'Anjali Didi says that this boy Salim's family is an old one, very cultured and well-to-do. Mallika told her that they did not move here from Pakistan. Their family has been here for generations.'

'Why can't Mallika Didi marry the boy she likes?' I asked fiercely, forgetting to keep quiet.

'Why are you interrupting our conversation? You are too young to understand these things. Let us, who have seen life, take care of these matters,' my father said to me in a threatening tone that I dared not disobey. The anger in his voice reminded me that I needed to closely guard all my secrets.

Feeling frustrated, I went out to the darkened veranda. I looked out into the night, the bushes and trees looking like black-shrouded ghosts. The air crackled with the static of summer lightning. The monsoons would be here soon. It seemed that everyone around me was afraid: Mallika, Rani, my mother, my father, Binesh Kaku, Anjali Mashi. And so was I. I felt a shiver of apprehension run up my spine.

That night, I dreamt of the giant banyan tree in the palace garden. The tree was full of birds that sang and twittered. Under the tree, Salim was singing my favourite song to Mallika: '*Mere sapnon ki rani, kab ayegi tu ...*' All of a sudden, a bolt of lightning from the sky split the tree in two. A deafening crack of thunder scared the birds and they rose in a dark cloud, flying away in one sweep, shrouding the palace gardens in sudden gloom. The thunder silenced their song and Salim's. Then Salim was gone. Only Mallika was left alone, standing under the tree. I woke up, shouting: 'Mallika Didi, Mallika Didi!' But no one heard me that night.

7

Saturday Evening. San Francisco.

The bar was now full. I paused, reliving the alienation and helplessness of the situation we had faced in those tumultuous years in Hyderabad. I did not realize that I had been staring at the votive candle in its little red holder for so long. As I looked away, little dots of light danced in front of my eyes and I felt a tightness in my chest and shoulders. I looked at Andrew as he sat silent. My drink lay half full. I took a sip of it and the liquor burnt a fiery path down my gullet. At this rate, I would be tipsy soon. Andrew followed suit and quaffed the dregs of his drink. He stared moodily at his empty glass, a little drunk. I was not there yet.

'Another round, guys?' The bartender had apparently been waiting for a chance to break into the conversation.

I looked at Andrew, raising my eyebrows, and shrugged. He shrugged too.

'Sure,' he said, not looking at the bartender, still lost in contemplation.

'One for the road,' I said, thinking of the road home. Would I go home alone and Andrew to his motel?

'Wow. That is heavy stuff, Rahul,' Andrew said, after a few minutes of uneasy silence. 'The horrible legacy of your country's Partition never really hit home, you know. Not even when I watched *Gandhi*. So much hatred! Is it still as bad for inter-religious marriages?'

'Yes, it is. The memories are deep and regularly reinforced by communal riots and the frequent bombings that are often the work of Muslim terrorist groups and Hindu fundamentalists. It's a crazy, swinging pendulum of intolerance and hatred. Of course, it's the ones who have nothing to do with the struggle for power, the innocent bystanders, who suffer the most.' I paused for a moment. 'And then, those who suffer turn on their own when same-sex relationships are concerned. It's almost like there has to be a pecking order.'

'Funny you should say that. Our most polite and upstanding churchgoers back home would never use a racist word. But they would not flinch or protest if their kids called a gay kid "faggot" and beat up a gay child at school.' Andrew's tone was unusually vitriolic. He had suffered so much frustration and pain, just like me. My heart went out to him.

'Here you go, guys.' The bartender put down a couple of Manhattans on the counter. Andrew asked him to close the tab and gave him some cash.

'To breaking the last socially sanctioned Nazi attitudes.' I raised my glass.

'Yes, to one day not having to worry about who is marrying whom and what religion, gender and sex they are.'

We clinked our glasses together and I took a big gulp, feeling the fire ignite my insides. I needed it to continue the rest of the story. As the irony of my situation hit me, I laughed out loud. Here I was, fighting to reclaim a relationship that was for all practical purposes destined to be as much a disaster as Mallika and Salim's.

'What's so funny?'

'Nothing,' I said. 'Let me go on with the story.' I tentatively reached for Andrew's fingers, but he did not respond by touching mine. He looked instead at the light coursing through the liquor in his glass. After caressing his hands for a few moments, I withdrew. Clasping my hands together, I faced the red glow of the candle and continued my story.

July 1973. Hyderabad.

After the horrors of Partition were revealed to me, I started to understand that the deep-rooted mistrust of Muslims that our parents had was going to continue to pose an obstacle to Mallika and Salim's happiness. I tried to think of a way to help Mallika, but nothing came to mind. A few days went by with me just whiling away time, worrying about the things I had no control over. Then, one day, the telephone rang. It was Ranjan.

'Hi, Ranjan,' I said, overjoyed that he had called. I had been waiting for a respectable break before broaching the topic of a Day Spend at Ranjan's house. 'I was thinking … we should have another Day Spend. At your house.' My words came out casually, but inside I was squirming. If I went over to Ranjan's house, surely I would meet Shubho.

'Oh, Rahul, that would be so much fun. But we are leaving tomorrow for Nainital to visit my grandmother. She has invited Shubho Dada and me to stay with her for the rest of the summer holidays. I am really excited. It is so nice and cool there and we go swimming in the lake every day!'

This meant that I would not see Shubho for a very long time. My spirits flagged.

'Oh, that is so nice,' I said, trying to muster up some excitement for Ranjan. His grandmother had a lovely cottage in Nainital and they went there every summer.

'Well, I guess I will see you when school starts again,' Ranjan said. 'That's what I was calling to tell you about. Bye!'

'Bye,' I said, sliding the phone back into the cradle.

I walked out to the lawn, staring at the lake shimmering in the distance. The stillness of the morning air was a harbinger of the heat that was soon to follow. The raucous crows were scavenging in the garden outside. The marigolds were bright in the morning sunshine and pale-green cabbage butterflies hovered delicately over the golden-orange blossoms. Dragonflies buzzed overhead, their diaphanous wings as finely spun as silver gossamer. But my summer looked bleak and hopeless. It was not fair, I thought bitterly.

'Rahul, Rahul, where are you?' Rani called from the portico.

I did not answer and kept walking.

I reached the lawn and took my slippers off, luxuriating in the feel of the warm grass under my feet and between my toes. All around me, the air was heavy and sweet with the scent of lilies, marigolds, champa and chameli. I lay on the grass and felt the heat rise through my clothes and skin. The tang of crushed grass was heavenly and I breathed deep. I thought of Shubho kissing Anamika in the garden and closed my eyes, gently touching my face with my fingers. They lingered on my lips and probed my mouth and, unbidden, my tongue reached up to touch them with urgency, tasting the salt on them. Desire stirred in me and I stopped, shocked and ashamed of my body. I sat up and quickly looked around to see if anyone had seen me. I missed Shubho, but I would have to wait until he showed up in my world again. Brushing the grass off my shorts, I walked further into the garden.

The morning grew hotter and the still air grew quiet as, one by one, the birds fell silent—to sing in this heat was too exhausting. All the birds except for the koel. It started on a low note and then grew louder and louder, rising in pitch until it sliced the air into thin slivers with its sharp edge, sounding like a frenzied woman calling out in her madness. Summer was exploding against the backdrop of the koel's cry.

That night, after a day spent in disappointment, I sat outside on the veranda steps, thinking about Mallika. I had not seen her since the time we had gone to Abid Road.

'I would love to go to visit Mallika Didi for a Day Spend. Please, please?' My voice sounded whiny and childish to my ears as I posed the question to my father over dinner. Then it broke. I stopped. It had never done that before. My father looked amused. I took a deep breath and continued in a lower voice, 'It has been so long since we spent time with her.'

'So you want to see your Mallika Didi?' Baba smiled. 'Achha, I will call Binesh and ask him,' he said unexpectedly. 'Looks like you are growing into a man, Rahul. Good.' He gave an approving nod. I was not sure what he meant. In any case, my grown-up request had been received well and I took note of that. 'It will certainly be good for all you children to spend time together,' Baba added, with a meaningful look at my mother. After dinner, he called Binesh Kaku.

'Binesh,' Baba said over the phone, 'Rahul and Rani want to visit Mallika and Shyamala for a Day Spend.' There was a long pause, then my father said, 'What? You sent Mallika to the tea estate in Assam for a few months? Don't you think that this might be a little too hasty? What about her studies? After all, she does need to finish her college, doesn't she? When do you think you will find ... one minute please.' Baba sounded surprised. He stopped and then turned to Rani and me and said, 'Mallika has gone to visit her grandmother. But Shyamala is there. You can visit her. Now go play.' As Rani and I lingered, he snapped, 'Go!'

Embarrassed, we rushed from the room, but stationed ourselves outside the door, just out of sight. Mallika had been sent off to her maternal grandmother's home so unexpectedly! I felt angry that I would not see her for the summer. Then I thought of Binesh Kaku and felt afraid for her.

'Now, Binesh. You are like my brother.' We strained our ears to hear Baba's voice. Why did you not consult us? Are you going to keep her there until the marriage? And have you found a boy yet?' He paused while Binesh Kaku said something in response, then continued: 'What if she contacts that blighter from there? Be careful that she does not run away.' He stopped again to listen to what Binesh Kaku was saying. 'I understand. I would do the same thing if my daughter tried to marry a Muslim boy. They think they know what is best for them, but we have our family honour to think of. We want to walk in society with our heads held high. We will talk more when we meet. You are doing the right thing. Have faith in Ma Durga.' I could hear the anxiety in my father's voice.

I broke out in a cold sweat. Mallika, isolated and held prisoner! What about her and Salim? I had a terrible vision of her leaping over a waterfall, disappearing forever from our lives. Rani said nothing, but her jaw was set and I could see her stubbornly resisting my father's ownership of her future life as an adult.

'I have news for you,' my father called out to my mother, who had cleared the table and was in the kitchen.

'Mallika is in Assam, at the tea estate. Luckily, there is no telephone in the house and her uncle is checking the mail, so there is no way that the bugger Salim can contact her. What a terrible thing for Binesh and Anjali to have to go through! I hope we never have to suffer anything like this …'

Sick at heart, we did not want to hear any more. Rani and I walked out to the garden and tried to think of ways to help Mallika.

'I hate Binesh Kaku. I hate Baba. They think they own us,' Rani burst out, her voice trembling with anger and helplessness.

'Why can't Mallika Didi be with Salim when she loves him so much? He is not like the rest of them, cruel and violent. I wish Binesh Kaku would just meet him once. Or if Baba met him, he could talk to Binesh Kaku,' I said, even though I knew that it was just wishful thinking.

'Sure. And then we will all live happily ever after. Grow up, Rahul! Life is not a fairy tale. Our family is not like Ranjan's. He and Shubho Dada are so lucky. But they are boys and can do anything they want. Can you imagine how horrible it will be if I am married off to a greasy, conservative Bengali smelling of mustard oil? A man who expects me to cook and feed him and his parents? I will run away on my wedding night if that happens,' she said defiantly.

We laughed in spite of ourselves. But we knew we were powerless in this game. Our parents decided our futures and determined who could love whom. I knew Mallika enjoyed going to her grandmother's tea estate. She had told me many times about the verdant hillsides and the colourful tea pickers. Most of all, I liked to hear about the elephants that roamed in the forests nearby and occasionally made an appearance. She had once seen a cow elephant and her baby and, for me, the next best thing to seeing it was hearing her describe it. But this time, it was different. Mallika had been sent there against her will.

'When we visit Shyamala, we will find out what really happened,' said Rani, still mutinous and angry. 'Did you hear what Baba said about me? I will not marry some idiot in an arranged marriage.'

We visited Shyamala that weekend. The house did not feel the same without Mallika. Shyamala and Rani did not gang up on me. We were all drawn together for the moment, united in our concern for Mallika.

'So when did they send Mallika Didi away?' Rani asked as soon as Anjali Mashi had gone to the kitchen.

'Come upstairs, we can talk there,' Shyamala said, leading the way up to the same room where a few weeks ago Mallika had shown us her billet doux, the rice paper crackling with promises of love.

We walked in and she shut the door, bursting into tears. 'It was horrible,' she said. 'Ma showed Baba the letters and he found out that the boy she was seeing was Salim. They asked Mallika to stop seeing him and she refused. Baba slapped her once, then again and again. I have never seen him so angry. He has not slapped us since we were children. Ma was crying. Mallika did not say a word. All she did was sob. They dragged her to her room and locked her in. A day later, they unlocked the door and went in to talk to her. An hour later, she came out. She looked like stone as she went with Baba and Ma to the train station. Baba went with her all the way to Assansol.'

We listened in horror. Binesh Kaku and Anjali Mashi were like our parents—it was difficult to imagine them being so cruel. It seemed as if this situation had somehow changed them into monsters, full of anger and hatred.

'What happened then?' I asked.

'I asked Ma why Mallika Didi could not marry Salim,' Shyamala continued. 'She said because then no one would marry me and people would look down on our family forever. As if I want to be married off to some stupid man they choose! I will run away when I am older.' She sounded very determined.

'I will too,' Rani said unhesitatingly.

'Mallika Didi gave me a letter for Salim. She asked me to give it to you both. Do you think you can find a way to get the letter to him?' Shyamala asked.

'Where does he live?' Rani enquired.

'Close to Mint House. In the Lakdi ka Pul area, just past the Khairatabad market, which is near your house. His uncle is a mullah in a mosque in your neighbourhood, maybe even the mosque behind Mint House.'

'Maybe his uncle can help Salim and Mallika Didi,' I said hopefully.

'Don't be stupid. Muslims are much more conservative than Hindus are,' Rani said impatiently.

'Anyway, make sure Salim gets the letter, all right?' Shyamala persisted.

'I am not sure ...' Rani sounded a little doubtful.

'Of course we will give it to him,' I said, interrupting her. It was unthinkable that we could not do this for Mallika. 'We will find a way.'

'Okay then, here it is,' Shyamala said, bringing out a letter in an envelope from under the mattress, where she had hidden it. Rani tucked the letter inside her blouse.

We went home, sobered by the gravity of the situation. I did not dare talk to my father about it. We all pretended that nothing had happened and Rani and I avoided mentioning Mallika in front of our parents.

Oh, how I missed Mallika! There would be no one to stand up for me if I got into trouble at school again and when Rani and Shyamala made fun of me. The sky grew dark that evening and inky black clouds with violet fringes piled up in the sky, turning crimson as they were touched by the fingers of the setting sun. The air was heavy and moist. The monsoons were very close now and I could smell them in the night air as I sat on the veranda that night. I knew we had to get the letter to Salim as soon as possible. He would find a way to rescue Mallika, I felt sure of that. But how would we get the letter to him? We had never left the palace alone before and never gone to Salim's house either. Even if we figured it out, the only time we could go on our own was on a Saturday or Sunday, when the Mint was closed in the afternoon and our parents were enjoying their afternoon siesta.

A purple-blue bolt of lightning illuminated the garden for a second, followed by a violent, thunderous crack that resounded all around. It was a fitting start to the last monsoons I would witness at the palace.

I woke up the next morning to the sound of rolling thunder coming from far away. I ran outside to the veranda to take a look at the sky.

It was still mostly clear, but a few wispy patches of grey indicated that this could be the day the rains started. I gobbled down my breakfast because I wanted to make sure that I was outside when the first drops of water fell. But the morning dragged on and soon it was lunch time.

'Ma, when will it start raining?' I asked.

'A watched kettle never boils, Rahul. You would do well to stop waiting for it to rain. It will happen when the time is right. Just like everything else. Here, take this chapati I just made. Put some butter on it and some sugar like *this*. I loved it when I was a young girl. Here,' she said, handing me a roll of freshly made chapati, sweet and salty and warm with the melting butter oozing from one end. Ma always knew what to do when I got impatient. I took the roll and went outside and walked to the lawn.

As I took off my slippers and felt the warm, dense grass under my feet, the sky grew dark. The air became heavy and humid as it settled like thick molasses over everything. The rumbling of clouds got louder as the rain approached. The sky grew blacker by the minute and the wind picked up.

I walked further out, to the middle of the lawn, stirred by the promise of the wild display of nature. The deluge was always preceded by a few moments of calm. Even the usually raucous crows were silent, the koel had stopped its feverish call and the sparrows were hiding in the rafters of the servants' quarters, their feathers puffed up.

A deafening clap of thunder reverberated through the sky, shaking even the old banyan tree. The trees trembled as their leaves rustled and shook. The rumbling increased, the clouds roaring like angry lions as clap after clap rolled through the skies. The thrill of joy and danger that the monsoons brought with them stirred in me strange feelings of passion. Random bursts of raindrops fell and the wind whipped my hair into my face, stinging it.

My mother was insistent that I get back into the palace, her strident voice calling for me: 'Come inside, Rahul!'

But I stayed out in the garden for as long as possible.

'Come in before you catch a cold and fall ill,' Ma screamed. I lingered outside a little longer, savouring every drop of rain that fell into my open mouth and upon my upturned face. Finally, I turned to go back into the palace.

'What will happen to the nest of the weaverbird? Will the babies die?' I asked Rani as I ran back. She was sitting on the veranda, enjoying the spectacle nature was putting on.

'Don't be silly,' she retorted. 'It is only the rain. The birds are used to getting wet.'

'I want to go check anyway!' I shouted as I started to run to the weaverbird's nest. It was being buffeted by the strong winds, but I was relieved to see that it looked as if it would weather the first rains. And then I saw it. A little baby weaverbird—dead, on the ground, its head stretched out and its beak open. The beak was still yellow around the edges and the early feathers looked like quills. It had to be the weaverbird that Ranjan had shaken out of the nest. I ran over with a cry of horror and knelt down to take a closer look. Thousands of ants were pouring out of the hollow sockets where its eyes had been. I stayed there for a couple of moments, overcome by sadness and anger. I wished I had never shown the magical treasures of my garden to Ranjan, who had proved to be so cruel. I bit my lip and willed myself not to cry.

And then the rain came down hard. By now, the entire garden was soaked. I was wet too, even though I had reached the shelter of the veranda.

The rooms were dark in this weather, the gloomy skies blocking out light from the cavernous spaces of the ceilings. The palace was so solid, so well-built, that even in the worst storms there was never a leak in the ceiling or walls. I wondered what it felt like to live in Colonel Uncle's apartment upstairs and see the approaching storm from above the treetops.

'Change your clothes now or you will catch a cold.' My mother was not willing to negotiate. I reluctantly followed her indoors and changed into dry clothes. The steady drumming of the rain on the window panes was rhythmic and hypnotizing. I heard a song by Mohammad Rafi on the radio wafting in from the sitting room, bemoaning the unreliable and deceitful weather: '*Aaj mausam bada beimaan hain ...*' A fitting song, I thought.

The phone rang late in the afternoon. My mother answered it.

'Anjali Didi, how are you?' she enquired. 'And how is Mallika?' A crack of thunder startled us. Then Ma said, 'It's only to be expected that she is angry and upset. Well, remember that boys and girls today are not as obedient as we were. They have a mind of their own nowadays.' The tea kettle started whistling and she hurriedly said, 'Anjali Didi, we can discuss all of this when we meet next.' She was about to hang up, but Anjali Mashi's response kept her at the phone. 'Yes, it is a difficult time, but I am sure you are doing what is right for the family and for Mallika too. Our children need guidance from us. Someday she will thank you for this. Start looking for a suitable boy, it could take some time.'

'Ma, why is Mallika Didi getting married so soon? Why can't she choose the person she wants to marry, like people do in America and England?' I asked when she finally put the receiver down.

My mother looked perplexed for a moment. Then she said, 'You know how you have rules at school?'

'Like not talking in class?' I answered.

'Yes, like not talking in class. If there were no such rules, there would be disorder and noise all day long. The teacher would not be heard and the students would not learn anything. Similarly, there are rules in our society.'

'Why do we need rules that tell us who can marry whom? Why can't anyone marry someone of their choice?'

'That is the way our society is set up, Rahul. Remember you studied about the caste system and how each caste performed a certain role in the ancient times? Well, people in those castes did not marry each other. They stayed within their groups. The parents arranged the marriages of their children.'

'Did you have an arranged marriage too?' I asked.

'Yes, I did.'

'Did you want your parents to arrange your marriage for you?'

'I did what was expected of me,' Ma said. She looked pensive for a moment and continued, 'And now I have the two most precious jewels of my life, Rahul and Rani.'

I looked at her, not quite sure what to make of her answer.

'Do not talk about this to anyone, understand?' she said again. 'Anjali Mashi and Binesh Kaku are doing what is best for Mallika and their family.'

I wondered what Mallika was doing in the tea estate in Assam. I could see her in my mind's eye, lovelorn and sad, her hair blowing behind her, torrential rains falling in bursts as she walked through the colonial mansion, singing '*Na koi umang hai, na koi tarang hai, meri zindagi hai kya, ek kati patang hai ...*' It would be just like Asha Parekh in *Kati Patang*, singing about the absence of joy in her life because it was just like a kite floating aimlessly in the sky, at the mercy of the wind.

Suddenly, I thought of Colonel Uncle. I wondered if his parents had tried to arrange a marriage for him. After thinking about him for a bit, I decided to go upstairs, treading the spiral staircase more confidently this time. The raindrops stung my bare legs as I climbed the slippery wrought-iron steps. The trees swayed in the wind, the branches bending this way and that. The bats were not out yet, even though it was twilight. Perhaps the strong winds and tempestuous night was keeping them indoors. I gingerly stepped over a broken branch, trying not to slip and hurt myself this time.

Colonel Uncle's room was brightly lit, a sliver of light shining on the wet terrace. I hesitated at the door and then decided to knock. At first, no one responded to my polite knocking. Then I knocked harder. This time, I heard his familiar, deep voice say, 'Kaun hai?'

Not waiting for a response, he opened the door, holding a wooden spoon and wearing a black silk dressing gown with Japanese cranes flying across it. A delicious smell of garlic and tomatoes cooking wafted through the open door.

'Hello, Rahul.' Colonel Uncle's expression rapidly softened from the hard frown he had been wearing when he opened the door.

'Hello, Colonel Uncle. May I come in?' I asked, careful to use the tone I used when I wanted to enter a classroom at school.

'Of course, come on in,' he said smiling. 'I hope you don't mind the mess. I am cooking.'

I walked in, full of excitement at being in Colonel Uncle's

apartment again. It was nice and warm, the windows steamed up, and I felt like I had been transported away to a different place altogether. I looked around appreciatively at the clean sitting room, the carefully arranged cushions on the sofa and the shiny, varnished furniture. The rug on the floor was soft and yielding as I walked on it and sat carefully on the edge of an enormous, silk-covered armchair, avoiding the cushions.

'Sit comfortably, Rahul. Those cushions are meant to be leaned on.' Colonel Uncle smiled at me.

I shifted back into the overstuffed chair, loving the way I sank into it. I propped my elbows on the arms, feeling very grown-up. 'What are you cooking, Colonel Uncle?' I asked, sniffing the air appreciatively. I loved the aroma coming from the kitchen.

'I am making a tomato sauce for spaghetti, the way I learnt in Italy. Have you ever had Italian food before?'

I shook my head. 'No, I have not,' I answered. 'Rani tells me that only girls should cook, not boys. When I go into the kitchen, she calls me a girlie boy. But my mother has told me that she will teach me to cook if I want to learn. She lets me peel boiled potatoes and mash them to make alu tikia. Did your mother teach you to cook?'

Colonel Uncle looked grave and sighed. 'No, when I was your age, if I spent time in the kitchen my father would punish me. In Rajput families, men never cook. Only women do. In Rajput culture, the place of a man is supposed to be on the battlefield. I grew up in a family of warriors who used to be in the king's army some generations ago. The Chauhans are still famous in the city of Jaisalmer—that's where I grew up. We lived in a large palace, almost as large as this one.'

'Tell me about your palace and what you liked to do there,' I said.

'I used to love to go to the kitchen to watch the cook make chapatis and curries and roast the spices. The cook, Padma Bai, used to be my nurse and loved it when I helped her in the kitchen. It was our secret. Then, one day, my father's valet saw me in there, sitting on the floor with the maidservants, cleaning the chaff from the rice and wheat, helping them make balls of dough for the chapatis.'

Colonel Uncle paused as he stirred the sauce on the pot one more time. He put a handful of spaghetti in a pot of boiling water. The stiff sticks of dried spaghetti started sliding into the pot as the boiling water softened their ends.

I sat upright. I knew something was going to happen to him in the story. Just like me, Colonel Uncle was going to be teased for behaving like a girl. I looked at him, tall and upright—his frame strong and proud. His grey hair and clipped moustache were trim and neat. I could see him on the battlefield, wearing a suit of chainmail armour, riding his horse, just like Rana Pratap rode his brave horse Chetak in the history books.

'That night, my father called me to his room. He was sitting in the men's quarters of the palace, with his friends. I entered the room nervously. He was smoking a hookah and laughing about something. His face turned to thunder when he saw me. He said, "Only girls work in the kitchen. No son of mine is a girl. Tomorrow, you will be sent to a boys-only military school. Now go, and come back to me next summer—a real man.' Colonel Uncle's voice grew soft with remembered pain as he gazed at a wall-hanging, his mind far away.

'What did your mother say? Didn't she stop your father? My mother would never allow me to be sent away to boarding school,' I said.

He laughed—a strange, bitter laugh. 'In those days, women could not say or do anything outside the women's quarters in the palace. I was sent away to Bikaner. I did not see my mother for a full year. When I returned, I never went back to the kitchen. I was forced to spend all my time with my brothers, riding horses and playing polo.'

'So who taught you how to cook?' I asked.

'I learnt many years later, when I lived alone, without servants. And, of course, I learnt Italian cooking from Claudio,' he said, his face tender as he looked at the photograph in its brown leather frame.

I looked at the picture, at their carefree, happy and smiling faces.

'This is a recipe he taught me. Would you like some?'

I nodded. 'Yes, Colonel Uncle.'

He placed two mats on the dining table, on either side of the candlesticks, which burnt slowly, their mellow golden light spilling onto the dark wood of the table. They looked like orbs of melting butter. He came back with two plates of spaghetti covered with a red tomato sauce. It smelt incredibly fragrant, just like the tulsi bush in the garden. 'This smells of tulsi leaves,' I said.

'Very good,' Colonel Uncle said. 'This is basil, which is often mistaken for a close relative of the tulsi.' He placed the plates heaped with spaghetti and fragrant sauce on the place mats. Then he pulled a chair out for me at the table. I perched myself on the corner and wriggled until I was seated properly. Colonel Uncle pushed the chair in towards the table and then sat across from me. I felt like an adult, awed by Colonel Uncle's gravity. I played with the spaghetti awkwardly. I never knew how to eat noodles, not even when we went out to dinner at Peking Palace.

'Here, let me show you how to eat spaghetti.' Colonel Uncle expertly twirled the long strands of pasta on a fork, using a spoon to hold it before slipping it into my mouth. 'Here, try it now.'

I tried and managed to twirl some of the spaghetti around my fork. It still slipped and slithered, but as I kept practising, I got better.

'Colonel Uncle, why are you a bachelor?' I asked suddenly, remembering why I was there.

He looked surprised for a second. He paused and said carefully, 'Because I did not want to marry anyone.'

'I do not want to either. But my father says that he will find me a wife when it is time, else I will be a lonely bachelor.'

'Ah … I see …' he said quietly. 'When I was your age, things were different. We were forced to marry the person our parents chose for us. I had to go to Italy during the war. When I left, my parents were already old. When I returned, they had passed away, so there was no one to insist. When you are ready to marry, you can make up your own mind. Remember, no one can force you to do anything. And one can have love in many ways, from many people, so one is not lonely even if one is a bachelor. I have had great love in my life from my Claudio—I still do.' He looked at the photograph fondly before looking serious again.

'But my Mallika Didi will be forced to marry someone,' I said. 'She loves Salim, but her parents won't let her marry him.' My voice rose and broke, sounding awkward, but I continued. I told him about Binesh Kaku, Anjali Mashi, Mallika and Salim. I told him about her being sent away to Assam alone, a prisoner against her will. I could not stop until I had told him everything—except about Shubho, even though I wanted to and felt somehow that he would understand.

Colonel Uncle's face hardened, his eyes grew cold and angry. 'How much fear and suffering for everyone—how unnecessary!' He was quiet for a few moments and then said in a softer tone, putting his hand on my shoulder and giving it an affectionate squeeze, 'Let us hope that your Mallika Didi can follow her heart.' He paused and added, looking straight into my eyes, 'Just as you must follow yours, Rahul.'

I did not understand what he meant. I was about to ask him when I heard my sister calling: 'Rahul, Rahul! Where are you? We are going to eat dinner.'

'Oh, I forgot about dinner. Ma must be looking for me.'

'I hope you do not get into trouble for coming here at dinner time without letting anyone know.'

'Oh, no. I won't. If I leave right now, I will not get scolded. I am sorry I am leaving in such a hurry, Colonel Uncle.'

'You may go now,' Colonel Uncle said, patting me gently on the head. 'Here, take this chocolate and share it with Rani.' I slid off the chair in a hurry. 'I will be going to take care of my estates in Rajasthan for a while.'

'When will you come back?' The thought of not having my new confidante around made me nervous.

'I don't know, but I will try to come back as soon as I can. You are always welcome here, you know …'

'Thank you, Colonel Uncle.'

'You can always come up here and talk about anything. I mean anything. I am here for you, Rahul.' Colonel Uncle's voice grew gentle and he swallowed. Then, with a firm pat on my shoulder, he gently led the way out.

I held the bar of Cadbury's chocolate in one hand and followed him to the terrace. 'I can go down from here, Colonel Uncle,' I said. 'I am not afraid of the stairs any more.'

The rain had slowed to a drizzle and the wind had settled down. Colonel Uncle guided me with his torch over the broken neem branch and over to the top of the wrought-iron staircase.

I held the banister carefully as I stepped down, one foot after the other. The turns of the stair were no longer menacing and strange.

Rani saw me coming down the stairs confidently and was so surprised that she could not say a word. Her mouth dropped open as I walked over to her and asked her airily, 'Want some Cadbury's chocolate? Colonel Uncle gave it to me.'

'You know, strange things happen upstairs. I heard a ghost walking around in chains the other night,' she said.

'I don't believe you. There is nothing there, no ghost or ghoul. Nothing there,' I answered, feeling brave and adult and angry that I had been so easily fooled.

That night, I could not eat much at dinner because I was already full.

'You are not eating enough.' Ma was concerned. 'Have you been eating before dinner again?'

'No,' I lied. Colonel Uncle was my secret. The Italian meal was my secret too. I could not stop thinking about Colonel Uncle and how wonderful he was. If I could be like him, I too would never marry and live in Italy in a beautiful house and have beautiful European antiques and lots of friends who loved me. I felt sorry for Rani because she was a girl and would be forced to marry someone our parents chose. I would never do that. I would be just like Colonel Uncle, I promised myself.

Later, as the pelting rain kept us indoors, Rani said, 'Remember we have to go deliver Mallika Didi's letter this coming weekend. We can go on Saturday when everyone will be taking their afternoon nap. Can you believe it has been almost a week since Shyamala gave us the letter? We need to get it to Salim as soon as possible.'

I took a deep breath as I realized that we had to be successful in our mission and that any mistakes would be disastrous for all of us— Mallika, Salim, Rani and me.

'We should be able to return in two hours if we take a rickshaw,' I thought out loud, feeling like a decision-maker. Both my parents loved their afternoon siesta in the hot summer. It would be the perfect time to embark on our mission. Rani nodded.

It would soon be time for the second picking of mangoes. I felt sad at the thought that Mallika was not going to be there, even though she had promised.

'*Allah ho Akbar* ... .' The mullah's poignant call echoed through the palace gardens, summoning the faithful to their prayers at sundown. The birds madly chirped their evening song and the normally melodious sound of the mullah's call made me unexpectedly melancholic. I walked around the mango orchard restlessly as I thought about Mallika so far away from us. What was she doing right now? Once we had delivered the letter to Salim, I would ask him to go rescue her so that they could run away, just like the irrepressible lovers in *Bobby*. I remembered what Shyamala had said about Salim's uncle being a mullah—was it his voice that I could hear? I had a mad desire to go running to him. Surely he would understand and talk to Binesh Kaku? Maybe he would go and get Mallika and marry her to Salim himself. I thought of Colonel Uncle. Would he be able to go and help Mallika? But then I would have to reveal my friendship with Colonel Uncle. And if Binesh Kaku got upset with Colonel Uncle, my parents would not allow me to see him any more. There was really no one I could turn to.

I looked up at the mangoes in the trees. They had started to droop low, almost ripe now, their skin splashed with touches of gold. The profusion of ripening mangoes meant that the harvest was going to be truly spectacular.

'This week is going to fly by as the summer vacation comes to an end, just like it always does,' I said ruefully to Rani later that evening as we sat on the veranda. The sky was a shade of rich violet, the dark monsoon clouds were piling up in the horizon. I did not tell her, though, that I was so excited about seeing Shubho at school again. 'I think the mangoes are going to be harvested this weekend.'

'How are we going to make sure that we can deliver the letter to Salim this weekend?' Rani asked. 'You know we always have to be there with Ma and Baba when they go to the orchard with Shankar,' she whispered and we both looked over our shoulders.

'Yes, but we always pick the mangoes on Sunday. We will go to deliver the letter on Saturday afternoon. Hopefully, Salim will be home then.' I took a deep breath. 'If they find out, Ma and Baba will be so angry! We have never gone out of the palace on our own before.'

'We have to do it. We have to go. This is the only way Salim will know what has happened. Are you planning to back out now?'

'No, of course not,' I said, horrified that Rani thought I would not go. I liked the fact that Rani was depending on me this time.

As the weekend came closer, we both nervously anticipated our trip to Salim's.

'Where is the letter? Are you sure you have it?' I asked, wanting to be sure that we were prepared.

'Yes, I have it,' Rani said, walked to the dresser, and pulled it out from the back of the drawer that contained old pens and other stationery. 'Let's read it first.'

Rani and I crept to the garden, to the ruins where no one ever visited. She pulled the letter out of the bag and began to read it out loud:

My dearest, darling Salim,

I hope you get this letter before you go to meet me in our special place because, my love, I will not be there. Salim, my darling, everything has changed since I last saw you.

Both Baba and Ma asked me about you. They read your letters and I could not lie any more. I told them that I loved you and wanted to marry you. Baba slapped me and dragged me to my room as I screamed and cried. I am helpless. By the time you get this, I will have been sent to my Didima's tea estate. They will find me a husband. My father has said that he will get you beaten by goondas who will break your knees and maim you if I ever see you again. They said that if I marry you, Shyamala will never marry into a good family. I don't know what to do. It is hopeless.

I beg you to forget about me. My heart is breaking as I write this. I will never love anyone ever again. If anything happens to you, I swear, I will kill myself. Meri kasam, swear that you will not come after me.

Forgive me for breaking your heart, my darling. I will be a walking corpse until the day I die from the pain of separation from you, from the memories of your touch, your lips, your love and your embrace.

I pray that this life is over soon so that I can be reborn to be with you.

I can never see you again. I shall think of you all the time, but please consider your Mallika to be dead. May Ma Durga protect you.

Yours forever,
Mallika

The letter was blotted with tearstains and blue ink had streaked all over the page. Rani and I were quiet.

'Poor Mallika Didi,' Rani finally said. 'You will never let something like this happen to me, will you, Rahul?'

'I will never be like our parents or Mallika Didi's parents. They are so cruel.' I was feeling as vulnerable as her.

When Saturday dawned, we were nervous all day and offered to clean the table after lunch, surprising Ma. We just wanted her and Baba to settle down for their siesta so that we could get out of there as quickly as possible and return before they woke up.

But then the phone rang and I cursed because we would have to wait now. 'Four-six-five-three-zero,' my mother answered. As the person on the other end replied, she said, 'Anjali Didi, how are you?' When Anjali Mashi said something in response, she nodded. 'No, later. I cannot talk right now,'

She paused for a second when Anjali Mashi said something again. 'Oh, you want us to meet the boy?' she asked. Cupping her hand over the receiver, she asked my father, 'Ogo, shunchho? Anjali Didi wants us to go to meet the boy and his parents.'

Like all Bengalis, my parents never called each other by name. Occasionally, my father called my mother by her nickname Supriya. But my mother never called my father by his first name. It was always 'Ogo, shunchho?' which meant, 'Are you listening?' An oddly intimate greeting.

'When?' my father called out from the sitting room.

'Tomorrow night,' Ma said.

'Achha. We will go.'

'Anjali Didi, we will be there.' She listened to Anjali Mashi's response and said, 'Of course! You know we are part of your family. How can it be any trouble?'

My mother soon joined my father. I tiptoed into the sitting room and listened carefully. My father's gentle snores and my mother's deep breathing assured me that they were asleep.

I looked at the clock on the wall. It said two o'clock. Only two hours to get there and back.

'Did you bring the letter with you?' I asked Rani.

'Yes, I did.'

The second exit from the palace was across the street from the India Government Mint and in the rear. We made our way to it after a circuitous route around the palace to avoid detection. I slid open the metal bolt and slowly opened the small door, praying that it would not creak. The sentries were in their kiosks, slouched over their rifles, napping in the afternoon heat. I knew they were trained to jump to attention at the smallest sound, so we crept out as quietly as we could.

This was the first time that Rani and I had been outside the palace on our own. Knowing that we could be grounded for the rest of or our lives for doing this made it scary but also empowering. It was our way of rebelling against our parents and, in some way, Mallika's parents too. Bicyclists, motorists, rickshaw drivers, cows and goats flowed by in a continuous stream of life. The ringing of bicycle bells blended with the impatient toots of car horns. Slow-moving rickshaws and lazy cows grazing on newspapers meandered through the streets. With Rani at my side, we crept away from the palace gates.

I hailed a cycle rickshaw. 'Lakdi ka Pul jaana hai? Kitna?' I asked the driver the fare to Salim's neighbourhood.

The rickshaw driver was an old man, aged by the sun and the streets of Hyderabad. He was dressed in a salwar kameez and wore a cap on his head.

'Address?' he asked in heavily accented English.

'Three-hundred Akbar Road,' I said.

'Achha, Sahib, aap Mullah Habib ke ghar ja rahe hain?' he asked. He knew the house well—it was the home of Mullah Habib. Shyamala had been right when she'd told us that Salim's uncle was a mullah.

'How much?' I asked.

'Sahib, roundtrip six rupees,' he said, holding up six gnarled fingers, the nails cracked and soiled with grease. I looked at the rickshaw doubtfully.

It was covered like all others, with a top that could be either put up or down. The sides of the top were like an accordion fan, the canvas soiled and tattered between the metal ribs that held the sides together. The body of the rickshaw was graced on one side by the face of Raj Kapoor and a painting of the holy black stone of Kaaba surrounded by inscriptions in Urdu on the other.

The rickshaw puller saw me hesitate and smiled, showing a few missing teeth.

'Let us take this rickshaw,' I said in hushed tones, anxious to get going.

'Yes, he seems like a nice person. I think it will be safe to have him take us there and back,' Rani replied.

'Sahib, okay, roundtrip five rupees,' the man said, holding up just one hand this time.

Moved by his generous offer, I climbed onto the rickshaw and the raised seat, followed by Rani. The cracks in the lumpy seat were old and the fibres escaping from it were black with age. We had not taken too many rickshaw rides before, so we were both excited and a little scared. We sat in the centre of the seat, trying not to fall over the side as the rickshaw puller expertly mounted it and started pedalling away, ringing his bell.

Within minutes, we were past the palace walls. Rani gripped my hand hard. We were travelling on a familiar road, the road to Khairatabad Market. The boundary of the market expanded and shrank with the size of it, located as it was on either side of the road. It was criss-crossed with tiny lanes and the kitchenware, vegetable, fruit, fish, meat and poultry sections were each in their own areas. As we entered the market, it was a world of chaos and cacophony. Vendors hawked their wares loudly as Hindi film songs blared from transistors. There were pictures of film stars plastered on the sides of the stalls. The smell of incense mingled with the smell of flowers and raw vegetables. As we passed the fish market, the odour of fish mingled with that of the open sewers that bordered one side of the market. The paan shop was abuzz with activity as always, the paanwallahs liberally applying chuna, kathha and supari. A piece of slowly burning rope hung from a nail outside the paan shop so that the cigarette and bidi smokers could light up.

Just past the market, we could see a small crowd outside the Khairatabad mosque and the temple. In one group, there were men in lungis and beards, carrying banners that read 'Build the Mosque' in English and also other slogans in Hindi and Urdu. Facing them was another group of men with the Vaishnavite symbol painted on their foreheads in vermillion and rice paint. A small group of sadhus in orange robes shook trishuls threateningly at their opponents.

My stomach tightened as I heard a row rumble of slogans and chants. *'Allah ho Akbar!'* and *'Jai Vishnu! Har Har Mahadev!'* shouted the crowds at each other in the age-old battle cries. A dozen policemen with lathis formed a cordon that separated the two groups.

As our rickshaw passed the demonstration, it slowed down to a crawl as market-goers, fear written on their faces, started to surge away from the scene of commotion. A stone flew through the air and hit a young woman in front of us. She fell to the ground, bleeding from a cut to her head as angry family members screamed at the crowd milling around to make room for her. Someone in the crowd pushed one of the people shouting at him and he pushed back—a sea of disturbance erupted as the protestors' slogans grew louder and more heated.

'Oh, God! Did you see that?' I clutched Rani's arm.

She nodded, looking pale, 'They are fighting about the expansion of the mosque.'

'If that stone had hit us, Baba would have been so angry,' I whispered, my voice shaking. 'Jaldi chaliye, Miyan,' I said to the rickshaw puller. I craned my neck, trying to see if a fight had broken out around the injured woman, but the scene disappeared from view as the rickshaw puller turned into a narrow lane between the slums.

'Mmhh ...' I said, covering my nose with the sleeve of my shirt, assailed by the stench of open sewers. A group of children in rags, with tangled hair and runny noses, stared at us with frank curiosity. We were suddenly conscious of our clean clothes and neatly brushed hair, realizing with a pang that this world was very different from ours.

After a few minutes, the traffic thinned out and we reached a filthy canal spanned by a wooden bridge. Large sows and piglets lay in the putrid black slush.

The neighbourhood looked and felt different from anything we had come across before. Instead of the dhoti or kurta–pajama worn by Hindus, almost all the men were dressed in salwar–kameez. The loose-fitting clothes were distinctively embroidered. Other men wore lungis. Most of the men had no moustache but full beards. Their heads were covered with small embroidered skullcaps almost without exception. The few women we saw were dressed in black burqas, covered from head to toe, with a mesh in the front of the veil that allowed them to see. The ubiquitous roadside temples of Hindu neighbourhoods were absent and a large old peepal tree stood forlornly without the vermilion coated rocks that Hindus ringed such trees with and worshipped. Instead of signs written in Telugu or Hindi, all around us were signs written in Urdu, which I could not read. There were stores for bicycle repair, fruits, vegetables and women's jewellery as well as ramshackle tea houses. Other shops looked secretive, their doorways covered by old, tattered curtains. Very soon, the buildings thinned out and we were in a modest and clean residential area. This was certainly not Banjara Hills with its spacious landscaped homes and chowkidars guarding the gates. Mallika and Salim's lives, we could see, were worlds apart. We stopped in front of a light blue house with a small garden in front. Dismounting, the rickshaw wallah pointed to the house. We had reached our destination.

I looked at Rani. She looked blank. I felt a sudden rush of confidence.

'Is this the house?' I asked the rickshaw puller.

'Yes, Sahib, correct address this,' he said in broken English.

I jumped off the rickshaw. 'Achha, we will be back,' I said as we entered through the gate and walked towards the house. Rani held on to my arm, clutching the letter in her free hand. It made me feel like I was the elder of the two.

'I hope Salim opens the door,' I said.

We rang the doorbell. After what seemed like forever, the door opened. It was Salim. He looked astonished to see us. He was dressed casually, in jeans and a T-shirt that said 'Woodstock'.

'Rahul, Rani,' he said in surprise. 'How are you? Are you here with Mallika?' He looked expectantly behind us, towards the waiting rickshaw puller. 'Khan Sahib, kaise hain aap?' Salim shouted out to him.

'Salaam, Salim Baba,' the rickshaw puller replied. 'Khuda ki marzi …'

Rani and I were surprised that he knew the rickshaw puller. 'How do you know him?' I asked.

Salim laughed, looking more endearing than ever. 'Khan Sahib used to take me to school when I was a little boy, much younger than you, Rahul,' he said. 'So, have you come with Mallika?' he asked again.

'No, Salim. Mallika Didi is getting married. You must help her and take her away,' Rani blurted out.

Salim looked confused for a second and then smiled mischievously as if he had discovered a joke. 'What? Oh, I see. Your Mallika Didi is a big practical joker and she has sent you to scare me. It is not going to work. Come inside. It is too hot here,' he said, opening the door and smiling indulgently at us. He walked ahead, confident and light, a spring to his step. He was clearly delighted to see us. He turned around dramatically on one heel and, pointing a finger at me, said, 'So? Do you want to tell me the real reason you are here? Your Mallika Didi is playing another of her tricks on me, isn't she? Anyway, so you were saying?'

Rani looked around the sitting room, frustrated. It was painted a light blue inside. There were a couple of comfortable and slightly worn sofas by the wall, tea tables at each end and a Persian rug on the polished grey slate floor. There were pictures all around the room, black-and-white pictures of a pretty lady and a younger Salim. Her head was covered with a stylishly wrapped dupatta in all the pictures. In some of the older pictures, there was a man who was presumably Salim's father. I wondered if his mother was home.

Rani turned to me and said with urgency, 'Rahul, tell him.'

Salim turned to me for confirmation. The look on my face made his smile fade.

'Salim, Mallika Didi's parents are marrying her off to another boy. She has been sent away to Assam. Here is her letter for you. She wanted you to read it.' I spoke quickly. Salim looked at Rani and me in shock. His face turned ashen. Rani nodded and gently shook the letter in her hand, confirming that I was serious.

'Wait, wait. What are you saying? When did this happen?' His voice rose, words tumbling out of his mouth. His eyebrows knotted in a frown as his mouth set in a stubborn, hard line. He stood rigidly, his feet spread slightly apart, his arms crossed across his chest.

'Munna, who's there?' A woman's voice sounded from the back of the house.

Salim abruptly uncrossed his arms, now looking very vulnerable. 'Friends of mine, Ammijaan,' he said in a strained voice.

'Will you send her a letter too? We will give it to Shyamala to give to Mallika Didi when her parents bring her back from her grandmother's home,' Rani said. I was speechless, terrified that she would be interrupted by his mother at any moment.

'Munna, who's there?' The woman's voice sounded anxious and closer. We heard footsteps. My body tensed. Salim took a deep breath and collected himself, squaring his body as if bracing for a blow.

'Meet us outside Mint House at the back entrance tomorrow afternoon at three,' Rani said, giving him the letter, which he stuffed into his pocket.

Salim nodded. The curtains parted as a woman entered the room. Salim turned to the doorway.

The woman who entered was the woman in the photographs, but older. She was dressed in a dark brown salwar kameez, her head covered by a dupatta. She had heavily darkened eyes lined with kohl. She was very beautiful and held herself regally. I looked at her and could see that Salim had got his eyes from his mother. He had also inherited her chin and lips.

'Adaab, Aunty,' Rani said, taking the lead. I echoed her greeting.

'Adaab,' she replied, raising her slightly cupped hand to her face, just as we had done. 'Munna, who are these children?' The woman searched our faces, a look of distrust in her eyes.

'Ammijaan, this is Rahul and this is Rani,' he said, avoiding looking at his mother. 'They are friends of my good friend Aziz from college. They were on their way home and decided to come and knock on the door. They have been here with Aziz before.' He turned to us. 'You will be late. Come, let me take you outside.'

We said our goodbyes as he quickly ushered us out of the room.

'Khuda hafiz, Aunty,' both Rani and I said.

'Khuda hafiz, Munna aur Munni,' Salim's mother said, her eyes narrowed and she went back inside.

We walked out of the cool sitting room into the bright afternoon sunshine.

'Salaam, Salim Baba,' the rickshaw puller called out, saluting him again.

'Take good care of Munna and Munni,' Salim said to him. 'Make sure they reach home safely. They are my friends.'

I thought about the dangerous mob we had seen as I turned to look at the gate behind us. Salim looked incredibly sad and shocked as he stood at the door, his hand raised to us in farewell. Both Rani and I had been filled with anticipation at the idea of seeing Salim, but now it seemed that he and Mallika would never be together again.

'I wish Salim would tell his parents about Mallika Didi so that they can go and talk to her parents,' I told Rani. In the films, sometimes the heroine's parents did go to the hero's parents to persuade them to agree to a marriage.

'Don't be so stupid,' she said. 'Hindus and Muslims can never get married. Remember what Ma said?'

'I hope we can make it outside Mint House again tomorrow,' I said.

'We have to.' Rani's voice was urgent. 'This is the only chance for Salim to write back to Mallika Didi.'

I looked out of the rickshaw. We were back on the bridge, crossing the canal with pigs wading in black slush.

'Which road shall we take? There are fights at Khairatabad …' I said to Khan Sahib.

'No worry, Sahib,' he said. 'I take home this.'

We went back through the same slum. As we headed towards the Khairatabad road, Rani whispered, 'If we get stuck in the mob again, we will get off and run through it. Make sure you hold my hand and keep the money ready to pay the rickshaw puller.'

I put my hand in my pocket and clutched the five-rupee note. A strange burning smell was in the air. It smelt like singed hair. The street was almost empty now. A few policemen were walking up and down. Khan Slahib pedaled as fast as he could, muttering 'Ya Allah,' under his breath as he shook his head dolefully, looking at a heap of burnt rubbish.

I saw a claw extending from a heap of burnt cloth. As I stared at it, the form took shape. Gnarled and blackened, it was clearly a hand— the burnt cloth hid a human body.

'Oh, God!' I whispered.

'My God!' Rani's voice trembled. She leaned over the side of the rickshaw and retched.

The rickshaw puller slowed down, but I waved him on, anxious to get away. The stench of burnt flesh stayed with us even as we entered the proper Khairatabad Market area. I held Rani's hand.

Both of us were shaking.

Soon, we could see the canopy of treetops and the tall palace walls in the distance.

'Look, Rani' I said, pointing to Mint House. 'We are almost home.'

Rani nodded in relief.

'Roko, roko,' I said, asking the rickshaw puller to stop before we pulled up to the palace gates.

He stopped and got off the cycle rickshaw. I gave him the five-rupee note. The rickshaw puller said, 'No, Sahib, I will not take money from Salim Sahib's friends. I used to take Salim Sahib to school when he was as old as you. He is like my son.'

'No, no. That is not right. He must take the money.' Rani was insistent.

We argued briefly and then the rickshaw puller reluctantly took the money, then pulled away. We were a few hundred feet away from the palace walls.

As we approached the gates, the sentries sprang to attention.

'You cannot go in there …' the sentry started to say, until he saw me and Rani, recognizing us. 'Salaam, Sahib,' he said in surprise and snapped to attention.

'Salaam,' I said and we walked in.

As we neared the palace, I could hear Baba's voice booming: 'Rahul! Rani!'

I felt a stab of terror. 'What will he say if he finds out we had gone by ourselves to Salim's house?'

'He won't,' Rani replied. 'Let us run to the far side, to the dhobi ghaat, and pretend we were playing there.'

'All right,' I said. We ran to the dhobi ghaat, ducking behind bushes and trees. We saw our father standing in the distance on the back porch of the palace, under the wrought-iron stairs that led to Colonel Uncle's house.

'Rahul … Rani …' he shouted, cupping his hands around his mouth.

'Coming!' we yelled back in Bengali.

'Oh, there you are,' he said, exasperated, when we finally reached him. 'Where were you? Your mother is worried sick. She woke up a while ago and has been looking for you the whole time. What were you doing at the dhobi ghaat?'

'Just playing,' Rani said.

'Well, come inside. It looks like it might start raining again,' he said.

I looked up. It looked like the sky was going to be dark as night very soon. Purple-grey thunderclouds had begun to gather on the horizon. The wind was picking up, leaves and twigs starting to stir on the tennis courts and the stairs leading to the back porch.

'Thank God it has not rained yet. We would be in such trouble if we were gone in the rain. Baba and Ma would be furious! Can you imagine what would happen if they knew we were almost in a riot?' I whispered to Rani.

She gave me a look of warning and motioned to me to keep my voice down.

'Why are you walking so slowly? Your mother is making her special Sunday snacks for us,' Baba said impatiently, looking back at us. 'What have you been doing, Rahul? Wash your hands first, they are filthy. Then go help her set the table.

I looked at my sticky hands. The grease from the sides of the rickshaw had stained my fingers and worked its way under my nails.

'Nothing …' I muttered and ran towards the bathroom, where I scrubbed my hands and nails.

The storm that night did not bring torrential rains. It was dusty and dry. Over dinner, the mango trees shuddered with dry heaves, waiting with parched impatience. Their branches were heavy with fruit ready to fall.

'It is time to ripen the mangoes,' my mother said, ladling out the dal on my plate at the dinner table. My father nodded.

'Rahul, tell Shankar to be ready at five o'clock tomorrow.'

I nodded as I thought of the mango rooms full of ripening fruit, their sweet smell overpowering. I had been waiting all summer for this time—a time of unbridled pleasure, when I could savour the delights of the different kinds of mangoes in the garden. But after the events of the day, I did not care.

That night, I felt very grown up as I lay in bed. I had gone outside alone without my parents, with only Rani beside me. The world outside was threatening and dangerous, but we had survived the trip. I felt a strange surge of strength and power—a good thing. I would need it.

The next day, we fidgeted about impatiently. The afternoon could not come around soon enough. Rani and I crept out to the back of the house. I opened the smaller door and walked out with false confidence. Rani followed. We did not make eye contact with the men on guard; they were not the same ones on duty the previous day. We hurriedly went around the corner and waited for Salim. I looked around for a familiar figure, smartly dressed in the usual jeans and T-shirt.

'Is that Salim?' Rani clutched at my arm, her voice in a horrified whisper. I looked over to the person she was pointing at. I saw a man in a rumpled kurta–pajama, unshaven, his hair unkempt, dark shadows under the eyes. I was shocked. It was indeed Salim. But gone was the Salim I knew, the confident, upbeat and charming Salim. This Salim looked beaten by life, his shoulders stooping, his face twisted in a bitter grimace. He came closer and then we saw the oozing, purple bruise with an angry-red, split-open mouth in the centre. He winced as he raised his arm to wipe the sweat from his forehead. His face was covered with scratches, his lip was cut and swollen, crusted with dried blood. His kurta was torn in several places and stained with mud. He looked like a hideous, frightful version of Salim. This was a face that would haunt me forever.

'Hello, Rani, Rahul,' he said, his valiant attempt at a smile awkward and painful. His lips barely turned up at the corners and no light touched his eyes. 'I have a letter for Mallika. Please give it to her.' His eyes held a look of deep pain and sorrow—he looked like a dog that had been cruelly hurt.

'Salim, why don't you tell your father to talk to Mallika Didi's father?' I said. Maybe Salim's father could make a difference.

Salim gave a bitter laugh. 'My father? Help me? I told my parents yesterday about Mallika. They were very angry. My father threatened to throw me out of the house. I went to Mallika's house to talk to her father. He came out and had the chowkidars beat me. We had a terrible argument and I left. I spent the night at my friend Aziz's home. I have not been home since we fought …' His voice cracked with pain and he stopped, biting back his anger and tears.

We listened in silent horror and shock. 'So what are you going to do now?' I asked. I was in awe of Salim's bravery. I would never have had the courage to say anything to my father, let alone to Binesh Kaku.

'I don't know. Mallika has asked me never to contact her again,' he said, and the quiet desperation in his eyes frightened me. He took out a letter in an envelope. I heard the sound that I knew so well, as his shaking hands gripped the letter. He put the letter in Rani's hand and put a hand on each of our shoulders. 'Help Mallika contact me when she returns, all right?' His voice broke and he turned away. We watched him walk away, his shoulders hunched over like an old man's. We watched him until he disappeared into the crowd. He never looked back.

Rani's hand tightened on my arm. 'Let's go inside,' she said. We walked back without another word.

Rani went to her room to hide the letter for Shyamala. I followed her. 'What has he written?' I said. 'I think we need to know what he is planning to do. Maybe we can help him.'

Rani took out the letter with trembling hands. The emotionally charged meeting with Salim had shaken us both.

Meri jaan Mallika,

I write this to you with a stone on my heart. Only yesterday, my world was happy and full of hope. I thought I was the luckiest man in the world. But now I am the unluckiest man alive.

I beg you to reconsider your decision. Please do not throw your life away because of all the things your parents say. We have to carve out a home for ourselves in this inhospitable desert that society has made for us and create love and hope where none is provided. Is your life worth less than Shyamala's? Does your happiness mean nothing to your parents? My parents have told me that they too will disown me, if we marry. But my dearest, if our families disown us, we will still have each other. I will give you so much love that you will not be unhappy for even one day. I beg of you to give me a chance.

I don't care if you are engaged to be married. Let me know if you want me to come and get you. I will.

My heart is broken. I don't know what I will do without you. I cannot bear to live in Hyderabad any more where every tree, every bird, every shop and every street reminds me of you. I cannot imagine going to college to study. I will be looking for you in the classrooms, the common room, the cafeteria, the gardens, all our secret meeting places ...

Oh, love of my life, I will wait for you, till the day I die.

Yours always,
Salim

We both felt the raw torment in his letter. Suddenly, I felt the need to see Colonel Uncle and ask him for help. I went to the back of the palace and climbed the wrought-iron staircase. This time, I paid scarce attention to the terrace, the resting bats or the squirrels that scattered as I tore through. I knocked on Colonel Uncle's door. There was no sound. I knocked harder, praying for a stentorian voice to say, 'Who's there?' But there was nobody home. Colonel Uncle was not back yet from his trip, I realized with a heavy heart, and I had no one to confide in.

Reluctantly, I went downstairs. I walked around the palace, through the lawn and to the gulmohar tree, and sat down in the comfortable nook by the branches, leaning against the solidity of the tree trunk for comfort. I thought of Salim and his grief and of Mallika—the unfairness of it all was overwhelming. There had to be a way out, but what? No answers came. I wished again that this was a film, a film where Rajesh Khanna would find a way to solve the problem. But there was no Rajesh Khanna here, just us and our parents, who ruled our world mercilessly. Lost in my thoughts, I slowly drifted into a deep, dreamless sleep …

'Rahul, Rahul, where are you? Ranjan is on the phone.' My mother's voice floated across the lawn. 'Where is Shankar?'

I jumped up with a start. It was probably five o'clock already. I ran to the palace to take the call.

'Hi, Rahul! We are back.' I was thrilled to hear Ranjan's voice after such a long time.

'Hi, Ranjan. You did not reply to my letter. Did Shubho Dada come back with you?' I bit my tongue, wishing that I had not blurted out Shubho's name in such a hurry.

There was a pause. 'Yes, he is back. He has gone to see Anamika.'

I felt a stab of jealousy. 'Well, I will see you next week,' I mumbled. I desperately hoped that Shubho would remember his offer to coach me for the football team.

School would start soon. I felt a sense of excitement as I thought about seeing Shubho again, even though I would hate the end of my freedom once term started. He was going to be the football captain and I could not wait to join the team. I thought of him in the Ajanta House colours, yellow and green, a striking figure with strong legs as he dribbled the football from one end of the field to the other … A burst of desire rushed through my body.

Shankar was sitting at the back of the palace, under the employees' bicycle shed next to the back gate. He was smoking a bidi along with the sweepers.

'Salaam, Sahib!' Shankar jumped up, throwing the bidi away. It lay next to his foot, sending up a blue-grey plume of foul-smelling smoke.

'Memsahib wants you to come pick the mangoes,' I said.

'Achha, Sahib,' said Shankar, setting off to get his homemade contraption to pluck mangoes.

Soon after, my parents came out to the mango grove where Shankar was waiting. Rani and I were there to participate in the yearly ritual, even though, for the first time, our heart was not in it. The nagging thought of Salim and Mallika's sadness enveloped me and I stood there, under the trees in the grove, lost in thought.

'Shankar, let us start at one end of the grove. That one. Good, now pluck the next one, no not that, the one next to it,' my mother instructed Shankar. I did not know how she knew which mangoes to pick and which ones to leave for later. Each mango had to be picked at the right moment, when the fruit was just beginning to turn yellow. If it was too raw, it would not ripen at all.

'Rahul, Rahul!' My mother's voice startled me. 'What has gotten into you? Why are you so preoccupied? Just like your father,' she said impatiently. 'I asked you to make sure that each bag of mangoes is tied at the mouth so that they don't spill out later.'

As I tied the bags, Shankar picked the mangoes, patiently going from branch to branch and tree to tree. I missed Mallika very much and remembered sadly how the last time we picked mangoes, for pickles, she had been there with us.

The mango-plucking operation would take days—this was just the first one. Not all mangoes were picked successfully that afternoon. There were accidents in which the mango missed its intended target—the open bag—and came crashing down to become useless. A bruised mango would always rot.

'Rahul, call the sentries at the gate to come and help Shankar carry the mangoes to the ripening room,' Ma ordered me.

I ran to the gate and called out for the sentries who stood at the back gate. I froze. The men were the same ones who had seen us come back unchaperoned when we had gone to Salim's house. Oh God, please let them not say a word, I prayed silently.

They arrived at the orchard, talking in low, agitated voices.

'Sahib,' one of them said, with a deep breath.

'Yes?' Baba responded, preoccupied with packing the mangoes properly for transport to the ripening room.

'Baby and Baba …' the guard faltered when he saw my pale face. 'Baby and Baba left Mint House on their own yesterday. It is dangerous out there, Sahib, and anything can happen.'

My father stopped what he was doing. 'Stay here,' he ordered me. 'Rani, Rani!' he shouted. Rani came running up, looking anxious. 'Did you go out of the palace yesterday?' he demanded.

'Yes …' we both replied together.

'Why? Haven't I told you to never leave the palace on your own?'

'Yes, Baba,' I stammered. 'We just wanted to …'

'It was my fault,' Rani said.

Baba turned his wrath on her. Ma was too horrified to say anything. 'Do you know how dangerous it is out there? You could get caught in a mob riot! Do you know that last week someone threw the severed head of a cow into the Vishnu temple in Khairatabad? There was a small riot yesterday and two Muslims were burnt alive by Hindus!' He turned to Ma. 'I told you it was time to send them to boarding school.'

We were speechless, afraid to say anything that would betray our mission.

'I don't know why you did this, and at this point I don't care. But if I ever find out that you put yourselves in danger like this again, I will send you both to a boarding school in Dehra Dun. Now go to the ripening room and lay out the straw beds.'

As we scurried away, we heard him say. 'This is how it starts. First Mallika has an affair with that scoundrel. And then these children start getting ideas of breaking the rules. I just don't know what to do. What if they turn out like her and disgrace us?'

'Do you think you can control them forever?' Ma snapped back. 'They will do whatever they want in a few years. Times are changing and things are not how they used to be. I am tired of hearing you and Binesh Dada constantly criticize Mallika and Anjali Didi. I have raised my children well. They can make up their own minds about how they want to live their lives when they grow up …'

We could not hear the words of his heated response as we walked out of earshot.

'We are so lucky that today the guards changed their shift right after we saw Salim,' whispered Rani. 'If Baba found out that we had gone out twice, he would demand to know why. You heard what Baba said. We will be sent to boarding school far away next time.'

We reached the ripening rooms. Shankar and the sentries had carried the mangoes in bags to the servants' quarters, where some of the empty rooms had been set aside as mango-ripening rooms. They deposited the bags and left, without making eye contact. Everyone had heard the altercation and all of us were embarrassed.

In the mango-ripening room, on a bed of straw some two feet deep, we placed each mango carefully so as to not touch another. Mangoes that touched each other when ripening would rot. After we had laid all of them out, we covered them with straw. Then we locked the doors to let nature take its course. In the warmth of the bed of straw, the mangoes would ripen, as nature had intended. But we had also set other wheels in motion—Salim would surely rescue Mallika, now that he knew what had happened ...

8

August 1973. Hyderabad.

First of August came too soon and, with a flutter in my stomach, I watched the old school bus as it appeared around the corner. The blue paint on the side of the bus seemed to have faded, though it was still the same royal blue. The letters HRA emblazoned in gold were a stern reminder that the new school year had begun. The wheezing bus stopped with a tortured squeal. I stepped on and looked around. The bus was full of students already—some excited and others quiet, all dressed in brand-new school uniforms.

'Hey, Rahul!' I took a seat next to Ranjan and smiled. 'How were the rest of your holidays?'

'Very good,' I replied smiling back, suddenly excited about meeting my other friends but also somewhat worried about the curriculum. This year, I was going to start algebra for the first time.

'Make sure you come first in class this year. I don't want to hear any nonsense about wanting to be a film star—or no more films for you this year.' Baba had been stern, his reading spectacles perched on his nose, the newspaper spread out in front of him as he drank his tea. He had overheard me telling one of his friends, Mr Roy Choudhury, that I wanted to be a film star and was livid that I would even consider this as an option. We middle-class Bengalis had only three career options—engineer, doctor or lawyer. He wanted me to be a decent, upstanding member of society having a respectable career. Just in case I was not clear about these expectations, I was made aware that the stakes were high, even before my first day at school.

But studies were not at the forefront of my mind right now. I was looking forward to seeing Shubho again and spending more time with him alone.

The bus hit a pothole and the jolt flung me from my seat, bringing me back to the present. 'I had such fun at your house at the Day Spend. Shubho Dada mentioned that you will train to be on his team this year,' Ranjan was saying as he slammed into me, both of us struggling to stay seated. The bus creaked and shuddered violently as the driver tried to avoid more potholes.

'Oh, good!' I could barely hide the glee in my voice.

'You, of all people, playing football is something I don't understand,' Ranjan continued. 'You have always hated sports.'

'I am sick of being teased by Suresh Khosla and his gang. I will show them,' I retorted.

'You know what they say ...'

'What?'

'Once a girlie boy, always a girlie boy. Remember what happened in class last year with Amit Puri? Hope nothing like that happens again.' Ranjan pretended to vomit.

My hands turned icy.

'Yes, it is better you don't draw too much attention to yourself.' Ranjan smirked as if he knew a secret.

'Can we just forget it? I mean, all that stuff. It will be different this year,' I snapped.

The bus turned into the gates of the school. The Hyderabad Royal Academy stood in front of us, the domes and spires rising up to the sky, surrounded by freshly mowed lawns and immaculate grounds.

The first day of school flew by quickly as we opened unfamiliar textbooks each hour. The teachers were new as well. Our Anglo-Indian class teacher, Miss D'Souza, was a beautiful, tall and confident lady. She had bobbed black hair and wore knee-length dresses to school with smart, patent-leather pumps.

'Did you see her legs?' Suresh Khosla asked Ranjan excitedly at break time, licking his lips in enjoyment.

'Yes, I did. I would love to look up that frock,' Ranjan said, his eyes glinting with an excitement I had never seen before. 'Watch me drop a pen and look up!'

'That is so rude. Why would you want to do that?' I said, disgusted.

'Oh, Rahul, you are too immature to understand these things,' Suresh said. He and Ranjan laughed, as if sharing a secret. 'You will understand someday—one can only hope!' Suresh smirked.

'Or maybe he will never understand,' Ranjan quipped. They burst out laughing even harder, digging each other in the ribs and looking at me patronizingly.

A sudden feeling of alienation overwhelmed me. I wondered why they felt this way about Miss D'Souza and got so excited about girls whom I saw just as friends and sometimes as sisters. I did feel the way they did, but only about Rajesh Khanna or Shubho.

The whole week slipped by as I was consumed by school and homework. Rani and I had not heard anything from Mallika or Shyamala or Salim for a month. All we overheard when we eavesdropped on phone conversations between our parents and Binesh Kaku and Anjali Mashi was that they were trying their best to find a good husband for Mallika. We dared not ask any questions. Since our escapade outside the palace, we had tried not to provoke my father any further.

'I wish we could go and see Salim again. Do you think he tried to reach Mallika Didi?' Rani asked me as we sat down to do our homework. I had just finished the first round of tests.

'I don't know. Wish we could find out. Did Shyamala say anything to you at school?'

'No, she didn't. She is very quiet these days. She told me she is too scared to mention Mallika's name at home because Binesh Kaku gets into a terrible mood. All she knows is that they might have found a boy for her. Mallika must be so angry and sad, being forced to get married like this. I would refuse to marry if I were her. I don't understand why she does not run away! I wish we were old enough to do something.'

'Oh no! Did Mallika Didi agree?'

'I don't know. I don't think they have told her yet. Shyamala wants to warn Mallika Didi, but does not know how.'

We lapsed into an unhappy silence.

Over the next few weeks, we did not go out much because we were forced to study and do homework. I rarely saw Shubho at school since his classroom was in a different building. I did pass him once, on my way to the gymnasium, as he walked by with his posse. I wanted to hang around him and be his friend, but I did not have any idea of how to go about it. I procrastinated when it came to starting football practice, afraid to draw attention to my lack of talent, but events finally forced my hand.

I had a choice of gymnasium or football. Gymnasium practice was easy. We could spend the entire class running up to the horse and vaulting over onto an overstuffed mattress or climbing a rope. There was no danger of being pushed and kicked by other boys. But the football players made fun of those who attended gym class.

I was on my way to the gym when I heard a taunting voice say, 'Hey, Rahul, sissy boy! Are you too scared to come and play football? Only girls learn gymnastics. Why don't you come and play football?' It was Suresh Khosla, unusually belligerent as I walked to the gymnasium, past him and his friends in their football gear. His podgy and pampered face leaned threateningly towards me. He grew red with excitement as I shrank back from his jibes.

He turned to his friends, licking his lips. 'Yaar, Rahul must be a homo too, I say!' He spat. His friends snickered.

'Oh, leave him alone. Yaar, he is such a sissy. If you tease him any more he will cry,' one of his sidekicks said, pouting like a girl. The gang burst out laughing.

My body tensed as I feared that I would be expelled like Amit if the teacher heard them calling me 'homo'. And then I would be sent for shock therapy and become like Amit, a dull, slow-moving person that people stared at. Shubho would never look at me again, except in pity. I had to apply myself to football. I would do whatever was needed to prevent a showdown.

I was nervous as I stood outside Shubho's class that afternoon. 'X C', it said above the door. The senior boys were bigger than me and I wished that my body was more developed like theirs. Some of them almost had moustaches while others had clearly started shaving. Their voices were low-pitched and manly. The school bell clanged, signalling the end of a period. The teacher sailed out of the door, her sari billowing behind her as she strode towards the teachers' room, holding a sheaf of papers in her arms.

And then, like magic, he was there. My tongue felt swollen and stuck to the roof of my mouth. Shubho walked by me with his friends, his arms around their shoulders.

'Shubho,' I said weakly. He did not hear me. I could not call him 'dada' at school. That was an out-of-school practice. The suffixes of respect were used in the Bengali social context; in the context of an English-medium education, everyone was called by their name alone. Just like the personal connection we had shared, they did not belong in school, in the presence of classmates.

'Shubho,' I repeated, much louder this time.

He turned around and, disengaging from his friends, walked back to me. His brows moved up quizzically and he flashed me a broad smile. 'Hey, Rahul,' he said. His eyes became soft for a moment and my breath got caught in my throat.

'Shubho,' I said softly, 'you said I could start football practice with you this year.'

He threw his head back and laughed, delighted that I was going to join his team. 'Wonderful, Rahul,' he said. 'Report to practice this week. We practice every Tuesday at 5 p.m. If you play well, you can be on the Ajanta team. How would you like that, eh, Rahul?' He slapped me on the back and rejoined his friends.

I glowed self-consciously, suddenly embarrassed by my own boldness.

As I waited for Tuesday to come, I was full of nervous anticipation. What if I was a bad player and got thrown out of the team on the first day itself? What if I never made it to the final selection? Then I would be teased even more for not making the cut. I eventually showed up for practice on the first day, consumed by anxiety. Fortunately, there were a couple of other boys also starting for the first time and I relaxed. We started with a few laps around the field. Breathless and ready to collapse, next we had to pair up and kick the ball to one another.

Shubho was a fair and impartial coach. He spent a lot of time teaching us to dribble the football across the field, head a ball off or score goals when we got a penalty kick. I learnt not to be so afraid of a football.

'Chatterjee!' Shubho shouted across the field. 'Pay attention to the ball. Be aware of your teammates. Remember, we have to get the school cup this time and Ellora House is practising hard too!' I felt special because he had singled me out this way.

At times, Shubho would come up to me and show me how to kick and dodge. I loved it when he did this. His firm hands held my foot and put it in the right place to kick the ball high and far. My body grew rigid with excitement at the sight of his glowing face, I breathed in the smell of his sweat, my skin tingled for a long time wherever he touched it.

Once, when my shoelace had come undone, he bent down to tie it. I had seen him do this for the others when he wanted them to stay in position. His hair was matted at the nape with sweat as he deftly tied the laces with his strong fingers. His football shirt clung to his shoulders, outlining his back, and I ached to taste the wetness. But others were watching, so I acted aloof, just like him.

On the field, he was a hard taskmaster. We both followed an unspoken code of conduct and I missed his banter. At times, I wondered if he would ever look at me in that special way again. At other times, I thought maybe he was upset with me and perhaps Ranjan had said something to him about me. My heart raced with dismay and longing through those training sessions, hanging on to any sign of redemption or damnation. Each session, I waited for some indication of affection, to console myself that things were all right. When we finished, he would say with a warm smile, 'Well done, boys.' I hated sharing that smile with the others players. I longed for the day when I would be able to show the bullies what a strong player I was. But first, I had to make the team.

One Tuesday evening, I arrived late. Practice had already started. 'Sorry, Shubho, I am late,' I said as I came running up to the field, pulling my green football socks up to my knees. They had slipped down my legs because I had not fastened them properly with the elastic bands that held them up.

'Chatterjee, you are late. Join the team in the conditioning exercises. You will have to practise your kicks later. Only two weeks to the game now.' He sounded disappointed.

'Sorry, Shubho,' I murmured, crestfallen.

That day, after everyone left, Shubho kept me on the field. He made me practise at a gruelling pace to make up for the time I had lost. It was getting dark and the crickets had started their evening chorus in the surrounding fields. The croaking of the frogs was a constant serenade, as was the annoying buzz of mosquitoes hovering in big clouds over our heads as we kicked, dribbled, tossed, headed and dodged the ball.

Finally, I was exhausted.

'What? Tired already?' Shubho's voice was teasing but not unkind. 'Okay, then. Let us go and change. I better call your parents and tell them I will bring you home. Wait here until I come back.' I collapsed on the grass, panting until my heart stopped hammering in my chest and my breathing returned to normal. I closed my eyes and enjoyed the cool evening breeze, luxuriating at the thought of all the attention I had received from Shubho. Suddenly, I felt him shake me gently. I sat up and he held a hand out to pull me up and we headed towards the changing rooms.

As we walked, he put his arm around my shoulders. I swelled with pride at being treated like a friend. His strong arm lay on my shoulder and his hand casually fell on my chest, absent-mindedly tracing a pattern with his fingers. There was no one around. Even the school cleaners had gone home after cleaning the bathrooms and sweeping the classrooms and hallways.

The lights were off in the changing room. Only a naked light bulb, hanging from the ceiling and protected clumsily by a wire cage, illuminated the concrete entrance. Thick honeysuckle covered the entrance and the sweet fragrance of the flowers filled the air. As we stepped inside the dark room, Shubho stopped. His hand was still on my shoulder, but his grip had tightened.

'Frightened?' he asked jokingly.

'No, Shubho Dada. I am not frightened.'

Shubho's arms fell to his side and then they wrapped around me. He gave me a tight squeeze and then loosened his embrace a little, as if scared of hurting me. His face bent down and his lips touched my forehead lightly. I was thrilled, scarcely believing what was happening. I had thought about his lips for so long, about wanting to be close to him, about feeling his breath and smelling his skin. But I had had no idea that it would feel so wonderful. I turned towards him and put my arms around him, holding him tightly, my head on his chest, my heart pounding, my breath coming in short gasps, feeling a stirring inside me that I had never felt before. I smelt his warm, male smell, of salty, crushed grass after a game of football. His skin was warm and smooth and slightly sticky. I could feel the wet tips of his damp hair brush against my forehead, cool against my skin. We were both drenched with sweat from our game and our football jerseys stuck to each other. Shubho bent down and kissed me on my shut eyes, my cheeks. And then I felt the soft fullness of his lips on mine. He moaned slightly and, at that moment, I knew that this was what I had wanted to do all along. This was the desire that I had felt for Rajesh Khanna when I had first seen him in a film. My heart was pounding like it did when I ran. I grew aware of my body and felt a raw, burning need for the first time. It was different from wanting to eat or play or do anything else. This was a desire that I instinctively knew I could never talk about to anyone—ever. But I lost track of my thoughts as Shubho's breath quickened, he kissed me again and again and his fingers ran through my hair, massaging my scalp and then gently tracing the outlines of my face, as if to memorize them. I moaned in response—I wanted him to kiss me like he had kissed his girlfriend.

The chorus of the crickets was suddenly interrupted by footsteps outside, accompanied by the thumping noise of a lathi rhythmically pounding the ground. It was the chowkidar making his rounds and using his stick to let the world know. Shubho released me abruptly and moved away, saying, 'Shh ...'

My eyes had adjusted to the dim light and I could see his finger raised to his lips. His alarm was contagious and for a moment I felt as if I was going to be caught doing something really bad. Then the footsteps receded slowly into the distance as the chowkidar continued walking on the concrete footpath that ran along the side of the changing room. Shubho did not seem so confident any more and I felt his fear, the fear of being caught in a transgression, seeping into me.

As the sound of the chowkidar's footsteps faded away altogether, Shubho heaved a sigh of relief and moved close to me again and held me once more. But his body was still tense. He relaxed a few moments later and buried his face in my hair, breathing my scent in. 'Let us keep this our little secret, all right?' he murmured.

I nodded, my face upturned and pressed against his chest, completely content in that moment. The hardness at his groin pressed against my stomach and I moved unconsciously, wanting more. I wanted this to go on, to not stop, to feel my excitement build more and more, and wished desperately that we were somewhere safe, where the fear of discovery would not bother us.

After what seemed aeons, Shubho gently loosened my embrace and said, 'Let me take you home. Chatterjee Mashima and Meshomoshai must be getting worried about you.'

I wrapped my arms around him again and he held me for a few moments more. He was right. My parents would certainly worry if I stayed out too late. Then Shubho moved away to pick up his books and school uniform. I did the same. We walked out, his arms around my shoulders. It was completely dark by now. Begumpet Airport glowed in the horizon and I heard the drone of a two-engine plane as it approached the airport. The lights twinkled in a distance and then dipped lower and lower as the plane descended, until it was suddenly hidden by the trees. The grounds of the school were dark now. Tube lights made opalescent-blue, symmetrical patches as the light shone through the scalloped arches that followed each other all along the length of the school buildings. The chowkidars patrolled the grounds, holding a stick in one hand and a torch in the other. In the distance, we could see the resident boys who lived at Hyderabad Royal Academy lining up for dinner in the students' mess.

Shubho disengaged from me and ruffled my hair after giving me one last squeeze. We got into the car and drove to Mint House. Neither of us said much, the comfort and ease we had felt enveloping us like a soft blanket. And I felt a wrenching sense of loss as we travelled up the driveway to the palace, my longing for the comfort I had felt when Shubho put his arms around me renewed.

Once I had got out of the car, Shubho waved to me and drove off. As the car pulled away, I experienced a heavy sense of terror. I knew that I could not tell anyone about this, the way I knew not to say the word 'fuck' in front of our parents, even though the boys said it at school. This was my secret.

I walked up to the portico, climbed the steps and knocked on the door, waiting for Rani to let me in.

The following Tuesday, I stood in line, heart pounding, with the others who had been practising for a place in the Ajanta house football team.

'Malhotra, Saxena, Rao …' Shubho's voice called out each name crisply. We stood at attention, waiting to find out who was going to be judged fit to play in the house matches. As each name was called, the boy stepped out in front of the line. The list was long.

'Choudhury, Stevens …'

I waited with sinking hopes for my name to be called. I was going to be passed over, I thought, and this time, Suresh Khosla and his posse would have a field day. The only thing worse than not playing football was to be officially deemed unfit to play.

'Chatterjee … Chatterjee!' I heard my name being called impatiently and my heart jolted. 'Step out in front, Chatterjee.'

Shubho sounded exasperated. I stepped out self-consciously. Shubho looked at me with a fleeting twinkle in his eye and his lips twitched for a moment. Then he dismissed the boys who had not been chosen.

'Okay, boys. This is the last time we will be practising before the match this week. Give it your best. Which house is going to be the football champion this year?'

'Ajanta house!' The roar was deafening.

'All right, then. You know what to do. Get started. Give me two laps, quick!'

We started running in a single file. It felt like a dream—I was going to play in the match after all!

The match was held on Friday. Classes ended early that day. It was scheduled to start at three in the afternoon, so we met at two o'clock for our final warm-up and practice.

I pulled on my new football shorts and jersey with shaking hands. I was going to represent Ajanta and play against Ellora house. I looked down with satisfaction at my newly toned legs, in white knee-high socks and football shorts. The jersey was bright green and yellow, emblazoned with the house symbol, a hand holding a torch aloft, reminiscent of an Olympian.

'Team, remember—the future of Ajanta rests in our hands now. You have all practised very hard. Now it is time to put that to good use. I have gone over the moves that Ellora is famous for. You know how to beat them and catch them by surprise.' Shubho walked by the team as we all stood at attention. His strong legs were muscular and brown, his calves tightly defined by the knee-high white socks. I saw how his white shorts fitted his thighs and his tight-fitting jersey and remembered how he had felt as he had held his body against mine in his room. A surge of desire coursed through my body. He looked strong and incredibly handsome, like Alexander the Great addressing his troops on the eve of war. He paused for a moment as he walked by me and his eyes softened. Then he walked on, continuing his talk, as expected from the team captain. 'Remember the tactical moves I have taught you. Above all, play fair. Each year, the Ellora team gets a record number of penalty kicks. This year, I expect them to do the same. They will try to win by all means, fair or foul. But I expect each and every one of you to be a good sport, no matter what happens.' With that, he dismissed us.

The match started at a brisk pace. Suresh Khosla, who played for the Ellora team, was surprised to see me playing. He lost no time in taking a dig at me, however. 'Psst … Rahul! So, when did homos start playing for Ajanta house?' he taunted as we battled for possession of the ball. His teammates snickered. 'Well, I guess we will certainly win this game, won't we, boys?' he continued. He was greeted by a volley of derisive laughter.

I felt my ears burn with anger and shame. But I pretended not to care and did not answer. I was confident that Shubho would lead us to victory.

In the first half of the game, neither side could score a goal. The sides were evenly matched. Again and again, the Ellora team tried to score, but our goalie was quick to defend and successfully headed off all attempts. I was able to pass the ball to my teammates a few times, but most of the time I was running from one end of the field to the other. When halftime came, I was exhausted. My breath caught in my throat like a hard rock and my heart hammered painfully against my ribcage.

After drinking water, we collected in a group in the shade of a tree. I looked at Shubho. His football jersey was streaked with sweat. Dark patches had formed under his armpits. His hair was wet and clung to his forehead. I had an overwhelming desire to brush the hair out of his eyes and kiss him. I pushed the thought away, conscious of both desire and the fear of being caught looking at him that way. He limped slightly from a fall he had taken earlier and his knee was scraped raw—the blood was drying—but he did not seem to feel it.

'Team, beware of Ellora's tricks,' Shubho warned us. 'Their tactic in the first half of the game was to tire you out. You all spent a lot of time running. Now is the time when they will try to score a goal, hoping that you will not be able to defend your positions as well as before. They will play dirty. Be careful.' With that last cautionary remark, he stopped and dismissed us. We ran out to the field to join the Ellora team.

As I walked up, I saw Suresh Khosla looking at me and licking his lips, the tell-tale sign I had come to know so well.

The second half was played much more offensively by the Ellora team, which played on our side of the field from the moment the whistle went off. No matter how hard we tried, we could not be on their side of the field long enough to score a goal. Our team was beginning to feel the pressure of playing on the defense. We were almost at the end of the game. Time was running out and we would have to score soon if we were to win. Please, please, please let us win, I silently prayed.

Suddenly, out of nowhere, I saw the ball flying towards me. One of Ellora's players had missed his block.

'Pass, Rahul, pass to Vishal,' I heard Shubho yelling at me from afar. I did not have time to think. I ran to the football and blocked it with my foot. I was just getting ready to pass it to Vishal when I saw Suresh Khosla coming towards me. He stuck his foot out, trying to trip me. In a moment, he was almost upon me. I could hear his breathing and see his nostrils flaring as his lips curled up in a sneer. I turned and passed the ball—not to Vishal but to Shubho—to outwit Suresh, who collided with me a moment too late. I felt the wind knocked out of my lungs as his foot tangled with mine. Both of us fell to the ground, the impact hitting me like a wall.

As I fell to the ground, I heard a roar. Then I heard the referee's whistle blow loud and clear, marking the end of the match. I was still lying on the ground, trying to get away from Suresh Khosla. I could smell his sour sweat and his fetid breath and felt revolted. My knees were burning from the scrapes I had got when I fell and my body felt bruised all over.

They won, they won, I thought despondently, too miserable to even try and get up again. And then, I felt a pair of strong hands grip my shoulder and pull me up to a sitting position.

'Rahul, you did it! You passed me the ball and I scored a goal!' Shubho's face was close to mine, his eyes shining with excitement. And then the rest of the team was upon us, shaking us, rubbing my back, slapping it. They hoisted Shubho on their shoulders and marched around, singing 'For he's a jolly good fellow'. I could not believe it. I had passed the ball to Shubho—and we had won!

'I did it, I did it!' I proudly proclaimed to my family when I got home that evening.

'Did you score a goal?' Rani asked.

'No, but I passed the ball to Shubho Dada with seconds to spare. Without my help, he would never have scored. Thanks to me, Ajanta house won the cup!'

Rani looked impressed.

'Just passed the ball but did not score a goal?' Baba was happy but not impressed. 'At your age, I was the football captain of our team. I hope you will make me even more proud next year. Now don't forget to pay as much attention to your studies.' He squeezed my shoulder. 'I know you will always be a son I can be proud of. After all, you are *my* son!' He smiled at me and then returned to the *Hyderabad Chronicle* editorial. I smiled back uneasily. I knew he would not be proud of me if he found out what Shubho and I had been doing together.

The next day, I walked by Suresh Khosla and his gang sitting on the lawn at school. They looked up, but did not say anything. However, I did not trust Suresh. I knew he was just biding his time. He would have his revenge sooner or later. But I felt less threatened in class as the teasing ceased. Instead, Suresh and his friends picked on poor Arun Malhotra—a small, slender boy, who bore their taunts silently, too scared to respond and too terrified of football to ever dare to play it. I knew how he felt and was sorry for him.

With the football match over, evening practice ended and the students turned their attention to the tests and exams. I no longer got to see Shubho like I had become used to and missed him terribly. All I wanted to do was be with him again. At times, I toyed with the idea of writing him a love letter, but then the terror of what would happen if it was found would paralyse me. All I could do was spend as much time as possible close to the seniors' building in the hope that I would see him again.

'I have some news from Shyamala,' Rani whispered to me in bed, a couple of weeks after the match.

I felt a rush of guilt. I had been so caught up with my life that I had thought little about Mallika. The rest of the year stretched barrenly ahead with her gone, with no trips to her home, no films to watch and no secret trysts to meet Salim.

'Binesh Kaku and Anjali Mashi have settled on the boy they found a few weeks ago. They will be setting a date for the wedding,' Rani said.

'How does she know? Is she sure? Mallika Didi would never agree to a marriage with someone else.' My voice rose a few octaves with my panic.

'Shh ... be quiet.'

Rani's information was proven correct when, that evening, she and I were sitting down to an early dinner. Our parents would eat later and were now talking in the doorway between the dining room and the kitchen.

'Binesh Dada and Anjali Didi have found a suitable boy for Mallika,' Ma said.

'Who is the boy? Have his parents met her already?' Baba asked.

'Anjali Didi called me earlier today. They found a good match through her relatives in Calcutta. The boy's name is Sanjib and his parents live here, in Hyderabad. They travelled to the tea estate to see Mallika, who agreed to marry the boy. The cards will be sent out soon.'

I heard the news with a heavy heart.

'Well, I am glad that this terrible matter is getting settled finally,' Baba said. 'What a terrible thing to do! That girl has caused her parents so much sorrow. I hope the wedding takes place before people start gossiping, especially that Mrs Khosla. When are we going to meet the boy they have chosen?' he asked.

'After the next Bengali Association meeting next week,' replied Ma.

There was no one I could talk to about this, except Colonel Uncle. So I went up to see if he was back. I knocked on the door, but there was no answer and the padlock had fresh cobwebs on it. Colonel Uncle had not returned. I slowly walked back down, consumed by questions. Where was Salim? Was he back in college? Had his parents disowned him? I wanted to go to his parents' house again in Lakdi ka Pul and contact him. I could not forget his sorry broken and bruised figure the last time we had seen him, even though I wanted to remember him the way he was when I first saw him—handsome, debonair, with eyes filled with love for Mallika.

As the second round of tests came around, I was very nervous. I had not been doing well in my algebra homework.

'Glad to see you are studying hard,' Baba said one day when saw me chewing on my pencil, deep in thought. 'We are Bengalis and have a fine tradition of excelling in everything. Some of the finest poets, artists and writers have come from Bengal. I am so glad you have started playing sports. But make sure you do not neglect your studies. You have to be competitive. The world is a hard place and life is full of struggle. You must do well in school so that you can get a good job.'

Unfortunately, as I had expected, I did badly in algebra. Seeing the results, my father sat me down for a talk. I shrank from the signs I knew so well—the frown, the tightening lips, the clenching jaw. 'Look at Shankar,' he said, frustration and worry written on his face. 'He is a gardener. Do you want to be a gardener? That is what you will be. You will be like him, tilling the ground with your trowel, while others drive by in their expensive cars to their offices. What will all my friends say? You have to do better at school. If you don't, I will send you to boarding school.'

'But I don't want to go to boarding school. I want to stay here, at Mint House …' My voice trembled and I tried to steady it, wanting to sound mature.

'Achha. Then make sure you do well at school. No more distractions.'

I was out of danger for the moment. But with that one threat, Baba had effectively squashed all plans I had of going to the movies. The latest Rajesh Khanna film was released with much fanfare that week, but I did not dare say that I wanted to go watch it. I had to do well in algebra and maintain my top position in class.

The following week, we were at the Bengali Association's monthly Durga Puja Committee meeting when Mr Roy Choudhury asked me, 'So, Rahul? Do you still want to be a film star?' His tone was slightly mocking.

'I want to be an astronaut or an aeronautical engineer,' I announced. The words 'aeronautical engineer' sounded important and impressive.

'Very good!' Mr Roy Choudhury's voice was more encouraging this time.

My father patted my shoulder appreciatively. I made a note to myself to say the right thing in the future and not share my personal opinions. 'Rahul is on his way to being the captain of the football team next year,' Baba declared. 'Like a true Bengali, he has taken to football,' he proudly announced to Mr Roy Choudhury.

But football practice would have to wait until next year. The days were growing shorter and we could no longer practise late into the evening. I did see Shubho from time to time, but aside from a cheerful hello and occasional pat on the head, he showed no signs of the special familiarity we had experienced together. It felt as if he was treating me just like his younger brother's friend, nothing more—and it hurt each time it happened.

After we came back from the Bengali Association meeting, we dressed up for our visit to Binesh Kaku and Anjali Mashi's house. My mother wore a blue sari with a thin gold border and tiny roses embroidered all over it. 'Hurry up, Rahul and Rani,' she said as she put on her make-up.

'I hope Mallika Didi will be there,' I said.

'No, she is not, but she will be back soon,' Ma said. 'We are going to meet the man she is engaged to marry. His name is Sanjib. He will be your future jamai-babu.'

A stunned silence fell over Rani and me. I wanted to say that I hated my future brother-in-law and wished Mallika and Salim could be together, but then all our secrets would be out in the open and Mallika would get into even more trouble.

'Mallika Didi really likes this boy,' Ma said, looking at my crestfallen face. 'That Muslim boy is not important. Your Anjali Mashi said that Mallika Didi is very excited about this boy, Sanjib.'

I wanted to tell her about the letters I had read, but dared not. My mother believed what Anjali Mashi had told her. I felt a surge of anger against this boy who would be married to Mallika, who was doing it because she had no other way out.

'Rahul, dress nicely.' My mother's voice broke into my thoughts. 'Wear that new Rajesh Khanna shirt your father bought you from his last trip to Bombay. And Rani, wear that new salwar–kameez. The purple one. We are going to meet Mallika Didi's in-laws-to-be. You don't want them to think that Mallika Didi's friends don't dress well for a special occasion, do you? Sanjib is an engineer. You can ask him questions if you like and let him know that you want to be an aeronautical engineer.' Ma was trying hard to get us excited about meeting Mallika's husband-to-be.

'So what does Sanjib look like?' Rani asked. 'Have they met already?'

'Yes, Sanjib and his parents just came back from the tea estate in Assam. They met Mallika there. She likes the boy and so do her parents. I am so glad that she has agreed to this.'

'I wish Salim and Mallika Didi could marry.' I blurted out, unable to keep quiet any longer.

Ma came over to my side. She held my hand and led me to a chair. She sat down and made me sit next to her. In a very gentle and loving voice, she said, 'You must not mention Salim in front of Sanjib or his parents. If you do, there will be trouble for everyone, even your Mallika Didi.' Her voice took on a more urgent and pleading note: 'Promise me, Rahul, that you will not mention Salim. Head promise, like you do in school?' She put my hand on her head.

That amounted to a promise which, if broken, would kill my mother. I reluctantly said, 'All right, I promise.'

'Good.' Her voice held a note of relief. 'Rani, will you promise too?' she asked my sister.

'Of course, Ma, I promise,' she said.

I dressed with care for the occasion. I arranged the curl on my forehead and wore my new Rajesh Khanna shirt. Then Rani and I plotted in whispers in the back seat to not become friends with Sanjib at any cost.

Soon, we pulled into the driveway of Mallika and Shyamala's house and the chowkidars opened the gate. I looked at them, hating them for what they had done to Salim.

'Bloody basket,' I muttered, using some of the worst words I knew.

'Not bloody basket,' Rani corrected me under her breath, suppressing a giggle. 'It is bloody bastard, but don't say that in front of anyone. It is a very bad word.'

'Fuck … shit …' I murmured. Rani stifled a snort and poked me hard in the side, warning me to keep my voice down.

Shyamala opened the door for us. She was dressed in a lovely churidar–kurta and looked taller than usual in high-heeled slippers. Her hair was pulled back from her face and her eyebrows were knotted in frustration. As my parents walked into the sitting room, we fell behind.

Shyamala urgently whispered to us, 'They are here. Mallika Didi has said yes. You know, don't you, that when Salim came here, Baba was so angry that he had the chowkidars beat poor Salim up.'

'Shyamala, Rani, Rahul … come in here. You can play later. Rahul and Rani, meet Sanjib, your brother-in-law-to-be,' Binesh Kaku interrupted us before Rani or I could say anything.

We dragged our feet to the sitting room.

The first person we saw was an elderly gentleman, dressed in formal Bengali dhoti–kurta, the border of the fabric a classic rust-coloured pattern. He had a greying moustache and heavy, black-framed glasses. A heavyset lady sat next to him. She was dressed in a cream-coloured silk sari with a heavy red border. Her hair was combed neatly into a bun and she was wearing a red bindi but no make-up. They looked like my father's relatives who lived in Calcutta. I felt out of place and overdressed.

'Nomoshkar, Uncle and Aunty,' we chorused, folding our hands and bowing our heads slightly in respect. We smiled with our usual familiarity at Binesh Kaku and Anjali Mashi.

'Nomoshkar.' Sanjib's parents smiled at us.

'And this is Sanjib.' Binesh Kaku, resplendent in a silk kurta–pyjama, gestured towards a lanky man. His hair was slicked back with oil and he wore the same heavy, black frames as his father, which made him look much older than Salim and very serious. He was dressed in a white kurta–pyjama.

'Hi,' we said to him.

'Hello,' he replied dismissively, turning away to say something to his mother.

If this was what engineers were like, no thanks! I would rather be a film star. I could not help comparing him to Salim, so handsome, clean-shaven and bright-eyed. Sanjib's slow, measured answers and stodgy Bengali personality contrasted painfully with Salim's quick sense of humour and flair. I decided then that I wanted to be like

Salim, the hero in my real-life film.

After a while, we sat down to a quintessential Bengali meal of luchi and alur dom, sandesh and rosogolla. Sanjib ate a lot and was urged to eat even more by his doting in-laws-to-be. I noticed that Binesh Kaku was nervous, almost fawning on Sanjib. I had never known him to be so loudly genial before. Anjali Mashi was charming and gentle as always, but it was clear that they wanted to make a good impression.

'Shyamala, clear the dishes,' Anjali Mashi said. 'Your Sanjib Dada will think your Mallika Didi does not do any housework either.' Everyone laughed as if this was a big joke. 'Mallika is a wonderful cook,' Anjali Mashi added. 'I am sure she will make Sanjib lots of tasty meals.' Everyone laughed again. There was an air of gaiety about the table.

'Rani and Rahul, help Shyamala. I have trained my children to be fully at ease in the kitchen,' Ma told Sanjib's parents proudly. 'Do you cook?' she asked, turning to Sanjib.

'No, Mashi, I do not,' he answered, looking surprised.

Sanjib's mother said stiffly, 'A woman's place is in the kitchen, not a man's. Cooking will be our daughter-in-law's responsibility.'

Ma looked annoyed and started to say something, but changed her mind and fell silent.

'Of course, we have raised our daughters to know their responsibilities. They know to keep the family well-fed,' Binesh Kaku said.

Shyamala, Rani and I cleared the table and took the dirty dishes into the kitchen. After putting them in the kitchen sink for the maidservant to wash the next day, we crept up to Mallika's room. We tiptoed inside and shut the door gently.

'Poor Salim!' Shyamala's words tumbled out in a mad rush. 'He came here to talk to Baba and was beaten so badly. It was horrible— I was so scared for him! You do know what happened?'

Rani and I nodded, but she continued with the painful story we knew so well.

'I never told you the details at school Rani, but this is what happened. Salim rang the bell and Baba opened the door. I don't know what he said, but suddenly I heard Baba shouting. He said, "No daughter of mine will marry a Mussalman. Get out of here. How did you ever find the guts to mix with a Brahmin girl? Mallika does not want to see you or hear from you. Do you understand?" Salim said something to him that I could not hear. Then Baba said, "How dare you say you love her and that she loves you? What do you know about our culture and customs?" Baba was shaking by now. I thought he would hit Salim right then and there. Ma and I watched from the dining room, hiding behind the curtains. Then he said, "You scoundrel, I will teach you a lesson." He yelled for the chowkidars, who came up with their sticks and started beating Salim all over. They pushed him outside the gate with their blows. It was sickening. Salim kept asking Baba to give them a chance, but he would not listen. I did not know Baba could be so angry. I am scared to do anything to upset him now.'

We listened, speechless.

'Did Mallika really agree to marry Sanjib? He is so ugly compared to Salim,' Rani finally said with a shudder. 'And so boring, with those horrible glasses! Just like a typical Bengali Babu.'

'Baba and Ma travelled to Assam last week. Sanjib and his parents met them at Didima's tea estate. I don't know what happened there. I asked Ma, but all she said was that Mallika liked Sanjib very much and wanted to get married as quickly as possible. The wedding is going to be in a few weeks. Mallika Didi is arriving here next week.'

'There is nothing we can do.' Rani sounded defeated. She sat there quietly, her shoulders hunched. Shyamala and I looked at each other helplessly, too dejected to say anything.

9

Saturday Night. San Francisco.

'You've always had nightmares, haven't you?' Andrew put his hand on my arm, his eyes soft for the first time since he had left. The bar was quite full now and I could barely hear him.

'Yes.' I shrugged.

He stroked the back of my neck. I leaned back, loving the way his fingers massaged my tense muscles. The bartender looked at us and then away.

'Baby,' I whispered to Andrew, 'it's getting crowded here. Let's go back to your motel. I want to be alone with you.' I reached out and played with the down on his chest. He did not pull back. It was a good sign, I thought.

We walked out of the bar and took a taxi to Andrew's motel. Once we got to his room, we started kissing. I could not believe that I had come so close to losing him. I burrowed my face in his chest and breathed in the musky scent of his skin. We staggered to the bed, intoxicated from the drinks we'd had. I lay on top of Andrew and kissed him long and hard. His tongue tangled with mine with urgency and he rolled me over to get on top of me.

Our lovemaking was short and intense, without our usual tenderness and foreplay. Andrew's touch was punishing, his fingers bruising my skin. I did not know what was going on in his head. We finished abruptly, our clothes still on, and then lay on our backs, panting.

'So,' Andrew said slowly, sitting up suddenly, his eyes narrowing. 'Have you told the girl's family not to come on Sunday?'

'No ... I haven't,' I confessed. 'I was hoping you would come home before I made that call.'

Andrew got up. His shirt was unbuttoned and the trail of blond hair on his chest, trailing down to his pelvis, sent a flame of desire through me. I reached out to touch it.

'No, stop it.' He pulled away and wrapped his shirt around his torso. His voice was a whiplash that made me flinch. 'So, are you waiting for me to come back first so that you won't be burning bridges by losing both me *and* your fake life? Fuck that.'

'Andrew ...' I stammered.

'No, seriously. *Fuck* that. I don't want you to do this just for me. I want you to do this for yourself. You have a community in this city. It is my community. Your community. Our community. And yet you act like you don't belong. Like you're an outsider.'

'Andrew, all I am saying is that I want you back in my life...' I faltered, trying to say the right words, but knowing deep inside that he was right. I felt an old knot in my stomach. 'I just need you to be there. For ... support ...'

'But I have been there for the past six months! It didn't change anything. You didn't even open up to me until I walked out on you! You know what they say—you can't sail in two boats at the same time. You have to pick one, you'll fall into the water and drown.'

I cringed at the harshness of his words.

'You need to leave now,' Andrew said, walking to the door.

I stared at him, realizing that things were not going to work out. The familiar pain of losing Shubho suddenly stirred inside me, paralysing me, sapping my strength.

'You don't get it, do you?' Andrew snapped. 'I am not coming home until you stop lying—to yourself, to your family. Please go now.' He held the door open, his eyes averted.

I had hoped that Andrew loved me too much to let go of me. But now I was forced to consider that perhaps I had made him despise me. I walked out, feeling hopeless and helpless, knowing that I may just have lost the greatest love of my life, hating myself for being a coward.

Outside, the fog swirled in thick wreaths around the lamp posts as it came tearing in from over the Golden Gate Bridge and Crissy Field and down to the Marina. I shivered and pulled my jacket around me. Damn this San Francisco summer. Why did it have to be so bloody cold? The street lamps glowed dull amber and the headlights of the cars looked milky. I stood there on the road, feeling that peculiar loneliness that comes with living in America as an immigrant. It is a poignant thing and one lives with it every day because, ultimately, here, one lives alone and dies alone. I wondered why I had bothered to make it my home. Wouldn't it have been easier in India, where life was pre-ordained and managed by family from birth to death? But in India, there was no place for people like me. The irony of giving up so much only to live a lie in America struck me for the first time.

I did not want to go home alone. The nightmares would come back and I could not face waking up without Andrew's arms around me, comforting me. I badly needed a drink.

I hailed a cab. The driver was Indian.

'Bhaisaab, Castro jaana hai.'

He turned around and gave me a look of real concern as we drove up Divisadero Street and neared California Street. 'Be careful, Sahib. I am telling you because you are desi too and seem like a decent, God-fearing man. Castro is not for good-character people. Full of homos and bad diseases.'

For a moment, I was back in the schoolyard again, being taunted by the other boys as I shrank with terror inside. I lost my temper.

'Stop the taxi, asshole. Who the fuck are you, calling me a homo?'

I got out of the taxi, shaking with anger and humiliation.

I caught another taxi and was dropped off at the Market and Castro crossing. It was a busy Saturday night. Men strolled arm in arm with each other. A group of young boys in tight jeans and spiked hair stood at the window of the Castro video store, pointing to the window and leering at the covers of porn movies. The Castro Theatre loomed large and stately, its marquee brightly lit.

I was still feeling rattled by my outburst. I needed a drink, I thought again, and walked into Rumours, the first bar I saw on Castro Street.

It was packed inside. The noise was deafening and everyone was trying to talk over the music being played by the house DJ. I stood by the bar, trying to get close to the counter.

The sexy bartender leaned over, bare-chested, his jeans hanging low on his hips. 'Hey, handsome, what can I get ya?'

'Black Label on the rocks, please.'

He came back with two drinks. 'Here, man, one is on the house for a handsome guy like you. Bottoms up!'

He thrust the two glasses into my hand. I swallowed one and slammed the glass back on the counter and gagged as the alcohol trailed a fiery blaze down my throat. I swallowed most of the other drink too in one gulp. My head spinning, I turned around to look at the crowd. Cruisy.

'Hey, baby.' A slim young man in a tank top and tight jeans slid over to me. 'Wanna dance?'

'No, thanks.'

He shrugged and walked off.

Nursing my drink, I went to the bathroom at the back of the bar. I needed to take a leak. The alcohol had gone straight to my head and I felt unsteady as I made my way through the gyrating crowd. I walked into a stall. The door was pushed open a few moments later. The man who entered was quite handsome in a rugged kind of way. He was wearing Levis and a tight V-necked T-shirt, like construction men preferred, and also had work boots on. I gave him an apologetic smile since I had not locked the door of the toilet.

'Sorry, I am using the toilet ...'

'It's okay. I can wait.' He leaned in as I zipped up. 'Hey, guy, want some coke?

He dug into his pocket and pulled out a vial. Unscrewing the top, he dug in the spoon and held a heaping mound of coke under my nose. 'No thanks,' I said. 'Please leave and wait to use the stall until I come out.'

'No worries man. Sure you don't want a couple of bumps?'

'Yes. Leave. Now!' I tried hard to control my temper and the alcohol was not helping. He was pushing my patience.

'Hey relax, stud.' Ignoring my request, the man took two deep bumps from the glass vial full of cocaine. He rubbed his gums with his coke dusted fingers. 'You're hot, man.' He leaned over, pushing me against the wall, and tried to kiss me. I pushed back, but he was heavier than me and ground me into the wall.

I felt his rough chin scrape mine as he forced his tongue into my mouth.

'What the fuck!' I pushed him with all the force I could muster.

'Hey, take it easy man. No need to get angry.'

I strode out of the stall, slamming the door behind me.

I made my way to a corner of the bar. I felt dirty and violated. God, what had come over me? What would Andrew say? Flooded by guilt, I walked out of the bar unsteadily, barging into the line of men standing outside, waiting for the bouncer to let them in.

'Careful, sexy,' a young man cautioned. I spun away, staggering down Castro Street.

I crossed the street, weaving a little as I avoided the stream of cars going up and down, and sat down on the pavement outside the Castro Theatre. Boys and men looked at me curiously, some with interest. I avoided looking at anyone and, as the buzz of the alcohol subsided, hailed a taxi to go to Club Folsom, where I knew my friend Richard liked to go on Saturday nights. I just wanted to forget all the terrible things that had happened all evening. I wanted to lose myself in music, be with a friend.

When the taxi dropped me off on Folsom Street, a line had started forming outside the nondescript building. As I paid the cover charge and walked up the stairs, I was greeted by a blast of trance and house music. The floor was packed with men and women dancing with each other. I heard a familiar voice call my name as I left the coat check.

'Hey, Rahul, how's it going?' Richard was shirtless, smiling broadly at me. 'Where's Andrew?'

'Oh, we're having some trouble. I don't know if we're together any more.' I looked at the floor, miserable and alone, wondering if I should have just gone home and tried to sleep after taking a few pills to knock myself out instead of coming to the nightclub.

'You're not serious, are you?' Richard sounded incredulous. 'You know, Andrew is madly in love with you. Lovers' tiff, man. It will be over before you know it. Christ, you look totally miserable. Poor thing. Now stand up straight like this. There … that's better. And smile a little. You look like you could do with some fun.' He stood behind me, massaging my shoulders. 'I know what you really need right now,' he whispered into my ear. 'A little pill and some fun dancing will chase the blues away.'

I looked at Richard, carefree and happy. Perhaps he was right—I needed to spend the night with a friend, not all by myself.

Richard discreetly slipped a pill into my hand and handed me his bottle of water. I casually put the Ecstasy into my mouth and, after a few moments, took a swig.

'Rahul!' Another familiar voice hailed me. It was Michael, Richard's boyfriend. I wished Andrew were there with me, like he had been on other nights at Club Folsom. Sadness descended on me like a dark cloud.

'Hey, hey,' Richard broke in. 'This is no time for feeling bad. It will all work out. Just hang with us tonight and have some fun.' He embraced me in a big hug. The brotherly affection was a balm to my sore nerves. 'Come, let's get to the dance floor.'

It had been a long time since I had gone out with friends like this. The floor was packed and we managed to squeeze our way through the crowd until we found a little free space. I watched entranced as the laser lights made an insane pattern through the fog exploding, cannonball-like, from the fog machine. The kaleidoscope of images frozen for seconds in the strobe lights hypnotized me as I looked at the sea of smiling faces around. Most of the men had their shirts off, the buff bodies clad in tight jeans making islands of opalescence in the black light. Many couples were dancing close together, others were even more intimate, dancing skin to skin. And still more men danced in groups, making little circles that expanded and contracted to allow for the wave of movement to ebb and flow. The music was heavenly and I felt a tingling in my scalp and chills run up and down my body as the Ecstasy took hold of me. The music started sounding far away and then very close and then far away again as the beats reverberated through the club. When Lady Gaga's 'Born This Way' came on, the dancers erupted in frenzy. I felt my eyelids grow heavy and flutter.

Through the haze of the fog, Richard appeared close to me and smiled roguishly. 'Looks like you're feeling it, buddy.' He turned towards Michael and they danced close, in an embrace, lips locked together.

I opened my eyes wide and looked around. Fluorescent colours flashed before my eyes and my eyeballs vibrated, as if zapped by a tiny electric current. Suddenly, I started to feel incredibly light and happy. All I was conscious of was euphoria—so much that I could not remember having ever felt unhappy. I felt love, saw love, experienced love as never before …

'Hey, gorgeous!' A handsome, dark-haired, young, collegiate type came up to me. 'What's your name?'

'Rahul,' I said as loudly as I could, cupping my hand to his ear. I could smell his sweat and the sweetness of his hair.

'What?'

'Rahul. RAHUL.' I boldly embraced him and traced the letters on his bare back, feeling his nipples brushing against mine.

'Casey,' he said, extending a hand and shaking mine. 'Man, you are hot! Let me look at you again.' He stepped back and held me at arm's length. 'Man, you are so very hot,' he repeated. Stepping in close, he started dancing, gyrating his hips to the beat.

He must be a salsa dancer, I figured, watching him move in close and step away, expertly keeping the beat. I looked at his broad chest and the clear outline of his pectorals, the six-pack defined and shadowed in the changing lights, the glint of his teeth as he smiled broadly at me. He was not shy and, for once, neither was I. Suddenly, I felt this surge of confidence that I had never felt before. I felt whole and complete. Desirable. Grounded. A few feet away, I saw Richard and Michael giving me a silent thumbs-up before turning back to each other.

The music continued, time stood still. I felt an indescribable burst of energy and affection from everyone. Faces were wreathed in smiles and there was acceptance, unconditional acceptance such as I had never experienced before in the gay scene. I felt as if someone had peeled away the layers of armour that I had built around myself, exposing me to the real people around. People who were happy with their lives, who revelled in their sexuality and the family they had created—with men and women from all walks of life and beliefs, creating a microcosm of the world they lived in.

Casey moved close. His lips brushed mine and I smelt the musky odour of his skin combined with the scent of cologne. It was all so overpowering that I walked to the edge of the floor and leaned against a wall.

Casey followed me. 'You are sweet,' he murmured in my ear. 'Are you single or do you have a boyfriend?'

I thought about Andrew, our love for each other, and my heart constricted. I knew I had to get back together with him again. I would do whatever it took.

'Sorry, Casey. I do have a boyfriend. He is not here tonight. We … we broke up … and I am still in love with him …' My voice trembled.

'Are you cheating on him?' Casey asked, frowning.

'No. He left me because I am still seeing girls for an arranged marriage to keep my parents happy.'

'Wait a minute. So you are not out to your family?'

'No.'

Casey looked stunned for a few moments. 'Man, he must feel like a second-class citizen in your life.'

I stared at him, nodding sadly.

'You seem like a really nice guy,' Casey said after a while. 'I would love to date someone like you, but you're taken. And you're not out yet, Rahul. Not even to yourself. I used to be like you. But now … Look around you. It is amazing once there are no more secrets. Life is easy and it flows.' He gave me a hug and walked away.

'Of course,' I said to myself. Suddenly, I wanted to go home. I didn't know exactly what had happened, but I felt … free. I was not afraid of sleeping any more.

The palest sliver of a moon hung in the sky, casting a light streak of silvery pink over a cloud, making it glow against the heavy, leaden sky. The street lamps were unusually bright and there was a purple ring around the moon. I breathed in the fresh air and smiled. I felt carefree and happy, confident that I would work it out with Andrew. I had hurt him, yes, but I knew that he loved me and I loved him. That was all that mattered.

The taxi ride back to the apartment was a blur while music from the club still echoed in my ears and I felt warm all over. And there was a lightness to my feelings, as if I had been cleansed.

10

Sunday Afternoon. San Francisco.

It was the sound of the cable car that woke me up. I looked at the clock. It was two in the afternoon I had slept dreamlessly for the first time in a very long time. As I replayed the events of the night, I looked out of the window. A thin finger of fog was snaking its way across the top of the Golden Gate Bridge. It would be another afternoon of summer mist. Opening the windows to air out the apartment, I felt the chilly breeze ruffle my hair.

In the bathroom, I turned on the shower. Hot jets of water hit me, stinging my skin, waking me up. I emerged, feeling clean and fresh, and started to get dressed. Looking in the mirror, I cocked my head to one side, like Rajesh Khanna, and smiled. I could not wait to show Andrew what I used to do in front of the mirror as a boy.

The lock turned and the door opened abruptly as Andrew walked in looking serious.

'Hi, Andrew.'

'I have come to get my things.'

'What? Why are you … ? I thought you were going to give us some time.' My head started spinning. 'Please, Andrew,' I pleaded. My euphoria of the past twelve hours ebbed with the shock of the finality in his face. This could not be how it would end … I had to show Andrew that I was not the same person he threw out of the motel room.

I reached out to him, but he pushed me away, walking to the closet to gather his clothes.

'No!' I blocked his path.

Andrew pushed me roughly. I fell, my head grazed the end table by the bed. The picture of Colonel Uncle and Claudio came crashing down on my head and then to the floor. I saw stars for a second. I tried to get up, but I felt dizzy and sank back onto the floor.

'Oh my God!' Andrew was on the floor beside me in an instant. 'Oh my God, Rahul, I am so sorry!' Now he was crying, cradling me in his arms. 'I did not mean to hurt you, I promise. I love you, baby. I don't want to leave you. I just don't know how I can stay …'

I lay there for a minute, trying to gather myself. I finally sat up, shaking my head, feeling disoriented. Darts of pain shot through my head like bullets ricocheting off an iron wall. My eyes fell on the picture of Colonel Uncle and Claudio lying face-down on the floor. On its back were the words Colonel Uncle had written—words I had long forgotten: 'To Rahul, the sweet prince of the palace. Think for yourself and you will be strong enough to face the world. And always follow your heart.'

In that moment, I knew what I had to do.

'Never mind.' I stood up, shaking Andrew's hands off. 'If you feel we don't have a future, Andrew, and want to leave, I am not going to fight you. I know I have hurt you terribly and disappointed you very much. But let me tell you the rest of my story—then, perhaps, you will give us another chance.'

Andrew shook his head. I don't think he believed me and I didn't blame him. My heart grew heavy again at the thought of losing him, but I knew that it was up to me to heal this relationship, to erase the pain I had caused. I thrust away my anxiety. I could not afford to lose focus.

Sometime later, Andrew and I both sat on cushions, facing each other, in front of the fireplace. I took his hands, he pulled them away. 'This is too intense,' he said. 'Let us figure out if we are going to be together before getting close again.'

I could not help feeling rejected. I guess I was trying too hard.

'You know, Andrew,' I said. 'At first, there was just the loss of Amit, which I managed to deal with. Then there was Mallika Didi's loss, which was harder. But there were more and more. And at some time, I started to feel as if it was all *my* fault. That I had somehow caused things to happen because I was bad. Do you know what I mean?'

Andrew was silent for a while as he stared at the sparks dying as they flew into the fire guard.

'Yes.' His face was sad. For a moment, he looked like a little boy, a wounded child. 'Your story is bringing up all those memories for me, you know. I remember thinking after my parents' divorce that it was all my fault. That *I* must have done something wrong. I remember asking my mom if my dad had left because I had used his power drill to drill holes in the garage wall.' His laugh was bitter.

I wanted to touch him, but I held back. Touching in America was a loaded action—a touch means intimacy, I had learnt. The most organic human action, to touch someone, was classified, labelled, quantified. Holding hands was for lovers only. A hearty pat on the back was the standard expression of affection between male friends. Anything more made them complicit in a shameful, suspect act of homosexuality. There were Americans who actually believed that all men in India were gay because they held hands. I had never got used to this kind of censorship. But Andrew was American and I lived in America. And so I had learned to adapt. Andrew had already indicated his comfort level for this conversation—I was not about to push it.

'You know, for a while, I not only believed that I was bad but that I was also possessed by the devil,' Andrew said.

'What? That is so fucked up! Why would you think such a thing?'

'Just like your community that met to plan the festival of your Goddess Dur … Durka?'

'Goddess Durga.'

'Sorry, Goddess Durga. Our community would also meet to celebrate our faith. My father forced us to go with him to church, where the pastor translated the Bible literally. *Literally.* And he said that feelings of homosexuality were caused by the devil. Our math teacher was gay and he was fired when the parents of some students found out that he lived with his life partner. He was such a wonderful teacher, you know. I would not have become an engineer if he hadn't nurtured my love for mathematics. But when that happened, I learnt to hide by being as invisible as I could. I used to pray for hours for God to exorcise the devil from me. It was hell, being part of that narrow-minded community. That is why I moved away as soon as I turned eighteen and got a college scholarship …' Andrew sighed. 'Anyway, this is about you, not me. So what was this Goddess festival about? It seems like you guys met in large groups to eat and celebrate whenever you got a chance. Did your priest talk about sin and repentance as well?'

'Not our priest. Our festivals are based on mythology and our rituals are symbolic. It was not until the Hindu–Muslim riots started that I came to understand that people can be so intolerant of each other's religions. But no, the pujas are not about sin and repentance. Durga Puja is the festival that worships and celebrates Durga, who is our mother goddess. It is the best time of the year for Bengalis. Our Christmas. New clothes, lots of food, fun. There is also music and dance and singing. And we kids loved it, as did the grown-ups. As the myth goes, the Mother Goddess comes to earth for ten days each year from her husband's home in the Himalayas. She has four children, Goddess Lakshmi, Goddess Saraswati, Lord Ganesh and Lord Kartik. The artists that came to Hyderabad from Bengal each year were very talented. Here, in the US, those poor, underpaid guys would have been stars. They built statues of clay and straw and then dressed them up in silks and jewellery. The idols towered over us, twelve or fifteen feet in height. The pantheon of Durga and her children would be stunningly life-like and incredibly awe-inspiring to my young eyes. I had no idea, however, that it would be so bloody traumatic at the festivities that year.'

'Is this the same Goddess whose picture you have on your altar? The one with several arms, riding a lion?'

'Yes! Very good, Andrew.' I smiled and went on. 'I used to look at the goddess with awe. She looked so fearless, like the heroine in an action film, her large, doe-like eyes filled with fire. She would ride her lion, a beautiful animal with a golden coat, its mane swaying in the wind, its mouth snarling as its paw ripped open a buffalo and the demon Mahishasura climbed out of its body … And then Durga's spear plunged into his chest.' I stopped to savour my memories.

'That sounds scary.'

'No, it isn't scary. It's the timeless story of the victory of good over evil.'

'This is all so different from Christianity's version of the same struggle.'

'Of course it is.'

'And I know you told me but I forget the name of the fat guy with the elephant head all over the apartment?' Andrew gestured around.

'Oh, yes, that is Lord Ganesha, my favourite.'

'Why do you have so many likenesses of him?'

'Because I like him. And because he is the remover of obstacles.'

'I am trying to understand. How can you relate to something so out of this world? A man with an elephant's head?'

'Our mythology has plenty of strange characters. Nothing unusual in that. Besides, I love elephants! And since he has an elephant head, I find him the most endearing of all our gods. He is very wise, you know. During Durga Puja, Lord Ganesh is married to a small banana tree.' I held up my hand. 'Don't ask me. I don't know why. It was always a treat to see the tree swathed in a cream-coloured cotton sari with a red border, the green leaves peeping shyly out from under the covered head.'

'Seriously, this is all fascinating—and so unreal!'

Andrew seemed to be lightening up a little, I noted with satisfaction.

'Why? That is India. This is America. Of course it is different. Anyway. Where did I stop my story before I digressed?'

'Let me think. You were telling me about … about … Mallika's marriage being arranged by her parents. So weird. I know it happens, but it is hard to get used to the idea. I can't believe that you are also playing the same game.'

I stiffened at the barb. I had to get through to him. 'Please, Andrew. You promised to hear me out.' I fought to keep the irritation from my voice. I did not want to risk another argument.

Andrew crossed his arms in front of his chest, defensive. After a few moments of silence, he said, 'Okay, so did Mallika get forcibly married to some jerk?'

'Yes …'

September 1973. Hyderabad.

The postman delivered a red envelope with gold lettering a few days after our visit to see Sanjib. I had never seen such a pretty envelope before—it had a picture of a Bengali bride in a palanquin embossed in gold—and it signified the death of Mallika and Salim's dream. This was not how this story was supposed to end. My real-life heroine would be given away to some stranger Binesh Kaku and Anjali Mashi had found, and I was powerless to do anything.

'Rahul, come and help me check on the guavas.' Rani's voice distracted me from the card. Relieved to have something to occupy me, I joined her in the kitchen, where we carefully cut little squares of cheesecloth to be used to wrap and protect the fruit. When we had enough squares, Rani and I ran out to the garden and raced each other until we reached the far end of the palace grounds, near the guava grove.

'Did you see the wedding invitation?' I asked.

'Yes, I did,' Rani said, swinging onto a sturdy guava tree, its dark-brown bark weathered by many monsoons. The year before, I had struggled to climb up with ease like Rani. This year, the trees looked shorter and were surprisingly easy to climb. I hauled myself up without any trouble.

Rani had carefully tied little pieces of cheesecloth over each of the baby guavas earlier so that they would be safe from marauding squirrels, bats and birds. Most of the time, this trick worked.

'This means that Mallika Didi will never be with Salim again,' I said sadly as I looked under little cloth tents, relieved to find most of the guavas intact and still growing.

Rani didn't reply. After a while, we looked around for signs of half-eaten fruit. There were a few of them on the ground, in the grass. As we walked back to the palace, I asked Rani if Salim would try to contact Mallika Didi if he found out she was back.

'I hope Salim talks to Mallika Didi when she returns,' she said. 'But if Binesh Kaku finds out this time he will have Salim killed. She will probably refuse to see him, though. She said in her letter that her mind was made up. I cannot believe she is coming back in just a few days.'

I remembered the red-and-gold envelope, waiting to be opened.

'Let us go and see if Ma has opened the invitation yet.'

We trudged slowly to the house, too dispirited to race each other. When we reached, I went to the dining room, where the wedding invitation lay on the table. My mother had already opened the envelope. I pulled out a bright red card with a golden silk band running through it. Inside, it said: 'Sri Binesh Bannerjee and Srimati Anjali Bannerjee request the pleasure of your company to celebrate the auspicious occasion of the marriage of their daughter Mallika to Sanjib, son of Sri Ashok Ganguly and Srimati Aparna Ganguly.'

'Rani, Mallika Didi is getting married on 20 September, just two weeks away.' I felt the hollowness in my stomach, staring at the crimson slash of the envelope as it lay on the table like a bleeding wound.

A few days later, the phone rang. I heard my mother pick up the phone and say, 'Anjali Didi? How are you?'

Anjali Mashi replied and Ma exclaimed in surprise: 'Oh, Anjali Didi! When did Mallika get back? Why did you not let us know she has been here for some time? Of course we got the card. How is she?' After a while, she said, 'She is probably tired with the clothes fittings and jewellery trials and that long train ride from Assam. Sorry to hear she is not feeling too well. That is to be expected, I suppose, considering everything going on. I am so glad she is being cooperative. Yes, we will come by today. Rahul and Rani are dying to see her and keep asking about her all the time.'

Hanging up the phone, she said to my father, who was reading the newspaper, 'Ogo, shunchho? Mallika is back for her wedding. Anjali Didi wants us to go and see her.'

We visited Mallika Didi that evening. There were many cars parked in the driveway. I wanted to run up to her room to talk to her, but the door was opened by a strange young man and the sitting room was full of many people—there was no sign of Mallika.

'Shyamala!' I said with relief, glad to see a familiar face. 'Where is Mallika Didi?'

'She is sleeping. She has been sleeping ever since we got back,' Shyamala complained.

'Come and help me in the kitchen,' Anjali Mashi said, beckoning to my mother. I followed them into the kitchen. Anjali Mashi led her to the pantry, and I heard them talking in a low voice.

'Mallika has been a little agitated since she returned.' Anjali Mashi's voice dropped to a whisper. I moved closer to the pantry entrance and peered under the kitchen table, pretending to look for something, as I strained to hear the conversation. 'She wanted to go out of the house to Abid Road to do some shopping on her own, but you know how dangerous that is. It is too close to the wedding. If she tries to meet that boy Salim, the wedding will be in jeopardy. We cannot have that. Dr Rao has given her some medicine so that she can rest. He said the medicine will make her relaxed and more cooperative. We have been adding the drops to her tea every morning. The doctor has said it is not going to harm her. There is just so much going on, with all the relatives arriving in droves. More are coming tomorrow.'

'And then there are all the special ceremonies to go through too, aren't there?' My mother's voice was understanding. 'Mallika will be very busy and surrounded by people the entire time. How is she dealing with so many relatives in the house?'

The man who had let us in brought some dirty dishes in. Anjali Mashi and Ma heard the clattering of dishes in the kitchen sink and came out of the pantry in a hurry.

'You don't need to do this,' Anjali Mashi said firmly as she guided Binesh Kaku's nephew outside. 'The kitchen is the domain of women. Let us do the work. I hope your wife does not make you work in the kitchen!' Anjali Mashi laughed and he smiled sheepishly and left.

Anjali Mashi slipped back in to the pantry with my mother and started talking faster: 'She has been really quiet and very obedient since we have been giving her the medicine. We *had* to get something to keep her calm. The relatives think she is just tired with all that is going on and let her sleep. In Assam, she cried a lot at first, but then she seemed to realize that there is no future for her with

Salim. Your Binesh Dada can be very firm and persuasive, you know. And then, once she realized that Shyamala's future was in jeopardy because of her foolishness, she got over this love nonsense. As if life is like a Hindi film!

'She agreed to the marriage with Sanjib very easily. I was not happy to see her agitation when she returned. She might have had second thoughts about the marriage—you know how young girls can be. I have not told her that the Muslim boy came here in her absence and have warned Shyamala not to say a word. I pray that he will not come here before the wedding. Otherwise, everything can fall apart. Your Binesh Dada has given special instructions to the chowkidars not to let him enter and to do whatever is necessary to keep him away. Thank goodness there is only a week before the wedding.

'It has been hell since this nonsense started with that Muslim boy. I thank Ma Kali that everything has been working out all right so far. I have made a promise that, if everything goes fine, I will make a pilgrimage to the Kali temple at Dakshineshwar. When I think of what would have happened if she had got even more brainwashed by that scoundrel of a boy and run away with him, it makes my blood run cold. My whole family's honour, even the future of my little Shyamala, was in such danger …'

'Don't worry, it will all be over soon.' My mother's voice was soothing. It reminded me of the times when I would fall and hurt myself and she would make everything seem all right again. 'Mallika will thank you for this one day. Do you like that boy Sanjib? His parents seem wonderful and friendly, but he seemed a little withdrawn. Perhaps he was nervous.'

Anjali Mashi sounded a little less frantic as she said, 'Everyone is nervous before marriage. I wanted Mallika to see some more boys, but she said yes to him right away. She said she would marry him. She is a good girl, she will adjust. Isn't that what we all had to do? Look at your Binesh Dada. He has his faults, but we both adjusted. When Mallika was young, he was a little restless and used to have a really bad temper. I used to be so scared of him. But now he has settled down and I can depend on him. We have to get our children married so that when they are old they are not alone and so that the family name can continue. When the romance and the honeymoon are over, we women have to raise the children and keep the household together. It is our duty in life.'

'Yes, that is true. Perhaps Rani and Shyamala will get married at the same ceremony, in two wedding ceremonies, side by side, with nice boys we find for them' Ma added.

I crept away from the table and silently left the kitchen. I climbed the stairs to Mallika's room, avoiding the groups of uncles, aunts and grandparents gathered everywhere. Mallika's door was shut. I turned the knob. It turned easily, but the door stayed shut even when I pushed hard. When I noticed the big brass lock on the door, I thought that there must have been some mistake, because I had never seen Mallika's room locked before.

Perhaps the saris and gold and jewellery were locked up in Mallika's room and she was sleeping in the guest room. But when I went to look, I saw that it was full of half-opened suitcases. Suddenly feeling anxious, I went back to her room and rattled the knob again.

'Mallika Didi, Mallika Didi,' I said in a low voice. But there was no response. I looked through the keyhole. I could just about see Mallika on the bed, her face peaceful. For one awful moment, I thought she might be dead, but then I saw her chest rise and fall softly. I called out to her again, but it was useless.

I went downstairs in a hurry to find Rani, but then it was time to have snacks. I could hardly eat, feeling nauseated with the knowledge that my beloved Mallika was locked up and drugged. I wanted to go upstairs to her room and shake her till she woke up. We would open the window of the bedroom and she would run away with a waiting Salim, just like Dimple Kapadia had done in *Bobby* … But this was not a film, and we left soon afterwards.

We attended the wedding the following week. All of us dressed with great care for the event. My mother wore her beautiful peacock-blue Benarasi silk sari, reserved for very special occasions. Her hair was piled high on her head—She had gone to the Sundari Beauty

Parlour on Abid Road to have it done. I watched her go to the prayer room, where my mother kept all her jewellery locked up. This was the safest place since it was seldom visited for any reason other than saying our prayers. Since my father was the most religious of the family, the rest of us rarely entered. Ma unlocked her trunk and took out her ruby-encrusted gold necklace with matching bangles and earrings.

'Ma, please wear that turquoise-studded Favre-Leuba watch you have,' I begged. I loved that watch—it was thin and delicate and a fine gold chain hung in a loop from the cunningly wrought clasp.

'All right!' She laughed and put the watch on.

My dhoti was a complicated affair—six yards of brown-cream silk, tied across the waist, meticulously pleated and wrapped. My father helped me dress. I stood impatiently, shifting from one foot to the other, while he muttered, 'Stand still and stop wriggling, Rahul.'

Rani was wearing a beautiful sharara, covered with sequins and a lovely long dupatta which was transparent and had golden-thread-embroidered edges. My father wore a white silk dhoti-kurta. I wished I had his gold buttons set with diamonds, but with my history of losing things, it was out of the question for me to wear anything so expensive. Both my father and I looked like Bengali babus.

'Rahul, you look just like I used to at your age.' Baba ruffled my hair. I wriggled away, not wanting my carefully arranged hair to get messed up. I had worked very hard on setting my curl just right.

As we drove up to Banjara Hills, close to where Ranjan lived, I remembered Shubho and wished I could see him again. I hoped he would be at the wedding. I wanted to see him all dressed up—and I wanted him to see me in all my finery.

The wedding was being held in the garden of the Bella Vista Club, an exclusive establishment open only to members. As we drove through the gates of the club, the light globes on their posts shone a milky yellow-white light on us. The driveway and the road outside were full of cars, mostly Ambassadors and Fiats. There were a few American cars too—Chevrolets and Buicks. A Lincoln Continental sedan with dark glass windows, covered by strands of fragrant jasmine and rose, was parked to the side. This was the car the married couple would leave the ceremony in.

The pandal was a very large affair. Gaily coloured stripes and scalloped edges decorated it all over. Tall bamboo poles held it up in the centre and on all sides. These were secured to metal stakes in the ground with thick and sturdy ropes. The Durga Puja festival was also always held in a gigantic pandal like this. I looked around me with great interest. There were hundreds of guests, speaking in Bengali, English, Hindi, Urdu and other languages I could not recognize. I had never been surrounded by so many people dressed in such finery. The women and girls looked like brightly coloured songbirds, their gold, diamonds and rubies flashing. The men were dressed in dark suits and looked like sinister crows next to the women. The Bengali babus were dressed mostly in dhoti–kurta, the yards and yards of gold-embroidered silk making a swishing sound as they moved. Servile waiters in fine livery walked around with trays of drinks and food.

A band played at one end of the lawn, where some people were dancing to 'Come September'. The band members were dressed in velvet jackets with gold braid and the conductor waved his baton with a flourish.

'Where is Mallika Didi?' I asked my mother.

'Why don't you and Rani go and see? She is probably in the pandal, sitting by the fire. The wedding mantras started a while ago.'

'Come, Rahul.' Rani held my hand and we walked into the pandal. On the way, I stumbled and the carefully arranged accordion folds of my dhoti tumbled out—I almost lost half of my clothes right there.

'Clumsy,' Rani said, laughing at my embarrassment. 'Why don't you walk more carefully? Here, let me fix your dhoti.' Disaster averted, we continued walking.

We wove our way through the crowd sitting around the couple by the fire, in front of the purohit-moshai. The rotund priest was wearing only a dhoti and sweating profusely. His bald pate and body glistened in the light of the flames. At specific intervals, he would pour ghee into the fire, and the flames would leap higher each time he did this. The priest was supposed to be chanting Sanskrit hymns, but because he was Bengali and his accent was very strong, the mantras sounded like Bengali too.

'Look, there's Mallika Didi! Isn't she looking beautiful?' Rani clutched my arm and asked me in an excited whisper.

Mallika did make a beautiful figure, in a sari of red and gold like all Bengali brides. She had garlands of fragrant flowers around her neck and a delicate crown made of pith. I could not see her face, which was partially covered. She looked like the heroine of a film in her scarlet silk and brocade sari next to Sanjib, who was dressed in a silk dhoti–kurta. He was heavily garlanded and also wore a crown of ornately decorated pith with tassels hanging on each side of his face. Mallika and Sanjib were facing the fire together. I thought of Salim and felt sad. He should have been sitting next to Mallika.

Shyamala waved to us with a small flick of her hand. She was sitting very close to the couple, at hand to help out if needed. Anjali Mashi and Binesh Kaku were watching intently. Sanjib's parents sat by their son, looking overjoyed.

'Look, it's time for the Subhodrishti—the auspicious glance!' Ma whispered excitedly as she seated herself behind me. The auspicious glance was the part of the marriage ceremony where the bride and groom looked at each other for the very first time and made eye contact. This had been a custom from the time arranged marriages had started—in those days, the bride and the groom never met until the wedding as the elders in the family made all the decisions. This part of the ceremony was supposed to be very romantic and was loved by Bengalis.

The air smelt of burning ghee and incense. The bride and groom stood up and faced each other. The women of the family held a silk cloth, like a tent, over the heads of the couple. With both hands, Sanjib raised the end of Mallika's sari, which was covering her face, and revealed her downcast eyes. Mallika was beautifully made up, her forehead covered with an ornate lattice of sandalwood paste. Sanjib looked at her with impatience, waiting for her to raise her eyes and look into his for that special moment, but she did not. I looked at my mother in confusion. She looked shocked. The auspicious glance had been withheld by Mallika.

At the very end, the couple had to walk around the fire seven times.

The groom led and the bride followed, a corner of his shawl tied to the corner of her sari. As each round was made, the priest chanted sacred verses and threw more ghee into the fire. The slow progression around the fire was final and irrevocable. As they completed each circle, they cemented their togetherness in all worlds forever. My dreams for Mallika and Salim dimmed at the finality of these vows taken in our presence.

After the last of the mantras had been chanted, the bride and bridegroom sat on two special throne-like chairs that had been set up for them. Many guests and relatives milled around the wedded couple. Anjali Mashi was busy tending to her daughter and new son-in-law. She looked harried but happy. I ran up to the bride as soon as I could.

'Mallika Didi, Mallika Didi,' I yelled.

She looked up at me, but I could not see her face because the heavy brocade veil covered it. She held out her arms to me. I walked over to her and playfully put my head under the veil. I saw tears streaming down her face and she grabbed my arms. I was pulled away by a pair of strong, determined hands.

'Mallika Didi needs to rest,' Anjali Mashi said, firmly leading me away. 'Dinner is being served and it will get cold. Go join your parents and sister.'

In the Bengali tradition, the wedding dinner had countless courses. Dinner was served on plates made of dried leaves and the guests sat in a row on the floor on a folded carpet, cross-legged. A continuous stream of food servers came by and each had a bucket of steaming food. They stopped to serve at every plate and moved on to the next one. There was barely time to finish one course before the next one arrived. We started off with beguni, followed by chorchori, shukto, chholar dal with little bits of coconut and various curries. All of this was served with fragrant pulao, drizzled with ghee and full of raisins and cashews. Numerous fish dishes followed, each one cooked in a different sauce such as curd, or tomato and onions or mustard. Sweet tomato chutney acted as the palate cleanser between meals. The finale was the dessert, comprising sweetened curd, dark-brown and creamy, rosogolla, gulab jamun and payesh. 'Bas, bas!' the guests would say to indicate that they had eaten enough, but their pleas went unheeded and more and more food was heaped on our plates.

On our way out, I kept looking for Shubho, but was disappointed. Perhaps they had not been invited. Finally, we got into the car and drove home, feeling sleepy.

'Mallika did not return the Shubhodrishti,' my mother remarked to my father. 'That is an ill omen.'

My father did not respond.

Mallika left on her honeymoon the next day. I waited impatiently for her return. Now that the wedding was over, I hoped that I could have my old Mallika back so that we could celebrate the upcoming Durga Puja together, like old times.

'I ran into Colonel Sahib outside today,' my father told my mother as he came back from the garden where he had been picking flowers for his morning prayers.

I sat up in bed, listening carefully, my spirits lifting.

'So, he is finally back,' Ma said. 'He has been travelling a lot to Rajasthan lately to take care of his family estate. I have heard that he has a lot of land and that many villagers till his fields. The palace, I think, sits empty. It is very sad. At his age, he is alone—he should be with a wife and children and grandchildren. He must be a lonely man.'

I wanted to jump up and say that Colonel Uncle was not a lonely, sad man. In fact, he was full of life and seemed to enjoy living by himself upstairs. But I remained silent. To say anything would be admitting that he was my friend—and I was determined to keep our friendship to myself.

The phone rang. My father picked it up. 'Oh, Binesh Dada,' he said. 'Congratulations. I am sure you and Anjali Didi are sleeping peacefully now.' He listened for a moment and laughed. 'Oh, I am sure the marriage will be a success. Our children forget that we always know what is best for them. Mallika will thank you once she realizes what a terrible mistake she was going to make. Wait and see how much she will have changed after the honeymoon.' He laughed again, as if the honeymoon would work magical wonders. 'I am glad to hear the artists are here,' he said, moving to the subject dearest to the Bengali heart. 'The next month is going to be a busy one, preparing for Durga Puja. Okay, then ... bye.' As he hung up, he said to my mother, 'The artists have arrived from Bengal and will start work today.'

I knew what that meant and was filled with delicious anticipation. I leapt out of the bed in excitement.

'When are we going to the tailor to get new clothes?' Rani, who was already up, asked my father with her most beguiling smile.

'Yes, when? May I get the latest Rajesh Khanna jacket with the round neck? Please, please?' I begged, hanging on to his arm.

'Arre, stop pulling on my arm! How old are you? You are too old to be acting as if you are eight. Go brush your teeth and comb your hair. At your age, I never thought about fashion and films. I knew that I had to study hard and make my parents proud,' Baba said, shaking me off. Seeing my scowl, he added, 'Fine, we will get you your Rajesh Khanna jacket once I see the results of your tests. If you don't do well, you will not get any new clothes this year.'

Rani glared at me for ruining her efforts.

Annoyed and embarrassed, I walked to the bathroom to brush my teeth and get ready for breakfast. If my father was not satisfied with my school performance, this would be the first time ever that I would not get new clothes for Durga Puja. I looked at myself in the mirror and kicked the bathtub in frustration. Growing older meant that I could not take my life for granted any more. I would have to work hard to earn what I wanted. I could not wait until I was old enough to do what I wanted!

'Oh, I forgot. I have invited Colonel Sahib to tea today,' I heard my father say when I came back for breakfast. 'Do we have any snacks? He must be pining for home-cooked food. As a bachelor, he probably eats very little—and poorly too. I don't understand why he did not marry, even if it was late in life. Every man needs a woman to take care of him and the household. From time to time, do send some food upstairs.'

'I'll go and take him food,' I said before I could stop myself.

My father smiled approvingly. 'All right. You can take him food sometimes … when your mother asks you to. Remember that some people are old and lonely and need our company and kindness. I am very lucky to have your mother. Colonel Uncle is not so lucky.'

I had never considered Colonel Uncle in that light. How could he be unlucky when he was so wonderful? I was pondering this later that afternoon when the doorbell rang. Rani had gone to visit a classmate for a few hours, but I was waiting. I ran to the door and opened it before I was asked to. The air was redolent with the fragrance of jasmine blooming in the garden, and the humming of bees and dragonflies was a constant drone in the background. And there stood Colonel Uncle, smartly dressed in beige linen pants and a pale-blue bush shirt, open at the neck. He looked cool and comfortable in the early autumn weather. In his hand, he had a box of sweets from the best sweet shop in town—Goyal Mithai, the box said in bold red letters, and it was tied with a string of red silk and gold.

Colonel Uncle's face creased into smiles when he saw me. His eyes twinkled merrily. 'Hello, Rahul,' he said. 'We meet again!'

I gave him a shy but conspiratorial smile as my father came up behind me. 'Colonel Sahib. What a pleasure to see you! This is my son, Rahul. You remember him, don't you? He was a baby when you last saw him and brought Rani that wonderful kitchen set.'

'Yes, but I have met him upstairs since.'

'Really? Rahul, have you been bothering Colonel Uncle?' It was my mother. She had also come to the door and was leading us all into the sitting room.

'No, no, Bhabhiji,' Colonel Uncle said. 'Rahul is such a well-behaved and smart young man. It is always a pleasure to talk to him.'

'Still … Colonel Bhai, I don't want him disturbing you if you are not ready to have guests. I am sure you are busy with so many things. Come, please have a seat. So, how is the family estate in Rajasthan? I must say, you are looking fit and fine.' She sounded a little surprised, as if expecting to see a starving and ill Colonel Uncle who did not have anyone to take care of him.

'Everything is fine, Bhabhiji. Here are some sweets.' Colonel Uncle offered the box to my mother.

'Arre, Colonel Bhai, why do you insist on all this formality?'

'No formality, Bhabhiji. It is for this festive season. Also, I am celebrating some good news I got in a letter from an old friend yesterday.' Colonel Uncle's eyes brimmed with joy.

'Good news? Please share it with us,' my father requested.

'Oh, it is a letter from an old friend in Italy who wants me to visit. You know, it is always good to hear from old friends.'

Colonel Uncle did not give any more details, but I knew he was talking about Claudio. A stab of worry shot through me. Was Colonel Uncle going to leave us again?

'Are you going away again?' I could hardly keep the panic out of my voice.

'Listen to Rahul!' My father laughed. 'He does not want you to go, Colonel Sahib. He must be very fond of you.' He patted my head affectionately and I pulled away, trying to save my hair.

'You can always visit me anywhere I am in the world,' Colonel Uncle reassured me.

'Come, help me bring in the snacks,' my mother said before I could respond. I followed her into the kitchen. She arranged the samosas stuffed with fresh coconut meat, some Parle biscuits and great mounds of upma on the plates.

'I will carry the dishes out,' I announced.

'Yes, of course. Poor Colonel Uncle. All alone and a bachelor at his age.' Ma sighed. 'I know he will enjoy these snacks. I hope he has a cook who prepares his meals. Men of his generation are so useless in the kitchen.' She was still convinced that Colonel Uncle was to be treated with a great amount of compassion and sympathy, almost as if he had only one leg.

I took the dishes out into the sitting room and, then, all of a sudden, heard the dreaded words.

'Rahul does not play much sport, though he recently did join the football team. I hope he continues playing. I want him to be the captain of the football team next year, just like I was at his age. He has more of an artistic temperament.' Baba laughed self-consciously, as if to dispel his discomfort. 'He is not like the other, typical boys of his age. I transferred him to Hyderabad Royal Academy to make him more of a man, but there have been some unsavoury incidents there lately. As the Trustee of the Board of HRA, you must have heard about that boy Amit Puri ...'

I slowed my steps, listening to the conversation. So Colonel Uncle was on the Board of Trustees! This was news to me.

'Yes, I did hear about the case. I cannot say I agree with the way it was handled.'

'But Colonel Sahib, how else could they have handled it? I thought that the school would be a good environment for Rahul, but I am not sure any more. After all, ours is a good family and this kind of behaviour is unacceptable to all decent society. I heard the boy had been sent off to an institution to cure him of his illness with shock therapy. Sometimes, I think Rahul would be better off at a boarding school, but how do I protect him from such sickness in his environment?'

'No, Chatterjee Sahib, do not remove him from home at such a young age.'

'What to do? Nowadays, children are getting so many ideas. They do not respect and obey their elders like they used to ...' Baba broke off as he saw me approaching with the snacks.

I felt a wave of terror go through my body. Did my father suspect that I was different from the other boys? Was that why he kept talking about sending me to a boarding school? My letter to Rajesh Khanna came to my mind again and I was relieved that Baba would never see it. Then I thought of how I good it had felt to touch Shubho, to be kissed by him ... I deliberately put on a nonchalant expression.

'Let him be,' Colonel Uncle said. 'I used to be like him too.'

I wondered if Colonel Uncle would still be on my side if he knew what I had done.

'Arre, Colonel Sahib, I am sure you were quite the sportsman in your school. Careful, Rahul,' my father cautioned as I gingerly laid the tray on the table, my arms trembling a little from the rush of anxiety.

'Rahul is growing up to be a fine young man. He must make you all very proud,' Colonel Uncle said with a conspiratorial nod to me. His eyes twinkled.

Ma joined us. 'Please, Colonel Sahib, there is no formality. Do help yourself to more tea and snacks.'

'Bhabhiji, how can I say no?' Colonel Uncle took some more snacks on his plate.

'So, Colonel Sahib, what are you going to do with the huge estate you have in Rajasthan?' asked my father.

'I will leave it to the Wildlife Society Trust,' Colonel Uncle said. 'There are so many rare species of birds and animals in the tracts of the forest—I want to make sure that they are protected forever. It is my duty.'

'That is very generous, Colonel Sahib. But don't you have any nephews or nieces that you can leave the estate to?' asked Ma.

'Oh yes, I have nephews and nieces. But they are greedy and will sell the trees to the highest bidders and destroy the land that has been in my family for centuries. So they get nothing,' Colonel Uncle said firmly.

My parents looked shocked, though my heart swelled with pride when I heard that Colonel Uncle was going to take care of the creatures that lived on his land. The conversation meandered on and I sat there with a big smile on my face. I was also very happy that Colonel Uncle had stood up for me.

'Look at Rahul.' My mother laughed. 'I have not seen him so happy in a long time. Colonel Sahib, you must come again.'

'I will, Bhabhiji. Thank you for inviting me.'

I smiled, delighted that Colonel Uncle was back from his trip. I did not feel so alone any more.

Too soon, his visit was over and he left amidst promises to visit again soon.

'Rahul, visit me sometime when you are free. And do bring Rani with you too,' he said to me as he left.

'Rahul, you never told me that you have been visiting Colonel Uncle,' Ma said half-admonishingly. 'I will send him some food through you soon.'

'He is a fine gentleman. I am sure he will teach you many things that he learnt in the military, like discipline and how to be a strong leader and a tough man,' Baba said.

I was glad that I did not have to hide my friendship with Colonel Uncle any longer. I had no intention of telling them when I would go upstairs, however. That would be my secret.

For the next two weeks, the midterm tests kept me busy. I scored top marks this time, even in algebra. Durga Puja was only a fortnight away.

'Well done, Rahul.' Baba smiled as he saw my tests results. 'We can go this Saturday to buy fabrics for your new clothes.'

Since all our clothes would be tailored, we would also have to go visit our family tailor. We had already decided what clothes we would be getting that year. And then, finally, we would get to visit Mallika.

First we had to go to Khairatabad Market because my mother wanted us to get vegetables and meat. Parking the car by the wayside, we walked carefully, avoiding puddles of water and excrement.

We visited the vegetable section first. The vegetable sellers were too poor to own stalls. They sat by the roadside, a tattered piece of cloth covered with onions, potatoes, ginger, squashes, gourds, tomatoes and other vegetables in front of them. An unwelcome sight awaited us as we neared Mohammed, our favourite vegetable vendor. Mrs Khosla, planted firmly in front of him, was flapping her arms as she argued shrilly.

'Nahin, nahin …' She was disagreeing with Mohammed and cut him short as we walked up.

'Namaste, Mrs Khosla.' My father greeted her with folded hands.

Rani and I looked at her in dismay and revulsion.

Mrs Khosla's cheeks quivered indignantly as she complained to my father: 'Mr Chatterjee, this man thinks I am a fool. What do these low-class and dishonest people think we are? Rich? He thinks he can charge whatever he wants from us hard-working people …' she broke off as she saw Rani and me approach. 'Hello, Rahul and Rani.

What has happened to your manners? Don't you want to say namaste to your Khosla Aunty?' She sounded hurt, as if we were the best of friends. In a moment, the vicious tone returned as she turned to Mohammed to say, 'Fifty paise a kilo. No more.' Mohammed was stunned. He would barely break even at that price.

Annoyed, my father had already turned to us in embarrassment. 'What has happened to you children? Don't you know how to show respect to your elders?'

'Namaste, Khosla Aunty,' we chorused reluctantly.

Rani squeezed my hand in warning. Suresh Khosla had clearly inherited his mother's beady eyes and scowl, along with her bad temper and meddling ways—I could see the resemblance.

'Memsahib, jo marzi aye de do,' Mohammed said, giving up the fight. He was tired of haggling with her. 'Hum gareeb hain, aapki dua hain,' he added softly.

Mrs Khosla was unmoved by his plea. 'Fifty paise,' she said again.

Mohammed sighed and placed the vegetables on one pan and the weights on the other.

'Ruko, ruko.' Mrs Khosla stopped him, asking him to show that the scales were not loaded.

'Memsahib kya bharosa nahin karte?' Mohammed said. He sighed again and removed the weights and the vegetables. Some vendors loaded their scales—not Mohammed, whose honesty made him Baba's favourite vendor.

Mrs Khosla carefully watched Mohammed weigh the potatoes and place them in a bag made from old newspaper. She grunted as she took the bag and carelessly flung a fifty paise coin at him, turning away before Mohammed had completed his gesture of thanks. 'I don't know what this world is coming to,' she grumbled to my father. 'The prices keep going up all the time. We still have to feed our children, no? And then there is the price of the books.' She leaned in close to my father, demanding a response.

'Yes, Mrs Khosla, what to do?' Baba agreed, shrinking back as we smirked.

Warming up, Mrs Khosla blocked our access to Mohammed and proceeded to discuss other matters on her mind. 'And then the education these days. I tell you, there is hardly any discipline. At least no one can say I did not raise my Suresh properly. Mrs Joshi, the principal, said that if it had not been for him ...' She paused and, looking at us, leaned over to my father and whispered something in his ear.

'I know. I heard. If my son did something like that, I would not be able to show my face in public either. Chhee, chhee!' Baba responded.

I knew what they were talking about. Had Suresh Khosla said something about me to his mother too? She would surely encourage him to make trouble for me. I nervously clenched my icy hands, praying that she would go away.

'Well, Mrs Puri is never going to be in the PTA again. I am going to make sure of that,' Mrs Khosla said with a virtuous nod of her head. I stared at her with burning resentment. The blackheads on her nose were showing through her make-up in the heat. She fanned herself with her plump hand, diamonds glittering on her rings. 'I saw your children the other day, you know,' she said. 'With Mr Bannerjee's daughter Mallika. I was surprised to see them alone with her. I don't know if you heard, but ...' Mrs Khosla again lowered her voice and whispered something into my father's ear.

I looked at Rani's pale face. We were both wondering if Mrs Khosla was going to get us into trouble.

'Oh no, no, Mrs Khosla,' Baba said, shaking his head. 'I am sure Mr Khosla was mistaken when he saw Mallika in the college café. She is a very good girl and got married just a few days ago. No, she was not mixing with anyone of bad character.'

Disappointed that she had not uncovered any fresh gossip, Mrs Khosla looked at the diminutive watch encircling her fat wrist and exclaimed, 'Oh, Mr Chatterjee! It is later than I thought. Don't let these dishonest people cheat you. Always pay a fair price, no more, no less!'

I was relieved when she left, cutting a swathe through the crowd with her ample figure.

'See how people talk?' Baba said to us. 'Always remember, if you do anything to shame our family, people will talk and we will have to hide our face in decent society.'

After paying Mohammed the price he asked, we left with our shopping bags full of the freshest potatoes, onions, sprigs of coriander and mint, ginger, garlic, green onions, hot green chillies and coconut.

'I don't want to go to the butcher's shop,' I said, remembering how horrible the carcasses had looked when I was there last.

'You are a young man now, Rahul. It is time you learnt not to be squeamish,' Baba insisted.

There were several stalls selling meat. A sawed-off tree trunk served as a chopping block in each stall. There were great iron meat cleavers on these blocks. Behind the butcher were rows of goat carcasses, hung by their hind legs. Depending on the portion requested, butchers reached behind them and carved off a section of meat. The tissue, lining and fat were still attached to the meat. I smelt the stomach lining and raw meat, freshly skinned, and felt nauseous.

'I think I will vomit,' I said as I looked upon a sight that I would never forget. There was a line of severed goat heads—black, dappled, white and in other colours, with eyes that were black, brown or yellow—staring at me balefully, their mouths twisted in a frozen grimace of death. Then I saw some live goats tethered next to the butcher's stall and got really upset.

'What must those poor goats be feeling?' I whispered to Rani.

She turned her face away and so did I while my father ordered some choice cuts. I knew I would not eat meat again.

And then we finally went to the fabric shop, where Rani picked out sequinned and embroidered silk while I had to pick out boring men's prints.

'It is not fair,' I complained. 'You have all the fun clothes.'

'Why don't you wear my frocks and pinafores?' Rani laughed. 'In fact, you should stay at home and cook in the kitchen with Ma, wearing a sari …'

'Rani is right. Rahul, you must start behaving like a young man,' Baba said, his mouth pursed in disgust. 'Or else people will say things about you that no person should mention in decent society.'

If Colonel Uncle could help out in the kitchen, I could too, I thought smugly, even as I knew that if my father found out what I had been doing, he would be terribly concerned.

We drove to Charminar, the ornate gateway adorned with four minarets that had been built hundreds of years ago. The air was hot and polluted in this old part of Hyderabad. It was a Muslim neighbourhood. Our family tailor—wizened and stooped, with a pair of thick spectacles—lived here, as his family had for generations. He was happy to see us always and, after taking our measurements, promised to tailor our clothes in the latest styles, as we had requested. By this time, I was beside myself with impatience to see Mallika. I wondered where Salim was at that moment. Did he know that Mallika was already married?

Once again, we drove across town to Banjara Hills and I pined for Shubho—I had not seen him in ages. I wished I could go to see him and breathe in his warm male smell again. Feelings of sadness mixed with the excitement of seeing Mallika again as we approached her new home.

Sanjib lived with his parents in a small, charming bungalow. The chowkidar jumped to attention and opened the wooden gate for us when we drove up. It was like stepping into an arboreal haven. The lawn was well-maintained, there were flowers blooming in geometrically precise beds and birds twittered in the well-tended trees. The sun was setting in the horizon and the evening was peaceful here, far from the bustle of the old city. An Ambassador was parked in front of the house.

We jumped out of the car even before it had stopped fully and raced to the door. We pressed the doorbell and I hopped impatiently, ready to ring the bell again. I was waiting for Mallika to come to the door, elegantly dressed as usual. Instead, it was Sanjib's father who opened the door.

'Nomoshkar, Ganguly Babu,' my father said from behind us.

'Nomoshkar, Uncle,' Rani and I repeated.

'Nomoshkar. Arre, why are you standing outside? Come inside. Have some tea. Sanjib, Bouma! Come and see who is visiting,' he called out to his son and daughter-in-law.

We were welcomed into a sitting room lit with tube lights. The furniture was old but nice. There were lots of pictures of Sanjib in frames—Sanjib as a baby, Sanjib as a toddler, Sanjib in various stages of growing up, more recent pictures of Sanjib, including a large one of him with Mallika. Her face was decorated with sandalwood dots and she was covered in garlands of flowers as she looked down demurely. I remembered the last time I had seen her, when I had hugged her after the Shubhodrishti, and my heart grew heavy.

The curtains parted and Sanjib came in, looking very severe. He was wearing a white cotton kurta–pyjama and those wretched Bata sandals with thick straps that all Bengali babus wore. He was quiet and respectful to my father as he greeted him, dismissive towards us. The smell of fish frying filled the air, flavoured with the pungent aroma of panch-phoron seasoning. Smoke from the incense sticks favoured by all Bengali households, Sugandha Shringar, also wafted through the curtains.

'How was the honeymoon?' My father's voice held a hint of teasing.

Sanjib put his head down, looking embarrassed, and said, 'It was wonderful, Mesho. We had a really good time. But Mallika was a little tired and ill most of the time. I wanted her to go with me and see the sunrise on Tiger Hill, but she did not accompany me.' He sounded a little resentful.

'I think the stress of the wedding and the travelling was too much for Bouma. Sanjib, you must be a little patient with her. After all, she is in a new home,' Sanjib's father said.

I could hardly contain my impatience to see Mallika any more. I expected to see her come floating through the curtain, ethereal, light, dressed in another exquisite summer frock, her legs and feet slender and bare, her nails perfectly painted.

The rustle of a sari indicated that Sanjib's mother was on her way. The curtain parted. A woman came through with her head covered.

'Nomoshkar, Mashima.' I jumped up with my hands folded and head slightly bowed.

'Rahul, Rani!' The voice was unmistakably melodious. It was

Mallika. I stared at her in shock. She looked happy to see us, but spoke in a measured tone I had never heard before. She was wearing a cotton sari with a brightly patterned border. She bent down and touched my father's feet.

'Shukhe thako,' Baba said, blessing her and wishing conjugal peace and happiness.

I was taken by surprise yet again. Mallika had never touched my father's feet or covered her head before.

She sat down rather demurely near me, her head still covered, the border of the sari framing her beautiful face. She looked like someone else—with her hair severely pulled back, a broad streak of sindur in the parting, her wrists covered with gold bangles and bracelets made of shell. The white of the conch shell bracelets was startling against her smooth brown wrists.

She held out her arms to me and said, 'Come here, Rahul.'

I reluctantly walked over to this strange, new Mallika and was hugged by her. I was acutely conscious that I was in the presence of strangers. The cotton sari felt hard and starchy on my bare legs, scratching them. Mallika's body felt foreign, swathed in so much cloth. She held me tightly, as if I were the only connection to the old life she had. I looked at her, but the edge of the sari hiding her face was like a barrier between us.

'So, how are you, Rahul?' she asked as I disengaged myself and sat down next to her. 'Look at you. Growing into a young man already, taller, and all this new fuzz on your face! Are you still reading Enid Blyton books? I miss playing board games with you.' She sounded strained, unused to having a conversation with me in front of Sanjib and his father.

'Fine, Mallika Didi,' I said stiffly as my voice cracked, fully aware that everyone could hear me. 'I am reading …'

I was interrupted by Sanjib's voice. 'Get them some cha, Mallika,' he ordered imperiously, just like I had heard Mallika's father order her about.

I wanted to talk to her about everything that had happened—about the mangoes and Colonel Uncle and Salim. But I sat there, not speaking a word, in that sitting room, with Sanjib, his father, Baba and Rani, as Mallika got up and walked with measured steps towards the back of the house, obedient and docile.

'Tell Sanjib Dada what you want to do when you grow up,' Baba prompted me, beaming proudly.

'An aeronautical engineer,' I said, the words sounding false and hollow.

'Very good,' Sanjib said approvingly as he turned to my father to say something about melting metals in the foundry.

Mallika soon came back with a tray in her hands, cups of steaming hot tea, Parle Gluco biscuits, sandesh and masala-coated peanuts piled upon it. Mallika served her father-in-law first, then my father, then Sanjib, and then, finally, Rani and me, following the hierarchy of age. I kept quiet and watched her going through the motions—it felt as though Mallika was there not as herself but acting out the role of a newlywed Bengali bride, with me as her audience.

'So, Mallika, are you going to finish your last year at college?' my father asked.

'Yes, I would love to. Then I can get a job ...' Mallika brightened up and sounded enthused for the first time, but Sanjib cut in and spoke for her.

'We are thinking of having a child soon. And then Mallika will be very busy. Besides, she does not need to work. By the grace of God, I have a good income.'

Mallika's face dimmed again. The awkward silence that followed was punctuated only by the clinking of tea cups on saucers as we ate the snacks, with nothing to say.

'Well, it is later than I realized,' Baba said suddenly.

I jumped up gratefully and we left after the required farewell greetings.

'Why was Mallika Didi so quiet? And why was she dressed in that heavy sari?' I asked my father. 'She never wore saris at home before.'

'Bengali brides wear saris. Unless Sanjib allows her to wear frocks or salwar–kameez, that is what she will wear. It is not respectful to the in-laws to talk too much or jump around like an unmarried girl. You must not expect your Mallika Didi to run around with you like she used to. You will understand all this when both of you grow up and get married.'

I looked at Rani's stricken face in silence.

One evening a couple of weeks later, my father showed up with a large package wrapped in newspaper. We always knew when our freshly tailored clothes arrived because the print would be in Urdu, not English or Hindi.

'Rani, Rani!' I yelled at the top of my voice as it broke with excitement. 'Our clothes have arrived.' My voice had started breaking a lot and I could control it best when I spoke in a low tone. I repeated in a lower octave, 'Our clothes have arrived.'

I tried to undo the knot that held the package, but it got tighter. I started ripping at the newspaper.

'Please don't behave as if you have never seen new clothes before in your life, Rahul,' Rani admonished me, all lady-like as she got a pair of scissors and cut the knot. She opened the package with deliberate and maddening slowness. I could not wait to see the clothes.

Oh, the joy of seeing the Rajesh Khanna jacket—folded and ironed, the smell of new cloth, the newly sewed-on buttons, the stiff collar— was almost too much to bear. I shook out the jacket, held it against my body and ran to the mirror to look. I loved it. It was silky and creamy and elegant, just as I had imagined it. A few bits of thread still clung to the cloth—Hussain Sahib had missed them in his final cleaning—but I didn't care. I looked at the stitches and the hem— they were perfect! I turned my eyes to the shirts and trousers and was thrilled anew. I could not wait to wear them.

Rani, having abandoned her lady-like manners, was hooting with joy as she danced around the table with her shararas.

'You better take me to the sari shop,' my mother said to my father in a mock-threatening voice. He had already received his Puja clothes. They had been sent to him from Calcutta by our relatives. My mother would get a selection of saris—rich silks from South India, finely woven cottons from Bengal or voiles from Bombay—

from her favourite shops on Abid Road.

'Yes, ma'am,' my father said, playing along.

I generally loved this time of year. Everyone was excited and happy, ready to banter and have fun. The year before, Mallika and I had taken two servings of prasad one day. The prasad was distributed at the end of each day and the portions were substantial. But we had wanted more and had accepted prasad from two different people to get double helpings. At the back of the tent, we had hurriedly stuffed our mouths, choking with laughter.

But this year, despite the new clothes and my excitement about them, I knew that things would be different. In spite of the gaiety and sweets and celebrations, everything had changed. Mallika would be with Sanjib. I would be alone.

11

Sunday Evening. San Francisco.

The log in the fireplace had burnt down to a few dying embers. I had not noticed that the apartment was almost dark. The fog-shrouded darkness outside muffled the rumble of the cable cars. They were running at thirty–minute intervals due to the Sunday-evening slowdown. Shrouded in shadow, Andrew's face was inscrutable. I looked at him, searching for a sign that he was opening up to me again. But all I could see were his eyes, staring at the fireplace, deep in thought and reflecting the fading light.

'Let me turn on the lamp. It's too dark in here.' I got up and stretched. Andrew did the same. I turned on the lamp in the corner and set the thermostat to heat the apartment.

Andrew went to the bathroom and came out a few minutes later.

'Want a glass of Pinot?' I asked, knowing that he seldom said no to his favourite wine.

'Sure. As long as you have one too.'

I took this as a good sign. Pouring out two glasses, I handed him one and set mine down on a table. I removed the fireguard and put a fresh log in the fireplace. As I blew on the embers, the dry log caught fire and soon a warm blaze lit up the room. I placed another log on top of the first one, replaced the fireguard and then sat down next to Andrew.

'Cheers.'

'Cheers.'

After staring at the fire for a few minutes, Andrew looked at me. 'You know, Rahul, it is hard to imagine how women's lives change once they get married in your country. It is not as if they are being denied education or a fair upbringing. But what is the point of that if it is all going to change after marriage? I mean, giving up one's profession, education, dreams ... is so *unfair*. And then being forced to go live with a man she has never met must be so traumatic. What if the man turns out to be a jerk or have an intolerable personality? Living with strangers and in-laws could be hellish!'

I laughed. 'Some things are universal. Of course in-laws are tyrannical. That is the pecking order. The in-laws torment the weak new bride. After they die, the no-longer-new bride becomes the matriarch and repeats the cycle all over again.'

The log suddenly crackled with an explosive sound. I jumped, my knee pushing against Andrew's, and he almost spilt his wine.

'Whoa ... steady!' he said.

'Sorry. That took me by surprise,' I apologized. It was time for me to return to my tale. 'There is a lot to tell you still ...'

October 1973. Hyderabad.

Durga Puja arrived in late October, and I greeted it with mixed feelings. On the day before the formal installation of the idols, Baba took Rani and me to see the statues of Goddess Durga and her children at the pandal. When we got there, the finishing touches were being applied. The artists were hard at work in the glare of spotlights. Bare-bodied and sweating, dressed in dhotis shortened and tightened around the knees, they were adjusting the hair, jewellery and clothes of the idols. We stared in awe and admiration.

On the first day of the puja, at the installation, the gods were welcomed in a special ceremony at the altar. The festival was too important and too big to be ignored, even for Hyderabad Royal Academy, which was closed for the last three of the five days of celebration.

The first two days of Shasthi and Saptami led up to Mahashtami, which was the main day of worship. On Saptami, I raced home after school and did not have to do any homework. Like most Bengalis, we waited for Mahashtami to go to offer our prayers. On that day, we rose early and, after a quick vegetarian breakfast, went to the site of the puja. There was a pile of slippers and shoes at the entrance to the pandal and we left ours there too. Men in billowing white dhoti–kurtas and women in flowing tussore silk saris with red borders sat on the carpet. The women's feet were painted with alta, the traditional red stripe of colour that bordered the base of the foot in a thick line. Children in new clothes ran all around as the priest recited prayers.

The sacred chants rose to a crescendo, leading to the Pushpanjali, the offering of flowers to the gods, as the dhakis drummed a hypnotic and pulsating beat on their dhaks. Fragrant smoke from burning frankincense billowed through the pandal. Durga was flanked by her family. Ganesh looked placid and benevolent like his two sisters. But it was Kartik's sculpted body and handsome face that caught my eye—I stared at him, at the line of his belt around his slim hips, and then turned my eyes away, feeling ashamed of my desire for an idol.

Women blew on conch shells, producing a soulful chorus. Other women chorused '*Ooloolooloo!*', a wailing ululation that went on and on, creating harmonious vibrations in the air. Men danced in the space before the idols, stripped to the waist. Their sinuous bodies, shining with sweat and gyrating to the beats of the dhak, entranced me. They held in each hand earthen lamps, filled with burning coals and topped with smouldering, frankincense-sprinkled coconut coir that glowed and crackled, producing thick clouds of smoke. Faster and faster the drums beat, and faster and faster the dancers moved. My breath caught in my throat as I looked on, my heart in my mouth. The dancers would be burnt if any of the coals fell from the brimming lamps, but they continued undaunted, their moves skilled, confident and graceful. Through the thick haze, I could see the goddess, primeval, ferocious yet protective, frozen in the moment of her triumph over evil.

'It is now time for the pushpanjali.'

The same purohit-moshai had led the prayers for as long as I could remember. He was short and rotund, his bald head shining with perspiration, his sacred thread stretched tight across his protruding belly. Tufts of hair sprouted from his shoulders and back, his ears and nostrils and above his eyes.

As was customary, the priest made offerings of incense, sweets, saris and other choice items to propitiate Ma Durga. Then a big basket of flowers was passed around. We each took a few and then repeated the mantras chanted by the priest three times.

'Say your prayers to Ma,' the priest said to us all. 'She will grant all your desires and prayers. Think of what you want for yourself and for those you love and care about.'

I thought of Mallika and Salim. I thought of my secrets and how different I felt from everyone. 'Please, Ma Durga.' My silent prayers were fast and furious, the words a jumble in my head. 'Please let Mallika Didi and Salim be together and protect me from getting into trouble for wanting to touch Shubho Dada and not being first in class. And please don't let anyone find out about the evening with him in the changing room.' I paused and looked at Ma Durga's loving face and whispered quietly, into my folded hands, 'And please let me be with Shubho Dada again.' I thought of what the priest had promised—surely the goddess would understand, even if no one else did?

'Come on, let's go and have the prasad. Oh look there's Mallika Didi!' Rani prodded me with her elbow. As I turned around to go with her, I saw that Mallika was with Sanjib and his parents. Mr and Mrs Ganguly walked ahead of the two, who were in deep conversation, and Sanjib was gesturing emphatically at Mallika. Her head was only partly covered, so I could see her face. She was biting her lip and her hands were twisting the fabric of her sari as she said something. Sanjib's face was grim and he did not look at her even once. He seemed oblivious to our presence and it was only when they were almost upon us that he put on a polite mask.

'Rahul, Rani!' Mallika exclaimed. Her face lit up and she hugged us hard.

'Go show your respect to your elders and get their blessings,' my father instructed us.

We walked over dutifully and greeted them with folded hands, heads bowed to show our respect. 'Nomoshkar, Uncle and Aunty,' Rani and I said together, as my father nodded approvingly. We reluctantly greeted Sanjib, even though I did not want to do anything nice for him.

'Come visit me soon. I will be visiting Ma and Baba at the end of the month,' Mallika said to us. I was elated. I could not bear to see her in a sari, so reserved and quiet, and looked forward to playing Snakes and Ladders with her and eating tuar dal and rice, just like before. Ma Durga would surely hear my prayers—the priest had promised.

'We are going to bow to the goddess,' Sanjib said to us curtly, and he and Mallika left. I saw them prostrate themselves at the feet of the goddess. After they had paid their respects, Mallika made an impatient gesture with her hands and walked away. She made her way to a far corner of the tent and sat down, facing away from the crowd, and opened her purse, looking for something. Sanjib strode after her and sat down next to her.

My parents, Rani and Sanjib's parents were busy in conversation, so I slipped away. Standing a little distance from Sanjib and Mallika, I strained hard to hear what they were saying.

'I cannot take this any more,' Mallika said, her voice breaking. 'I will tell them … about what you did to me last night. If you beat me again, I will tell them everything … the unspeakable things you have done …'

My heart racing, I moved closer.

'If you dare say a word, I will divorce you. I will tell them that you are still having an affair with that Muslim bastard. They will believe me, just wait and see.'

'You are truly a monster—threatening me in front of Ma Durga!'

Sanjib laughed a nasty laugh. 'We'll see who will marry Shyamala once there is a divorcee in your family.'

He moved closer to Mallika—to the world, they probably looked like a newly married couple enjoying a little chat. But I heard Mallika's sari rustle and then her sharp exclamation of pain. There was the tinkle of bangles breaking and falling to the ground.

'Oh, look what you have done!' Mallika's voice was simmering with anger and hurt and was louder now. 'My favourite bangles from Abid Road, they are in pieces!'

'Come on. Let's get back to my parents,' Sanjib said curtly. 'No more nonsense and hysterics. Or I will have to teach you a lesson again tonight.'

As they left, I crept to the corner and picked up the pieces of broken bangles one by one. Then I quietly rejoined my family. No one except Rani had missed me.

'Where did you go?' she hissed through her teeth. And then, after taking a good look at me, she whispered, 'What happened? You look as if you are going to cry.'

'Tell you later,' I said quickly.

'Well, I am starving. Let us go and eat prasad. I was waiting for you to come.'

I looked around to see if Mallika was going to join us, but she had disappeared. Sanjib was waving at his parents, asking them to join him, so they left too. Then my parents, Rani and I moved to the area where the prasad was being served. It was a delicious meal—hot khichuri, different vegetable curries, fruits and sweets, served in leaf plates. We sat on the carpet that covered the grassy field inside the tent and ate our prasad. For the first time ever, however, I did not enjoy the meal. Instead, I played the scene I had witnessed over and over again in my head.

On the way home, Rani and I sat silent in the car.

'Did Anjali Didi say anything to you?' I heard my mother ask my father.

'No,' Baba replied. 'I did talk to Binesh, though.'

'Did he say anything?'

'About what?'

'About the marriage, you know.'

'Why? Did Anjali say anything to you?' my father asked.

'No, she was very quiet, very preoccupied.'

'So what? You are imagining things. I am sure she only misses her daughter.'

'My intuition is telling me something else. I don't think Mallika is happy.'

'Wouldn't she tell us if something was wrong?'

'No, I don't think so. Remember, they forced her to marry that boy.'

'Well … we all saw Mallika with Sanjib and his parents at the pandal,' Baba remarked. 'It is not as if she is housebound.'

'And?'

'And what?'

'Did you notice anything strange? You did say Mallika was very quiet when you visited her. She seemed very quiet to me too.'

'All brides are supposed to respect their in-laws and not talk much in front of them. Sanjib did seem a little stern, though.'

'I am telling you, something is not right.'

And then we were home. The car idled by the gates as they swung open slowly. I heard them close behind us with a loud metallic clang, then the sentries clicked their heels in attention and we drove up the long driveway. A canopy of darkness shrouded the drive. The wind whispered secrets I could not understand.

On Dashami, the last day of the pujas, the idols of the goddess and her children were immersed into water, symbolizing that she was being sent back to her husband's home. We duly went to bid her and her children farewell for the year. Mallika too had left for her husband's home after her wedding—would she also come home just once a year for a few brief days, before leaving again? I wondered sadly about this, watching the spectacle as, with heaving cries, the statues of Ma Durga, Lakshmi, Saraswati, Ganesh and Kartik were borne aloft on the shoulders of devoted volunteers and then loaded on to a lorry. Surrounded by a throng of devotees, the lorry slowly inched its way through crowded streets and open boulevards towards the river. Drummers drummed and the dancers deftly weaved in and out of the crowds of people gathered on the road to watch the procession. Huge plumes of fragrant smoke rose from the lamps they held. The procession slowly weaved through town. When it reached the river, the faithful lifted up the gods and goddesses and slowly took them down to the bank. The priests chanted mantras, amidst which the idols were immersed in the water, one by one. It was a lesson in detachment, I thought, to watch the hard work of the artists, the beautiful decorations, saris and jewellery, all disintegrating and flowing away in the fast-moving currents of the water, swirling into the dusk. And so, to the sound of women ululating and the melody of conch shells, the goddess returned to her husband's home for another year.

It was a few days after Durga Puja when Mallika finally visited her parents.

'When is Mallika Didi coming back?' I asked my mother every day in the meantime.

'She is not coming back, Rahul,' Ma explained patiently. 'In the future, your Mallika Didi will visit her mother's home for just a short while.'

Hearing her old home referred to as her mother's home sounded as unfamiliar as thinking of Mallika as Sanjib's wife. It was as if the old Mallika was a person of the past, someone who had left, never to return. Everyone now acted as if she was Mrs Sanjib Ganguly, a new person altogether, who would dress like a Bengali bride and act and talk like a Bengali daughter-in-law and wife. I wondered if Rani would turn into a stranger as well when she married a boy chosen by my parents. And when they picked a bride for me, would they want her to leave her old life behind and turn into someone else too? Would I be expected to act like a Bengali babu like Sanjib?

At last we made plans to go see Mallika when she visited her parents. I was impatient throughout the day we were going to see her. Classes seemed to go on forever and Shubho was his usual distant self when I saw him during football practice from the edge of the field. I longed for him to put his arms around me again, but I was never alone with him nowadays. He was always with his classmates and just waved to me casually when he saw me. Anyway, when I finally got home that day, I quickly changed into my drainpipe pants and the shirt with extra-long collars like Rajesh Khanna had worn in *Dil Daulat Duniya*. I arranged my hair carefully as well. I wanted to dress nicely for Mallika. I wanted it to be just like the old times. She would be in her summer frock, her hair smelling sweet and flowing down to her waist. We would play Snakes and Ladders and she would feed me tuar dal with fragrant basmati rice and melted butter.

I could not wait.

We got into the car and my father drove us all to Mallika's house. The chowkidars opened the gate for us. I looked at them and felt a wave of anger rise within me again—I could not forget Salim's bruised and swollen face.

At the door, I heard loud voices. My parents were walking behind me and could not hear the commotion. I hesitated for a moment, looking at Rani, who raised her finger to her lips, asking me to be quiet and try to listen. We could hear Binesh Kaku's demanding voice booming as Mallika's shrill voice responded, defiant.

'Ring the doorbell, Rahul,' my mother said, seeing me just standing there. 'Don't you want to see your Mallika Didi?'

I reluctantly rang the bell. The voices, which had been getting louder, stopped abruptly. I heard someone run up the stairs and the sound of a door slamming.

Binesh Kaku opened the door, his face mottled. He looked angrily at me for a second.

'Nomoshkar, Binesh Kaku,' I said timidly.

Binesh Kaku grunted in reply and then granted me a tight smile when he saw my parents and Rani.

'Where is Mallika Didi?' I asked.

'She is upstairs. She will be down soon,' Anjali Mashi said, coming up behind her husband. 'Mallika!' she called out loud, smiling at me and looking slightly relieved. 'Look who has come to see you.'

We went into the sitting room. There were newly framed pictures on the table of Mallika and Sanjib, taken at their wedding. Mallika's face was almost hidden—she was swathed in silk and brocade and garlands. Then there were the family pictures, taken with the parents of the bride and groom. Everyone else looked overjoyed, but Mallika's face had not even the hint of a smile.

'So, Binesh—one daughter married off, one to go,' my father joked.

'God willing, Dada, your Rani and our Shyamala will also be fortunate enough to get good husbands,' Binesh Kaku said.

Rani and Shyamala looked aghast.

I heard Mallika's familiar footsteps coming down the stairs before she came in. She was wearing a blue salwar-kameez with embroidered sleeves that came down to her wrists. In the old days, she would have been wearing a sleeveless summer frock on an evening like this. But her hair was down, just like before, and I could recognize my Mallika the way she used to be. She was not the docile, stilted new bride here, she looked more at ease.

'Nomoshkar,' she said to my parents in a flat voice. 'Rani, Rahul. How lovely to see you!' I realized then that her smile was strained and did not light up her eyes. They looked puffy and red, like she had been crying.

'Doesn't she look lovely?' Anjali Mashi said quickly. 'Oh, the honeymoon days are the best!'

I jumped up from the sofa and ran to Mallika. She gave me a big hug and held me tightly for a moment and, finally, I saw the smile reach her eyes.

'Oh, Rahul. How are you? I have missed you. You have to tell me all about school, the books you've been reading … and everything you have been up to!'

I beamed. 'Mallika Didi, let's go play Snakes and Ladders.' I was anxious to get back our special ritual.

Mallika took me by the hand and we went up the stairs. I heard Shyamala say, 'Rani, let's go upstairs and practise the lines from our play.' Shyamala and Rani were in the school play that year. They followed us upstairs.

Once we reached her room and shut the door, Mallika sat down on the bed, her face in her hands, a picture of despair. I went to her and knelt on the floor, my head in her lap, my arms around her legs.

'We heard shouting when we first came. What happened?' asked Rani in a low voice.

'I gave Mallika Didi Salim's letter and told her what happened when Salim came here,' Shyamala explained.

Mallika looked up, her eyes flashing. Her voice quaked with fury and unshed tears. 'I found out what Baba did. Damn, damn, damn! Why did Salim come here? I told him not to. I hoped he would understand that we could not be together. It is too late now anyway. I should have run away before the marriage.

'Ma and Baba tried to convince me that the right thing to do would be to marry Sanjib, but all they wanted was to save the family reputation. Oh, God, Sanjib is so different from Salim! He has a horrible temper and even his parents are scared of him. He wants a good, Bengali, village girl who will obey his commands, like his mother obeys her husband. He won't even let me finish college. My life is over! I had such dreams … Now, all I am is Mrs Sanjib Chatterjee, a bloody housewife, and a beaten one at that,' Mallika finished bitterly and broke into sobs.

We all put our arms around her and held her until she calmed down. Her sobs finally subsided. Rani and Shyamala were in tears too, and so was I. It was so hard to see my beloved Mallika suffer like this. I had never seen her cry before—it was heart-rending. This was just like the scene from *Bobby*, when the lovers find out that they can't be together. Except, in the movie, they miraculously survived the jump over the waterfall. But this was real life and Mallika was married and she and Salim would never be together. There was no generous parent waiting on the other side of the rapids, repenting past harshness and finally accepting the lovers.

'Mallika, come downstairs with the other children for some jol-khaabar,' called Anjali Mashi.

'Go on downstairs. Tell them I am in the bathroom and will be down in a minute,' Mallika said urgently. 'I need to splash some water on my face and blow my nose.'

We quickly went downstairs. Anjali Mashi was very quiet, and so was my mother. Anjali Mashi's eyes looked red and weepy like my mother's—I could always tell when my mother had been crying. I wondered if Anjali Mashi wished that she had let Mallika marry Salim. But then, why would she be sad about the marriage when she was so happy about it earlier? Binesh Kaku and my father did most of the talking as the meal was served, oblivious to the fact that their wives were very quiet. Anjali Mashi had made us a mini-feast, but I had lost my appetite. I could think of little else other than Mallika's raw grief and tears. Mallika entered the room with a smile painted on her face. Her eyes were swollen, but she had her hair down and it concealed her expression.

'I have made all of Mallika's favorite dishes,' Anjali Mashi said lovingly, stroking Mallika's beautiful waist-long hair. 'I don't want her to pine for my cooking and get thin. Look at her, she has lost so much weight. I am making sure she eats to her heart's content.'

I stared at my plate glumly. 'Rahul, you are not eating properly.' Anjali Mashi's voice startled me. 'I thought you liked kochuri and alur dom.'

I started eating quickly, not wanting to draw attention to myself. I did not want anyone to know that we had seen Mallika breakdown like that.

'So, Rahul,' Anjali Mashi said with feigned brightness. 'I heard you have started playing football like a good Bengali boy ...'

'Did you score a goal?' Binesh Kaku interrupted. 'When I was your age, I could kick the football so hard that once it flew all the way into the village square from the football field. And the village head was so angry that he took the ball and threw it into the fire.'

'And I kicked it so hard once that it exploded,' my father added with a laugh.

'Now, now, Chatterjee Dada, there is no need to exaggerate,' Binesh Kaku said with a friendly jab at my father.

Their laughter sounded forced. I gave a polite smile and continued eating, wanting the meal to end so that we could leave the table. Baba and Binesh Kaku continued to make aimless conversation.

After finishing my food, I said to Mallika, 'Let us go upstairs and play Snakes and Ladders.'

'Mallika, why don't you play Snakes and Ladders with Rahul at the kitchen table?' my mother suggested. 'I have not seen you for so long.'

'Achha, Mashi,' Mallika said obediently. 'Rahul, will you bring the board from upstairs? You know where it is.'

I ran upstairs as fast as I could. I opened the top drawer of the dresser where all the board games were kept—Ludo, Snakes and Ladders, Monopoly, Chinese Checkers, and more. I pulled the Snakes and Ladders board out of the drawer, making sure that I had the dice, the counters and the dice thrower. When I got back to the kitchen, I opened up the folded-up board. We had never played there before, but it felt good to be playing the game with Mallika after so many months.

'You roll the dice first,' I suggested.

She rolled the dice and moved the counter. She got a ladder after the first throw and moved further up. Then I rolled the dice, but ended up staying on the same row. Before we knew it we were climbing ladders and gaining on each other or being devoured by snakes and falling behind. My mother and Anjali Mashi were busy chatting as they put the dirty dishes in the sink for the servant to wash the next day.

'Oh, no!' exclaimed Mallika. She had rolled the dice too hard and it had bounced off the board and fallen on the floor, under the table. Mallika leaned forward to pick up the dice from the floor. As she did so, her blue sleeve drew back and I saw a huge purple bruise on her forearm. She quickly straightened up, pulling the sleeve back over her arm. She looked around to see if anyone else had seen it. My mother and Anjali Mashi quickly looked away, but I heard my mother's sharp intake of breath.

'Mallika …' Ma started to say, turning back, when Anjali Mashi grabbed her firmly by the elbow.

'Didi, did you see the beautiful tea set Sanjib's parents presented to us at the wedding?' Anjali Mashi asked as she spun my mother around and marched her off to the pantry.

'Mallika Didi, what happened to you?' I asked.

'Shh … nothing,' she said quickly. 'I … I slipped and fell on the wet bathroom floor and hurt myself. I am so careless sometimes.'

I heard muted whispers from the pantry. Then, either my mother or Anjali Mashi turned the tap on in the pantry sink, drowning out their words.

We returned to our game of Snakes and Ladders, though my mind was in turmoil. Mallika won the game and, like the old days, she laughed, throwing her head back, her dimples appearing suddenly, her eyes sparkling. For a brief moment, it was as if nothing had changed. I did not mind losing. I wanted her to win and be happy. For a little while at least, she seemed to have forgotten her cares and worries.

'So, Rahul,' she said, after we had folded the board and put the game aside, 'have you read any more Enid Blyton books? You should start reading the *Hardy Boys*' mysteries. I loved those stories, even though they are boys' books.'

'Yes, my friend Ranjan loves the *Hardy Boys*. It will be such fun to read them together. How long will you be staying here, Mallika Didi?'

'Just two more days. Then I go back,' she said, looking serious. 'You will visit me with Rani and your parents, won't you?' Her smile had faded and the pain had returned to her eyes.

'I will, Mallika Didi,' I promised as she gave me a long hug.

As we left, my mother said to Mallika, 'Come and visit us in Mint House any time. Come with your husband and his parents.' As we walked out of the house, Mallika and Shyamala walked out with us. Shyamala and Rani walked ahead with my father.

'I know it is hard to adjust to a new home,' Ma said to Mallika, quietly. 'Just remember—if you ever need anything, come to me. I am your mashi, just like your mother.'

By then, we were at the car. We waved goodbye to each other, promising to meet again very soon. As we drove home, Rani and I listened to my parents talking.

'She is having difficulty with her husband,' Ma said.

'Yes, Binesh told me. He said Sanjib had beaten her. He has a bad temper. She does not want to go back to his house, but Binesh has told her she has to return to her husband's home—it is her home now. If she stays with her parents, what will people say?'

'I don't think she should go back.'

'Binesh is upset about Mallika but also worried about Shyamala,' Baba replied. 'He knows that he will never be able to find a good boy for Shyamala if Mallika's marriage does not work out. You know, once the rumours start that the Bannerjees are a bad family, no one will want to be associated with them in that way.'

'I told Mallika before I left that she could call me any time she needed anything,' Ma said.

'Don't get involved in other family's matters. Tomorrow, people will say that we broke their marriage up. You know how people are.' Baba sounded very annoyed.

I wanted to ask my father why Mallika could not leave Sanjib, but kept quiet, fearing his temper for talking about things that I did not understand.

A few days passed by. I was busy studying hard. Before the third round of tests, Ranjan suggested I go to his house to study with him. I was very excited about the invitation—at the possibility of being alone with Shubho.

This time, my father drove me to Ranjan's house. Rani did not come. She was going to a class picnic with Shyamala. As my father's white Fiat drove all the way to Banjara Hills and up the winding roads to Ranjan's house, I felt a flutter of excitement.

'Study hard and do not inconvenience Bose Mashi in any way,' Baba warned me. I nodded, feeling anxious and happy as I wondered if Shubho would be home.

'Rahul! Glad you made it.' Ranjan ran down the steps to greet us.

My father drove away, the wheels scattering loose gravel, and Ranjan and I entered the house. His mother, Dr Bose, was at the door, looking businesslike and severe, as if she were still at work at the mental hospital. She was very proper, spoke little and only when necessary. I'd always found her rather unapproachable. She intimidated me because my mother was loquacious and expressed affection very easily. I wondered if Shubho was scared of his mother too. Dr Bose's hair was pulled back tight in a bun and her glasses perched on her prominent nose, making her look beaky. As usual, she was dressed in a dull-coloured sari, unlike the bright colours my mother wore—it was like suddenly seeing in sepia instead of colour. And, though beautifully furnished, with lots of antiques, the house too was monochromatic and dark, with no respite for the eyes. Ranjan's mother had brought everything from her ancestral home in Bengal and it was difficult to go anywhere without bumping into exquisitely carved and polished pieces.

I stood stiffly, on my best behaviour. The walls were covered with black-and-white pictures of grandparents, great-uncles and great-aunts, looking disapproving as they stared at me from the other world. Somehow, my Rajesh Khanna shirt did not belong in that house. The dining room was gloomy too, its walls covered with dark teak panelling. The table in the centre of the room, usually set for four—Ranjan, Shubho and their parents—was massive and could seat ten people. The rooms upstairs were more cheerful though, with large windows and light-coloured walls. Ranjan and Shubho had their own rooms. I felt the urge to run to Shubho's room and find him, but I controlled myself as I stood in the dim foyer.

'Rahul, how nice to see you,' Dr Bose said formally, sounding stiff. 'How are your parents? It has been a long time since I saw them. And how is Rani? I thought she was going to come with you.'

'They are fine, Mashi,' I said. 'Rani had to go for a school picnic.'

'Would you like some nimbu pani?'

'Yes, Mashi,' I answered.

'Ranjan, take Rahul to your room and start studying for the tests,' Dr Bose instructed. 'I hope you cleaned your room like I asked you to. I will be coming up to take a look at it later this morning.' Dr Bose was very exacting with her sons. There was a penalty each time they disobeyed her.

As we stood up to leave the sitting room, Dr Bose said, 'Ranjan, please try to learn something from Rahul today. He studies hard and comes first in class. You are never able to get past second place.'

I felt uncomfortable. I hated being compared to Ranjan.

'Yes, Mum,' he replied sulkily. I glanced at him from the corner of my eye to see if he was getting angry. He was—I could tell by the way his lower lip jutted out.

Dr Bose left to go into the kitchen to continue with her baking and Ranjan glared at her. Then he looked accusingly at me and turned on his heel and walked up the stairs to his room. I followed, wanting to appease him. He grabbed me by the hand and pulled me in, shutting the door with a sharp click. Taking a look around, he took a deep breath and forced a smile. He said, 'If Mum sees this, I will lose my pocket money this week. I have to clean this up first.'

I looked around. The room was a war zone. Books, clothes, magazines and shoes were piled up everywhere. The bed was unmade, and on the wall, even the pictures of Ranjan's favourite cricketers were askew. It was as if a freak storm had gone through the room, scattering everything.

'What happened here?' I asked.

'Oh, nothing. I had not cleaned my room for a week because Mum was out of town attending a psychiatric conference. And now she is back and I need to straighten it up.' He added impatiently, 'Come on, help me.'

We started tidying. In about half an hour, it was tidy enough to pass muster. Ranjan had been quiet all this while. I hoped he was not still angry because his mother had suggested that he needed to learn from me.

'Where is Shubho Dada?' I asked, trying to sound casual.

'Oh, he is out with his girlfriend. I think they went to Anjali Shopping Centre in Maredpelly. Why do you always ask about Shubho Dada?' Ranjan said somewhat resentfully. 'It is not as if you are friends with him. He is always with his friends or his girlfriend and never spends any time with me any more.'

I felt my face flush and turned away, my disappointment crushing. I had hoped that I could at least talk to Shubho—he would, for once, not be with his friends and ignore me. I wanted so badly for him to hold me again …

Ranjan walked over to the mirror on the wall and examined his face. It was covered with acne, but the shadow on his upper lip was thicker than before. 'Damn pimples,' he muttered. 'But see, I am starting to grow a moustache,' he boasted. 'I have been shaving with my father's razor, but he does not know it. Girls like boys with hair on their bodies. What about you? Let me look at your face.' He swaggered over to me and examined my face closely. 'Some beard, but not as much as mine. Not bad, Rahul, but I am ahead of you on this one.' He laughed, suddenly cheerful.

'Is he coming back to have lunch with us?' I continued, unable to help myself. I tried to speak as nonchalantly as I could while I straightened the books on the table.

'Who?'

'Shubho Dada,' I said. I knew I was pushing my luck.

'I don't know. He is probably with Anamika right now.' Ranjan was preoccupied with his face again. Then his voice suddenly rose with excitement. 'You know, I wish I had a girlfriend like her. She is so sexy! Hey, you know that girl who lives across the street? I think she likes me. I cannot wait until my parents let me start dating. So, do you have your eyes on any girl?'

I was at a loss for words again. He was talking about things that I did not ever think about. 'No,' I said.

'Oh, come on! What's the matter with you? Are you a homo or something? Everybody in our class wants to do it, you know. Especially with Miss D'Souza.' Ranjan winked at me conspiratorially.

'Do what?'

'You know ...' He lowered his voice and said, 'Fuck. Have sex.'

'What do you mean?' I asked, willing to risk looking ignorant, even though I had a good idea of what he meant.

'Well, you do know how babies are made, don't you? When a man and woman get married, he puts his thing in her thing,' Ranjan said in a whisper.

'Really?' I said, recoiling at the idea, though not for the first time.. 'How do you know?'

Ranjan laughed scornfully. 'You are so ignorant! No one ever talks about it because it is a dirty thing that our parents do. Our parents don't like discussing these matters with their children because we are supposed to be too young to know about them. If you say the word "fuck" in front of them, they will be furious!' he said. 'Well? Don't you want to do it with Miss D'Souza?'

'That is disgusting, to think of doing it with Miss D'Souza!' I said before I could stop myself.

Suddenly, I was an outsider in Ranjan's world. He looked at me strangely, his eyes narrowed. 'You better not be a homo like Amit, or you too will get into trouble at school and get expelled. And I don't want to be best friends with a homo either. Then everyone will think I am one as well.'

Ranjan's mother arrived right then, without any warning, and opened the door. She surveyed the room, looking for mistakes, her expression disapproving. 'Are you boys going to talk or study? Your room looks neat enough, Ranjan, though you could do better. Look at how well your brother keeps his things. You need to be more like him. You will not go very far in life if you cannot even keep a room clean. I am sure Rahul knows how to keep a room neat and tidy. And look what a good student he is!' With a look of grudging approval at me, she left the room.

'I am sick of being compared to others,' Ranjan muttered, his brow furrowed in anger.

'Let's study,' I said, changing the subject.

We started studying. Then the maid brought the nimbu pani and curry puffs. The puffs were crisp and flaky on the outside and filled with a variety of curries. After finishing our snack, we started solving algebra problems at the back of the chapters in our textbook.

'I have finished!' Ranjan's voice interrupted me as I sat working on one of the problems.

'Good,' I said. 'Hold on, let me finish mine too.'

'I finished first and I got it right. You better improve your speed if you want to get top marks in the next test.'

'Let me finish solving the problem. Then we can continue with something else. Remember, we have history and geography to do as well,' I said in a placating tone, anxious to avoid another accusation of cheating, like the Monopoly incident at Mint House.

The rest of the morning was like that. Ranjan was determined to beat me at every exercise. It was a competitive study session and I felt like I was in an examination hall, writing my final exams. By the time we heard the lunch bell tinkle in the dining room downstairs, I was pretty tired.

We walked downstairs to the dining room. In accordance with Dr Bose's British-style upbringing of her children, every meal was very proper, with tablecloth, napkins, forks and knives. We always used our hands to eat at home and used forks and knives only at restaurants and on formal occasions. I could not imagine what it would be like to have to use them for every meal—the joy of eating was in using my hands. It was as if my taste buds were on my fingertips, they sampled the texture and temperature of the food before it reached my mouth. But that was what Ranjan's family was like—modern, formal and cold. Except for Shubho. He was warm and comforting and so exciting to touch. I hoped he would be there for lunch.

When we reached the dining room, there were four place settings, but only the three of us. I was horribly disappointed that Shubho was not there.

'I guess Shubho is not going to be sitting with us at lunch,' Dr Bose said, her lips set in a tight line. 'We cannot wait for him all day. And I have things to do this afternoon. I am sure you boys are hungry too, after all that studying.'

Lunch was different from the meals we had at Mint House. There was a Russian salad, cold cuts, baked vegetables and stew, followed by a freshly baked sponge cake with ice cream to finish it all off. The cold cuts looked revolting and I did not have any. The memory of my visit to the butcher shop was still fresh in my mind. The three of us sat in the dining room at the dining table for ten while the maid served us. My chair felt hard and I sat stiffly in it. Conversation was stilted, punctuated by the clink of knives and forks against porcelain plates. Shubho's place sat empty, a gaping void—I wished he would magically appear and fill it.

'I need to go to the market to buy some tatting thread for a lace tablecloth I am making,' Dr Bose said as we were polishing off the last of the cake and ice cream from our matching dessert plates. 'Ranjan, I need you to come with me. On the way back, we can stop at the tailor's shop, where you must have another set of school trousers stitched for you. I don't know what you do in your school uniform—the maid showed me huge rips in the knees. Rahul, would you like to come with us? We should be gone for less than an hour. Or you can stay here and take a nap or study.'

'I would …' I started to say, wishing that Shubho were here, when I heard loud footsteps coming up the front stairs. The front door opened and shut with a bang. The sound of running feet preceded a dishevelled and breathless Shubho as he materialized in the doorway to the dining room.

'Hello, everyone. Mum, I am sorry I am late. Anamika wanted to buy some bangles on Abid Road and it took her forever. Rahul, how are you?' he asked casually, walking behind my chair and messing up my hair. I felt my face flush with pleasure. 'So what are you doing here with Ranjan? Are you here to have fun or study for the tests?'

'Rahul and Ranjan are studying for the next round of tests,' Dr Bose answered for me. 'But first they are going with me to shop. Shubho, go wash your hands and have your lunch.'

Shubho went to the washroom, humming a tune under his breath. He came back as we were getting ready to leave the table and said, 'Are you all going to leave me here to eat alone? Rahul, at least you can stay behind and give me some company, right? I will tell you about my plans for your next position in the football team. Mum, why don't you go with Ranjan and leave Rahul behind? You know I hate eating alone.'

Dr Bose, for all her dryness, was not immune to her son's charms. 'All right, Rahul, you can stay here and give Shubho company if you like. You will probably have a better time here than with us in this heat.'

And that is how simple it all was. One moment, I was going out in the afternoon heat, running around town with Ranjan and Dr Bose; the next, I was to be alone with Shubho.

Ranjan and his mother left soon. As we heard the revving of the Ambassador fade away and the noise of the churning gravel quiet down, I knew that I was going to get exactly what I had been hoping for.

I washed my hands and sat down at the table across from Shubho. He looked at me and smiled that indulgent smile that confirmed our little secret. It was as safe with him as it was with me. I felt a warm pressure on my bare calf. It was Shubho. He had slipped off his sandals and was slowly rubbing my calf with his bare foot.

'I am fine. You don't need to wait here.' Shubho dismissed the maid waiting in the corner. She left the room smiling, glad to be free to enjoy her own lunch.

Shubho ate slowly, chewing deliberately and relishing the meal. I watched him, fascinated by the way his muscles at the temple and jaw rippled under his smooth brown skin. We did not say much to each other. He seemed absent-minded—as if he was trying to make his mind up about something. Suddenly, he pushed his plate away and said, 'Want to go upstairs?'

I nodded, full of anticipation. My body felt charged and my mouth tasted salty. I felt aroused and excited. Shubho stood up quickly. He ran up the stairs and I followed, both of us anxious to be alone, knowing that Ranjan and Dr Bose would be back soon.

Shubho led me to his room, which was at the other end of the house. It was full of light and airy, just like Ranjan's. The walls were pale yellow and a large window opened to the front of the house. I could see the chowkidar standing at the gate of the gravel-covered driveway. The roughly hewn stones that bordered the window were covered with ivy and a few strands curled and swayed in the light afternoon breeze. Posters of Sunil Gavaskar and Pele holding the World Cup hung from the walls and the actresses Mumtaz and Zeenat Aman smiled seductively in low-cut, sequinned gowns. Pens and papers lay neatly arranged on the desk, in sharp contrast to Ranjan's messy desk. School books were stacked on one end. I read the titles—*Advanced Physics*, *Intermediate Biology*, *Calculus* and some others that I could not recognize.

As I took this all in, I felt Shubho's arms come up around me. I turned to face him and buried my face in his chest. I nuzzled him, parting the opening between the buttons in his shirt with my nose to breathe in the smell of his skin. The fine hair on his smooth chest was soft, like down. I had wanted to do this for so long—I could not believe it was finally happening! The fragrance of Lifebuoy soap mingled with his distinctive male smell, making me dizzy with delight. His hands squeezed my shoulders, my neck and then my back, softly massaging, feeling my body. It was the most arousing thing I had ever experienced. I wanted him to kiss me, so I turned my face up to his. Standing on tiptoes, I just managed to reach his chin and jawline and pressed my lips to his skin. It felt taut and warm, soft and prickly, all at the same time, a strange combination that inflamed my senses.

Shubho laughed and then, looking out of the window furtively, led me to his bed. We lay next to each other, my arms around his chest, his arms around mine, his face buried in my hair, his breathing ragged. His lips were burning hot and his breath was uneven. We faced each other and my lips touched his. His body pressed close to mine and I could feel his heart thumping loudly against my own. He suddenly held his fingers to his lips, asking me to be quiet. He slowly raised his head and looked out of the window to see if anyone was coming. The coast was clear—he dropped back down to the bed and held me tight again. I felt safe, warm and excited as never before. For that moment, even though I knew we were doing something that had to be hidden from everyone, I wanted it more than anything in the world. I buried my face in his shirt and nibbled on his button, wanting it to come undone.

'Oh, you rascal!' Shubho laughed as he proceeded to unbutton his shirt. It was open now, displaying his soft skin. A light dusting of hair made its way down from his chest, disappearing into his jeans. I followed the trail with my fingers and felt his body harden with urgency. I felt like I was on the brink of an adventure, even as terror gripped me hard.

Shubho rolled me on my back and lay on top of me, taking care not to crush me. He slowly relaxed his weight onto my body. His lips touched mine and I felt the flicker of his tongue in my mouth. I opened my lips to taste him better, my tongue pushing back against his with a will of its own. I was dimly aware of his body gently rubbing against mine as he kissed me. I opened my eyes and looked at his face, damp with perspiration, his eyes closed. He slowly unbuttoned my shirt and trailed his fingers down my body. Suddenly, our bodies were rubbing against each other, skin to skin, and it was the most incredible sensation I had ever felt. Then he moaned and shuddered and a small cry escaped him. I felt an almost unbearable tightness building up in my groin and I ground and thrust my hips helplessly against his.

Spasms ran through Shubho's body and he convulsed, his breath harsh and loud against my ear. Then he pulled away. The spell was broken, and I felt like I had been pulled back from the brink of ecstasy.

'Shubho Dada, what is happening to you?' I asked in alarm when I saw a stain on the front of his pants. I wondered if he had urinated in his pants, but that did not make sense. Is that why he looked so shamefaced? He started pulling his shirt out of his waistband—it was rumpled from our embraces. He looked down and, brushing the front of his pants, covered the stain with the ends of the shirt.

'Shh ... nothing. I am fine.' He looked very sheepish.

I wanted him to come back and lie on top of me again and keep rubbing and thrusting against me. But I did not know how to say it to him, even though I was very disappointed. Somehow, I was sure I had been denied some unknown and incredible experience.

The faraway squeak of the gate as the chowkidar opened it shattered the silence. We heard the Dr Bose's Ambassador slowly lurch up the driveway, crunching gravel and stones.

'Oh, shit!' Shubho jumped up.

I jumped up as well and straightened my clothes, hiding my arousal. I did not need to be told what to do. Shubho smoothed out his bed and his hair. He turned me around and straightened my hair too. In that moment, I knew that I loved him for caring for me that way. He quickly gave me a kiss on my forehead and whispered, 'Not a word to anyone. Remember, this is our secret. Go to Ranjan's room and sit down with your books.'

I could hear Dr Bose's voice in the foyer as she spoke to the maid. 'I'll go and see where Rahul is. He must be waiting for us.'

I quickly slipped into the corridor, running towards Ranjan's room. Dr Bose's footsteps sounded very close as her voice grew louder: 'Rahul ...'

She had caught me before I reached the room. I froze. 'Yes, Mashi?' I said, terrified that she would suspect what I had been up to.

'What are you doing? And why is your hair so messed up?'

I turned around slowly, smoothing my hair. 'Nothing. I ... I ... just went to the bathroom ...' My heart was pounding and my voice sounded strained and high. Heat rose in my face.

'And your clothes are rumpled. Oh, you must have taken a nap in Ranjan's room!' She laughed as if it was something very funny. 'Well, I always say nothing like a nap after lunch. I think I will go take one too.'

I laughed nervously and, grateful for the reprieve, slipped into Ranjan's room. I rumpled the bed cover and pounded the pillow. I could feel a damp stickiness in my underwear, but I did not have time to dwell on it because I could hear Ranjan running up the steps. I picked up the history book in a rush, holding it upside down. As he entered the room, I panicked and put it away.

'What are you doing?' Ranjan asked suspiciously.

'Oh, nothing. Just reading history chapters for the test. I took a nap after you left.' I straightened my shirt ends so that they covered the front of my pants.

'Mother has promised me a new bike if I come first in class, so watch out, Rahul!'

Ranjan was in a good mood for the rest of the afternoon. It crawled by slowly as my body and mind were agitated after my experience with Shubho. I wanted more than anything else to go up to his room, which I knew was impossible. Instead, Ranjan and I spent the hours learning by heart historical dates of medieval dynasties of North India.

At about five o'clock the bell rang downstairs, signalling tea time. The cook had baked fresh scones and we had them with clotted cream and strawberry jam. A beautiful porcelain teapot had tea steeping in it. Shubho did not join us for tea. As we were finishing, I heard him coming down the stairs.

'I am going to see Anamika,' he yelled as he ran out of the house. I felt a bitter flood of jealousy course through me.

Ranjan and I went out to the garden to play after that. I kept hoping that Shubho would return before I left, but he did not. Very soon, my father arrived to pick me up.

'Did you study well?' he asked. 'I am sure Ranjan wants to beat you this time in the tests.' His voice grew stern. 'Make sure you come first again in the next round.'

I desperately wished that my parents and Ranjan's would stop pushing us like this.

That night my body felt different as I touched myself, thinking about Shubho. I could not wait to see him again, to feel his touch.

We would meet secretly again, sooner or later—of this much I was certain.

November 1973. Hyderabad.

The air had grown cooler. The birds were sluggish and did not sing as much. Some of them had flown off to warmer regions. Others, like the crows and sparrows, stayed around but puffed up into balls of feathers to keep warm. Migratory birds arrived from colder lands, preferring our climes to their winter. They nested in rushes by the lake. The sun rose late in the morning now and my bed was no longer warm when I woke up. I hated the gloominess of the mornings.

Other things were changing too. My khaki pants, which had been comfortable and well-fitting the year before, now barely made it to my ankles. But thrift demanded that I make do with the same clothes this year too. I hated the dullness of my clothing as well, since the only coloured sweaters we were allowed to wear to school were navy-blue. The sweaters were serviceable rather than comfortable, prickly around the neck and tight on my arms.

School had become even more demanding. Everyone was busy studying for the last round of tests that would be held a few weeks before the finals for the first half of the school year. I practised my algebra, geometry and arithmetic daily and also had to study history, geography, civics, science, English, Hindi and Sanskrit. I wanted to see Shubho very badly, but there was no way for that to happen now that the early evenings had put an end to football practice. Ranjan was still my friend, but he was spending more and more time with Suresh Khosla and the other boys who made jokes about looking up Miss D'Souza's skirt.

Then I got a call from Ranjan that made me very, very happy.

'Hi, Rahul. We are going to have a birthday party for Shubho Dada. Mum asked me to invite you and Rani.'

My throat tightened with nervous excitement. 'When is it?'

'Coming Saturday. Make sure you come. And bring Rani too.'

'Dr Bose has invited me to her house for Shubho Dada's birthday party,' I announced to my parents. 'And she has invited Rani too.'

'When is it?' asked my father

'Coming Saturday,' I said, praying silently that my visit would not be vetoed.

'All right, I will drive you both over,' Baba said. 'What do you want to buy your Shubho Dada for his birthday?'

'Oh …' I was nonplussed. What would I buy for Shubho? 'A football jersey,' I said in a sudden burst of inspiration.

'We can go to the sports shop on Abid Road then, before I drop you off at the party.'

I also wanted to give Shubho another gift. One that I would myself make. Packing all my art materials in a bag, I tucked it under my arm and strolled out of the palace. I did not want Rani to see the card I was going to make.

I sauntered towards the dhobi ghaat at the far end of the palace and sat in the warm afternoon sunshine to make a birthday card for Shubho. I loved this place with its rough-hewn granite tanks and the steep steps that led into them. The brass faucets were covered with a thin patina of green. In summer, lilies bloomed in the smallest tank, which was always kept full of water. I sometimes liked to imagine the family of dhobis all around me. Huge pots of water boiled in my imaginings, with tough washerwomen on their haunches beating the dirt out of the clothes. After the clothes dried on the line, the dhobis pressed them with irons that hissed and puffed, like mechanical dragons, as water drops evaporated on the blistering hot metal, leaving behind crisp, starched cottons.

But, alas, the ghaats lay empty and deserted in the winter sunshine and I was the only one there. My family's clothes were washed in the large tiled bathroom close to the laundry room in the palace. Shaking my head free of thoughts, I took out the pink cardboard and scissors from my bag and got to work.

I had dried autumn leaves and summer flowers from the deciduous trees in the garden the year before. I decorated the pink card with flowers and dry leaves and liberally sprinkled it with gum and glitter. Then I carefully trimmed away the extra paper and errant leaves and turned it around to make sure it looked perfect for Shubho, fervently hoping that he would like it.

Inside, I wrote:

> Happy Birthday, Shubho Dada! Thank you for being my friend. I
> love doing fun things with you. I think about you all the time and
> want to see you again.
> Love,
> Rahul.

I put the art materials back in the bag and placed the card carefully
in an oversized envelope.

When I went back to the palace, Rani was suspicious as she saw me
carrying the bag. She asked about it, but I lied to her about an art
project. I could not let anyone see the card.

I dressed with care the evening of Shubho's birthday and wore my
new drainpipe pants with a bright red sweater that my mother had
knitted for me the year before. It was a bit short at the wrist now and
I pulled at it in irritation.

'Hurry up, slowpoke!' Rani said. She was dressed up and looking
impeccable as always. Her hair was brushed to one side and a hair
clip with a large orange flower matched her orange sharara. But it
was not her hair that I stared at. Her lips were orange—a bright
orange. I had never seen Rani look like this before. She looked just
like the actress Mumtaz.

'Oh, Rani!' I exclaimed. 'You look beautiful.' She preened in the
mirror and followed me to the dining room.

'Arre. What are you wearing on your lips? Is that lipstick?' Baba
demanded when he saw her.

Rani did not respond, taken aback.

'Why are you wearing lipstick?' my father persisted, sounding
unusually angry as he flung aside the newspaper he had been
reading. 'Ogo, shunchho? Our Rani is wearing your lipstick.'

Ma came to see what the ruckus was about. 'Oh, Rani, that is such a
nice colour you are …'

'Have you all gone crazy?' Baba slammed the table with his fist.

'Well, I am going to a party and it matches my sharara, so …' Rani's voice trailed off.

'Well, take it off. It looks terrible! You are still a young girl. Stop trying to act like an adult. Go!'

Rani left the room with a rebellious flounce of her sharara.

'See? All this bad influence ever since Mallika fell in love with that blighter,' Baba said to Ma. 'I will not tolerate any of this nonsense in my house. Binesh told me that Anjali spoilt her daughter and see what she ended up doing. Chhee … chhee …'

'Let them have fun. They are only children,' Ma snapped as she left the room as well.

I sidled towards the veranda, wondering if I would be scolded for something as well. Rani reappeared in a while, her lips wiped clean.

Our trip to Abid Road was conducted in stony silence.

'I will stay in the car. You go. I don't want to pick out a jersey for Shubho Dada. In fact, I don't want to go to this stupid party any more,' Rani said to me when the car had stopped.

'You children are getting unmanageable,' Baba muttered angrily under his breath as he and I walked to the sports shop.

I picked out a jersey for Shubho carefully. It was green and yellow, the colours of Brazil. I was thinking of the poster of Pele on the wall of Shubho's room and hoping that he would really like his gift.

When we got to Ranjan's house, there were already many cars parked in the driveway.

'Have a good time,' Baba said.

Rani got out without a word and I said a hasty goodbye as I tumbled out of the car. I could not wait to give Shubho the card and the gift that I had chosen so carefully for him.

Seeing us arrive, Ranjan ran over to us. 'Why are you so late?' he demanded. 'There is no one of my age here and all of Shubho Dada's friends are too busy with each other to talk to me.' He looked at Rani admiringly and whistled softly. 'My, Rani, you look smashing!' He looked her up and down, his eyes lingering on her chest.

Rani preened. 'Why, thank you, Ranjan,' she replied, looking coy. I stared at her simpering smile. Her mood had lifted at Ranjan's admiration and, linking her arm in his, she walked with him towards the house. I did not care. I had Shubho to think about.

The trees in the garden were starkly outlined against the dark winter sky and I felt a chill in spite of my warm sweater. I remembered how thick the leaves had been on the trees the last time I was in Shubho's room … My heartbeat quickened.

Shubho was in the centre of the drawing room, dancing with Anamika. 'Hey, Rahul,' he said when he saw me, but he did not leave Anamika's side.

Rani and I went over to give him his gift. 'Happy Birthday, Shubho Dada,' we said in unison and then started laughing.

I did not give him the card. I wanted to give it to him when we were alone.

'Thank you, Rahul and Rani,' Shubho said with a stiff bow and turned back to Anamika.

'Thank you for inviting us,' I said to him and to Dr Bose, who had come up to greet us. Shubho did not seem to hear me and I was disappointed. But I was sure he would be warm and friendly once he saw the beautiful card I had made for him.

Dr Bose was in a good mood. The table was laden with all kinds of pastries, samosas, pakoras and other snacks. A big cake covered with white frosting sat in the middle of the table.

Through the evening, Beatles songs kept playing and Shubho kept dancing with Anamika and his friends. Rani and Ranjan were busy moving to the music and having a good time. I was with them, but I was watching Shubho, waiting impatiently for a moment when I could be alone with him.

Finally, my moment arrived. I saw Shubho whisper something in Anamika's ear and make her laugh. He squeezed her hand and left the room. I followed him. He ran up the stairs, and so did I. He heard my footsteps behind him, just as he was at his door. He stopped humming the Beatles song playing and said, 'Hey, Rahul, what are you doing up here?' He opened the door and entered his room.

I slipped in behind him.

'Shubho Dada …' I began, but he cut me short with a wave of his hand.

'Rahul, I hope you have not told anyone about what happened here the other day.'

'No, I haven't,' I said, happy that he wanted this secret to be just between us.

I went up to him and, standing on my toes, gave him a kiss on his cheek, breathing the familiar scent of his skin.

'Careful,' he warned, stepping away. I did not understand why he was being so aloof. I wanted him to hold me, brush his lips against mine and stroke my hair.

'I made you a card,' I said, giving it to him.

He opened it, frowning as a few leaves and some glitter fell on the floor. He read the card and his face contorted with anger. 'Are you crazy?' he demanded. 'What if someone sees this card? Do you know what will happen to us if someone finds out? They have a word for it, you know. Homo!' He spat out the word.

'But Shubho Dada ...' My voice cracked. 'I thought ...'

'Thought what, Rahul?' This was not the genial and happy Shubho I had known and loved. 'If anyone finds out, we will be expelled from school. What was the name of that boy in your class? The one who was expelled?'

'Amit,' I whispered. I was terrified by Shubho's anger. My world was falling to pieces around me—and I did not know how to stop it.

'Yes, Amit. His family's reputation is ruined forever! You should hear my mother talk about him. I have been thinking a lot since the last time you were here. Do you know that people can be jailed for this? Yes. People turn in others all the time. This thing we have ... It must stop. Now.' There was a note of finality in his voice.

I reached out for him again, wanting him to touch me tenderly like he had the last time, but we heard voices and footsteps outside and Shubho moved away from me.

'Shubho! Shubho!' It was Anamika.

'Oh shit!' Shubho said and pushed me hard behind a curtain that covered an alcove in his room. It was full of coats. I fell as he pushed me, scraping my knee, and my temple hit the corner of a shelf where his clothes were stacked. Oddly enough, I felt no pain. I was numb with shock. Shubho drew the curtain back and leapt for the door, even as Anamika opened it

'Hey,' he said breathlessly. 'I was just coming downstairs. You took too long and we need to go downstairs or they will wonder where we are.'

I heard the door shut and the room fell silent. I waited for a few minutes and then came out of my hiding place. My heart was hammering against my chest and … I hurt, deep inside. I looked into the mirror and saw a stranger. I tried to straighten my clothes and mechanically arranged my hair, covering the cut on the temple. Luckily, only a thin trickle of blood showed. It was already darkening, the tiny droplets of blood congealing. I was feeling a bit dizzy as I turned towards the door and tripped on the dustbin. That's when I saw it—my carefully made card ripped into pieces and balled up at the bottom of the bin.

I opened the door and walked out slowly, trying not to limp, and went downstairs. Everyone was singing '*Happy Birthday, Shubho!*' I entered the dining room, trying not to draw attention to myself. Shubho was wearing a birthday hat and laughed as he cut the cake. He took a piece and put it in Anamika's mouth. She squealed with pleasure and broke off a piece and fed it to him amidst much clapping and cheering.

I tried to act as normal as possible, but my heart was breaking and I wanted to cry. A lump the size of a large rock had lodged itself in my throat. I politely refused the cake and any offers of food.

'What is the matter with you?' Rani was annoyed that I was acting so strangely.

'Nothing,' I muttered.

The evening could not end soon enough for me. Ranjan could never suspect anything, so I put on my best face. Shubho looked at me a couple of times from the other end of the room, but quickly looked away when I caught his eye.

I had never been so happy to see my father as I was that evening. He dropped in as the party was winding down, politely refused Dr Bose's offer to eat anything and we said our goodbyes and left. I was anxious to avoid Shubho, so I slipped out with my father, putting my hand in his, grateful for my family.

I was miserable that night. Shubho's anger and fear had been palpable. He was not the charming and carefree Shubho I knew any more, and I struggled to understand it. We would never be close again. Fear was transforming everyone around me. I felt hot tears of sadness and humiliation flow down my cheeks. I knew now how heartbroken Sharmila Tagore had felt in *Amar Prem* when she realized that her love for Rajesh Khanna was doomed.

On Sunday morning, I woke up with an aching sense of loss. I still could not believe that Shubho had been so angry and cruel. After a half-hearted breakfast, I sat in my favourite chair, curled up with a book. I did not want to talk to anyone and just wanted to be left alone. I skimmed the pages of a Perry Mason mystery. Of late, Enid Blyton characters had begun to seem too childish to hold my interest.

'I used to read a lot of those before I met your mother,' my father said, glancing over at me to see what I was reading. 'Aren't those books a little adult for you?'

'No, I understand them just fine,' I answered, anxious to appear normal. 'Do you have any more Perry Mason mysteries?'

'I did. I don't remember giving them away to anyone. I bought at least one a week for a long time, so I know I have plenty of them. If they are anywhere, it would be the box room.'

'Ogo, shunchho?' My mother's voice floated out from the kitchen. 'Arre! Are you forgetting that there are all kinds of books in the box room? Rahul does not need to see them.'

'I know. I know. You can read those books when you are grown-up, Rahul. Besides, the room is filthy and has not been used since before you were born.'

'All right,' I said, pretending to be obedient but making my mind up to explore the box room. Next to the dining room was the prayer room. A door led out of this room to the box room, but it was bolted shut. However, I was determined. There were books there that my parents did not want me to see. Books for adults only. Maybe I could find something that would explain to me exactly why Shubho thought being a homo was so terrible.

I slowly tiptoed into the prayer room, looking fearfully at the altar. The gods stared back at me, silently accusing me of trespassing. I knelt and bowed, touching my forehead to the ground and gently banging it in supplication. After atoning in advance for the coming transgression, I prepared myself to enter the box room.

It had not been opened for years and dust and age had fused the doors together. I slid the rusty metal bar of the latch out of the slot and, after a hefty push, with a creak of wood and old paint cracking, the doors opened. It was dark inside and smelt of years of stagnancy. As I walked forward, guided by feeble light coming from the prayer room, dust rose in little puffy clouds making me choke.

I stumbled against a crate in the semi-darkness and fell, hurting the knee I had bruised the night before. I found a light switch at last and got to work opening the crate with a crowbar. It was full of books by authors whose names I recognized—Agatha Christie, Erle Stanley Gardener, James Hadley Chase, Alberto Moravia, Pearl Buck, Charles Dickens, the Bronte Sisters and Oscar Wilde. But there were also other names I did not know. I realized that I had discovered a world that was a window into my parents' minds.

As I rummaged through the contents of the crate, the partially naked man and woman embracing each other on the cover of one book immediately caught my eye even though it was hidden at the bottom of the crate. I dug it out with some difficulty and turned it over in my hands. It was a very thick paperback, titled *It's Never Too Late to Love—Everything You Wanted to Know about Sex*, by a Barbara Golding. The word 'sex' loomed up at me. I remembered what Ranjan had said about how babies were made—had my parents hidden the book because it was about sex? I wondered who it belonged to. Perhaps Ranjan had been right when he said that our parents did not want us to know about sex because it was a dirty secret.

I looked at the cover carefully. I could not help noticing with excitement the man's body and how it resembled Shubho's body, though it was fair instead of brown.

I turned the book over. The back cover said, 'Barbara Golding is one of America's earliest sex experts. Find out everything you need to know about sex or making your sex life fun once again. Millions of men and women have found out how to live healthy and exciting lives after reading this book.'

I flipped through the pages, my heart racing. It was a book about sex and Barbara Golding was an expert on the subject. I had to find out what she had said about homosexuals. Surely an expert would say that it couldn't be dirty to be a homo? It was with hope that I went to the index. Running my fingers down the list, I finally stopped at the word I was looking for: 'Homosexuality'. I turned to the page number listed.

Words leapt out at me from the page: 'Homosexuality is an abnormal condition. Male homosexuals are often effeminate. Parents need to look to see if their children are teased in school for being too feminine or masculine. Boys who are homosexual like to play with dolls, hate sports and prefer quiet activities to active ones. Girls who are homosexual like to play rough sports and do not play with dolls like normal girls do. Early signs of homosexuality are obsession with a friend who is of the same sex and a lack of desire and interest in the opposite sex. It is treatable by electric shock and aversion therapy. Homosexuals live on the fringe and are very unhappy people. Parents are advised to start treating this condition early in childhood.'

I felt physically sick. I had been right to hide it from everyone after all. I had an abnormal condition. My thoughts were in a jumble. I could now understand why Shubho had been so angry. He did not want to be an unhappy person. Would I be given electric shock therapy? Certainly I would be jailed—what shame that would bring to my family! Reading the words over and over again, I felt that familiar sense of despair and terror. Ranjan was right. The boys were right. I could be expelled for this—or worse. If my parents found out, what would they do? What would their friends say?

I looked through the book and read about intercourse and orgasm and erogenous zones and impotence. I understood then what Ranjan and the boys were so excited about. All the information was very helpful and supportive for men and women who were attracted to each other—heterosexuals. There was no mention of homosexuality anywhere else.

I read the part about homosexuality over and over, then I put the book back at the bottom of the crate. I took the other books that I had carefully stacked and threw them in as fast as I could. I was disgusted with myself and knew now why Shubho had been so repulsed the evening before when I had tried to touch him.

I wanted to leave this horrible, dusty old room. Baba and Ma were right. I should never have entered this room. I knelt on the marble floor, the dust and grit grinding into the cut on my knee. But I could not feel anything other than the frenzied beating of my heart, the blood rushing in my ears. I picked up a pestle and started pounding away at the lid of the crate, trying to seal it again. I forgot about being quiet. I just wanted to get out of there. My knees were shaking so hard that I had to steady myself against the wall.

Finally, when I had calmed down a bit, I bolted the doors behind me and went to the bathroom. I locked the door and looked in the mirror. I saw a dusty figure, covered with cobwebs from head to toe. The blood and dirt on my knee looked painful, but I could not feel anything. I soaked a towel in the sink and started wiping my arms and legs, my hands and face, my knee and my hair, in a slow rhythm. My knee finally stung with pain as the grit and dirt ground into the open wound, but it did not matter. When I was clean, I went out to the garden.

'Rahul ...' My mother's sleepy voice came to me from her bedroom.

'I am going to the garden,' I called back to her as I ran out, limping slightly. My mind was still in turmoil. Thoughts raced through it, punctuated by jagged bursts of fear. I sought out my haven of safety, the gulmohar tree, and sat down, leaning against the bark. I breathed deep and slow, trying to regain control over the chaos in my head. As my pulse steadied, I realized that no one needed to find out about me. If I hid my attraction to Rajesh Khanna, Amit Puri and Shubho, no one would be the wiser. I had an abnormality—I simply could not let anyone know about it. I would be good. I promised myself that I would study hard, do well and never, ever, do anything that would expose my secret.

The sound of the pestle hammering the nails into the crate reverberated through my head all evening.

At dinner that night, my father was sombre. I was still thinking about the past two days when my mother said in a serious voice, 'Are you going to tell the children?'

'What?' I was scared that my father had discovered my secrets.

'Achha ... Rahul, Rani ...' Baba looked very serious. 'The government has decided to expand the mint. Since there is no land available except for the land around Mint House, the ministry in New Delhi has decided that the palace needs to be demolished.'

Everything froze, like in a movie still. Rani's mouth was open in shock and I looked desperately for signs that this was a joke. But it wasn't.

'I told them that this was a historic building and should not be demolished,' Baba continued. 'I was hoping that the Ministry of Archaeology would certify that since this was the Nizam's palace it should be preserved. But the Nizam did not live here and so it does not qualify. I have asked for a transfer to Bombay. We will know more in the next few months.'

'But ... Baba, what will happen to the palace?' Even as I said it, I knew that just as I had been powerless to stop what happened to Mallika, what had happened with Shubho, I was powerless to stop this too.

'What to do?' Baba's words were really a statement of complete helplessness.

'But this is our home! We have lived here for so many years,' I protested.

'India needs to have greater manufacturing capability. Otherwise, we will continue to be a backward country like our neighbours. This is the first phase of the expansion. The palace and the gardens will be replaced by the extension and ...' Baba's voice trailed off as he saw the misery on our faces.

'When are we leaving the palace?' I could barely absorb the news.

'It is only a plan right now. Don't worry about it. It could be a few months,' Baba said soothingly. 'I have started looking at schools in Bombay for you and Rani. We will probably leave before any of this expansion and demolition starts.' He reached over and tousled my hair, reminding me of Shubho. 'You can see Rajesh Khanna in Bombay. And all the other film stars too. Don't you want to do that?'

For the first time ever, I was not excited at the thought of seeing Rajesh Khanna, even in person. I kept eating my dinner and did not respond. My mother did not say anything. Rani was also speechless.

I finished the food quickly. I had not tasted anything and I did not care. I was devastated. My world was changing forever.

That night, as I lay in bed next to Rani, restlessly tossing and turning, I overheard my parents talking at the dining table.

'I don't want to leave,' Ma said to Baba, her voice quivering.

'I know, I know,' he responded. 'But I cannot stop it. I cannot do anything to change this. What to do? What to do?'

I finally fell asleep. I woke up the next morning in a state of shock which was to last for days. I tried to behave as if it was all a dream, determinedly pushing away all bad thoughts and building an armoured fortress of denial. But reality crept in insidiously through cracks, even as the examinations loomed closer and closer. I welcomed the distraction they offered. Everything else was too painful to think about.

12

Even though relatively early in the season, it was the coldest onset of winter that even the old people could remember.

'Cover your ears. If you don't, you will catch a cold,' Ma advised.

I had to wear what was called a 'monkey cap'. The cap covered the head, ears and neck, leaving the face exposed, very much like a chainmail headdress, and I hated the prickly wool, which made my skin itch. The school bus would be full of boys in similar caps. Rani, however, did not wear a monkey cap. Her Cleopatra-style fringe would be immaculate when she left the house and when she returned.

'Here, Monkey Baba,' she would shout out loud as I returned from school, following it with a monkey howl. And then, one day, it happened. The real monkeys arrived.

We were sitting in the veranda outside the dining room and I was dangling my legs off the edge. Rani was sitting behind me, against the wall, reading a book. The late morning sun was a welcome relief after the morning chill.

'Don't sit like that,' Rani ordered me. 'And stop fidgeting like a monkey.' She laughed.

'Why?'

'Because you will slip and fall, that's why. And though you look like a monkey, you are, unfortunately, not one.'

'No, I won't fall.'

We were bickering thus when I was distracted by a blur of brown on the roof of the servants' quarters. Behind us, inside the dining room, mounds of dirty dishes and cutlery bore testament to a big, lazy breakfast. The shelf in which my mother kept the food to protect it from flies had a large bowl of bananas and apples perched on top of it. Ma was in the kitchen.

'Did you see that?' I asked Rani excitedly.

'See what?' she replied, looking up from her book.

'The brown animal that just whizzed by. I think it was a monkey.'

'Don't be stupid. We don't have monkeys here, and you know that. Actually, that is not true. We do have a monkey here, and that is you!'

'Look!' I yelled, pointing to the branch hanging over the roof of the servants' quarters.

Rani turned in the direction I was pointing. 'Ma!' she screamed.

Right there, in front of our eyes, was a large, brown rhesus monkey. He was sitting on the branch staring at us fearlessly. I was sure he was the leader because behind him were fifteen or twenty monkeys, a mixture of adults, juveniles and infants. His expression was peculiar. He had a woebegone face with small eyes and many scars on his face, the result of past skirmishes, I thought. One of his ears was partially missing. His long tail dangled below his formidable, muscular body and he seemed to be surveying us with as much curiosity as we were.

Suddenly, he jumped off the branch onto the rooftop of the garage, which was right under the tree, while the other monkeys watched him. Screaming in terror, Rani and I ran away, expecting an attack. Seeing us run, he chased us on to the veranda. I stopped and turned to face him in a moment of sheer bravado.

'Go away!' I yelled, waving both arms at him.

Surprised, the monkey skidded on the veranda floor. But he was not intimidated for more than an instant. He rebounded and jumped at me, his teeth bared, a deep growl coming from his chest. That did it. Rani and I ran into the house and shut the door behind us, locking the monkey outside. It was a long time before we opened the door to the veranda and we did that only after making absolutely sure that the monkey was gone.

This incident laid the groundwork for our future relationship. The monkey leader, having established himself as the victor, soon succeeded in scaring all the residents of the palace grounds. From then on, he went wherever he wanted to, ate what he wanted to eat and did exactly what he desired.

A few days later, as Rani and I sat around the tea table, the leader appeared at the dining room door, taking us by surprise. He walked in on all fours, looked at us, then at the fruit on top of the shelf. Before we could absorb what was happening, he was off with a banana. We jumped up shouting a few seconds after he disappeared through the door, his tail smacking the frame as he exited in a hurry.

'What happened?' Ma came running into the dining room, terrified that someone was hurt.

Monkeys were not unusual in Hyderabad. When I had gone to the Tirupathi temple, one of the holiest shrines of Sri Venkateswara, it had been impossible to ignore them. They were everywhere, inside and outside the temple compound, boldly willing to take what they wanted from the pilgrims. But we had never had an invasion of monkeys at the palace before. The evergreen trees in the gardens were thick and green, their upper branches forming a rich and well-knit canopy that provided sustenance to many feathered and furry creatures. These canopies proved to be an irresistible attraction to this team of monkeys, who appeared to have left their old haunts looking for a better environment and had decided to settle in the palace grounds.

The encounter in the dining room was the first of many. The leader of the troop had little fear of humans, but his troop was shy. I would look up into the tall trees and find them sitting on branches, jumping around, constantly chewing on something. Most exquisite of all were the babies with their miniature faces, bodies, sad little eyes and tiny fingers. The mother monkeys would walk on all fours, on the rooftop of the servants' quarters or the garage and sometimes in the garden, while the babies clung to their chests, hanging upside down. I was always concerned that one of them would fall and get hurt, but they never did. The first hint of major mischief came one morning when one of the monkeys stole a pair of glasses from an office worker. It took quite a bit of trickery on Shankar's part to get them back; he eventually bribed the culprit with a banana.

The monkeys made the palace more exciting for me and were a welcome distraction. The pressure was on at school. Impatient to get home, I was first in line for the bus, for the days were getting shorter. As I walked from the front gates to the lawns, to the servants' quarters, to the back of the palace, the mango grove, the guava grove, the ruins and other areas, I would look up, my eyes scrunched, looking for the troop. I found them every day before I had finished searching the grounds. Each time, I heaved a sigh of relief. I could no longer imagine the grounds without them. When the darkness fell, the monkeys inevitably retired to the trees behind the servants' quarters.

At school, the results from the last set of tests before the final examinations were handed out. All my hard work had paid off.

Miss D'Souza handed out the corrected papers for the various subjects after.

'Rahul has scored the highest marks in algebra.'

And so it went. I could not believe my ears. I had scored the highest marks in four subjects. Each time, Ranjan grabbed the paper from my hands and stared at it in disbelief, comparing his incorrect answers to my correct answers. He was sulky all day and ignored me, hanging out with Suresh Khosla and his gang.

It was almost the end of the day when the bomb dropped. We were waiting for the last period to start. Ranjan turned to me and asked, 'Where is my pen?' His eyes glinted in a strange way.

'I have not seen it,' I replied, feeling uneasy. 'I have no idea, but I can help you look.'

We looked without success under the chairs in the classroom.

'Quick, quick, Miss D'Souza is coming. Get back into your seats,' the class monitor warned us, and we scrambled into our chairs.

The class continued as usual. I saw Ranjan speak to Miss D'Souza during the class when we were all busy reading a section of English composition. She looked surprised, and then at me. I knew right away that something was up.

At the end of the class, Miss D'Souza spoke. 'Ranjan's pen is missing. Has anyone seen it?'

The class did not volunteer any information.

'Has anyone taken it? If you have, come forward now.'

No one moved.

'Okay … So you are going to make this difficult,' she said. 'Rahul?'

'Yes, Teacher?'

'Ranjan says that you have stolen his pen.'

I felt as if the ground had opened up and I was sinking into a deep, deep abyss. 'No, I have not,' I said, my voice tense and high, my heart pounding in my throat.

'I want you to return it to Ranjan if you have indeed taken it. Perhaps you borrowed it and did not tell him?'

'But I do not have it.'

'Frankly, Rahul, it is hard for me to believe that it is true. Ranjan?'

'Yes, Teacher,' Ranjan said, a pained look on his face.

'Are you sure that you saw Rahul take it? Rahul says he does not have it.'

'Yes, I am sure. If it were not my expensive pen …' He looked at me, then turned to her again, a sincere expression on his face. ' … I would not have mentioned it.' He sounded heartbroken.

'Okay, then,' Miss D'Souza said reluctantly.

Everyone knew that Miss D'Souza prided herself on being a sharp teacher—so sharp, in fact, that she regularly warned us not to underestimate her. 'Don't try to pull wool over my eyes. I am fair but no fool,' she would say when confronted with a shifty student. 'I don't care if your father is the chief minister or if you are the class prefect. If you break the rules, I will punish you. I will make an example of you.'

Her usually soft mouth became a thin, hard line and her voice took on a note of steel. 'Let us clear this matter once and for all. Rahul, please empty out your school box.'

I looked at my school box. It lay on its side and was unlatched. A sick feeling came over me. Someone had opened it.

'But Teacher …'

Miss D'Souza saw my hesitation and her voice grew sharper. 'I will have to ask you again to empty your school box. You are making me lose my patience.'

Ranjan smirked. I still hesitated.

'I don't care,' Miss D'Souza snapped. 'I don't care if you kiss the ground—you still have to return his pen.'

The class giggled. It was a fall from grace for me—from being first in class to the ignominy of being labelled a thief. I looked at Ranjan. He was clearly enjoying himself. I knew at that moment that my friendship with him was over.

'Well, hurry up,' Miss D'Souza said impatiently. 'I don't have all day.'

I could not believe how angry she was. Ranjan must have said something terrible about me to her. Had he told her I was a homo? Then why had I not been summoned to Mrs Joshi's office? My hands started shaking.

I opened my school box. I could see no pen. Mrs D'Souza took it from my hands impatiently and started rummaging around.

'Ranjan, is this the one?' she said, holding up an expensive monogrammed Sheaffer pen.

'Yes, Miss D'Souza, it is,' Ranjan said, looking pleased.

Miss D'Souza handed the pen to Ranjan. 'Meet me after class,' she snapped at me and turned to the blackboard. Titters rose in small waves through the classroom.

I sat down at my desk, feeling alone and miserable. After all my efforts to avoid extra attention, I had ended up in this awful situation.

Class dragged on forever. Ranjan avoided eye contact with me and left as soon as the bell clanged. Soon, only Miss D'Souza and I were left in the room. My feet felt leaden as I dragged one behind the other on my way to her desk.

I stood in front of her, scared and worried. But not guilty. She looked up from the papers she was shuffling on the desk.

'Rahul, I am so disappointed in you. You are such a good student— I am shocked that you would do anything like this! I could not believe my ears when Ranjan told me that he saw you take his pen and hide it in your box.' Her voice was stern. 'There are a few things that will not be tolerated in this school. Students are expelled for those actions. This is one of them.'

My heart sank. So this was it. An ignominious end to my glorious run at school.

Miss D'Souza handed me some papers. 'Take these to your parents, please, and bring them back tomorrow with their signatures.'

'But Miss D'Souza,' I said, my voice a bare whisper as I choked back tears, 'I did not steal the pen. I am not a thief.'

'The evidence is against you. Only Mrs Joshi can revoke punishment in this matter.'

That afternoon, I sat in the bus feeling miserable, not knowing what to do. I looked at the handwritten note. It was addressed to my parents. The words in Miss D'Souza's characteristic flourish made my heart sink.

Rahul stole another boy's pen. It was found in his bag. Please call Mrs Joshi, the headmistress, to discuss this matter. We take theft very seriously at the Hyderabad Royal Academy.

I remembered Mr Puri picking up Amit's bag and the empty chair that was left behind—no one could save me from the same fate. I went home with the most horrible feeling of dread.

'Rahul, are you all right?' my mother said when she saw me. 'You look sick.'

'I am fine, Ma.'

'Is something the matter?'

'Nothing,' I said and quickly went into my room to wash up and change. I did not go out into the garden to see what the monkeys were doing—I had to think of a way to get out of this mess. Looking for a place to hide, I ended up on the back stairs, clutching the note from Miss D'Souza, halfway up to Colonel Uncle's apartment. He never took the back stairs and Rani was still not back from school. It was a safe spot. I lay the paper next to me, hugged my knees and put my head in my lap, feeling sick with fear. What if I was expelled? What if I was sent to boarding school by Baba as punishment? Why had Ranjan been so cruel? The anger and humiliation of the afternoon welled up inside me and I cried, my body racked by guttural sobs.

'Rahul?' I was startled by the familiar voice. 'I was out on the terrace and thought I heard you. What is the matter? Are you all right? Come on up. Don't sit there, boy.'

I looked up to see Colonel Uncle peering at me from the top of the stairs.

'Come on up,' he repeated, his voice gentle, holding his hand out.

I slowly climbed the remaining stairs, clutching the note in my hand, feeling relieved and ashamed at the same time.

'When did you come back, Colonel Uncle?' I asked.

'Just a couple of days ago,' he replied.

'Were you at your estate?'

'Yes, I was. It is good to be back, Rahul.' Colonel Uncle smiled comfortingly at me. He looked as if he was ready to go to a tea party. He wore a cream-coloured shirt with dark-brown woollen pants and shiny, patent-leather loafers. His maroon-and-cream Argyle sweater added a dash of colour to the ensemble. His military moustache was trimmed neatly.

Colonel Uncle held my hand in his and put his other arm around my shoulder. The door to his apartment was open and we stepped in. When Colonel Uncle had visited us, he had commended me for being almost a young man and I was trying hard to act like one. But his gentleness moved me and I started to cry instead.

I tried to smother my rising sobs, embarrassed by my childish behaviour, and ended up gasping for breath.

'Rahul, what is the matter? Come, come,' Colonel Uncle said as he led me to the sofa and sat next to me. He stroked my hair with one hand and held me to his shoulder with the other. 'Shh … It is all right. You can tell me,' he crooned softly as I shed my tears all over his lovely Argyle sweater.

Calming down at last, between sobs, I told him what had happened at school. I was dying to tell him about my other great fear—that I was abnormal—but I did not dare.

Colonel Uncle took me by the shoulders and looked straight at me. 'Did you steal Ranjan's pen, Rahul?'

'No, I did not. I am not a thief.'

'I know. I wanted to ask you myself before I take care of this matter. I am on the board of Trustees of the Hyderabad Royal Academy, you know. My family has been a prominent donor to their scholarship fund for decades.'

I nodded. 'Will you please speak to Mrs Joshi?' I pleaded.

'Yes, I will. Do not take this to your parents. I will handle this. Have you eaten? Your face looks so thin. I baked a cake this afternoon—would you like a slice?'

I nodded, suddenly aware that I was hungry since I had not eaten since lunch break at school. Colonel Uncle went into the kitchen area and reappeared bearing a plate with a generous slice of chocolate cake on it. It was the best cake I had ever eaten.

'I have to go to a party,' Colonel Uncle said as I walked to the door, daring to hope that perhaps the nightmare was over. 'But don't worry about anything, Rahul.'

I went back downstairs with a kindling sense of relief. I knew that Colonel Uncle would be as good as his word.

'Rahul, where have you been?' Ma was annoyed. 'I have been calling for a while now. You know it is cold and dark outside. I don't like it when you go away like this.'

'Sorry,' I muttered as Rani smirked into her plate of food.

By bedtime, my sense of apprehension had started to build up again. What if Miss D'Souza asked for a signed note in the morning? I slept badly that night, tormented by strange dreams.

When I walked into class the next day, Ranjan and Suresh Khosla, who were in deep conversation, made it a point to lower their voices while looking at me and then laughed out loud. Soon, the first class started, but Miss D'Souza did not call out my name. Ranjan looked disappointed by mid-morning. He asked Miss D'Souza if he could move to a different seat to protect his belongings and she let him. I wondered if he was angry with me because he suspected something about me and Shubho. Or perhaps he was just angry because he would not get the bicycle his mother had promised him if he came first in class.

The day went by without incident. So did the next. In a few days, it was clear that Colonel Uncle had settled the matter. I hoped he had spoken to Mrs Joshi in his steely voice. It was deeply satisfying to think of that.

After the incident, I avoided talking to Ranjan altogether. I simply did not trust him any more, and he spent more and more time with his new friends. I felt a familiar sense of anger and helplessness grow within me every time I saw him. Even Miss D'Souza had believed him, not me. I wanted to ask him why he had lied to get me into trouble. Dr Bose had been the secretary of the PTA in past years and she and Mrs Joshi were friends. Obviously, Mrs Joshi was not going to punish Ranjan. And, besides Colonel Uncle, there was no one to stand up for me. Though I had not been punished further, the whole class still thought I was a thief. What if Colonel Uncle had been away that day? Would I have been expelled from school? I felt very alone for the next few days, unable to confide in anyone at home about my near-catastrophic experience.

A few days later, I saw Mrs Joshi walking in the corridor. 'Good afternoon, Teacher,' I said.

'Good afternoon, Rahul,' Mrs Joshi said tartly, slowing down. 'You were lucky the last time. I will not tolerate bad-character boys in this school. I will be watching you closely. If I hear any more complaints, you are out,' she hissed. Her spindly fingers were clenched in frustration and her eyes glittered through her glasses. I could hear the thin gold bangles rattling against her bony wrists.

I kept walking, glad that no one else had been there to witness the scene. If Ranjan told her I was a homo, she would surely contact my parents directly.

In the coming weeks, as the examinations drew closer, everyone seemed to have forgotten about the incident of the lost pen. Everyone except me. The threat of more accusations loomed so great that I barely spoke to anyone any longer.

Meanwhile, the cold snap ended as suddenly as it had begun. After the incident with the spectacles, the monkey became very bold. We started hearing reports of the Mint factory workers' tiffin boxes being stolen by a very aggressive monkey. I was sure it was the leader of the group living on the grounds. The monkey would watch the workers when they arrived in the morning and wait for lunchtime. Then he would swoop down, grab the tiffin box out of his unsuspecting victim's hands and run up a tree. He would open the tiffin carrier, which was no mean feat considering that it involved turning knobs and opening locks, ignore any meat or animal products and help himself to all the vegetables, dal and chapattis. Once he was done, he would fling the tiffin container at its owner and leap from branch to branch to disappear into the green trees. From there, he would attack again, jumping on another victim. He had a voracious appetite and would also share his food with the other monkeys in his troop, who were too timid to steal like him. So, in the course of a single day, numerous attacks would take place.

'Sahib, this monkey is making life miserable for us,' Mr Sayeed said one evening, echoing the complaints of his colleagues. Mr Sayeed worked at the Mint in the Metallurgy Research Department. He had made a special trip to Mint House after work to discuss this very urgent matter since it was not work-related. He stood respectfully in the portico, his bald head shining with sweat from the exertion of the long walk from the back gate to the front of the palace. His hands were clasped behind his back, his fingers interlaced and twitching with nervousness.

'What to do, Mr Sayeed,' my father said.

But this response did not appease Mr Sayeed. His eyebrows furrowed in frustration and he shook his head dolefully.

'Maybe you need to scare him so he stops doing this,' Baba added, anxious to get back to his tea, which was getting cold. He was delegating and putting the matter back in Mr Sayeed's hands.

The next day, Shankar came up the veranda stairs and said to me, 'Sahib, come and see what fun Mr Sayeed is having with the monkey.'

I threw my schoolbook down on the table and ran out.

Taking my father's suggestion to heart, Mr Sayeed had decided to teach the monkey a lesson. He had taken a banana and peeled the top. Then he had taken some chicken droppings and applied them to the banana and replaced the peel. He had taken the banana and put it into a container in his tiffin carrier and was now walking around, looking nonchalant. The tiffin carrier swung to and fro in his hand. As expected, the monkey leapt down from the tree at lightning speed and snatched the tiffin carrier from his hands. The group of factory workers watching the incident clapped their hands, knowing that their plan was swinging into action. They watched as the monkey leapt up confidently to the lowest branch of the tree. He opened the tiffin carrier and took out the banana.

When I joined the crowd looking up the tree, I saw that the monkey sitting still with a piece of the banana in his hand. His nostrils were flared and he was looking with dismay at his hand smeared with chicken droppings and banana pulp. He raised his hand to his nose, wrinkling his face in disgust. He wiped the offending substance from his hand and smelt it again, still looking revolted. As he proceeded to wipe and smell his hand over and over again, he found the smell of chicken droppings was still there. He began to wipe his hand with increasing madness.

'Oh, Mr Sayeed! What have you done? This is taking it too far. He will cut his hand open if he continues,' said Mr Radhakrishna, a devout Hindu. He was a soft-hearted man and much more tolerant of the monkey's antics than the other Mint employees.

Mr Sayeed and the rest of the people watching were, however, doubled up with laughter. They were very happy to see the monkey's discomfort.

The poor monkey could not stop wiping his hand clean. Small flecks of blood had appeared on his hand now. Suddenly, he stopped and looked at the laughing crowd. He seemed to understand what was happening. He lay down, both his arms clasped behind his neck, his legs propped up on the branch, and closed his eyes and proceeded to sleep, looking incredibly human.

Mr Sayeed decided that the monkey had learnt his lesson. Indeed he had, for the attacks stopped after that.

And then, there were just two weeks left before the final exams. Ranjan and I were still not on talking terms. Everyone was preoccupied and I was relieved that the other boys were leaving me alone. We only had half day at school each day and spent the afternoons studying at home.

One Saturday morning, my studies were rudely interrupted by a cacophony of screeching and howling.

It appeared that a troop of travelling rhesus monkeys had moved into the palace garden and attacked the resident troop. Now there were two troops of monkeys in the garden and they were fighting over territorial rights. The leader of the invading monkey troop was smaller and younger than the leader of the resident troop. His face had greyish markings and he looked very mean to me. But as he fought the leader of the resident troop, I realized that what he lacked in size he appeared to make up for in strength and viciousness.

Open-mouthed, I watched the monkeys battle it out. Bites, scratches and blood appeared on their bodies and inhuman howls rent the air. The males of the invading troop were trying to forcibly copulate with the resident females and the babies were screaming in terror. I shouted at the invaders, worried that our monkeys would be seriously injured. At first, our monkeys seemed to be losing but, though severely hurt, in the end, they managed to route the invaders. The ground was littered with leaves and broken branches. The mothers tried to soothe the wailing babies.

Then, one of the invading monkeys snatched a baby from its mother and flung it to the ground. It hit the earth with a sickening thud. The mother went crazy, attacking the monkey that had snatched her baby. I ran to the baby to look at it. I lifted it up, but its head fell to one side like a rag doll, its neck broken. A faint trickle of blood flowed from its nose, otherwise it looked like it was sleeping peacefully. The mother hurled herself at me, stopping a few inches away, baring her fangs.

'Rahul!' Rani screamed. 'Come back or she will attack you!' Scared, I put the baby back on the ground and stepped away.

The mother grabbed her limp baby and leapt up to a high branch, away from the fight that had started again.

'This is so sad,' I cried. 'Why are they so cruel to each other?'

'They belong to different troops and only care about their own. There is nothing we can do, Rahul. It is nature and the law of survival,' Rani consoled me softly.

I did not eat that night, haunted by the image of the dead baby in its mother's arms, where she held it for the rest of the day. The leader of the resident troop was hurt as well.

At school too, the boys had formed their own troops. The Muslim boys hung out together and did not invite any of the Hindu boys to join them. Ranjan and Suresh Khosla spent a lot of time in the playground, laughing at their own jokes and smoking cigarettes during the lunch break with other members of their posse. If Mrs Joshi knew about this, she turned a blind eye. I tried my best to stay out of situations where I could be harassed, but, not satisfied with accusing me of theft, Ranjan continued to make trouble for me.

The last week before the final examinations started, I went out to the schoolyard one day for the afternoon break. Ranjan and his new friends were crowding around the edge of the yard and I could hear them whispering as I walked by. Then, suddenly, Suresh Khosla called out: 'Homo!'

My head swung around involuntarily.

'See, what did I tell you?' Ranjan hissed. 'He does not ever look at Shubho's girlfriend. He knows what he is. He turned around.'

How I wished to God I had not turned around.

'Hey, Rahul! Did Amit Puri write you a love letter too?'

Suddenly, as if on cue, the entire schoolyard went quiet. The words echoed off the walls of the buildings, floated through the scalloped entrances, ricocheted off the pillars. I waited for the babble of voices to start again, but there was silence. Then the giggles started and turned into uneasy laughter. Suresh Khosla laughed the loudest. Soon, most of the boys were laughing and pointing at me as if I were a freak. I stood there, frozen, my ears burning. I hated everyone at that moment. Then I turned quickly and walked back to my class. I sat in my seat, my heart pounding, feeling guilty for no reason and hoping that no teacher had witnessed the scene.

That evening, as I studied, I toyed with the idea of deliberately making mistakes in the exams so Ranjan could get higher marks. It would be a small price to pay for him to stop hating me so much. But having to face my parents' disappointment would be worse and so I kept at my books.

Sunday Evening. San Francisco.

Andrew's phone rang. The electronic jangle startled me, bringing me back to the reality of the present crisis.

'Andrew Borghese. Oh, hey, Julian. No, I am not at the motel any more … Oh, about going out tonight …'

'You are not going out tonight, are you?' I interrupted even as I tried to keep the irritation out of my voice and failed. The dull throbbing in my temples had turned into a steady pounding now. Julian was Andrew's ex-boyfriend.

'Let me call you back?' Andrew said and hung up. He turned to me. 'Do you really think that I would go out tonight? Well, thanks for trusting my commitment to the relationship.'

'Well, here I am pouring my heart out to you and you've already made plans to go out without bothering to hear me out!' I said. 'I thought you were going to give me a chance to at least share my story with you.'

'I'm still here, am I not?' Andrew's voice was icy. 'I'm here, and listening, even though you wanted me out of here. If you really cared a whit about me, Rahul, you would never ask me to leave this place—even for an evening.' He glared at me, his body tense, looking ready to walk out again.

This was not good. I had to get through my story, I had to make him understand. Basically, I had to shut up and focus. I exhaled slowly, forcing myself to calm down. The headache was overwhelming now and I started to massage my temples. 'I am sorry, Andrew,' I said apologetically. 'I overreacted. You know how I feel about Julian—it seems as though he will keep butting in between you and me as long as he is single.' I sighed. 'I hate the thought that you have been discussing me with him.' Damn this headache, damn the whole bloody weekend. I hated being so needy, giving voice to words that I regretted even as I uttered them.

'Yes,' Andrew snapped. 'I know how you feel about him. For some reason, you think that I will run into his arms at the first opportunity!' He sounded positively furious now. 'Look, Rahul, while we are sorting this stuff out, you *have* to get this—I am not looking to get out of this relationship to get together with Julian or anyone else. I want this to work. That is why I agreed to hold off on moving out. Do you understand what I am saying? Can we get clear on that?'

I nodded.

'And yes, Julian is my ex,' said Andrew, 'and I do consider him a friend. You are going to have to respect that relationship.'

'Yes.' I was being chastised and it was galling. God, I loved Andrew so much. What would life be like if he left me?

'Is your head hurting? Do you want to take a break?'

'No, I'm okay. Let me just get some Ibuprofen before I continue.'

I walked to the medicine cabinet. The air in the apartment felt icy cold on my face after the heat of the fire. I rummaged through the cabinet, found the pills, then walked back to the fireplace. Andrew was on the phone.

' … Yes, I know I said I would go out, but I changed my mind. I have to work on the relationship tonight.' He paused. 'Well, I'm sorry you feel that way, Julian. But you know that this comes first. Okay. Gotta go.'

We sat by the fire again. I was overjoyed that Andrew wasn't going to meet Julian. I ached to touch him, kiss him, but I knew better than to reach out to him right now.

'So …' Andrew flashed me a brief smile. 'Back to your tale, Rahul. Loved the monkeys—such a riot! Hated the part about you finding out about homosexuality, though. I can't imagine how it must have felt. When growing up, it was bad enough being teased by bullies, but at least our school counsellor tried to get me to embrace who I was and feel good about myself. And there you were, with no one to talk to, looking at some obscure homophobic sex therapist's book. And drawing conclusions imposed on other people out of ignorance and personal bias.' Andrew's voice was warm with sympathy.

'Yes, it was horribly traumatic. Though, after the incident with Shubho, I felt totally numb. But it all hit me like a ton of bricks as the months went by. And I also got to see for myself how society treated the parents of gay children. From that point on, I pretty much went straight back into the closet. I could not imagine bringing shame to the family … I don't think you've ever dealt with that kind of shame.'

'Not true. Parents disowned their children for being gay when I was growing up. That speaks volumes about their shame, you know.'

'Maybe you're right. We have a word called izzat back home. I don't think there is an exact translation for that word in English. It means … personal honour—family honour, honour of one's position in society and much, much more. Without izzat, a man cannot leave his home and face the world. That is the level of shame I am talking about—disowning one's kids is not enough. Have you heard about honour killings?'

'When a family kills a member? Yes, that is brutal.'

'Well, that is the level of shame I am talking about. Anyway, by the time that year ended, I was completely in denial and lived in terror of losing what I had left.'

'Maybe that is why you feel so threatened by Julian …' Andrew mused. 'Do you think you will lose me to him?'

'Yes, I guess.' I shrugged, embarrassed at having admitted my fear. 'Though, you know what? I am tired of living with this fear.'

'You carry so much unnecessary baggage with you, Rahul.' Andrew's voice was gentle. 'But only you can get rid of it. I have to say, though, that I love the palace as you describe it! What a shame if you lost that too. If I had to leave a place like that, I would end up in therapy for years.'

I smiled wryly. 'Who has the luxury of therapy in India?' There was a strange bitterness in my voice.

'Rahul, you have to let go! Your past is ruining your life, do you get that? It is costing you so much—your peace of mind, our relationship, your freedom to be happy …'

I was silent for a while. Andrew was right, of course. The tightness in my chest relaxed as I breathed out, determined to move forward. The past did belong in the past. It was over. Suddenly, for the first time since I had been a boy of thirteen, I had the unshakeable sense that I would be all right. That I could face whatever came my way.

With or without Andrew. The peace from the night before came upon me again—a heavenly benediction.

'Hmm. So where did I stop when Julian called?' I wanted to get on with my story now, unburden myself to Andrew.

'Let's see. You were telling me about the boys in the schoolyard calling you names.'

'Oh yes. That was just before the final exams …'

13

December 1973. Hyderabad.

The week of the examinations was a blur of studying, writing the finals, going home and studying again. We usually had one exam a day, for three hours. When the last day arrived, I could not wait to finish. The winter holidays were beginning after a long wait, but I was already dreading going back to school the next year.

During the winter break, the days dawned clear and crisp. The sun shone brightly at us even though it was low in the sky and I spent all day watching the monkeys. They had by now got used to my presence as I followed them around from one tree to another. The babies had grown and most of them did not cling to their mothers any longer, but they still stayed close. In the afternoons, they would sit and bask in the sun's warmth, grooming each other, picking out lice and eating them. I tried to make the days last as long as possible, but they slipped by too soon.

The semi-annual PTA meeting of the HRA was a reminder that the winter vacation was coming to an end. Held in late December, just before classes resumed, it was attended by the parents of all students, including mine. The students themselves were not supposed to attend the meeting, so I stayed home with Rani.

Rani and I were playing Monopoly that evening when we saw a stream of headlights making its way along the driveway. I recognized our Baby Ford as it stopped in front of the garage.

'Ma and Baba are home,' Rani exclaimed, 'and they have brought back guests.'

We ran to the sitting room and straightened it out, arranging magazines on the coffee table and turning on the lights.

Under the lights of the portico stood my parents, Professor and Mrs Khosla and Ranjan's parents, Mr and Dr Bose. Seeing all these people together stunned me momentarily.

'Hello, Rahul, how are you?' A chorus of polite hellos poured in. I figured then that none of these people knew what had been going on in school. Relieved, I invited them in and stepped into the kitchen to help my mother.

Carrying out a tray with tea, biscuits and some homemade sandesh, I heard Mrs Khosla say with a nasty laugh, 'Arre, I must say that it was a relief that this PTA meeting was not as unpleasant as the PTA meeting in our daughters' school. When Mrs Puri ran for office, she did not get one vote. Not one vote, I tell you.' Her eyes glittered with righteous satisfaction.

'Why? Mrs Puri was quite a good president last year, wasn't she?' my mother asked.

'Well, she might have been a good president, but she was a terrible mother. After all, what kind of mother raises her son to be … you know …' Mrs Khosla's thin, pencilled eyebrows danced with implication, a smirk on her lips. Her jowls swung in disapproval on either side of her face.

'Well, we all know that her son was not normal,' Mr Bose chimed in. 'But you can't blame the mother for an abnormal son. They are lucky the child was not jailed. Such things are illegal you know, as they jolly well should be.'

'Arre, Mr Bose. You are too nice. That is not abnormal behaviour, ji, it is a sickness. A moral sickness. Sickness that runs in the family, if you ask me. Hunh!'

'All I can say is that I am glad that that disgusting boy is not in my son's class now.' Dr Bose pressed her thin lips together in a prim line and pushed her spectacles up her large beaky nose. They slid down again on her oily skin. 'One bad apple spoils the rest.'

'I agree,' my mother chimed in. 'There is nothing worse than bad company. You know, at this age … When we put Rahul in Hyderabad Royal Academy, we heard rumours about an all-boys school, you know … But we never thought that a boy in his class would do that … *be* like that.'

'Her daughter is in Madhu's and Rani's school,' Mrs Khosla said. 'I hope she is not like her brother, you know a … chhee, chhee … I cannot even say that dirty word.' She made a vomiting gesture, reminding me of Ranjan's reaction to Amit Puri. 'This perverted behaviour can ruin our children. Thank God my son brought this to Mrs Joshi's knowledge, you know. Today, a love letter to another boy, tomorrow something more disgusting. At least I raised my son with good moral values.' Mrs Khosla patted her own back, revealing a large sweat stain under her armpit.

'I say that we should not include her in any social functions or the PTA,' Professor Khosla added. 'Why expose our children to this bad family?' He took a deep breath. 'Achha, let me be frank. There are good families and bad families. Theirs is not a respectable one. Anyway, to be safe, I say we keep a very close eye on our children, just in case they are learning bad habits. Better to nip the corrupting influence in the bud.'

'I agree,' my father said as I started to slink away, cold with dread. So this is how people were talking about Amit's mother and family. I could *never* cause my mother to suffer like this.

I went and sat on the veranda outside. It was a cold and dark evening. My breath was like a white wisp of cotton as it condensed in the air. It was silent outside, the silence of a cold winter night that blankets everything, stifling every sound, every chirp, every whimper and moan. I sat with my legs hanging over the edge of the veranda, feeling a deep, chilling fear. I saw clearly the future of my parents' social standing if anyone were to find out about me. I resolved again to never put myself or my family in danger of disgrace and said a silent prayer of thanks that I was still safe.

The next day, the unthinkable happened. The monkeys disappeared—every single one of them.

'Did you see the monkeys today?' I asked Rani.

'No, I did not. Ask Ma.'

'Ma, have you seen the monkeys?' I asked with a sense of foreboding.

'No, Rahul, I have not. Go ask Shankar.'

I went looking for Shankar, confident that he would know, and found him. 'Shankar, where are the monkeys?' I asked.

'Sahib, they are gone.'

'Gone? Where? When? Did someone hurt them? Did someone frighten them?'

'No, Sahib. Nothing happened. I have heard that monkeys travel from one area to another. Maybe they did not find enough food to eat. It is winter and there are no fruits around. Maybe the other monkey troop will attack again. It is for the best, Sahib.'

'For the best? What do you mean?'

'Sahib, those monkeys will eat anything they can find. There will be no mangoes, no papayas, no jamun, lemon, oranges, guavas ... nothing will be left uneaten. So it is good they are gone. Lord Hanuman has guided them to a good place.'

I looked for them as I ran from one part of the garden to the other. I peered around the servants' quarters. I looked up at every tree, from the great banyan to the guava grove near the dhobi ghaat. There was no sign of them, nothing at all. Just the bare branches of the deciduous trees and the green boughs of the evergreens, swaying lightly in the afternoon sunshine.

My heart grew heavy with the loss of my unlikely friends.

January 1974. Hyderabad.

'India is going to be a third-world country forever if we do not advance technologically,' my father lamented as he read an article about a satellite that the United States had launched successfully into orbit. 'Look at the United States. They are so ahead of us. One day, you will have to go there and get an education.'

The first day of school was coming up on me. I readied myself for another lecture.

'That is why I want you to be an engineer, so that you can do your higher studies there. We are all doing our part. Even though I disagree with the expansion plan for the Mint, I have to agree that is the only way to increase factory production. There are many gardens and palaces, but only one opportunity to make this Mint the largest one in the country.'

I was at my desk, covering my text books with brown paper and labelling my new notebooks. 'Why do we have to lose our home?' I asked, irritated. My voice jumped an octave and then broke. I hated my voice these days—it was impossible to speak in normal tones. Clenching my jaw in frustration, I stopped folding paper for a moment. I was tired of being pushed all the time. 'Why don't you stop them from demolishing the palace?' I said, trying to sound persuasive like Rani.

Baba's voice was a whiplash. 'Have I not made myself clear? Enough of that talk. As I said, the matter is settled and out of my hands and I have applied for a transfer.' He sent me a warning look. 'In any case, you will have to study hard this year.'

I remained quiet as I folded the edge of the brown paper, making sharp creases that would protect the cover of my Social Studies book, stubbornly refusing to agree.

Baba sighed. 'We will be leaving for Bombay as soon as I get transferred. It will be fun in Bombay. It is a great city and you will make lots of friends.'

There was obviously nothing I could say to change my father's mind, to stop the destruction of the palace.

'Unless of course you want to stay behind and be a boarding school student?' Baba asked, surprising me.

I thought of being at school day and night, dressing like all the other boarders, in their uniform during the day and the formal dinner jackets every night. I thought of being discovered as a homo. If I left the Hyderabad Royal Academy and started all over again at a new place, no one would know about me. If I was expelled from the Academy, on the other hand, I would not be able to bear the humiliation for myself or my family.

'No, Baba, I don't want to stay behind.'

'Are you sure? Won't you miss your friends?'

'No … I mean, yes …'

I would probably have opted to stay behind if I did have any friends. But I had none any more and could not share with my father the escalation in harassment over the past few months.

'I have heard of dirty things that go on in the dormitories, so I am glad you have decided not to stay behind,' Baba said. 'Do you know what I am talking about?' He was looking at me carefully over the top of the newspaper, his reading glasses perched at the end of his nose.

'Oh ...' I didn't know whether to agree with him or not. I was sure that, acting on Professor Khosla's suggestion, Baba was testing me to see if I had been exposed to any 'corrupting influences'.

'Well?' Eyes narrowed, Baba put down the paper, taking his glasses off.

'No, I don't know what you mean,' I lied, squaring my shoulders and widening my eyes innocently as I looked at him. I had learnt well at school how to pretend.

Baba relaxed and said, 'Glad we can talk man-to-man now, eh?' He smiled. 'I will have to teach you how to shave soon, and get rid of the scraggly beard. It is beginning to look untidy.'

I touched my face and felt the down-like fuzz and longer stray strands that covered my chin and upper lip. 'I would like that,' I said, relieved at the shift in conversation. I knew, however, that I would never be able to talk to him man-to-man about how I felt, about the things I had done.

Baba looked at his watch and pushed his chair back, ending the conversation. 'It is time to go to the office.' He wore a satisfied expression on his face as he left.

The phone rang, shrill sound strident in the silence. Rani ran to get it, but my mother beat her to it.

'Oh, Mallika, how are you? It has been such a long time!' Ma's voice was warm. 'This evening? Yes, we will be at home. Rahul will be so happy to have you visit. Rani is going to a friend's party.' She lowered her voice. 'After I heard the parents of his friends talk about the bad influence in school, we have been worried about him. And now this ... He has always spent so much time playing in the gardens. You know it will be impossible to find a paradise like this anywhere, let alone in Bombay.' She nodded her head a few times and added, 'I don't know how he will adjust.'

That evening, my father left to drop Rani at her friend's party and then visit with his friends. Mallika arrived soon after. She was dressed in a beautiful, green silk sari with a red border. A Kashmiri shawl with heavy paisley embroidery in maroon and yellow was wrapped around her shoulders.

I had not been with Mallika since we had played Snakes and Ladders in the kitchen at Anjali Mashi and Binesh Kaku's house. I was shocked at the way she looked. Her eyes looked twice as large in her wasted face. The skin over her cheekbones was stretched taut and thin, accentuating them. The dark circles under her eyes were hidden expertly by make-up, but her face looked hollow and gaunt.

'Mallika Didi!' I cried out.

She wrapped her thin arms around me and hugged me to her chest. I held her so hard that it must have hurt, but she did not let go. There was so much to tell her, but I dared not. The secrets, the betrayal, the shame—I desperately needed a confidante. But I knew that it could not be Mallika—she looked fragile, ready to break.

'Oh, Rahul! It is so good to see you,' she murmured. Holding me at arm's length, she tilted her head back to look at me. 'I can barely recognize you, you know. You are growing into such a handsome man!' She put her hand on my cheek.

My mother carried in a tray laden with tea and snacks. 'So, Mallika, how are you?' she asked.

'Mashi, I am all right.' Mallika lost her smile for a moment, looking pensive, and then changed the subject. 'How are you?'

'We are fine. It is a very exciting time for us. You know, Rahul's father is going to be transferred to Bombay? It is a very big promotion.'

'Mallika Didi, the government is having the palace demolished. And the gardens. There will be a factory here.' The words rushed out and my voice broke again, annoying me—I wanted to sound grown-up and even-toned to Mallika.

'Mashi, it is so beautiful here. It will be so sad if that happens.'

'The government wants the Mint to be increased in size and double its daily production. This is the only way it can be done. Even Rahul's father has been unable to sway the government in this matter.' Ma sounded frustrated.

'Oh, I will talk to Chatterjee Mesho. There has to be another way. I have not been here for so long, Mashi ... Everything is changing so fast.' Mallika's voice was filled with despair.

I thought of how much had happened in the past six months and silently agreed.

'Mallika, what is the matter? Why are you so thin? And these shadows under your eyes ... Are you well?'

'Yes, yes. I am fine, Mashi. I have been very busy lately ... taking care of my mother-in-law, who is suffering from high blood pressure.' She turned towards me. 'I have a surprise for you.' The familiar twinkle was back in her eyes as she pulled out a game of Snakes and Ladders from her bag.

It felt good to be with Mallika again. That night, we played many games of Snakes and Ladders. Time was running out for both of us and we clung eagerly to each throw of the dice, each move of the blue-and-yellow counters on the squares on the board. In a few months, I would be in Bombay, far away from Hyderabad, from the palace and all that I loved.

I went upstairs to see Colonel Uncle the next day. I wanted to know where he would go when the palace was demolished.

Rani was busy reading and did not notice me leave. It was late in the afternoon and I hoped that Colonel Uncle would be home. He had been gone most of the winter vacation and I had missed him.

I climbed up the wrought-iron stairs. It took me a moment to recognize the terrace. It looked very different from the last time I was there. Gone were the twigs and branches. Someone had swept the terrace. I gingerly stepped towards the bat room. I could smell the odour and felt relieved. The colony was still there. But the urns and pots full of flowering plants the last time I had been here had only a few shrivelled stalks. It felt as if everything was in limbo, waiting for some sign to start living again.

I went up to Colonel Uncle's door and knocked confidently. An early evening mist hung in the chilly air and the doomed peepal tree looked like a gargantuan skeleton, its bare branches splintered the watery sky, and steel gray shards hung in space, suspended in jagged slices, changing colour with the setting sun. It was dormant for now—a sleeping giant that would awake soon for the last time and rule the grounds both above and below the earth, its massive root system deciding what would grow and where. A few birds still chirped, but the deathly silence of January shrouded the palace grounds. The frogs and crickets were somewhere deep below the earth, waiting for spring to break their slumber. But that was still a few months away. I wondered what would happen to all of them. Would they be stifled to death under a blanket of concrete? Would powerful bulldozers and shovels destroy their homes too?

A pair of squirrels raced around, their fluffy grey tails raised in the air, their graceful, smooth bodies gliding past me. I saw the flash of their stripes as they chased each other and remembered the story about why they were special. 'Legend has it that the grey-white stripes on their bodies were left by Lord Rama as he lovingly stroked their backs in the jungle when he was banished for fourteen years,' my mother had told me once. I loved the way they flicked their tails and ran away when I got too close and how they chased each other in an unending game of hide-and-seek. What would happen to them?

The door opened.

'Rahul! Come in.'

Colonel Uncle was dressed in a charcoal-coloured suit. His maroon silk tie was knotted expertly.

'Colonel Uncle, are you going out?

'Yes, I am going to a wedding reception. But you can come in for a little while. What would you like to drink? I have Coca Cola and Fanta.'

'I would like some Fanta, please.'

I heard him open the refrigerator in the kitchen. It was chilly in his room and I shivered in spite of my prickly woollen sweater and muffler.

'Sorry it is so cold. Let me turn on the heater.' Colonel Uncle switched on the heating lamp. The lights in the sitting room dimmed as soon as the lamp came on and it soon felt warm and cosy.

'So, how are you, Rahul?'

'Colonel Uncle, do you know the palace is to be demolished. And the gardens. Can you stop the government, please?' I spoke fast, wanting to tell him everything. Surely Colonel Uncle could talk to someone in the government and save the palace just like he had saved me at school?

Colonel Uncle listened to me patiently. He looked sad when I finished. His face was dark and weary when he spoke. 'Yes, I know. I have been told that I have to leave because of the demolition. Before independence, the British destroyed our forests and animals for fun and money. Now, we Indians are doing the same thing because we want to be powerful in the world. Right now, the plan to build a factory here is a very big project.' He stopped and sighed, 'Nothing lasts forever, not even this palace.'

'Where are you going to live, Colonel Uncle?'

Suddenly, Colonel Uncle's face glowed. 'Remember my friend Claudio? His wife died last year and his sons are in Rome and Milan. He has invited me to stay with him. After living here on and off for so many years, I don't think I can live anywhere else in Hyderabad, except Mint House. So I am going to Italy instead.'

'Oh no!' I exclaimed. 'You will go so far away …' My heart grew heavy even though I knew that Colonel Uncle was going to be very happy with his beloved Claudio.

'Yes, Rahul, I will be far away. But you can always come and stay with me, no matter where I live. And I will come back from time to time.'

'What will happen to the birds and animals that live here when all of this is gone?'

'They too will go away and find new homes. Nature will guide them to a safe place, Rahul. There will be a home for everyone. Don't worry.' Colonel Uncle put his arm around my shoulder and gave me a squeeze.

It was wonderful, I thought, that Colonel Uncle always knew exactly what to say to make me feel better.

February 1974. Hyderabad.

As the winter vacation came to a close, I began to dread the beginning of classes more and more. I badly wanted the next few months to be free of any incident. Too soon, school had started again, and there I was, waiting for the bus every morning. But I took comfort in the fact that the familiar blue-and-gold of the bus also heralded my last few months at Hyderabad Royal Academy. At school, I avoided Ranjan and his gang as much as possible.

'Remember, you have to do very well in the second half of your school year. Otherwise you will not get admission into St Stephens's School in Bombay,' Baba told me sternly. 'It is the best school for boys, you know.' His concerns were predictable and annoying, but I just nodded my head. Anything to avoid yet another lecture.

The days passed by and, back at the palace, the first stirrings of spring sent vibrations of life echoing through the entire garden. Tiny green leaves appeared everywhere and the team of gardeners, led by Shankar, got busy planting seedlings in the scores of flowerbeds.

The air smelt sweet and clean again. The faint, misty haze that had shrouded the afternoons and evenings these last months was now replaced by bright sunshine and blue skies, followed by orange-gold sunsets. The crows cawed, the sparrows chirped and the butterflies flitted around the gardens like liquid splashes of colour. The days grew warmer and, as I ran through the palace grounds, looking to see if everything was fine after the long, cold winter, I saw that everything was fresh and full of life. It was as if every flower bloomed longer, every tree grew fuller and every bird sang harder to appease the gods. Even though the gods had determined an unhappy destiny for my magical palace with their hearts of stone.

I was consumed by the demands of my teachers in the first few weeks of February. There was hours of homework every day. Each weekend, however, I spent time in the palace grounds, making note of the thickening foliage and the sound of the wind as it breathed life into the canopies of green. The ornamental lake fed by rainwater in the monsoons was one of my most favourite spots at this time. Thousands of dragonflies fluttered above the water as it got warmer, their wings creating a shimmering lattice of iridescence. Turtles sunned themselves on the rocks, extending their wrinkled faces to the warm sunshine.

When it became too painful to think about losing all this, I devoted time to my school books, grateful for the distraction.

March 1974. Hyderabad.

By March, I was preparing for the last round of tests, followed by final examinations. In the palace gardens, spring gave way to early summer. The scorching heat of the Hyderabad sun was back, silencing the birds by mid-morning. The mango grove was once again bedecked with the powdery, snow-white flowers.

At school, the afternoons were unbearable and the ancient British-era fans did little to alleviate our misery. We went in a daze from the annoying drone of Mr Swaminathan teaching civics in the torpid heat to the nasal speech of Mrs Desai explaining the difference between the Andes and the Appalachian mountain ranges—all of it was dreadfully boring. Only the history lessons kept me engaged—I devoured with fascination detail after detail of the kings and queens of medieval India.

Shubho was still the football captain, but I never spoke to him any more. Rani and I had stopped competing to see who was taller. It seemed childish and we did not argue like we used to. Asking my father for new trousers to replace my almost-new ones caused me more worry—I was outgrowing them rapidly. I had also started shaving once every week with my father's fluffy shaving brush and razor blade and loved feeling the faint prickle of a stubble on my chin. My voice did not see-saw any more and had settled down into a surprising baritone that I was still not used to. I felt awkward in my new body.

In class, I was a loner. I discovered that it was safer to be alone and have no friends because then I did not have to agree or disagree with anyone. It was easier to blend in when I said nothing. I guess I really started shutting down around that time. I still maintained my position in class, but had learnt to ignore the ribald jokes and jibes every time I scored high marks. I was much taller than before and had started filling out, so the bullies too were now turning their attention to easier prey.

I worried about Mallika constantly though, and was frustrated that no one seemed to be doing anything to help her. She rarely visited her parents these days. And when she did, we heard from Shyamala that she slept a lot. Any time we heard that Mallika was at her parents' home, we made it a point to visit. Each time we saw her, she looked thinner than before. She had stopped wearing make-up and colourful clothes and her hair was no longer lustrous and thick. And there was very little conversation to be had with her—she seemed completely lost in her own thoughts. In the early months after her marriage, she had struggled and railed against her life and it had been horrible to see her so upset. But her current silence and apathy were even more distressing. It was as if she had given up on everything, even herself. Anjali Mashi and Binesh Kaku too had changed. Nowadays, they rarely left their house and did not socialize like they used to.

It was in the last week of March that Mallika visited her parents' house after almost a month's absence. I was appalled to see how wan she looked.

'Mallika Didi, let's play Snakes and Ladders,' I suggested, trying to get her to act like her former self, even though I did not really feel like playing the game any longer.

'All right, Rahul.' Mallika sighed. She forced herself to go through the motions of getting the game out. We sat in the kitchen while our mothers talked about this and that. Mallika seemed preoccupied as I set the game up.

I threw the first dice and moved my counter up a ladder.

'Mallika Didi, your turn,' I said gently.

She stared vacantly into space.

'Mallika Didi,' I said, louder this time.

She jumped and said with a flush, 'Sorry, Rahul,' and threw the dice. She moved her counter forward.

I wanted her to clap her hands each time she moved up the board and exclaim with mock disappointment when I did better than her, just like old times. But she did not seem to care about the game and it dragged forever. Finally, we finished. I had won.

'Rahul, you are a much better player than me.' Mallika smiled weakly.

I smiled back. 'No, Mallika Didi, you are a better player than me.' I bantered, hoping for a rejoinder. But to no avail.

Mallika did not offer to feed me my favourite tuar dal and basmati rice either, and my heart filled with disappointment. The old Mallika was gone, replaced by a gaunt and silent stranger.

Just as I was about to propose another game, she got up and said, 'I am so tired. I am going to my room.' She came over to me and gave me a long hug. I clung to her thin frame, willing silently for her to get better.

Mallika slowly walked up the stairs to her room, one step at a time. I heard the door shut with a click. I started putting the dice and board away.

'What is the matter with Mallika?' my mother asked Anjali Mashi.

'Oh, Didi, I don't know what to say! She is wasting away before my eyes. When I asked her about her marriage, she said everything was fine. And then she asked me if I really cared whether she was happy.' Anjali Mashi's voice broke, and she was quiet for a moment trying to regain her composure. She wiped the corner of her eyes with the end of her sari and the keys tied to it jangled harshly. 'As if I don't understand. But what can I do, Didi? I do worry about her. She hardly eats and does not talk much about her marriage any more. Your Binesh Dada wants her to make it work. But she has changed so much that I hardly recognize her. If suffering is in her destiny, no one can change that. I have to leave it all in the hands of Ma Durga.'

'Yes, Anjali Didi. That is all you can do. I will try to talk to her as well.'

My mother went upstairs to see Mallika and shut the door behind her, leaving me in the landing, wondering what was going on. When she came out, she looked very serious.

'Poor Mallika,' my mother remarked to my father in the car.

'Binesh is upset that she is not happy. He feels she is too independent and headstrong.'

'I think Sanjib is a very difficult person. The girl is miserable.'

'She must learn to adjust,' Baba snapped.

The next day, as I was leaving for school, a team of men arrived. They were carpenters and they set about measuring the furniture.

'What are they doing?' I asked my father.

'They are here to build crates and moving boxes for our furniture.'

'What are the bales of straw for?'

'To pack around the glass tabletop, the almirah and other breakable furniture. They will take measurements and then start packing everything in May. We will leave on 28 May, right after your final examinations are over.'

The thought of the impending departure was overwhelming. In less than two months, we would be leaving for Bombay.

The call from Rani's headmistress a week later was unprecedented. I came home from school to find my parents standing on either side of a mutinous-looking Rani, whose hair was tangled and face and elbow were covered with scratches and bruises. The clear line of her fringe was uneven, her hair was tangled and her eye had been punched hard.

'Chhee, chhee … What kind of behaviour is this? Is this how we raised you—to be a harridan?' my father asked.

'It was not my fault. Madhu Khosla was horrible to Shyamala, and I had to teach her a lesson. She deserved it!'

I was astounded. What could have made Rani so angry that she had fought Suresh Khosla's sister? Rani, whose hair was always in place, whose pencils and pens were in mint condition and whose erasers were never misplaced—how could she have done this?

'This is the first time you have been given a warning at school. What has happened to you children?' Baba yelled angrily.

When Rani finally got away, I asked what had happened.

'Madhu Khosla was gossiping about Mallika Didi.'

'What did she say?'

'She said that Mallika has a Muslim boyfriend even though she is married. I have no idea where this gossip is coming from. And then she said that you were a homo.' Rani looked around to make sure our parents were not listening.

I looked away, trying to think of the right thing to say. Anything that I came up with was sure to lead to more questions. But then,

Rani surprised me. She reached over, took my hand and squeezed it.

'I don't care what those horrible people say,' she said firmly, kissing me on the cheek. 'I will gladly beat up anyone who says mean things about you.' She pinched my cheek playfully, her eyes twinkling. 'But I will always be stronger and taller than you!'

I looked at her in astonishment, unable to hide my smile. She looked like a hooligan, with scratches on her face and arms and a big bruise that was turning purple over her eye.

'Rani ...'

'Yes?'

'I ... Oh, it doesn't matter any more.' I tried to swallow the lump that had formed in my throat. Trying hard to speak normally, I said, 'Do you think it is a bad thing to be a homo?'

'Depends on whom you ask. Oscar Wilde, Leo Tolstoy and Michelangelo were all homosexuals and geniuses. I know because we heard about it in class when we studied their biographies. Anyway, who cares about what is good and bad? Don't you think that Mallika would have been happy with Salim? He was supposed to be a bad person. And look at the "good" match that they approved. Poor Mallika Didi! She should have just run away. I will run away too, rather than be married off to a boy like Sanjib.' Her voice shook with anger.

I looked at her admiringly. She was almost sixteen now and appeared very confident and poised. I did not want her to suffer like Mallika.

'I will never let them treat you like they treated Mallika Didi,' I said, squeezing her arm.

Rani smiled. 'All right, then. I stand up for you and you stand up for me. This way, they will be forced to deal with both of us. It's a pact.'

'Head promise,' we both said with our hands on each other's heads and burst out laughing.

'So, tell me. Did you teach Madhu a lesson?' I asked.

'Oh, I gave Madhu quite a trouncing.' Rani grinned. 'And she retaliated by pulling my hair and scratching my face. The girls made a circle around us, cheering and screaming. We were rolling around in the dirt, hitting each other as hard as we could, when the headmistress interrupted us. I had to go to her office and was then sent home with a letter. But I don't care. I am so glad we are leaving this small town with its small-minded people! I cannot wait to go to Bombay and wear what I want and do what I want. It is a different city, you'll see.'

'I wish the palace and the gardens did not have to be destroyed,' I said, my heart aching.

'Yes, that is a pity. But look around you—the palace is old. If the government does not want to save it, it will fall apart anyway.'

I looked around me and, for the first time, really took in the signs of age. Cracks were visible in the plaster and the floors were uneven. The outlets in the walls were old and outdated. Stains and discoloured patches showed where there had been water damage. Frayed electrical wires looped around the top of the walls. But it was still my precious palace and it did not deserve to be reduced to rubble, and replaced by cold machines and sterile walls. I turned away, sick at heart, feeling as if I had betrayed my friend.

That night, as I lay in bed, I replayed the day's events. Rani's positive take on homosexuality had been a big surprise. But I also knew that she did not write the rules of conduct we were supposed to follow. If anything, it underscored the fact I would have to protect myself and my family from disgrace as long as I lived.

The dry summer storms came then, without warning. Yellow lightning streaked the sky, which roared with roll after roll of thunder. The tempests shook the trees until the mangoes fell. The ground was carpeted with shivli flowers, the bright saffron stalks, a stark contrast to the milky white flowers. The wind wailed. Rani and I snuggled in our beds, glad to be inside.

I stood first in the tests again. And then the final examinations were around the corner.

Sometimes, I would, from a safe distance, watch Shubho practise as he trained the new team, whistle in his mouth. Despite the way he had treated me, I still wanted him to touch me, to hold me again. I wished I could tell him his secret was safe—I knew that he would not tell anyone. He was as scared of discovery as I was. But he never came over to say hello to me and always left with his friends at the end of practice. And since Ranjan and I were no longer friends, I could not see Shubho at his home either.

April 1974. Hyderabad.

The next set of summer storms brought rains. The first clouds arrived, angry at being forced inland before their time.

'Be careful. Do not let Rahul and Rani go to school without their raincoats. The monsoons are arriving early this week. I will be gone for three days.' My father was going to New Delhi on a trip.

'Don't worry. We will manage just fine.' Ma laughed.

The night my father left, the storm roared through the palace gardens in a fury. The windows shuddered and the winds lashed the branches of the old banyan tree, tearing young leaves from them. As electric-blue flashes illuminated the sky, the lamp posts in the garden flickered and then went out. The power surged and ebbed a few times. Finally, the waning voltage subsided and the lights went out in the palace too. I looked out at the garden from the veranda. It was pitch-black outside, the canopy of trees illuminated by split second snapshots of lightning. Creaks of protest erupted from the branches of the jamun tree as they rubbed against each other.

'Rahul, what are you doing outside? Come inside at once! I cannot find the torch. Where are the candles?'

'In the laundry room, in the top drawer in the hutch,' I said to Ma.

She went around the sitting room, the dining room and the bedrooms, checking each door and window, making sure that everything was shuttered firmly.

'Go to bed. It is late,' she said to Rani and me.

There was little else to do. We changed into our nightsuits and jumped into bed, glad to be tucked in and safe. I could hear the faint crashing sounds from stray window shutters between the rolls of thunder. A lone candle flickered on the dresser in the bedroom and the flickering flame created exaggerated shapes and figures on the wall.

Ma came to the bedroom. 'Rahul, I will go and see which window is loose. I will light another candle and take it with me.'

I was just falling asleep when a loud pounding on the door woke me up. Thinking that I had imagined the noise, I closed my eyes, but it started again, insistent. I squinted in the light of the candle my mother held.

'Rahul, there is someone at the door. Come with me. I do not want to open it alone.'

I followed Ma into the sitting room, padding behind her in my bare feet. She went to the door and said, 'Kaun hai?'

'Memsahib, there is a girl here to see you.' The sentry was shouting to be heard above the howling wind and the water pouring off the palace terrace and eaves.

I watched Ma draw back the heavy bolt. She pulled the door open, sheltering the flickering candle in her hands. The chowkidar had a torch; the light from it illuminated a shrouded figure at the door, a shawl wrapped around the shoulders. It took us a moment to recognize the figure of a woman, dripping wet, clothes clinging to her thin frame. As she uncovered her head I gasped in surprise.

'Mallika! What happened? Come in, come in, you will catch a cold.' Ma took her by the hand and pulled her into the sitting room.

'Please don't tell my parents I am here, Mashi,' Mallika said. She was pale and was shaking and there were dark circles around her eyes. The sindur in her parting coursed to her temples in bloody streaks.

Wanting to comfort my poor Mallika, I put my arms around her, holding her shaking frame tight. She finally grew still. 'You will get wet,' she said as she gently slipped out of my embrace.

'Come, come. Change into some dry clothes.' Ma had brought out a dry salwar kameez and took Mallika to the prayer room to change. Ma looked distressed and angry, her eyebrows knotted in a rare frown, and did not say a word while Mallika changed. She sat instead at the dining table, wringing her hands and biting her lip. This was a different Ma, one I had not seen before. I went to her and put my hand on her shoulder, letting her know that she had my support. I knew deep inside that she would not send Mallika back to her parents. She straightened up and, gripping my arms so hard that they hurt, said, 'Never cause so much pain to anyone, Rahul. Do you understand? Never.'

'No, Ma,' I answered seriously.

'You are a grown-up boy now, Rahul. Let us help Mallika Didi. I am so glad I don't have to do this alone.' She smiled, her eyes shining with unshed tears.

I felt proud to have been trusted with her confidence.

When Mallika returned, she was dressed in the clothes my mother had given her. Her hair was still wet and covered the side of her face.

'Where is Sanjib?' Ma asked.

Mallika's face crumpled and she started sobbing. 'Mashi, I cannot live like this any more. I don't know what to do. Ma and Baba will not let me leave him. He will kill me if he finds out I am here. Please help me. At first, I thought that it was my fault that he lost his temper with me all the time. I have tried so hard. I gave up Salim to make my parents happy and trusted them to do what was right for me, but ... Is there no escape from this hell?'

She pulled her hair back from her face to show a swollen bruise on her forehead. 'Today, he hit me again and dragged me on the floor by my hair. It is getting worse. His mother does not say anything to him. He accuses me of being unfaithful and seeing Salim secretly. Everyone is afraid of his temper. Tonight, after he fell asleep, I decided to leave him. I need some money, Mashi. I left all the jewellery they gave me back at the house. I will pay you back. I promise.' Her voice grew louder and more frantic as she spoke.

A loud roll of thunder silenced her.

'Shh ...' Ma said. 'It is all right, Mallika. You have come to your mashi for help—and I will not let you down.' She walked over to Mallika and sat her down on a chair. 'Mallika, you are like my daughter. Tell me the truth. Have you been in touch with Salim?'

'No, I haven't. I have heard that he lives in Madras now. He left Hyderabad before my marriage, to start a new life. The last thing he told me in a letter was that he could not bear to live here any longer. This city holds too many memories for him.'

The tea kettle started whistling, its strident cry audible even over the wailing of the winds. Ma went into the kitchen. 'Here, have some hot tea,' she said, bringing Mallika a steaming cup of tea with ginger, cardamom and cloves.

She then went to the prayer room and unlocked the trunk in which her jewellery was kept. I watched carefully, my eyes wide open. Ma came back with a bundled handkerchief in her hands. She untied it to reveal several hundred-rupee notes, all folded neatly. 'Here, take this. There are at least five thousand rupees here. I have been saving them for an emergency.'

'No, Mashi, I ... I cannot take this.' Mallika stammered, her eyes brimming with tears.

'This is the emergency. Please do not tell anyone about this.'

'I will pay you back, I promise, Mashi.' Mallika started sobbing again. 'Oh, this is so horrible! I wish I had never been born, Mashi.'

'I am like your mother—listen to me. Take this money, go to Madras. Start a new life. I will give you the address of my old college friend and a letter to take to her. We lived together in the YWCA when I worked in Madras. She is an executive in an advertising agency. She can help you get started. Don't tell anyone where you are going. You can contact your parents once you are settled. It is late now. You can sleep in the guest room. I will give you some warm milk to help you sleep. Rahul, go to bed.'

I stood up, but I knew I could not leave yet. I wanted to know that everything would be all right.

Mallika started shaking. 'I can't do this, Mashi. I can't ... If he finds out, he will kill me. And what about Shyamala? Who will marry her? I have ruined two lives, mine and hers. Should I just go back? Oh, leaving him is a mistake, isn't it?'

'No, Mallika. You have to trust me. Do as I say.' Ma's voice was firm and strong. 'Everything happens for a reason. Ma Durga will take care of everything. I know how to convince your parents. Your duty now is to take care of yourself first.'

Mallika stopped sobbing and started twisting the end of her dupatta. After several moments, she sat up, took a deep breath and squared her shoulders, bracing herself for the challenges that awaited her. 'All right, mashi,' she said finally. 'I am ready to do it. I will start a new life. I will not let that bastard have the satisfaction of beating me to the ground.' She smiled weakly at first, then her face grew determined. After a long, long time, she reminded me of my old Mallika, and I knew she would not turn back.

I went over to her and gave her a hug, then left to go to bed.

As I was falling asleep, I heard my mother in the kitchen, heating milk and speaking to Mallika in a soothing voice.

I overslept the next day and woke up to the sound of birds chirping. Rani had slept through the entire incident. The storm had blown over. The electricity was restored.

When I went to the guest room, Mallika was gone. I ran to my mother and asked her, 'Where is Mallika Didi?'

My mother looked serious and raising her fingers to her lips, whispered, 'Never ever tell anyone what happened last night, Rahul. If your father finds out, he will be very angry. And it is dangerous for your Mallika Didi too. You saw the way your Sanjib Dada had hurt her. If he finds out where she is, he can kill her. Promise me, you will never tell anyone. Not even Rani. This is our secret.'

I nodded in understanding. 'Where is Mallika Didi?' I asked again.

'She is safe and will let us know soon. Remember, if your father finds out, he will be very, very angry.'

I understood the need to keep a secret. I had been doing it for a year, after all. I suddenly felt very adult, a part of this subterfuge and secrecy—Ma's secret and mine, which no one in the world would be privy to. Not even Rani.

'I promise, Ma.'

The phone rang that afternoon, just after my father returned from his trip. He was reading the newspaper and drinking a cup of tea. I pretended to read my book.

'Anjali Didi, how are you? What? Are you sure? You mean she did not come to you? No, I have not heard from her. What is Sanjib saying?' Ma managed to sound genuinely shocked.

I could hear Anjali Mashi's sobs, loud and broken, even over the telephone.

'Why don't you come to see us tonight?' Ma finally said and then hung up.

Baba lowered the newspaper and looked over the top of his reading glasses at Ma. 'Well?' he said expectantly.

'Mallika is not at her husband's. She left last night in the storm and has not returned. Sanjib is livid and went to Anjali Didi's house to look for her. But they do not know anything.'

He sat up straight, took off his glasses and exploded. 'What a terrible thing to do! Such a selfish and ungrateful daughter Mallika turned out to be! I don't understand these children. Give them all the best opportunities in life—and they think only of themselves in the end! If our Rani ever behaved like this …'

Ma turned and walked out of the room.

Anjali Mashi and Binesh Kaku arrived that evening. The moment Anjali Mashi saw my mother, she burst into tears. Ma embraced her.

'There, there …' she gently comforted her. 'What has happened is terrible indeed, but have faith. It is always as it is meant to be.'

'Rahul, Rani, go inside with Shyamala,' Baba ordered.

We trooped away obediently to the dining room, but stood at the door, listening. Shyamala looked shaken up. But we were all happy for Mallika for leaving Sanjib. I ached to tell Rani and Shyamala the secret, but I knew I could not. Too much was at stake.

'But Didi, what if she is dead? What if she has been attacked and killed in some bad neighbourhood? A girl all alone, and so beautiful too. How will she manage?' Anjali Mashi was saying in anguished tones.

'Mallika is intelligent and educated. She probably had some money saved up,' Ma said in a soothing tone.

'She has brought disgrace to us. She has rubbed black shoe polish on our faces. Everyone is going to be laughing at us! And who will marry Shyamala after this? It is a mistake, a big mistake to let our daughters think for themselves. What am I going to tell Sanjib? He will divorce her. My daughter, a divorcee!' Binesh Kaku's voice shook with anger. 'I bet she has run away to be with that no-good blighter of a Muslim boy.'

Anjali Mashi burst into a fresh torrent of tears on hearing this.

'Binesh Dada, this is no time to be angry.' Ma tried to placate him. 'She will surely contact you soon. If she left her husband's house, she must have been really unhappy.'

'She is a wilful and disobedient girl! Sanjib is a good man, despite all his faults. He is a good provider and she is lucky to be married into a solid, traditional family like his,' Binesh Kaku retorted.

'This is indeed terrible. Chhee, chhee ...' Baba shook his head dolefully.

After a few minutes, my mother said, 'Let me make some tea for us all.'

As we heard her walk towards the kitchen, we ran quietly to the veranda, where we heard from Shyamala all that had happened that day.

'Sanjib Dada arrived this morning. I have never seen him so furious. He looked as if he had come straight from bed. His kurta pyjama was wrinkled and his hair was wild and tangled. He started shouting for Mallika Didi the moment he arrived, as if she was hiding somewhere. He looked in each room, under the beds, even in the prayer room. It was a long time before he believed that she was not there. After that, he made threats that he would divorce her if she did not come back by the end of the day. I hid upstairs until Ma asked me to come down and swore on my head that she had not seen Mallika Didi. I think that is when he finally believed her. He left in a towering rage.'

I wished I could tell them my secret and reassure them, but I had to keep my promise.

'I hope she has found Salim,' Rani said softly. Shyamala and I nodded fervently.

As they left, Anjali Mashi wiped her eyes with the edge of her sari. Shoulders hunched, his eyes far away, Binesh Kaku looked old and defeated.

We did not hear about Mallika for a month. My final exams were knocking at the door and I was studying hard in the study.

'Sanjib has filed for divorce,' my mother told my father in the next room.

'Chhee, chee ... What is going to happen to that family now? Mallika has really made sure that they cannot hold their heads high in society any more.' Baba was appalled. 'Binesh is very angry with Mallika. He says he has disowned her already.'

'How can he do this to his own daughter?'

'I understand why he did it. Mallika has destroyed his good name in the community.'

'So, because she left Sanjib after he abused her, she is to be punished for that?' Ma snapped.

'Marriage is forever. Once a man and woman are married, they need to be together, no matter what happens. What will happen to Mallika now? Do you think she will ever get married again? She will be a bloody divorcee.'

Baba said the word 'divorcee' in a tone that reminded me of the way Ranjan and the boys had said the word 'homo'. There was such disgust and revulsion in the word that I remembered how I had felt when I discovered that I was different from the boys in my class. It was becoming clear—it did not matter whether one was in school or at home, the one who broke the rules was always the one who paid the price.

'I support her no matter what.' Ma's voice was steely.

I felt very proud that she had had the courage to speak the words in my heart.

'Don't talk like this in front of Rani and Rahul. I don't want them to get any ideas.'

'Are you telling me that I cannot give my daughter good advice? I think she needs to know that she has options. Do you want her to end up stuck in a marriage that she cannot escape? A marriage in which her husband beats her? Times are changing, and we need to be flexible.'

I froze in the study, alarmed by the coldness of my mother's tone. My parents were about to start fighting. I was scared again. Would my father disown my mother and sister like Binesh Kaku was threatening to disown Mallika? It was a deeply unsettling thought.

I left for the garden, searching for the comfort of the gulmohar tree. Climbing up to my perch, I looked around at the limbs covered by leaves. It was too early for the sweet-scented, bright orange-and-yellow flowers. I knew I would never see my tree in full bloom, burning with a sunset-gold fire, ever again.

Everything was changing so fast … It was all falling apart. Angry, I yelled and rocked the branch I was sitting on, back and forth, kicking it in frustration until it creaked in protest. I stopped, ashamed of taking my frustration out on my old friend. I was not looking forward to going back to the palace if my parents were still fighting.

But when we sat at the dining table, it was as if nothing had happened. They had made up.

'Are you preparing well for your exams?' Baba asked me as I passed the vegetable curry to him.

'Yes, Baba, I am.'

'Good.' He nodded his head approvingly. 'Don't let Ranjan get higher marks than you.'

I thought bitterly of how Ranjan and I were barely civil to each other in class. I would never be able to explain all that had happened in the last year to my parents.

May 1974. Hyderabad.

One evening, as I was studying for my exams, the phone rang.

'Rahul, get the phone.' Ma was busy in the kitchen.

I ran to get it. It was Anjali Mashi.

'Nomoshkar, Anjali Mashi,' I said.

'Rahul, where is your mother?' Anjali Mashi trilled.

Ma came to the phone.

'Oh, this is such good news,' she exclaimed. 'So, she is in Madras now? Did she tell you where she is staying?' As Anjali Mashi responded, Ma covered the mouthpiece with her hand and whispered to my father, 'Mallika is well and in Madras. She is working there and has her own place.'

She returned to the conversation with Anjali Mashi. 'How is Binesh Dada? Oh, let him be angry. He will come around in time. So when are you going to visit her? Next month? Good. I have told you this before and I will tell you again—destiny must be fulfilled. If she had stayed with Sanjib, he would have killed her. You saw her poor health and depression yourself. Don't worry, Anjali Didi. Have faith in Ma Durga, she will take care of Mallika. Shyamala is still very

young, it is too early to worry about her marriage. Times are
changing. It is not as it used to be when we were young.'

She was happy for the rest of the evening, singing her favourite
Lata Mangeshkar songs. Her melodious voice floated through the
palace rooms, reminding me of Madhubala in *Mughal-E-Azam*.

Relieved, I went back to study in my room. It would be the last
room to be disturbed since I needed to use it every day. Every other
room was topsy-turvy. The move had been set in motion. Furniture
had been removed and packed by careful hands. My mother had
packed the crockery and glassware herself—she had put each egg-
shell-thin porcelain dish and cup, wrapped up in newspaper, with
great care in the big, sturdy metal trunk. Large crates filled with
packing materials and straw lay piled up in the empty servants'
quarters and the carpets had been rolled up. Our voices echoed high
up in the rafters in the bare rooms. The hands of the clock were
moving, faster and faster, inexorable, towards the day we would be
leaving Mint House forever. Each day, when I returned from school,
the rooms looked a little emptier than before.

I came first in the examinations again.

'Congratulations,' Ranjan said to me in class after the results were
announced. He had heard that it was my last day at HRA; he was
probably overjoyed that, with me out of the way, he would now be
the undisputed king of the class. He had come a very close second in
the finals.

'Thank you, Ranjan,' I said, feeling wary.

'Will you write to me?' Ranjan surprised me again.

'Yes, I will, if you do.'

'Of course, Rahul, I will,' he said. 'Here, let me write my address
down for you. So, who will be living in Mint House after you
leave?'

'Oh, no one. The palace is being demolished. And the gardens too.'

'What a pity! I will miss all the fun we had during the Day Spend
there.'

'Yes, I will too. Oh, the school bus is here. Time to go.' I was
remembering happier times spent with Ranjan and realized that I
would miss him.

I watched the old school bus as it approached, its familiar blue and gold colours bringing a lump to my throat—I would not take this bus again. I looked around me, at the symmetry of the buildings, the scalloped doorways, the clock tower, the carefully tended gardens, the playgrounds and, in the distance, the honeysuckle covered changing room where I had first touched Shubho. I was going to be leaving all of this behind. The pain hit me like a wave crashing through my carefully cultivated nonchalance.

Goodbye, HRA, I whispered in my heart as the bus slowly lurched out of the campus, wheezing as it approached the road. I ran to the back of the bus and stared and stared out of the window until the spires and domes of the school were eclipsed by the gates and walls. A plane getting ready for its final descent roared overhead, the twin propellers making a faint whirring sound that quickly receded.

I looked at the faces of the boys around me. Some were from my class, some from other classes. They were all excited about the school year being over and were chattering merrily. 'Happy hols!' they cried at every stop as someone alighted. The months of summer vacation stretched out ahead, a time to have fun, play and relax. For everyone except me. I had already spent the last summer I would have in Mint House and would be in Bombay soon.

'Happy hols, Rahul!' my friends shouted to me as I got off the bus. My schoolbox, battered and dented, bumped loudly against the open doorway for the last time.

As I walked up the driveway, I saw that three huge trucks were parked in front of the palace. The veranda was filled with trunks, crates and numerous cardboard boxes. Men heaved and grunted as they moved the heavy stuff, scraping the mosaic of the marble floors. Many of the packages containing glassware and furniture bore stickers saying 'Fragile: Do Not Drop'. My parents were directing the operations.

I walked through the palace. It looked and felt forlorn and deserted, the way empty houses always do. The air was heavy with a sense of abandonment. The back rooms of the palace were open today, including the box room. Windows and doors that had not been unlocked in decades were flung wide open. They would never need to be closed again—we were leaving the next day, and the demolition crew would be starting its work the very same week.

I could not bear to hear the hollow echo of my footsteps as I walked around, dragging my fingers along the walls. Memories of my childhood were imprinted on them. On one wall was a picture that I had drawn with a crayon at the age of six. My mother had strategically placed an almirah there, to cover the spot; now, with the almirah gone, the drawing stared sadly at me. On the veranda post were marks made by Ma from when she measured my and Rani's height every few months ... I went to the back of the palace and climbed up the back stairs, taking them two at a time, smiling as I remembered my abject fear of only a year ago.

Colonel Uncle's door was open and I walked in. The apartment was empty. I went from room to room, shouting, 'Colonel Uncle, Colonel Uncle!' But there was no reply. The beautiful ruby-red Persian carpets were gone. So was the bust of Apollo and the kitchen's gleaming copper-plated pots and pans. I was suddenly gripped by fear that I would never see Colonel Uncle again.

I walked out to the terrace and went into the room of the bats. I looked up but could not see a single one. The smell of bat urine was still fresh. I walked through the dry droppings and rotting, partially eaten fruit, looking for them to no avail. I walked out into the sunshine, the air above the terrace shimmering in the heat. The waxy green leaves of the peepal shivered in the slight breeze and the koel started its fevered call.

Colonel Uncle appeared suddenly. He was wearing tan cotton slacks and a light cotton bush-shirt, holding a brown paper parcel in his hand. His face relaxed into a smile of pleasure when he saw me.

'Rahul.' He held his hand out to me. I walked over and took it. 'I thought I heard your voice,' he said. 'I am leaving today. All my furniture has been packed and moved.'

'Where did it go?'

'I sent it all to the palace in Rajasthan where I grew up. It will be safe there. I cannot take it all with me to Italy.'

'Take me with you, Colonel Uncle.' I clung to him, momentarily forgetting all about my parents and Rani. He was the only one who understood me.

Colonel Uncle smiled indulgently at me. 'When you are a young man, you will visit me, won't you?'

'Yes, I will.' I was determined to do as I wished as soon as I was a little older. 'Where are the bats, Colonel Uncle?' I asked as I remembered the empty room.

'What do you mean?'

'I went to the bats' room and there was not a single one. They should be resting in there, shouldn't they?'

'Actually, Rahul, I have not seen them for the last two days. I usually wake up before sunrise and see them flying in as the sun comes up. But not yesterday and today. They must know.'

'Know what?'

'That their home is about to be destroyed.'

'So where are they? Are they going to be all right?'

'Whoever guides them is taking care of them, Rahul, don't worry. I remember when I was young … In the hunting season, the deer would hide in the sanctuary of the nearby swamiji's ashram. He was a devotee of Pashupati—Lord Shiva, the protector of all animals. The swamiji was an old, loving man, covered with ash, and the little children were terrified of him because of the markings on his forehead and the gigantic trishul he carried. But the animals knew he would protect them. Somehow, they know these things.'

I nodded, reassured. 'So, you will write to me, Colonel Uncle?' I asked.

'Of course I will. Here is my address, written on the back of this parcel. This is for you,' he said, handing the parcel to me.

'What is it?' I said, holding the gift carefully.

'Open it later, when you get to Bombay. And make sure you don't lose my address.'

'I won't, Colonel Uncle.'

He gave me a long hug. When he stepped back, his eyes were glittering with tears. He squeezed my shoulder so hard that I winced. He swallowed hard a few times, then stood upright in a military fashion and gave me a quick nod, as if he were saluting an officer. He turned away and walked briskly towards his rooms, his back straight and his carriage erect. At the door, he stopped, turned around and waved. Then he vanished into the darkness of his apartment.

As I went downstairs, I felt like I was being torn away from everything I was familiar with. I wanted to run away, right then, away from loss. But I went downstairs instead, for our last meal at the palace—khichuri with fried potatoes—quick food that was easy to make and eat. Food for the times when one's whole world was ending and a new one was about to begin.

I carefully put away Colonel Uncle's package with my clothes in the trunk. It would go with us in the train. Our bulky pieces of furniture would take two weeks to reach by truck.

The beds had been dismantled and packed up. So I slept on a makeshift mattress made by my parents that night, my last night in the palace. I looked up at the dark ceiling and the shape of the fan as it lazily rotated, the blades throwing darker shadows on the walls. The bedroom felt like a cavernous shell without the usual furniture.

I had a vivid dream that night. At first, I thought I was in the Salarjung Museum, the rooms full of antiques and valuable bric-a-brac. The carpets covering the marble floors were thick and luxuriant. There were gold-framed paintings on the wall. There was no one around. Then, as I looked at the open door and recognized the portico framed by the gigantic pillars, I realized that I was in the sitting room of the palace. The ceiling was covered with glittering gold leaf. Huge chandeliers hung from it, the rainbow lights casting a rich kaleidoscope of colours on the walls. I wandered from room to room, passing a floor-length painting on the wall. The ornate gold frame held the picture of a handsome prince with a jewelled turban on his head, his eyes dark and mischievous. He was dressed in rich silks and brocades and the ruby on his turban glittered. It was the same prince, the sulky prince who sat in the carriage as it rolled out of the driveway because his grandmother would not allow him to live there. The prince moved as I did and I realized that I was looking at myself—the painting was a mirror. *I* was the prince. I had always known it, and here I was, dressed in all my finery. As I glided through the palace, I found myself in the box room. But this was no cobweb-covered room with dim lighting. The chandelier hanging from the ceiling sparkled and the murals on the wall were glowing. In the middle of the room sat a familiar box full of books. I opened it, looking for the book that I knew lay at the bottom. I pulled out piles of books by Erle Stanley Gardner, James Hadley Chase, Oscar Wilde and Shakespeare, but there was no sign of the book that I was looking for—the book by Barbara Golding. Instead, at the bottom of the box, I saw a brown-paper parcel, just like the one Colonel Uncle had given me. I knew what it was even before I tore it open. I recognized the sepia print, the cracked brown leather and then the photograph of Colonel Uncle and Claudio. On the back of the frame, written in a bold and strong hand, were the words: 'To Rahul, the sweet prince of the palace. Think for yourself and you will be strong enough to face the world. And always follow your heart.'

From the veranda, the gates were visible in the far distance, but the sentries were gone. In the garden, the birds were twittering, butterflies flitted from flower to flower and insects hummed in the grass. And then, a huge black cloud arose from the trees. Crows, finches, sparrows, pigeons, peacocks, egrets, wild hens, lapwings, koels and many other birds—they all rose in a mighty tumult, letting out loud, painful cries. The branches of the banyan shuddered and shook, the palms quivered, the rich canopy above the driveway trembled with the force of thousands of beating wings. Feathers wafted down as the birds flew away in a flurry. Another black cloud emerged from the top storey of the palace. Thousands of bats joined the birds, swooping through the sky and fanning over the palace grounds. And then, all at once, they were gone. The garden grew deathly quiet. The premonition of destruction silenced every creature, every leaf, every blade of grass.

I woke up with the deafening silence ringing in my ears. Today, I was to leave my magical palace.

'Rahul, come and eat breakfast. It is not the usual kind. I made some special treats for you,' Ma called gaily to me.

I lay in bed, unable to respond.

'Cheer up, Rahul,' Rani said, her voice sympathetic. 'We will have an exciting life in Bombay, just wait and see.'

'I think the change is too much for him,' my mother told my father.

'There is so much to look forward to Rahul. New friends, new school, new home. Look how excited we all are about the possibilities of the future!' Baba was trying to cheer me up, but I turned away, sick at heart. Nothing could comfort me. 'It is all right.' I heard Baba trying to reassure Ma. 'He is still a child. He will soon be distracted by something else.'

When I went out to the veranda, the trucks were gone. Only the empty driveway stretched into the distance, long and lonely. The birds too were silent in the summer heat. But the koel kept calling, louder and louder, more plaintive each time, reaching impossibly high notes. It did not stop all afternoon. And yet, the crows, sparrows, finches and parrots were nowhere to be seen. Had they left already, like the bats?

When I entered the palace through the portico, there was no one around and my footsteps sounded loud and hollow in the emptiness. I heard a peal of laughter coming from somewhere. It was Rani. She and my mother and they were talking excitedly.

'You will see the ocean for the first time! We will go to Juhu Beach and eat pau bhaji. You will love it! And then there is the Marine Drive. It's called the Queen's Necklace because it glimmers like one at night ...' Ma was excited.

'And then there are all the actors and actresses. My friends at school said that you can see them shopping, just like real people! Rahul, imagine what fun it will be to finally meet Rajesh Khanna.' Rani tried to include me in the conversation when she saw me.

I turned away, incredibly sad. I was going to be losing my palace, my friend. All the treasures of Bombay could not replace Mint House. I was not scared at the thought of a new life. I now knew how to blend in, and Rani and I had made a pact and I would never be alone. But I was miserable at the thought of leaving Mint House, my home, the one place where I had always felt perfectly comfortable and safe.

'Rahul, I have put out your clothes for the train ride on your bed. Everything else has been packed. Be ready to go at seven this evening.' My mother had taken care of everything as usual.

The rest of the afternoon was spent in visits from a stream of family friends from the Bengali Association and workers from the Mint, all of whom were coming to bid us farewell. I was overwhelmed by the number of people who showed up. The people from the Mint brought gifts and flowers, sweets and photographs, mementoes of appreciation for my father, the Mint Master, who was going to expand the Mint, ensuring better jobs, promotions and prosperity for the workers. I saw the tears of gratitude and pain that they shed as they said goodbye. The vacuum left by my father would be hard to fill—he was greatly respected and admired by the people working under him.

Everyone was rejoicing in the expansion plan and the benefits to the community. No one, it seemed, cared about the trees, birds and animals that lived there. Rani and my mother were busy putting the gifts away and saying goodbye. They looked sad, as did my father, but they were also excited at the thought a new life in Bombay. I knew at that moment I could not explain how I was feeling to anyone but Colonel Uncle. But he was gone as well.

Seeking solace, I went to the gulmohar tree and sat in my secret place for the last time. The wind was warm and brisk and there was silence all around. I laid my cheek against the rough bark and closed my eyes, taking in the moment as the faint tremor in the trunk from the branches swaying above went through me. I wanted to store this moment forever in my memory.

I walked around the palace grounds one final time. The papaya grove, the mango grove, the lake, the dhobi ghaat, the guava trees, the banyan tree, the servant's quarters, the lawns, the thicket of trees with the empty baya nest ... Everything was still, shimmering in the late-afternoon heat. I breathed in the summer scent.

'Rahul, Rahul!' Rani called.

'What?'

'Come on, slowpoke! It's time to leave. The taxi is here.'

I glanced around one last time. 'Goodbye,' I said to my friends.

I went back to the palace. The last bags were gone.

I looked at the sitting room, so forlorn and empty. 'Don't leave us,' the walls whispered as I turned to leave. I went to the nearest wall and kissed it. The plaster was cool and smooth against my lips. I felt the walls breathe against my face as they sighed slowly. My hands stretched out, my fingers gently stroking the wall, wanting to imprint in my memory this last impression.

'Hurry up, Rahul!' Rani cried.

'Let him be.' Ma's voice was stern. Her tone became gentler as she said to me, 'Rahul, beta. Come on now. We will be late for the train.'

'Goodbye, Mint House,' I murmured. The walls moved against my fingers, I felt them sigh once more and reach out to me …

And then I was in the taxi. It slowly backed out and we drove towards the gates. The sentries clicked to attention. I looked at them. They stood erect, looking straight ahead, but tears were streaming down their faces.

I looked back at Mint House. It was already in the distance but still looked gigantic to me. And then it was lost in the canopy of trees …

14

Sunday Evening. San Francisco.

I could not see the fireplace or the flames through the tears which spilled from my eyes and coursed down my cheeks. I brushed them away angrily, wishing that Andrew could not see my pain.

'Oh, baby,' he whispered. 'Come here, honey.' He held me as I gave way to the pent-up tears and emotions that had been bottled for years. I did not speak for a long time. 'There, there, baby,' Andrew softly crooned to me through it. 'Let it go, let it go …'

I could feel his skin through the soaked T-shirt as my sobs finally subsided.

The door bell rang.

'Shit!' I jumped up. 'They must have arrived. The girl Anu and her uncle from San Jose. Fuck! I forgot to tell them not to come. Damn!'

'Do you want me to go into the other room?'

'No. Please stay here.'

I ran into the bathroom, splashed water on my face and looked into the mirror. I looked like a mess. I ran my damp fingers through my hair, trying to tame the unruly curls but gave up.

I opened the door to the apartment. A very Bengali-looking gentleman stood there. He had greying hair and a thin moustache and his pants were pulled well up to his chest. He looked impatient, like an aggravated Binesh Kaku. I instantly felt a surge of childish fear of being chastised by him, but a moment later, that fear was relegated to the past, where it belonged. I squared my shoulders, took a deep breath, folded my hands and said, 'Nomoshkar, Mr Ganguly.'

The gentleman nodded and walked in. The girl with him indeed reminded me of Mallika. She had the same sparkling eyes and smile and an easy spring in her stride.

'Hi, I am Rahul,' I said smoothly, as I had said many times before to many girls that I was supposed to meet.

'Hi,' she said, smiling shyly.

'Please, have a seat. What will you have? Tea, coffee or a soft drink?'

Mr Ganguly looked around the room, taking in the framed Herb Ritts posters and the modern furniture. His eyes lingered briefly on the dresser covered by framed pictures of Andrew and me. His heavy framed glasses glinted at me as flames from the fireplace danced on the lenses. He looked at Andrew, who was still standing by the fireplace where I had left him.

'Oh nothing, we are all right. Please do not take any trouble,' Mr Ganguly said and his niece echoed his sentiments.

After a very brief exchange of pleasantries, Mr Ganguly got to the point. 'So, your mother knows my sister in Bombay and thought it would be a good idea for you two to meet. This is my niece, Anu.' he said, gesturing towards the girl.

I felt the old and trite responses at the tip of my tongue. I knew exactly how to make small talk and lead the meeting in the direction I wanted it to go. I knew how to manipulate and make promises and end the evening on a good note, before I sent a note to my mother. It was always the same note, telling her what a nice girl she had sent, but I really felt that she and I were not compatible and that she was too modern or too old-fashioned or too shy.

However, today, instead of seeking refuge in subterfuge, I said, 'Mr Ganguly, I am sorry to have wasted your time. You see, my mother does not know that I am ... I am ... gay. Andrew here ...' I looked around. Andrew had left the room. 'Andrew!'

Andrew walked in, looking tense.

'Mr Ganguly,' I said softly, 'I am terribly sorry to have wasted yours and Anu's time. Andrew here is my life partner. I have not told my parents yet, and that is why you had to come here for nothing ...'

'But ... but ...' Mr Ganguly stammered, perplexed, and I watched his face grow mottled. He finally pulled himself together. 'Chhee,

chhee! How can you behave like this? You belong to a respectable family. We are not just Indians, we are Bengalis! We have a duty to maintain our parents' good name in society. So this is what you have learnt in America! To be perverted ...' He started shaking with his outrage.

'Mama ...' Anu said and moved towards him.

Mr Ganguly dismissed her with a wave of his hand. 'So this is what you young boys do when you come here,' he continued. 'I am sorry I ever set foot in your house. Wait till I tell my sister in Bombay. Don't think you can hide this dirty secret any longer!' With that, he turned and marched out of the door, waving at Anu to follow him.

Anu silently mouthed a 'sorry', her face a picture of chagrin, her hands raised to her mouth in horror. The door slammed shut and I heard their footsteps recede down the corridor.

I sat down on the sofa, my face in my hands, overcome by the events of the past few days. Andrew sat next to me and hugged me, his eyes wet. We sat like that for a long time, silent and pensive. Then Andrew stroked my head and whispered in my ear, 'Rahul, you must write this story. Others need to hear it.'

I shook my head. All I could think about was the email I had to send my mother that night. An email that was long overdue.

15

Six Months Later. San Francisco.

I sit at my desk, my shoulders aching and stiff from the hours of typing on my laptop. I am finally at the end of my project. I start a new page and type the word 'Epilogue'.

Epilogue

I have never returned to Hyderabad, the city of my magical palace. We moved to Bombay, I got busy with school and new friends. Years went by, college followed, things changed …

I hear that Mallika lives in London now, with Salim. Binesh Kaku finally accepted her marriage to Salim and they visit each other every now and then—nothing changes arrogance like old age and infirmity. I have never seen Mallika since that fateful, stormy night, though, and my mother and I have never spoken about it.

Ranjan and I sporadically sent each other cards for the holidays while we were still in school. And then that petered out too. Ma tells me that Shubho's marriage to Anamika ended in a divorce and he has not remarried.

Colonel Uncle moved to Montepulciano to be with Claudio. His picture sits on my desk even as I type this, his message is imprinted deep in my heart. I still plan to visit him one day, if it is not too late.

Many years after I left Hyderabad, I finally realized that, to follow one's heart, one has to break the rules sometimes, just like my mother, Mallika and Colonel Uncle did. And sometimes, one has to leave and go far, far away.

Sometimes, when the wild wind from the Pacific Ocean comes tearing across the foggy city where I live, I forget that I am not in Hyderabad any more. In the middle of the night, when the rain pelts the windows and makes the door to the balcony shudder like a tortured soul hammering and begging to be let in, I sometimes rise in my sleep and say 'Kaun hai?' I open the door, expecting to see a woman, her head covered, drenched in the rain, just like that fateful night when we broke all the rules. But there is nobody there. Only the wind asking questions.

Andrew walks up behind me and massages my shoulders. It feels good and I breathe out in relief. The apartment is warm and filled with the smell of onions, tomatoes and garlic. Andrew is making his special pasta sauce, just like Colonel Uncle used to. He hugs me, leans close to my ear and whispers, 'Baby, dinner is ready.'

Acknowledgements

Like most works of fiction, the creation of *My Magical Palace* was a journey. I was the traveller and my destination was a moving target which went through a series of metamorphoses.

The only constant in this journey of non-stop change has been the support and encouragement I have received from several communities, friends and family members. They have held the space for me to create the novel you hold in your hands today.

My thanks and gratitude to:

My parents Durga and Parijat—who taught me to live with passion and nurtured my interest in books from the start. I am blessed to inherit their passion for writing and their faith in my ability to fulfill my aspirations.

My sister Alaka—for her support and good wishes.

Linda Watanabe McFerrin—my 'angel-muse' and guide who saw the potential of this novel in a short essay I wrote as a class assignment. Without Linda's unwavering vision and mentorship, I would never have written this story.

V.K. Karthika, Publisher of HarperCollins India—for her expert guidance, vision and commitment to a quality product.

Pradipta Sarkar—for her editorial support and partnership.

Ann Kircher, Carol Jauch, Unity Barry, Joanne Stein—for co-founding Writing Out Loud, a writing group, ten years ago and providing me the kind of steady literary support structure that most writers yearn for, but few experience.

Nidhi Singh and Karen Llagas—for their intuitive and unique perspective over the years. Nidhi Singh's dedication to this project from the very start and her superb editorial feedback were both invaluable.

My aunt Indrani Mukherjee—for her enthusiasm and passion for this story that kept me going. She has always been a powerful influence in my life and continues to be so, and for that I am eternally grateful.

My dear cousins, specially Deepanjali and Neelanjana—for steadily cheering me on and connecting me with creative professionals.

Anne Woods, Diane O'Connell, Vivian Groman, Byron Russell—for contributing to the manuscript and supporting me in so many ways.

My coaches, guides and fellow course-mates at Landmark Corporation—for giving me possibility.

Daniel, Nathan and Allen—for your commitment to the fulfillment of my dreams.

And to my extended family members (you know who you are)—for your contribution to my life and creative endeavours. Please forgive me for not mentioning you all by name. This project is a testament to your enthusiasm and faith in my dreams.

Photo credit: Heather Hyryclw at www.hchphoto.com